LARGE
PRINT

Also by Jan Karon

A Common Life

The Mitford Years

In This Mountain

JAN KARON

BOOKSPAN
LARGE PRINT
EDITION

ISBN 0-7394-2686-9

This Large Print Edition published in
accord with the standards of the N.A.V.H.

Soli deo gloria
To God alone be the glory

And in this mountain
The Lord of hosts will make for all people
A feast of choice pieces,
A feast of wines on the lees,
Of fat things full of marrow,
Of well-refined wines on the lees.

Isaiah 25:6, New King James Version

Acknowledgments

Warm thanks to:

Bishop Andrew Fairfield; The Reverend Frank Clark; The Reverend John Yates; *The Anglican Digest,* a great resource and a consistently good read; Langford at Farmers Hardware; Murray Whisnant; Dr. Peter Haibach; Barbara Conrad Pinnix; Kenny Isaacs; Betty Newman; Jeff Harris; Bishop Keith Ackerman; The Reverend Edward Pippin; Rick Carter, Esq.; Ted Carter; Don Mertz; Dr. Chuck Colson; Kent Watson; Ron Humphrey; Wayne Erbsen; Graham Children's Health Center, Asheville, NC; Janet Miller; Ivy Nursery; The Reverend Gale Cooper; Cheryl Lewis; The Reverend Christopher Henderson; Dr. Karen DiGeorgis; Dr. Chris Grover; Alice Boggs Lentz; Richard A. Propst; Dharma Benincasa; The Reverend Harry N. Hill; The Reverend Jeffrey Palmer Fishwick; Joni Roseman; Nancy Briggs; Dr. David Ludwig; Janet Cherchuck; Stephen

Shifflett; Jeffrey Garrison; Sharon Vandyke; R. David Craig; and Jerry Burns, man about town.

Special thanks to:

Dr. Paul Thomas Klas; The Reverend James Harris; Dr. Sue Frye; Nancy Lou Beard, Joke Queen; Michael Thacker, my right hand; and to my valued readers and booksellers for your boundless enthusiasm and encouragement.

In memoriam:

Sonya Massi, sister in Christ, 1934–2001; those lost in the Pentagon and World Trade Center catastrophes, and the Pennsylvania plane crash of September 11.

Contents

xiv   *Contents*

In This Mountain

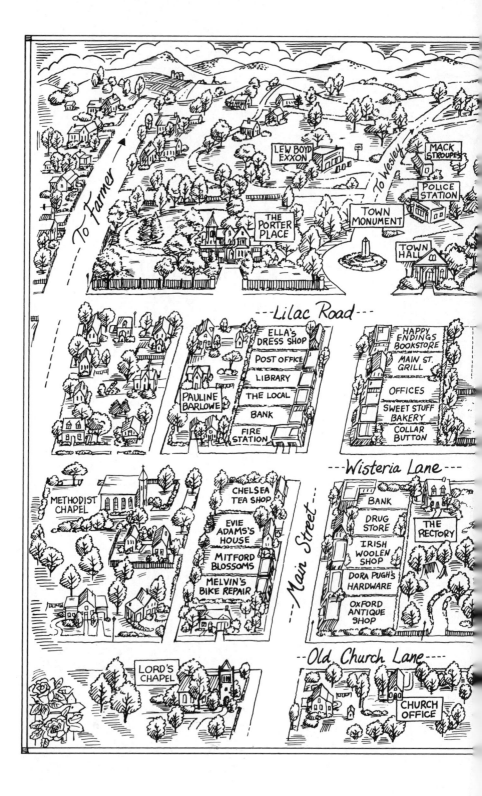

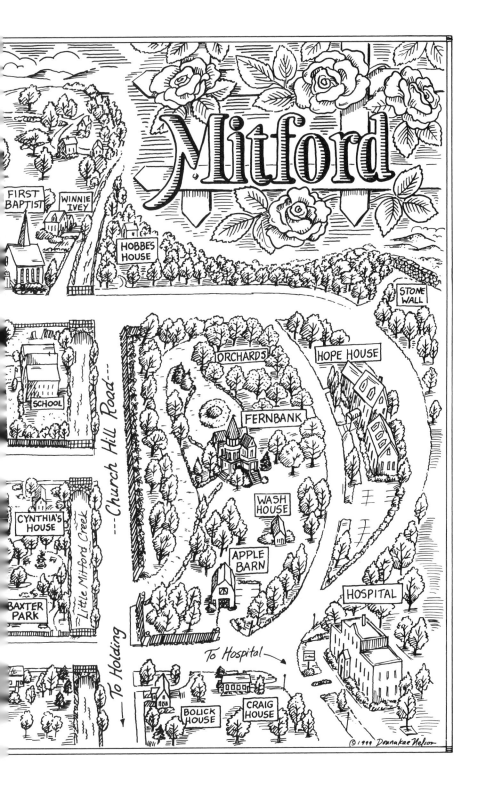

CHAPTER ONE

Go and Tell

Moles again!

Father Tim Kavanagh stood on the front steps of the yellow house and looked with dismay at the mounds of raw earth disgorged upon his frozen March grass.

Holes pocked the lawn, causing it to resemble a lunar surface; berms of dirt crisscrossed the yard like stone walls viewed from an Irish hilltop.

He glanced across the driveway to the rectory, once his home and now his rental property, where the pesky *Talpidae* were entertaining themselves in precisely the same fashion. Indeed, they had nearly uprooted Hélène Pringle's modest sign, *Lessons for the*

Piano, Inquire Within; it slanted drunkenly to the right.

Year after year, he'd tried his hand at mole-removal remedies, but the varmints had one-upped him repeatedly; in truth, they appeared to relish coming back for more, and in greater numbers.

He walked into the yard and gave the nearest mound a swift kick. Blast moles to the other side of the moon, and leave it to him to have a wife who wanted them caught in traps and carted to the country where they might frolic in a meadow among buttercups and bluebells.

And who was to do the catching and carting? Yours truly.

He went inside to his study and called the Hard to Beat Hardware in Wesley, believing since childhood that hardware stores somehow had the answers to life's more vexing problems.

"*Voles!*" exclaimed the hardware man. "What most people've got is voles, they just think they're moles!"

"Aha."

"What voles do is eat th' roots of your plants, chow down on your bulbs an' all. Have your bulbs bloomed th' last few years?"

"Why, yes. Yes, they have."

The hardware man sighed. "So maybe it is moles. Well, they're in there for the grubs, you know, what you have to do is kill th' grubs."

"I was thinking more about ah, taking out the moles."

"Cain't do that n'more, state law."

Even the government had jumped on the bandwagon for moles, demonstrating yet again what government had come to in this country. "So. How do you get rid of grubs?"

"Poison."

"I see."

"'Course, some say don't use it if you got dogs and cats. You got dogs and cats?"

"We do."

He called Dora Pugh at the hardware on Main Street.

"Whirligigs," said Dora. "You know, those little wooden propellerlike things on a stick, Ol' Man Mueller used to make 'em? They come painted an' all, to look like ducks an' geese an' whatnot. When th' wind blows, their wings fly around, that's th' propellers, and th' commotion sends sound waves down their tunnels and chases 'em out. But you have to use a good many whirligigs."

He didn't think his wife would like their lawn studded with whirligigs.

"Plus, there's somethin' that works on

batt'ries, that you stick in th' ground. Only thing is, I'd have to order it special, which takes six weeks, an' by then . . ."

". . . they'd probably be gone, anyway."

"Right," said Dora, clamping the phone between her left ear and shoulder while bagging seed corn.

He queried Percy Mosely, longtime proprietor of the Main Street Grill. "What can you do to get rid of moles?"

Percy labeled this a dumb question. "Catch 'em by th' tail an' bite their heads off is what I do."

On his way to the post office, he met Gene Bolick leaving the annual sale on boiled wool items at the Irish Woolen Shop. Gene's brain tumor, inoperable because of its location near the brain stem, had caused him to teeter as he walked, a sight Father Tim did not relish seeing in his old friend and parishioner.

"Look here!" Gene held up a parcel. "Cardigan sweater with leather buttons, fifty percent off, and another twenty percent today only. Better get in there while th' gettin's good."

"No, thanks, the Busy Fingers crowd in Whitecap knitted me a cardigan that will outlast the Sphinx. Tell me, buddy—do you know anything about getting rid of moles?"

"Moles? My daddy always hollered in their holes and they took off every whichaway."

"What did he say when he hollered?"

Gene cleared his throat, tilted toward Father Tim's right ear, and repeated the short, but fervent, litany.

"My goodness!" said the earnest gardener, blushing to the very roots of what hair he had left.

He heard the receiver being crushed against the capacious bosom of his bishop's secretary, and a muffled conversation. He thought it appealingly quaint not to be put on hold and have his ear blasted with music he didn't want to hear in the first place.

"Timothy! A blessed Easter to you!"

"And to you, Stuart!"

"I was thinking of you only this morning."

"Whatever for? Some interim pulpit assignment in outer Mongolia?"

"No, just thinking that we haven't had a really decent chinwag in, good heavens, since before you went down to Whitecap."

"An eon, to be precise." Well, a couple of years, anyway.

"Come and have lunch with me," suggested

his bishop, sounding . . . sounding what? Pensive? Wistful?

"I'll do it!" he said, decidedly spontaneous after last Sunday's Easter celebration. "I've been meaning to come for a visit, there's something I'd like us to talk over. I may have a crate of moles that must be taken to the country. I can release them on my way to you."

"A crate of . . . moles."

"Yes." He didn't want to discuss it further.

But he couldn't catch the blasted things. He prodded their tunnels with sticks, a burlap sack at the ready; he shouted into their burrows, repeating what Gene had recommended, though in a low voice; he blew his honorary Mitford Reds coach's whistle; he stomped on the ground like thunder.

"I give up," he told his wife, teeth chattering from the cold.

He noted the streak of blue watercolor on her chin, a sure sign she was working on her current children's book starring Violet, the real-life white cat who usually resided atop their refrigerator.

"But you just started!"

"Started? I've been working at it a full half hour."

"Ten minutes max," Cynthia said. "I watched you, and I must say I never heard of getting rid of moles by shouting down their tunnels."

He pulled his gloves off his frozen hands and sat on a kitchen stool, disgusted. His dog sprawled at his feet and yawned.

"I mean, what were you *saying* when you shouted?"

He had no intention of telling her. "If you still want them caught and crated up, you do the catching and crating, and I'll haul them to the country. A fair division of labor." He was sick of the whole business.

Cynthia glared at him as if she were his fifth-grade teacher and he a dunce on the stool. "Why don't you just stop fretting over it, Timothy? Let them have their day!"

Have their day! That was the artistic temperament for you. "But they're ruining the lawn I've slaved over for years, the lawn you dreamed of, longed for, indeed craved, so that you might walk on it barefoot—and I quote—'as upon a bolt of unfurled velvet.'"

"Oh, for heaven's sake, did I say such a silly thing?"

He rolled his eyes.

"Timothy, you know that if you simply turn your head for a while, the humps will go down, the holes will fill in, and by May or June, the lawn will be just fine."

She was right, of course, but that wasn't the point.

"I love you bunches," she said cheerily, trotting down the hall to her studio.

He pulled on his running clothes with the eagerness of a kid yanked from bed on the day of a test he hadn't studied for.

Exercise was good medicine for diabetes, but he didn't have to like it. In truth, he wondered why he didn't enjoy running anymore. He'd once enjoyed it immensely.

"Peaks and valleys," he muttered. His biannual checkup was just around the bend, and he was going to walk into Hoppy Harper's office looking good.

As the Lord's Chapel bells tolled noon, he was hightailing it to the Main Street Grill, where a birthday lunch for J. C. Hogan would be held in the rear booth.

Flying out the door of Happy Endings Bookstore, he hooked a left and crashed into someone, full force.

Edith Mallory staggered backward, regained

her balance, and gave him a look that made his blood run cold.

"Edith! I'm terribly sorry."

"Why don't you watch where you're going?" She jerked the broad collar of a dark mink coat more securely around her face. "Clergy," she said with evident distaste. "They're always preoccupied with lofty thoughts, aren't they?"

Not waiting for an answer, she swept past him into Happy Endings, where the bell jingled wildly on the door.

"'Er High Muckety Muck traipsed by a minute ago," said Percy Mosely, wiping off the table of the rear booth.

Father Tim noted that the slur of her perfume had been left on his clothes. "I just ran into her."

"I'd like t' run into 'er . . . ," said the Grill owner, "with a eighteen-wheeler."

If there was anyone in town who disliked Edith Mallory more than himself, it was Percy Mosely, who, a few years ago, had nearly lost his business to Edith's underhanded landlord tactics. It was clergy, namely yours truly, who had brought her nefarious ambitions to utter ruin. Thus, if there was anyone in town whom

Edith Mallory could be presumed to despise more than Tim Kavanagh, he didn't have a clue who it might be.

"Ever' time I think I've seen th' last of that witch on a broom, back she comes like a dog to 'is vomit."

"Cool it, Percy, your blood pressure . . ."

"An' Ed Coffey still drivin' 'er around in that Lincoln like th' Queen of England, he ought t' be ashamed of his sorry self, he's brought disgrace on th' whole Coffey line."

J. C. Hogan, *Muse* editor and Grill regular, slammed his overstuffed briefcase into the booth and slid in. "You'll never guess what's hit Main Street."

Percy looked fierce. "Don't even mention 'er name in my place."

"Joe Ivey and Fancy Skinner are locked in a price war." J.C. pulled a large handkerchief from his hip pocket and wiped his face.

"A price war?" asked Father Tim.

"Head to head, you might say. Fancy had this big sign painted and put in her window upstairs, said, *Haircuts Twelve Dollars, All Welcome.* First thing you know, Joe puts a sign downstairs, says, *Haircuts Eleven Dollars.*"

Joe Ivey's one-chair barbershop was located in a former storage room behind the kitchen of his sister's Sweet Stuff Bakery. The only other game in town was Fancy Skinner's uni-sex hair salon, A Cut Above, which rented the upstairs area over the bakery. "Poetic irony," is what one Grill customer called the arrangement.

"So Fancy cranks her price down to ten bucks and has her sign repainted. Then Joe drops his price, changes his sign, and gives me an ad that says, 'Haircuts nine-fifty. Free chocolate chip cookie to every customer.'"

"Cutthroat," said Percy.

"I don't know where this'll end," said J.C., "but if you need a haircut, now's the time."

"Happy birthday!" Father Tim thought they should get to the point.

"Right. Happy birthday!" said Percy. "You can be one of th' first to order offa my new menu."

J.C. scowled. "I was used to the old menu."

"This is my an' Velma's last year in this hole-in-th'-wall, I wanted to go out with a bang." Percy stepped to the counter and proudly removed three menus on which the ink was scarcely dry and handed them around. He thought the Wesley printer had come up with a great idea for this new batch—the cover showed the Grill motto set in green letters that were sort of swirling up, like steam, from a coffee mug: *Eat here once and you'll be a regular.*

"Where's Mule at?" asked Percy.

"Beats me," said Father Tim. "Probably getting a haircut."

"So how old are you?" Percy wanted to know.

J.C. grinned. "Fourteen goin' on fifteen is what Adele says."

"Gag me with a forklift," said Mule, skidding into the booth. "He's fifty-six big ones, I know because I saw his driver's license when he wrote a check at Shoe Barn."

"OK, give me your order and hop to it, Velma's havin' a perm down at Fancy's and I'm shorthanded. Free coffee in this booth, today only."

"I don't want coffee," said Mule. "I was thinkin' more like sweet ice tea."

"Coffee's free, tea's another deal."

J.C. opened his menu, looking grim. "You spelled *potato* wrong!" he announced.

"Where at?" asked Percy.

"Right here where it says 'tuna croissant with potatoe chips.' There's no *e* in *potato.*"

"Since when?"

"Since ever."

Look who's talking, thought Father Tim.

"I'll be darned," said Mule. "Taco salad! Can you sell taco salad in this town?"

"Taco salad," muttered Percy, writing on his order pad.

"Wait a minute, I didn't say I *wanted* taco salad, I was just discussin' it."

"I don't have time for discussin'," said Percy. "I got a lunch crowd comin' in."

Father Tim noticed Percy's face was turning beet-red. Blood pressure, the stress of a new menu . . .

"So what is a taco salad, anyway?" asked Mule.

The *Muse* editor looked up in amazement. "Have you been livin' under a *rock*? Taco salad is salad in a taco, for Pete's sake."

"No, it ain't," said Percy. "It's salad in a bowl with taco chips scattered on top."

Mule sank back in the booth, looking depressed. "I'll have what I been havin' before th' new menu, a grilled pimiento cheese on white bread, hold th' mayo."

"Do you see anything on this menu sayin' pimiento cheese? On this menu, we don't *have* pimiento cheese, we ain't goin' to *get* pimiento cheese, and that's th' *end* of it." The proprietor stomped away, looking disgusted.

"You made him mad," said J.C., wiping his face with his handkerchief.

"How can a man make a livin' without pimiento cheese on his menu?" Mule asked.

"'Less you want to run down to th' tea shop and sit with th' women, there's nowhere else to eat lunch in this town . . ."—J.C. poked the menu—"so you better pick something offa here. How about a fish burger? Lookit, 'four ounces breaded and deep-fried haddock filet served on a grilled bun with lettuce, tomato, and tartar sauce.'"

"I don't like tartar sauce."

Father Tim thought he might slide to the floor and lie prostrate. "I'm having the chef's salad!" he announced, hoping to set an example.

Mule looked relieved. "Fine, that's what I'll have." He drummed his fingers on the table. "On the other hand, you never know what's in a chef's salad when you deal with this chef."

"I'm havin' th' tuna melt," said J.C., "plus th' fish burger and potato skins!"

"Help yourself," said Mule. "Have whatever you want, it's on us." He peered intently at the menu. "'Chili crowned with tortilla chips and cheese,' that might be good."

"Here he comes, make up your mind," snapped J.C.

"I'll have th' chili deal," said Mule, declining

eye contact with Percy. "But only if it comes without beans."

Percy gave him a stony look. "How can you have chili without beans? That's like a cheese-burger without cheese."

"Right," said J.C. "Or a BLT without ba-con."

Father Tim closed his eyes as if in prayer, feeling his blood sugar plummet into his loafers.

So what are you doing these days?

It was a casual and altogether harmless question, the sort of thing anyone might inquire of the retired. But he hated it. And now, on the heels of the very same question asked only yesterday by a former parishioner . . .

"So what'n th' dickens do you do all day?"

Mule had left to show a house, J.C. had trudged upstairs to work on Monday's layout, and Percy stood beside the rear booth, squint-ing at him as if he were a beetle on a pin.

After nearly four years of retirement, why hadn't he been able to formulate a pat answer? He usually reported that he supplied various churches here and there, which was true, of course, but it sounded lame. Indeed, he once said, without thinking, "Oh, nothing much." Upon hearing such foolishness out of his mouth, he felt covered with shame.

In his opinion, God hadn't put anyone on earth to do "nothing much." Thus, in the first year following his interim at Whitecap, he'd given endless hours to the Wesley Children's Hospital, second only to the church as his favorite charitable institution. He had even agreed to do something he roundly despised: raise funds. To his amazement, he had actually raised some.

He'd also worked on the lawns of the rectory and the yellow house until people had been known to slow their cars and stare. Occasionally, a total stranger would park at the curb and ask if they could take a picture.

During the second year, he'd given a hand to their new mayor, Andrew Gregory, and supplied pulpits in Wesley, Holding, Charlotte, Asheville, Morganton, Johnson City, and, for a span of several months, Hickory. Somehow, it had been enough. Almost.

He was never unaware that something was gnawing at him, he couldn't say what. Perhaps it was nothing more or less than his masculine ego needing a good-size feeding; in any case, there was a certain restlessness in his spirit, something of feeling unworthy and not quite up to things anymore.

His wife suggested they go to the Dordogne, or even Africa, and he tried to get excited about traveling to faraway places, but couldn't.

In the end, why beat around the bush? A church! That's what he needed. He was homesick for his own flock to feed, to herd around. Occasionally he even missed typing a pew bulletin, though he would never have confided such a peculiarity to another living soul.

Why had he retired, anyway? He might have stayed on at Lord's Chapel 'til the cows came home. When he finally severed that comfortable connection, he was hugely up for freedom and adventure, yet now he wondered what he could have been thinking.

Sometime during the winter, a compelling thought had occurred to him, something for which he and Cynthia had since been seeking God's wisdom. Not knowing exactly how to press forward with such a notion, he decided to discuss it with Stuart. That would help settle things.

In the meantime, he'd begun doing what any self-respecting retired clergyman ought to do: He was writing a book, notably a book of essays that he'd begun on the first day of the new year.

The only problem with this was, he couldn't tell anyone about it.

Percy leaned into the booth and squinted down at him, knitting his brows. Father Tim could practically feel his hot breath. "So do you lay up in th' bed of a mornin'—or *what*?"

Percy wouldn't know an essay if he met it on the street; thus he found himself reporting a list of activities so monumental in length that Percy yawned in his face. Later, he wished he hadn't included the part about cleaning mildew off his old shoes and organizing his socks by color. He also felt that his confession of cooking *and* washing up most evenings was a little over the top—in fact, certain to be fodder for idle gossip from one end of Main Street to the other.

Another thing that dogged him was the uneasy suspicion that writing essays was an indulgent and egocentric thing to do. For that reason, he considered changing horses in midstream and writing his memoirs.

Didn't memoirs have a certain cachet these days? In some circles, they were a positive rage. However, he couldn't imagine saying to anyone, *I'm writing my memoirs*. Writing about one's life presumed that one had a life worth writing about. And, of course, he did, but only since marrying his next-door neighbor at the age of sixty-two. Now, *that* was memoir.

But no, he wasn't a memoir man; when push came to shove, he was an essay man. He had longed, rather childishly, to reveal his secret to someone; after all, he was more than ninety pages along and very much liking the momentum he'd gained.

When Mule didn't show up for breakfast the following morning due to a treadmill test at the hospital, Father Tim impulsively decided to reveal his personal tidbit to J. C. Hogan, who was as close to literati as Mitford was likely to produce in this lifetime.

"Say that again," said J.C., cupping his ear as if he'd misunderstood.

"Essays!" he repeated, suddenly feeling like a perfect idiot. "I'm . . . ah, writing a book of essays."

The *Muse* editor had a blank look as he forked a sausage link. "I've read a couple of essays," he said, shoving the sausage into his mouth and following it with half a buttered biscuit. "Doo fimmity glogalong. Doo muss ahtoo."

Father Tim sighed. "That's one way of looking at it."

"So," said J.C., "what kind of business do

you think Edith Mallory will bring in here when Percy retires?"

"Heaven only knows. It's anybody's guess."

"I could go for a shoe repair," said J.C., coaxing the last of the grape jam from the container. "Or a dry cleaner. I'm over goin' all th' way to Wesley to get my pants pressed."

"You wouldn't have to get 'em pressed if you'd quit hangin' 'em on th' floor," said Percy. Percy had visited the editor's bachelor quarters prior to his marriage to Adele and had been thunderstruck.

No matter how hard he tried, Father Tim couldn't imagine meeting J.C. and Mule at the tea shop. It just wouldn't be the same. Besides, Percy had declared he wouldn't be caught dead in the place, which was wallpapered in lavender forget-me-nots with matching ruffled curtains.

"Percy!" J.C. yelled in the direction of the grill, "who d'you think Godzilla will move in here when you retire?"

Percy looked disgusted. "A pet shop is what Ron Malcolm said was comin'." The very *thought* of that smell blasting out onto Main Street was enough to make a man throw up his gizzard.

"No way!" said J.C. "People in Mitford don't get pets at a pet shop. They wait 'til somethin' shows up at their back door. Idn't that right?" he asked Father Tim, who, after all, should know.

❧

"'O Lord, You are my portion and my cup . . . ,'" he recited in unison with Cynthia and the other congregants at St. Paul's in Wesley. "'It is You who uphold my lot. My boundaries enclose a pleasant land; indeed, I have a goodly heritage. I will bless the Lord Who gives me counsel; my heart teaches me, night after night. I have set the Lord always before me; because He is at my right hand I shall not fall.'"

Cynthia slipped her arm around him as they shared the Psalter. "'My heart, therefore, is glad, and my spirit rejoices; my body also shall rest in hope. For You will not abandon me to the grave, nor let Your holy one see the Pit.'

"'You will show me the path of life; in Your presence there is fullness of joy, and in Your right hand are pleasures for evermore.'"

His heart felt warmed by the familiar words, words he had memorized—when? How long ago? Had he been ten years old, or twelve?

He looked upon his wife and was moved by a great tenderness in his breast. The boy who had recited those words before a hushed

Sunday School class in Holly Springs, Mississippi—what a miracle that he was standing now in this place in Wesley, North Carolina, more than half a century later, feeling the arm of his wife about his waist and knowing a fullness of joy he'd never believed he might experience.

Stuart Cullen didn't appear to be a venerable and much-esteemed bishop. Indeed, at the age of seventy-one, he looked like a man who had just come in from tossing around a football on a back lot.

Father Tim felt oddly proud that his bishop and best friend from seminary looked young and vigorous and entirely without airs; it was a sight to make a man puff out his chest, hold in his stomach, and step smartly into the room where Stuart looked up from the antique walnut desk and smiled.

"My friend!" Stuart exclaimed.

They met in the middle of the room and embraced, the bishop feeling fond of his longtime favorite priest, the priest feeling glad he'd never had the ambition to rise to the top, though he knew perfectly well that's where the cream resided in the jug. In truth, he was glad someone else was willing to shoulder the staggering weight of higher church life and leave him in peace.

"You look terrific!" said Father Tim, meaning it.

"And old," Stuart said.

"Old? What is old? Old is a matter of—"

Stuart chuckled. "Now, Timothy, don't preach me a sermon. Have a seat."

He had one, amused to see that he and Stuart were dressed almost identically, both of them wearing khakis, a sport shirt, and a collar. "Gold Dust twins," he said, indicating their gear.

"Except you're not old, Timothy."

"What is this business about being old? I'm creaking in the joints like a hay wagon."

"I always liked your rustic imagery," said Stuart.

"Too much Wordsworth at an early age," replied Father Tim.

"Speaking of rustic, did you drop your moles off in the country?"

"A failed mission," he admitted. "We never caught any to drop off."

"I despise moles. Or is it voles? And what's the difference, anyway?"

"You don't need to know," said Father Tim. "Now tell me what's up. You're looking quizzical. Or perhaps philosophical."

Stuart sat in a leather wing chair opposite his retired priest and gazed out the window to the garden that his wife cultivated and he puttered in. A pink dogwood in early bloom trembled in a gusting wind. He turned his gaze on his visitor.

"I want to build a cathedral."

"Ahhh." Father Tim reflected a moment on this striking pronouncement. "Building cathedrals isn't a job for the aged."

"Thinking about it has made me face my mortality; it strikes me that I may never live to see it finished. In truth, considering the funds we'll need to raise and the time it will take to raise them, I may not be around for the groundbreaking, much less the dedication. We're not going to borrow a cent, you see."

"Well, then, we may both be dead and gone."

"I'll be seventy-two in eleven months, at which time, as you know, they'll chase me off with a broom. I've always regretted our strict retirement policy. I've never felt better in my life. Why should I be forced to retire at seventy-two?"

"Beats me," said Father Tim.

"In any case, I'm getting a very late start on a cathedral!"

"If you don't mind the platitude, it's never too late."

"I also wonder whether this notion is merely a self-serving desire for immortality, some . . . strut of the flesh."

They pondered this together, quietly. The clock on the mantel ticked. "Do you think," asked Father Tim, "that the desire for immortality was the driving force behind Michelangelo's David or da Vinci's *Mona Lisa*?"

The bishop crossed his legs and appeared to gaze at the toe of his shoe.

"Or behind, shall we say, Handel's *Messiah*?"

"I don't pretend to know what's behind much of anything we humans do. There are days when it seems that everything we do is for unutterably selfish reasons, then come the days on the mountaintop when we're able to know the galvanizing truth all over again, which is that we earnestly seek to do it all to the glory of God."

"What has God said to you about this thing?"

"Quite a lot. Actually, I think it's His notion entirely. I'm clever enough, I suppose, but not quite so clever to drum up the . . . particulars of this idea. I must confess that when it all came to me, I wept."

"Then it has nothing to do with seeing your name chiseled over the door? St. Stuart's on the Hill?"

Stuart laughed. Ah, but Father Tim liked hearing his bishop laugh!

Stuart's secretary opened the door and poked her head into the room. "I'm off to lunch. I don't suppose the two of you need anything?"

"Only a bit of humility, seasoned with patience and fortitude," said the bishop.

"On whole wheat or rye?" asked his secretary, closing the door.

"Some of us," said Stuart, "are interested in initiating only what we'll see come to fruition, but I've always looked beyond the present, beyond the day, a propensity that's both a blessing and a curse."

"Niebuhr spoke to that," said Father Tim.

"Indeed. He said, 'Nothing that is worth doing can be achieved in our lifetime; therefore we must be saved by hope. Nothing which is true or beautiful or good makes complete sense in any immediate context of history; therefore we must be saved by faith.'"

"'Nothing we do, however virtuous,'" quoted Father Tim, "'can be accomplished alone; therefore, we must be saved by love.'"

Stuart leaned forward slightly in the chair. "I have enemies, you know."

Father Tim didn't say it, but he did know, of course.

"As you're aware, ours is the poorest of the southeastern dioceses. So far, the idea of a cathedral has been largely dismissed as flamboyant, self-seeking, a display of spiritual pride, and a flagrant waste of money which could be used for higher purposes."

"And that's just for openers, I'm sure."

"The diocese exists in a culture in which a cathedral smacks of European decadence, though the Baptists down the road just built a church to seat two thousand and nothing was thought of it, nothing at all."

"Where will the cathedral be built?" asked Father Tim, looking on the bright side.

Stuart rose from the chair, grinning, and buttoned his jacket. "Come. I'll show you on our way to lunch."

❧

"This is a cow pasture, Stuart!" He knew for a fact that he'd just stepped in something.

"Ah, Timothy, open your eyes! A cow pasture, yes, but one that slopes down to a magnificent view of the city! Look where we're standing, for heaven's sake! It's a habitation for angels!"

The wind swept words from their mouths; their coats billowed and flapped like sails.

". . . transept," yelled Stuart, pointing toward the brow of the hill. ". . . cruciform!" he shouted, waving with outstretched arms. Though it was nearly impossible to distinguish what Stuart was saying, his bishop's countenance spoke volumes; he was as radiant as the youth Father Tim remembered all those years ago in seminary.

They hurried back to the car, swept along by the chill wind at their backs.

"So here are the particulars," said Stuart, forgetting to put the key in the ignition. "We'll build our cathedral of logs."

"Logs."

"Yes! Honest materials straight from our own highland forests, with scissor trusses of southern yellow pine, a roof of hand-split shakes, oak pews constructed by local artisans. . . . I can't tell you how this excites me, Timothy! *Plus* . . ."

His bishop had a positive gleam in his eye.

"Plus, such materials are exceedingly cost-wise!"

"Aha."

"We think we can do it for six million," said

Stuart. "A pittance, all things considered. At last we'll have what we've needed for so many years—a common meeting place for our scattered diocese, a center of learning, and one day, I trust, a great choir school."

The bishop started the car and they rolled slowly down the hill along the tree-lined street. "Pray for me in this," he said quietly.

"I've been praying for you more than forty years, my friend."

"Don't stop now. You know, of course, that you are faithfully in my prayers, and ever will be."

"Yes," said Father Tim. "And I'm grateful."

"But I've talked too much about my own interests. Forgive me, Timothy. Tell me what brought you today, what's on your heart."

The discussion of a great cathedral was a tough act to follow, but there was hardly a beat between the question and his answer.

"The mission field."

Stuart winced visibly. "You're not keeping busy enough, retirement generally gives too much time to think."

"Don't talk down to me, Stuart." He hadn't treated Stuart's dream lightly, and he didn't take kindly to having his own casually dismissed.

"You're right, of course."

"This is important to me, and to Cynthia. Besides, the commission is to go and tell, not sit home and fossilize."

"I reacted that way because you're diabetic. You don't need to be stumbling around in some bleak outpost with no medical assistance."

"I take two insulin shots a day, monitor my sugar closely, eat at regular intervals, exercise twice a week—it's no big deal. Actually, my doctor would forbid a bleak outpost; we won't go far from home."

"Any idea where?"

"Somewhere in Appalachia," he said. "It's where the Dooley Barlowes and Lace Harpers come from."

"Who is Lace Harper?"

"An exceptional young woman who's the adopted daughter of my doctor and his wife, off to her first year of college this fall. It wasn't long ago that she was living in the dirt under her house."

"Whatever for?"

"To escape a drunken father who beat her senseless."

"Dear Lord."

"Until the Harpers took her in, she was almost completely self-educated, thanks to the county bookmobile. Now she's one of the brightest stars her private school has ever seen. We're exceedingly fond of Lace, we cherish the notion that someday she and Dooley might . . . well, you understand."

"I see. And your boy, Dooley, he's doing well, isn't he?"

"A freshman at the University of Georgia, where he'll study veterinary medicine. If you recall, Dooley's the son of an abusive father he scarcely knew, and of a formerly alcoholic mother who gave her children away. Pauline has since come to know Christ and has married a believer; the transformation is wondrous. All this is to say I've seen what a difference it can make for kids like Dooley and Lace to be given a break, to be loved. In truth, it makes all the difference!"

Stuart braked, waiting to turn left, and looked at his old friend. "An English missionary said, 'Some want to live within the sound of Church and Chapel bell; I want to run a rescue shop within a yard of hell.' You have my blessing." Of all his clergy, Timothy Kavanagh had been the one he could depend on completely, the one whose theology never wavered and whose friendship genuinely counted.

"I'll need your help, Stuart, your input about the ministries we should consider."

The bishop wheeled into the restaurant parking lot and switched off the ignition. He looked at Father Tim and nodded his assent. "You'll have that, too," he promised.

CHAPTER TWO

Mixed Blessings

Lady Spring's Coy Flirtation Fails to Amuse
—BY HESSIE MAYHEW

For three days in mid-February, Lady Spring cajoled our wintry spirits with zephyrs so balmy that we found ourselves utterly deceived. How quickly we forget, year to year, the heart-wrenching extent to which this frivolous and unrepentant lady betrays us.

Our power lines felled by ice storms in March! Our rooftops laden with snow in April! Our lilacs lashed by bitter winds on May Day! One shudders to think what June may bring, the dear June that once gave us roses and clematis!

On the southerly slopes of the mountain, where the japonica has long since shed its crimson petals, we, hapless stepchildren that we are, must find delight in adorning our homes with sprigs of withered berries!

However much the heart may yearn toward Lady Spring's vernal passage, hearken, I implore you, to the one bit of counsel that, come what may in this earthly life, will never, ever betray you:

DO NOT PLANT UNTIL MAY 15!

Hessie Mayhew's annual spring angst. . . .

He sighed and dropped the newspaper to the floor.

Once he'd clipped along through the *Mitford Muse* in twenty, thirty minutes, max. Looking at his watch, he was dismayed to learn he'd just spent an hour and a half with the darned thing, as absorbed as if it were the *Chicago Tribune.*

He'd even studied the classifieds, something seldom done in this life, and found his interest sincerely piqued by a walnut chest of drawers listed at a yard sale in Wesley.

Retirement. That was the culprit.

He snatched the latest *Anglican Digest* from the table by his chair and went at it, head down.

"Mail call!" crowed his wife, never happier than when the mail had been chunked through the slot in the front door.

And who wouldn't be ecstatic? he wondered. Scarcely a day passed that her devoted readers didn't express their admiration of her talent, beauty, wit, intelligence, and general benefit to mankind.

She sat beside him on the study sofa and busied herself with sorting.

"Fan letter, fan letter, fan letter, bill . . . bill, bill, fan letter, junk mail, bill . . ."—she was, he noticed, piling the bills in his lap, not hers—"junk mail, junk mail, fan letter, bill—"

"Doo wap, doo wap," he said.

She stopped sorting and tore open an envelope.

"Oh, lovely, it's not a fan letter, it's from Marion!" Marion was their good and faithful friend from their interim on Whitecap Island; he always relished Marion's long, newsy letters.

"Oh, my!" She burst into laughter.

"What?" he said.

"Ella Bridgewater's bird, Louise . . . remember the canary that serenaded you? Well, it's not Louise at all, it's Louis! Marion has no earthly idea how Ella discovered this surprising fact, but it's the talk of St. John's."

"Aha."

"Marion's going online and wants our e-mail address."

"That will be the day."

"And she and Sam send their love."

"That's all? Louise is Louis and they send their love?"

"That's all, dearest, it's just a little note."

"Oh," he said, disappointed. His wife moved quickly to other matters, using her letter opener to slice the flap of a white envelope.

"My goodness," she murmured, reading. "Well, then . . ." She appeared briefly saddened, then looked at him and smiled.

"What is it?"

"I've been asked to tour the country with four other children's book authors and illustrators."

"Tour the *country*?" The thought chilled his blood. He remembered her trip to Lansing several years ago to read at a school. She had arrived home very late, just as he was calling the police to begin a statewide search.

"With a program called READ," she said, glancing again at the letter, "an acronym for Readers Earn Author's Day. Let's see . . . umm . . . what a grand idea! Schools compete to read so many books, and those who reach or exceed the mark are eligible for a visit by Davant Medal authors. It all raises money for local literacy programs, and look . . . the other authors are my *favorites*!"

Her bright countenance frightened him.
"But . . ."

"But of course I can't go," she said.

"And why not?"

"Because it's the first of August, and we'll be in Tennessee."

"Right!" He was flooded with relief. "Of course!" They were going to Tennessee in less than two months, to join forces with Our Own Backyard, the mission project they'd long prayed might present itself. Dooley would finish his freshman year at college, spend a few days with them in Mitford, and head to Meadowgate for the summer to assist Hal Owen in his veterinary practice.

Then Father Tim and Cynthia would tool across the state line to their year-long ministry in the newly formed OOB. The concept for this project, which was warmly endorsed by Stuart Cullen, had been developed by Father Roland, whose research had uncovered dumbfounding truths about the extent of poverty and deprivation in an area around Jessup, Tennessee. There they would find alcohol and drug abuse, violence, severe medical and dental problems, families without transportation, unpaved roads, a high rate of school dropouts—bottom line, an area not unlike

Mitford's Creek community before it had become a shopping center.

Theirs would be a simple ministry and, as far as he was concerned, that was among its attractions. Along with Father Roland and a zealous young Kentucky priest and his wife, they would live in the remote community much like other mountain families; except that, each afternoon, they would open the doors of their homes to whatever young people might come. There would be art classes and singing, Bible stories and books, food and games—a safe place, a good place; and on Sunday, he and the other two priests would celebrate and preach in the several widely scattered mission churches formed in the last century by ardent Anglican bishops.

The move itself would be the soul of simplicity: They would load the Mustang with kitchen gadgetry, a bolt of mosquito netting, five suitcases, four pillows, and a heap of blankets. They would ship thirty-six pounds of art supplies and two hundred books by truck. On arrival, they would set up housekeeping in a sparsely furnished metal building with a cement floor.

His wife had paled when told about the metal building, and had nearly reneged on the whole deal when the subject of cement floors arose.

"But," she had said, "it's not about cement floors."

He patted her hand that held the letter. *I'm sorry,* he wanted to say, but didn't. And he really was sorry, for he liked nothing more than to see his wife able to give something back in her own way, in a way not connected to being a priest's wife.

He looked into her earnest face and was shamed by his feelings. He was unutterably selfish; deep down inside he knew it, and no, he could never confess it to her, not in a thousand years.

At Mitford Blossoms, he asked Jena Ivey for a dozen roses; long-stemmed, without wires, ferns, or gypsophilia, please, in a box lined with green paper and tied with a pink satin ribbon.

"Oh, I remember how she likes her roses!" Jena looked him in the eye, smiling. "And it's been ages since you've done this."

He blushed. He was still smarting from the dark recognition that he desperately feared being separated from his wife. It had made him feel suddenly weak and frail, like a child. All those years alone, a bachelor who seldom yearned for the hearthstone of a wife's love, and now . . . he was a man beset with a dreadful mixture of anxiety and humiliation over the depth of his attachment.

"Make that . . ." The words lodged in his throat. "Make that two dozen!"

Jena blinked, unbelieving. She had never known but one other man in Mitford to buy two dozen roses at a whack, and that was Andrew Gregory, the mayor. Every time he and his Italian wife had an anniversary, Mr. Gregory hotfooted it to Mitford Blossoms and laid out cash money, no matter what the going rate.

"Why, Father! Cynthia will think . . . she'll think you've gone 'round the bend!"

He forced a grin. "And she would be right," he said.

"Tim?"

It was John Brewster, director of the Children's Hospital in Wesley.

"Yes, John, how are you, good fellow?"

"Couldn't be better, I have some great news."

"I'm eternally interested in great news!"

"We've finally got the funds to hire someone, someone strong, savvy, good at encouraging our donors—the kind of person who can really make a difference around here."

"Terrific! This has been a long time coming."

"A long time coming, and I'm asking you to consider the position."

There was a brief silence.

"We can talk about the particulars later. You're the absolutely perfect person for the job, Tim—heaven-sent, if you ask me. I hope you'll say yes."

"Ah." He was oddly shaken. Yes, it was something he would like doing and would, in fact, be pretty good at doing. But . . .

"It's too late," he told the director. "I've recently made a commitment, Cynthia and I will be going up to Tennessee to work with a children's program, we'll come back to Mitford most weekends, but . . ."

"I hate to hear this." He thought John sounded as if he might burst into tears. "I'm terribly disappointed, everyone agreed that I should call you at once. Is there any chance the other thing . . . could fall through, not work out?"

"I don't think so. I'm sorry, too, I would have liked . . ."

John sighed. "Well, then, we've got to dig

deep over here and reset our thinking. Ah. Well, then. Darn."

He thought the director seemed fairly stricken. *It's not the end of the world*, he wanted to say. "It's gracious of you to ask, John, I'm flattered, really."

And he was. He felt a spring in his step as he went down the hall to Cynthia's studio and sat on her small love seat and told her what they'd just turned down.

She came and sat in his lap and kissed the top of his head and hugged him, wordless.

Dear Stuart:

I've just recalled that Mahatma Gandhi said, "First they laugh at you, then they fight you, then you win."

In His brotherhood,
Timothy

"Father!"

Hélène Pringle dashed across the driveway and into the yard of the yellow house. He observed with some fondness that she bobbed when she dashed, rather like a small hare across an open field.

She clutched a parcel in her hands, which she transferred to his. "Bread!" she exclaimed, huffing a bit. "Just baked. I hope you and Cynthia will enjoy it."

"Thank you, Hélène!" The seductive warmth of the loaf seeped through the brown bag. "I just might eat the whole thing standing right here!"

His neighbor laughed with childlike merriment. What a transformation had occurred in this small, once-faint-hearted Frenchwoman who had moved next door from Boston two or three years ago. He hardly ever thought of it now, but they'd gotten off to an exceedingly rough start—Hélène had not only stolen a valuable bronze off his mantel, she'd sued him for big bucks—and all the while living in and renting his house. Thank heaven he'd dropped his charges, she'd withdrawn the lawsuit, and he and Cynthia now had the finest neighbor on God's green earth. In truth, Hélène Pringle had grown in grace and stretched her wings considerably.

"Warming up!" he said of the weather, and was glad to hear such words from his mouth.

"*Oui! J'adore le printemps!* Oh, excuse me, Father, I always speak French when I'm excited!"

"I saw Françoise yesterday, she looks strong

and happy." Hélène had managed to bring her mother from Boston and install her at Hope House, where, though plagued by several complications of heart disease, she was flourishing.

"Mother loves your visits, Father, thank you for all you and Cynthia do for us. One day, I promise I shall repay you in some important way. *Absolument!*"

"Don't even think it! Merely observing your happiness here gives us a double portion."

"Three new students, Father! That's fifteen, now, and I think I mustn't accept more. I never thought I'd be able to say such a thing." Hélène consulted her watch. "*Ça, par exemple!* It's nearly time for Sophie Hawthorne's eleven o'clock."

Hélène's piano teaching had introduced a pleasing new dimension to Mitford. He felt personally proud of her success, though he'd had nothing at all to do with it.

"Please help yourself to your roses when they bloom, Father, I must tell you I'm grateful to live in the home of a gardener! Well, *à bientôt!*"

"*Au revoir*, Hélène! Oh, and *merci!*" He estimated that his French vocabulary now included a whopping ten or twelve words.

She gave a fluttering wave, then darted

across the driveway and over the lawn of the rectory and up the steps. He smiled. Precisely like a hare!

As he walked into the hall from the front door, he observed his wife standing by the living room window.

"I saw you talking with Hélène, I thought she might eat you with a spoon on the very spot where you stood!"

"Spying on me!" he said.

"It's true, darling, but only while washing a smudge off the windowpane. I think she's mad for you, but in an altogether decent way, of course."

He judged Cynthia's eyes to be precisely the color of chicory blossoms, soon to appear in the fields around Mitford. He set the bread in a chair and bounded to her and took her in his arms. "Why would you be jealous of me, for goodness' sake?"

He was laughing as he said it, but he really wanted to know, needed to know; he suddenly craved to hear her say something that would knock his socks off. She was good at that . . .

"But I'm not jealous of you at all!"

"You're not?"

"Of course not! Hélène is a lovely woman who's scarcely ever known a decent man until she met her neighbor. Which is exactly the way I felt when I started popping through the hedge."

Ah. Popping through the hedge. That had been the modus operandi of their courtship; he felt positively nostalgic just hearing her mention the hedge.

"Besides, Timothy, I know you'll love me 'til death do us part, and then forever."

She put her arms around his neck and he kissed her tenderly, inhaling her warm scent.

But since she'd brought it up, he would have liked her to be jealous—if only a little.

He broke the news as they sat at the kitchen table.

"Not again!" wailed Puny. "Y'all jis' *went* off a little bit ago, I cain't even *think* about you goin' off ag'in!"

"Just for a year," he said, feeling like a traitor.

"Yessir, Rev'ren', seems like we ain't hardly got settled down from th' last time you went off," said Harley. Harley Welch was his friend, his handyman, his brother in the Lord, his neighbor who lived in Hélène Pringle's basement.

"We're going to work with children who've been terribly hurt by their circumstances,"

Cynthia explained. "It's a wonderful program that will help families find healing."

"But you got children right here," said Puny, struggling to understand. "I mean, they're not really hurt or anything, even if I did spank Sassy somethin' awful for playin' with matches."

Puny's red-haired twins, Sissy and Sassy, had been part of the Kavanagh household since birth. Now they usually came home each day to the yellow house, from Mitford School's second grade.

Father Tim glanced at Cynthia, who was clearly sobered by the gloomy response to their news. Didn't they have a perfect right to do whatever they pleased? Didn't they deserve the freedom to pursue God's plan for their lives? And here were two lower lips positively hanging to the floor.

Harley shook his head and sighed.

"Now, *listen!*" Father Tim said in his pulpit voice.

Aha! That was the ticket, that got their attention. From now on, it would be tell, don't ask!

"We're going to Tennessee, but we can't do it without you. No, indeed, we'd be in a pickle. In truth, if the Lord hadn't provided the two of you to care for things around here, I doubt if we'd be able to answer this call.

"Harley, you're to keep the two yards mowed, pruned up, and fertilized.

"Puny, you're to do the outstanding job you did while we were in Whitecap! We'll come home on frequent weekends as hungry as bears, so load up the refrigerator and don't spare the tomato aspic!

"Harley . . ."

"Yessir?" Harley had snapped to.

"Be sure and take Dooley's granpaw his livermush, as Dooley will be at Meadowgate with the Owens this summer. Further, I'd like you to go out to the farm now and again and let Marge Owen feed you some chicken pie, she said she'd look forward to it."

Harley stood bolt upright from the chair. "Yessir, Rev'rend!" He thought Harley might give a salute.

"Puny! You can handle the job?"

"Oh, yessir, I can, and be glad to!" Color was back in her cheeks and adrenaline was pumping; the place was humming again, as if power had been restored after a blackout.

"Well, then, go to it, and thank God for both of you!"

His wife turned and looked at him, smiling.

"Darling," she murmured with evident admiration, "you could have been a Marine!"

"For you," said Cynthia, going about her daily task of mail call.

He eagerly opened the envelope postmarked from a federal prison.

Dear Father:

Thanks for your letter of last month. I haven't responded as quickly as usual, for a great deal is going on here. God is working in very unexpected ways.

The short of it is this:

After eight years, I am being released on good behavior. My hand is trembling as I write this, as I didn't know whether I would ever be able to share such glorious good news.

It is my hope that I might be welcome in Mitford. If you could help me find a place there, I will be always grateful and will work hard to earn your trust, and the trust of everyone in Mitford. As I have said many times, I never felt so at home anywhere else. I will need employment and will appreciate it if you will keep your eyes open, though I know there's not much of a job market for convicted felons.

Pray for me, Father, as I go through these next few weeks, I should be arriving in Mitford, if that is all right with you, the middle of June.

I don't know what to tell you about my job skills, as I would never again be accepted within the university system. My main interests are living this merciful new life for Christ, and reading. I can play a little softball and restore antique cars, which, as I look at what I just wrote, is a pretty pathetic resume. I would be eager and willing to learn a trade, anything short of breaking wild horses . . . well, even that.

Enclosed is the monthly check for the Children's Hospital. I have saved nearly all the rest of my income from working in the prison laundry, and so will have some means, however limited, to make a go of things.

Please note the new address they've assigned me until my release. I look forward with hope to your letter.

Yours in the One Who is our faithful shield and buckler,
    George Gaynor

"You're beaming," she said.

"George Gaynor is being released from prison."

"Thanks be to God!"

"He's coming to live in Mitford. We must find him a job."

"Yes! Terrific! And a place to live," she said, her wheels already turning.

He snapped the red leash on Barnabas and walked up the street, whistling. He hadn't surprised himself by whistling in a very long time, probably not since his jaunts on the beach at Whitecap.

He was in a visiting mood. If Homeless Hobbes hadn't moved to the country when the Creek community was uprooted by the shopping center, he'd trot over there for a chinwag. He often missed Homeless's comfortable companionship and hard-won wisdom. In truth, his visits to the shack on the creek had once been a great getaway. . . .

He hailed Avis Packard, who was smoking a cigarette in front of The Local; he stuck his head in the door of the Collar Button and spoke to the Collar Button man, who was taking inventory and looking grumpy; he veered into the Sweet Stuff Bakery and said hello to Winnie Kendall, averting his eyes from the bake case and trying not to inhale too deeply as her husband, Thomas, removed a tray of chocolate chip cookies from the oven.

Walking on, he hooked the leash around the iron leg of the bench outside the Grill and went in for a large order of fries and chicken tenders, plus a Little Debbie snack cake. Then, clutching the bag, he trotted to the old Porter place, a.k.a. the town museum, to visit Uncle Billy and Miss Rose.

Uncle Billy Watson hoisted himself from the chair with his cane, shuffled to the back door, and looked out, grinning. "Law, if hit ain't th' preacher! Rose, come an' look, hit's th' preacher!"

He called to his schizophrenic wife of more than fifty years, who was nearly stone deaf but refused to wear hearing aids. "There's aids enough in this world!" was her common reply.

Miss Rose appeared behind her husband, wearing a chenille bathrobe and a turban adorned with . . . maybe a mashed-flat silk tiger lily . . . or was it a gladiolus?

"You leave that dog outside," she shouted. The gladiolus bobbed as she spoke.

"Yes ma'am," he said, "I was going to do that."

"And don't strap him to my lawn chairs, he'll haul them off every whichaway."

"Yes ma'am."

He attached his patient dog to the post on the porch stoop and went in with the sack from the Grill. "A little something to add to your supper menu," he said. He loved to bring fries to Uncle Billy, though he had to monitor Miss Rose or she would eat the whole caboodle and leave her husband holding the bag.

"What is it?" asked the old woman, looking especially fierce.

"Chicken, fries—"

"Bill Watson won't eat chicken thighs!" She snatched the bag from Father Tim's hand and bolted down the hallway. "He likes white meat!"

"I be dadgum," said her husband, sounding plaintive. "Rose! You come back!"

They heard the bedroom door slam and the lock click.

"Eh, law," sighed Uncle Billy.

"Well, well," said Father Tim, not knowing what else to say.

"Some days is worse than others, don't you know."

Father Tim thought Uncle Billy looked exceedingly fragile, like a dry leaf blown on the wind.

"You feel like going down to the Grill before they close? We'll sit there in peace and you can have whatever you like. I'll tip in a chocolate milkshake."

Uncle Billy's filmy eyes appeared to sparkle. "I'd be beholden to you, yessir, I would."

"And I'd be beholden to you," said Father Tim, eager for his old friend's company.

Walking down the street with Bill Watson was slow going, but he didn't mind. After all, he had nowhere to hurry to, and Barnabas seemed happy enough.

"We'un's'll be a whole lot older when we git there," said Uncle Billy.

He was helping Uncle Billy negotiate the curb when he looked up and saw her getting out of the Lincoln, several buildings away. It never failed; no matter how often he'd seen her over the years, it was always the same: His heart hammered, his mouth went dry, and he wanted to run for his life.

She glanced his way and appeared to stare for a moment as he helped Uncle Billy along the pavement. He turned his head at once, and when he looked again, Edith Mallory had disappeared into the Sweet Stuff Bakery.

On his way home from Uncle Billy's, where Miss Rose was still cloistered in the bedroom, he dodged into Happy Endings.

Margaret Ann, the orange cat, was sprawled on the counter by the register; Hope Winchester sat on a stool reading . . . he couldn't see what.

"What's new?" he asked, thinking that Hope looked unusually attractive today, rather like a youthful Jane Austen character dressed in jeans.

"Something old," she said, holding up the book for his view. "Angela Thirkell!"

"Anything on the rare books shelf that I haven't seen?"

"I have something coming next week, you'll find it uncommonly egregious."

"Give me a clue."

"Oh, I'd like it to be . . ."—she thought for a moment—"a peripeteia."

"Aha," he said. "Call me when it comes in. And by the way, a friend of ours is moving to town in June, he'll be needing a job. If you hear of anything . . ."

"What are his skills?" Hope adjusted her tortoiseshell-rim glasses.

The truth about George Gaynor would be out the moment he hit town, so Father Tim might as well start the ball rolling.

"Do you remember the Man in the Attic?"

"Why, yes! Who could forget? And he's coming to live in *Mitford*?" Her eyes fairly shone.

If she was this excited about a convicted jewel thief living among them, he thought, maybe the rest of the village would feel the same way. In truth, the whole town had taken to George Gaynor for the way he'd turned himself in to authorities during a Sunday morning service at Lord's Chapel. He recalled that Mitford School's first grade had sent drawings for George's jail cell, and his unusual confession of wrongdoing had been lauded in several local sermons.

He took Hope's bright countenance as a good sign.

Why go for a medical checkup now? Why not a day or two before their trip to Tennessee? That way, everything would be up-to-the-minute. He trotted to the downstairs powder room where he stashed his glucometer, opened the kit, shot the lance into the tip of his left forefinger, and spilled the drop of blood onto a test strip.

Barnabas came in and sat at his feet, curious. "Hello, buddy."

He slid the strip into the glucometer and waited for the readout: 180.

Not good. But not terribly bad, either. He could bring it back into line.

He went to the study, called Hoppy's office, and rescheduled.

"Mail call! Mail call!"

Cynthia came down the hall and into the study, trailed by Violet, and dumped the pile onto the sofa. Her letter opener, in permanent residence by the potted gardenia on the coffee table, was snatched up and held at the ready.

"OK, darling. Bill, bill, fan letter, fan letter, junk mail, junk mail, junk mail, ugh, junk mail, fan letter, *Southern Living,* fan letter . . . oh, my."

"Oh, my, what?" he asked, taking a sip of tea.

"This is from the awards commission." Violet leaped onto the sofa and settled in Cynthia's lap.

"Awards commission . . ."

"Yes, of the Davant Medal. No one in New York has said anything to me. Surely they would have said something. . . ."

She opened the letter slowly and began to read.

" 'Dear Ms. Coppersmith:

" 'We are delighted, indeed, to inform you that your most recent Violet book, *Violet Goes to the Beach,* is being awarded the prestigious

Davant Medal, which will be presented at a formal dinner on July 14, at the Plaza Hotel in New York.

"'Congratulations!

"'We are thrilled that this will be your second Davant Medal, and though this acknowledgment of your outstanding work is no surprise at all to a distinguished awards committee of your peers, we do hope it will be a most pleasant surprise to you.'"

His wife looked faint.

"Oh, Timothy . . ."

He reached out to her as she burst into tears.

Local Pastor's Wife Grabs Big Award

He rolled up the latest editon of the *Muse*, put on his cap, and, ignoring his dog, went at a pace down Wisteria Lane and hooked a right on Main Street.

He blew past the bakery, made the front windows rattle in the two-story office building, and charged into the Grill, where he marched to the rear booth, opened the door to the back stairs, and bolted up them two at a time.

"J.C.," he said, speaking through clenched teeth.

The editor looked up from his layout table. "What?"

He shook the rolled-up newspaper. "My wife is not a pastor's wife. . . ." He regretted that he was puffing and blowing.

"You could've fooled me," said J.C., looking bewildered.

"She is her own person, she has a name, and I would greatly appreciate seeing you use it henceforth. She has just been given one of the most distinguished awards in publishing, and you have demeaned this high honor by removing her name from the headline and casting her as my *wife*!"

"Are you *drinkin'*? She *is* your wife!"

Father Tim lowered his voice. "This award was not won as a pastor's wife, it was won as a hardworking writer and illustrator who has slaved over a drawing board for more than twenty years and has earned the right to be called by *her own name*."

"I called her by her name, dadblame it."

"In the *headline*."

J.C. glared at him. "You're goin' to fall down with a stroke if you don't watch out."

He saw that his hands were trembling, put them behind his back, and drew a deep breath.

"I just wanted you to know," he said, and turned around and went down the stairs and through the Grill and out to the street, where he stopped and wiped his forehead and wondered what, exactly, had just happened to him.

"Hey, Granpaw!"
"Hey, Granpaw!"
Twin girls, twin tousles of red hair, twin hugs—and yet, two thoroughly individual hearts, souls, minds, and spirits.
"Hey, yourself!" he exclaimed. "Come and tell me everything."
Ah, but he fancied the grandchildren Puny had allowed him to adopt as his own. There was, however, no Granmaw in the household; no, indeed, Cynthia did not take to this folksy appellation, it was just plain Cynthia for all comers, regardless of age or station.
"This is for you!" said Sassy, removing something from her book sack. "It has my name on the bottom."
He looked at the watercolor—a man sleeping in a wing chair with a huge black dog at his feet. The man possessed a large nose and was not wearing shoes.
"That's you!" she said, looking pleased.
"Umm. Are you sure my nose is that big?"
"Miss Cynthy says it looks just like you!"

"An' see, Granpaw, this is mine!" Sissy held up her own watercolor—a man lying on a sofa with a huge black dog sprawled beside him on the floor. "It's you an' Barnabas, I put Vi'let under the sofa, that's her tail, do you like it?"

There was that turnip-size nose again. He reached up and felt the thing that extended from his face. "I couldn't like it better. Why on earth were you painting me today?"

"Miss Hellman said do somebody, *not* your mama or your daddy, that you like really a lot."

"Well, if that's the case, maybe you wouldn't mind being seen around town with me." The twins began to jiggle on the balls of their feet, entering into an after-school game the three of them often played.

Father Tim scratched his head in mock puzzlement and inquired soberly, "But where on earth could we go?"

"Sweet Stuff!" they shouted in unison.

"I didn't know you had grans!" Ada Rupert, who was buying a dozen oatmeal cookies for a visit of her own grandchildren, looked suspicious.

"I don't," he said. "Well, not exactly. I borrow my grans, you might say."

"Humph," said Ada. "I guess when there's nothin' to do all day, borrowin' grans helps pass th' time. As for me, I've got all I can say grace over without grans comin' this afternoon to spend two days!"

He noticed Ada was huffing and blowing as if she'd run to the bakery from the top of the hill.

"Chocolate chip cookie!" said Sassy, standing on tiptoe and placing her order with Winnie.

"Cream horn!" proclaimed Sissy, indicating her choice by touching the glass case and leaving a smudge.

"Well!" said Ada, collecting her purchases and turning to leave. "You can borrow mine anytime! Help yourself!"

He was ashamed to realize he'd fallen victim to Ada Rupert's notoriously sharp tongue. Nothing to do all day? Nothing to do, indeed!

His face flamed as the bell jingled on the door, and he reached into his pocket and removed his wallet. "A cream horn, a chocolate chip cookie, and . . ." He stared into the case, stricken.

"And?" asked Winnie, peering at him.

His heart hammered. "And a *napoleon!*" he said, surprised to hear the forbidden order issue forth in his pulpit voice.

After dinner at the yellow house, he knocked on the rectory's basement door.

Harley opened it, looking sheepish. "Law, Rev'ren', you done caught me fryin' onions! Step on in, I hope you don't mind th' smell."

"Smells good! Won't take but a minute, just wanted to say a friend is coming to town. He'll need work and a place to live, says he can re-store old cars and he's willing to learn a trade. If that rings any bells, or if you hear of any-thing . . ."

"I'll keep m' eye out. Can you set down an' visit?"

"Can't do it tonight, thanks, we're going to take a little stroll through Baxter Park. His name is George Gaynor. He's . . . a convicted felon, out on parole after eight years in prison."

Harley looked dismayed, then dropped his gaze to the floor.

"What is it, Harley?"

"Well, Rev'ren', they's one thing I ain't never tol' you. I was meanin' to, but . . . th' reason I didn't never tell you is 'cause you didn't never ask me." Harley raised his head and looked his landlord in the eye. "I served time."

"Aha."

"What done it is, I was runnin' from th' *po*lice back when I was haulin' liquor. I didn't want t' run, nossir, but I was s' scared, I couldn't think whether I wanted to keep a-goin' and maybe git caught som'ers down th' road, or stop an' face th' music."

Harley sighed. "I kep' a-goin'. They run me all th' way to Cumberland County with fifty gallons of lightnin' in m' fender wells, an' th' harder they run me, th' madder they got, 'cause I had a '62 Chevy V-8 that went like a scalded dog." Harley sighed again. "Pulled three years. Hit sobered me up, in a manner of speakin'."

Father Tim nodded.

"I hate t' tell you that, hit pains me."

"What's done is done."

"When they let me out, I never hauled another drop. An' not too long after that, I quit drinkin' th' lowdown stuff—just quit foolin' with liquor all th' way around."

He put his hand on Harley's shoulder. What would he do without this good man the Lord had dropped in his lap? "That hard thing had a bright side, then."

Harley nodded, then grinned with relief, displaying pink gums entirely vacant of teeth.

"Keep your ear to the ground for George, if you will. He'll be arriving sometime in June. You'll like him, he's a strong believer."

"I'll do it. An' Rev'ren' . . ."

"Yes?"

"I wouldn't want th' boy t' know, hit'd not be right f'r th' boy t' know what I tol' you."

"He won't hear it from me." He turned to go.

"Rev'ren'?" Harley swallowed hard. "I thank you f'r . . . lettin' me tell you that."

"I thank you for telling me," he said.

He'd done everything possible to trace Dooley's missing siblings. Sammy and Kenny had, in fact, been missing for more than nine years, and nothing, no matter what he did, seemed to result in useful clues. Dooley's stepfather, Buck Leeper, was doing his share: He'd worked on a false lead to Kenny for a full year and it had turned into a dead end.

Locating the first two Barlowe children had been miraculously simple. Father Tim and Lace Turner had hauled Poo out of the Creek community, and Jessie, then five years old, had been traced to Florida. On the oddest of hunches, he and Cynthia had made the long trip to Lakeland with Jessie's mother, Pauline, and now, thanks be to God, three of the five siblings were safe and accounted for. More than anything, yes, more than anything, he wanted to see the whole family reunited with their utterly transformed mother who had surrendered her life to Christ and married a believer who loved her kids.

He tried not to despair over the mounting discouragement he felt, and firmly denied the thought that occasionally came to him; the thought that, deep down, he had given up hope.

"Sit still," he told his wife. "I'll get it."

He'd always rather liked a ringing doorbell. One never knew what surprise or even amazement might be waiting. It was a great deal like the mail in that regard.

He could scarcely see Jena Ivey, owing to the enormous basket of flowers she was delivering to their threshold. Jena ducked her head around the ivy that trailed profusely from one side.

"Congratulations!" she crowed, shoving the vast thing into his arms. He staggered backward from the weight of it.

"Congratulations? What did I do?"

"Nothing, as far as I know, it's for Cynthia!" The hardworking owner of Mitford Blossoms was positively beaming.

"Of course! Yes, indeed. Good gracious. . . ."

"It's the most money anyone *ever* let me spend on an order," she called after him. "I used everything but the kitchen sink!"

He trotted down the hall, peering carefully around a thicket of maidenhair fern so he wouldn't crash into a wall, and delivered the basket to the study.

"There!" He set it on the hearth, nearly poking his eye on one of the several lengths of grapevine stuck capriciously into the moss. "I don't know what it is; possibly a complete shire from the west of England!"

"How *wonderful*!" His wife bounded from the sofa, streaked to the thing, and buried her face in it, wreathed in smiles. "Heaven! Oh, my! What joy!"

He observed that she was now down on all fours, crawling around the basket, which was fully the size of Johnson County and loaded with everything from yellow tulips and lavender foxglove to pink roses and purple verbena.

"Umm! Oh, goodness! Look, dearest, could

it be heliotrope? And there! See the tiny mushrooms growing in the moss?"

"Who's it from?" he asked, squatting down to where the action was.

She removed the card from the French wire ribbon. "Let's see. . . . Well! Have you ever?"

No, he had never. "Who?" he asked.

"Dear James!"

"Dear James?"

"You know, darling, my editor."

"Aha."

" 'My dear Cynthia,' " she read aloud from the card. " 'Please accept this smallest of tokens for the joy you have brought so many. Congratulations!' "

"*Dear* James, *dear* Cynthia?" This inquiry, spoken with uncharacteristic sarcasm, was out of his mouth before he knew it. His face flamed.

Just as it took very, very little to make his wife happy, it took very little, indeed, to wound her deeply. She looked as if she'd been dashed with ice water.

"I'm sorry," he said, dumbfounded by his feelings. Where had that sudden, bitter jealousy come from?

He reached toward her, but she drew back. "I've never heard you . . . speak that way before," she whispered.

Tears sprang to his eyes. "I don't know, I'm sorry, please forgive me." He felt oddly lost, bereft, as if a great chasm had opened between them.

She leaned her head to one side and looked at him for a long moment. Then she smiled. "It's all right, dearest," she said, taking his hand.

CHAPTER THREE

The Future Hour

He settled into his chair in the study, swiveled around to the desk, and tore off several calendar pages.

May 21st, vanished!

May 22nd, defunct!

May 23rd, out of here!

Where had time gone? He hadn't penned a word in nearly a month. But there'd be no guilt; he'd sworn to enjoy the process and not kick himself for failing to churn out a predetermined volume of work. The book would happen when it happened.

He put his mind to the thing before him.

"'Enough, if something from our hands

have power,'" he recited aloud, "'to live and act and serve the future hour. . . .'"

This new essay would address the couplet from Wordsworth; it put forth an issue he'd been searching in his heart, whether indeed he'd done anything in nearly forty years as a priest that would truly serve the future hour. He needed to know the answer, the honest answer. Writing to search the soul had often helped; more than once this had enabled him to arrive at a better understanding of a personal issue. He thought, too, that the whole subject might be of interest to others—didn't everyone fervently desire to leave a mark, to make a difference? In truth, mortality had been one of mankind's most devouring disappointments—having only a brief time to make a difference, one forever felt the pressure to get cracking.

He picked up the black pen and relished its solid heft; for years, he'd wished for a fine pen, something more than the annual Christmas ballpoint from The Local, or the sundry poor excuses in his pen cup that multiplied like wire hangers in a closet. And now, in honor of this book of essays, his good wife had given him a black roller ball with a white emblem on the cap; he couldn't imagine what it might have cost—it had bucks written all over it. Maybe he'd use the pen today instead of his type-writer; after all, had Montaigne used a type-writer, or Proust, or Emerson?

He peered at the decrepit Royal manual that had served him well for longer than he could remember. It had gone through his sixteen-year tenure at Lord's Chapel and was still working like a clock, except for the lowercase *i,* which often printed *ii;* he'd always meant to have that fixed and now nobody repaired typewriters anymore.

Dooley trotted down the hall to the kitchen, which opened directly to the study, and examined the contents of the refrigerator. He popped the top on a Coke and glanced at Father Tim. "Hey."

"Hey, yourself." Father Tim felt the grin on his face.

"What's going on?" Dooley asked.

He opened his mouth to answer, but Dooley didn't wait for an answer; the question was rhetorical. He vanished down the hall, the soles of his tennis shoes squeaking on the pine floor.

Dooley. *Of course!* It was Dooley who, through whatever bumbling influence he'd had upon the boy's life, would serve the future hour. Yes!

He felt the sting of tears in his eyes and got up and crossed the study and went to the kitchen and peered down the hall, hoping to see Dooley before he reached the front door. He wanted to tell him something, he couldn't think what, exactly. But Dooley was gone.

His wife was gone, too, he'd forgotten just where, and his study was quiet as a tomb, the whole house seemed in a kind of repose which he should savor, but he could not. He listened to his dog snoring in the corner and observed Violet sleeping on the sofa. Violet, who was no longer a spring chicken, had lately begun to snore, as well. He stood for a moment listening to the odd cacophony, the delicate whiffle from the sofa, the bass rumble from the corner of the room near his desk. If he didn't watch out, he'd join the throng any moment. In truth, the world was standing still until Cynthia came in the door; it was as if half of him were missing—his better half.

Better half! He'd once found this term as quaint as *missus.* But he was wiser now, and wasn't she indeed his better half? The half that laughed more easily? The half that didn't take life so seriously? The half that was more spontaneous and free, more expectant of God's blessings, more certain, at times, of His love?

He heard the tolling of the bells at Lord's Chapel, a mere block away, and checked his watch. Three o'clock. Thirsty, he was very thirsty, but returned to his desk and sat as if asleep until he heard her come into the kitchen and set something on the counter. It was a glad sound; he wanted to rush to her, to see her face, but it was this very need that nailed him to the chair where he sat.

"What are you *doing*, dearest?"

"Thinking!" he said.

"Thinking? But you've been thinking for hours. You were thinking when I left!"

He picked up a piece of paper, trying to feign scholarly absorption. In truth, there was absolutely nothing on the paper; it was blank. He put it down and fumbled in his desk drawer.

"It's a gorgeous day, Timothy!" Rustle of bags in the kitchen, a few things from The Local, he supposed. It was her night to make dinner.

"Just gorgeous!" she crowed.

His wife wanted someone to play with, he could tell—a walk around Mitford Lake, perhaps, or a drive on the Parkway with the top down. Couldn't she see he was busy with something important? He grabbed a book off the stack by his desk and opened it. At once he felt filled with authority, as if he were knowledgeable and wise and she a child without purpose.

She came and stood by his chair and looked at him fondly. "Timothy, you think too much!"

He couldn't believe he was hearing those

words from his wife, words he'd heard since childhood—from his mother, his teachers, his first bishop, even from Stuart Cullen. What was too much? Who was to say which chalk line one should think up to and then come to a screeching halt? What if Wordsworth had never thought too much, or Shakespeare or Milton or Cranmer or Socrates? And what about Beethoven or Edison or . . . *Madame Curie*? Why was thinking such a crime?

"Why is thinking such a crime?" he asked, oddly angry.

"Oh, pfoo, darling!" She threw up her hands and walked back to the kitchen.

He didn't want her to leave the room, he wanted her to stay, he wanted her to . . . sit on his lap and ruffle what was left of his hair. He felt suddenly small and bereft. In a fleeting moment, she had become the authority and he the child without purpose.

Dear George,
    As you know, we won't be here when you arriive on June 15, as we leave June 1 for Tennessee. Everything iis finalized for your arrival. Our upstairs tenant at the rectory, Helene

Priingle, has approved your moving into the basement apartment with Harley Welch, and ii believe the two of you wiill do fine together. Harleyi is a pretty darned good cook and hi s brownies can't be beat. He'll be glad for the company. Anything you can do in the yard for Miss Pringle will be appreciated.

harley wiill take you to a body shop I n Wesley, where he thinks there may be a job available. he could Drive you each morning before he goes to work at his job in Mitford. I also have a few friends looking out for you, and have mentioned iit to Avis Packard of the Local, who is going to replace his delivery truck driiver at the end of June.

Rodney Underwood is still our police chief and is aware that you're coming. He invites you to stop by the station and say hello to the guys who attended your baptiism ceremony, they're all still there except the good fellow who gave you the socks.

the rectory basement isn't
the Ritz, but we Believe you'll
be comfortable. The mattress on
the sofa bed is a little lumpy
but only on the left siide.
Remember the orange marmalade
cake you called 'the finest
cake you ever ate in your
life'? that same good
parishioner has offered to put
one in the basement
refrigerator for your arrival.

Mmay God bless you George as
you go about the considerable
business of making a new life.
Cynthia and I deeply regret
that we can't be here to
welcome you but we'll be home
on leave for a long weekendi in
September, and home for good in
June of next year.

Hal and marge Owen invite you
and Harley out to Meadowgate
Farm for homemade chicken pie
any Sunday iin July. Take my
word for it, you definitely
don't want to miss this great
treat.

In closing ii think back on
the portion of psalm 126 which
ii quoted at our parting eight

```
years ago. he that goeth forth
and weepeth, bearing precious
seed, shall doubtless come
again with rejoicing, bringing
his sheaves with him.
    how good it is that God would
have you come again, my friend...
this time with rejoicing.
    in the love of Him Who Loved
Us fiirst
```

☙

On his way to the Grill, a strange thing happened. Out of the blue, he had an idea that was so perfect, so right, that he couldn't imagine why he'd never thought of it before. Of course. *Of course!* The only problem was, how would he present it to Dooley?

☙

"I got to do somethin' to rake in business."

Percy slid into the booth, looking . . . Father Tim pondered what Percy was looking . . . Percy was looking old, that's what; about like the rest of the crowd in the rear booth. He sucked up his double chin.

"Maybe I ought t' mess around with th' menu," said Percy, "an' come up with a special I could run th' same day ever' week."

"Gizzards!" said Mule.

"What about gizzards?"

"I've told you for years that gizzards is th' answer to linin' your pockets."

"Don't talk to me about gizzards, dadgummit! They're in th' same category as what goes over th' fence last. You'll never see me sellin' gizzards."

"To make it in th' restaurant business," said Mule, "you got to set your personal preferences aside. Gizzards are a big draw."

"He's right," said J.C. "You can sell gizzards in this town. This is a gizzard kind of town."

Mule swigged his coffee. "All you got to do is put out a sign and see what happens."

Percy looked skeptical. "What kind of sign?"

"Just a plain, ordinary sign. Write it up yourself an' put it in th' window, no big deal."

"When me an' Velma retire at th' end of th' year, I want to go out in th' black, maybe send 'er to Washington to see th' cherry blossoms, she's never seen th' cherry blossoms."

"That's what gizzards are about," said Mule.

"What d'you mean?"

"Gizzards'll get some cash flow in this place."

"Seem like chicken livers would draw a better crowd," said Percy.

"Livers tie up too much capital." J.C. was

hammering down on country ham, eggs over easy, and a side of yogurt. "Too much cost involved with livers. You want to go where the investment's low and the profit's high."

Mule looked at J.C. with some admiration. "You been readin' th' *Wall Street Journal* again."

"What would I put on th' sign?" asked Percy.

"Here's what I'd put," said Mule. "*Gizzards Today.*"

"That's it? *Gizzards Today?*"

"That says it all right there. Like you say, run your gizzard special once a week, maybe on . . ." Mule drummed his fingers on the table, thinking. "Let's see . . ."

"Tuesday!" said J.C. "Tuesday would be good for gizzards. You wouldn't want to start out on Monday with gizzards, that'd be too early in th' week. And Wednesday you'd want something . . ."

"More upbeat," said Mule.

Father Tim buttered the last of his toast. "Right!"

"Wednesday could be your lasagna day," said J.C. "I'd pay good money for some lasagna in this town."

There was a long, pondering silence, broken only by a belch. Everyone looked at Mule. "'Scuse me," he said.

"Do y'all eat gizzards?" Percy inquired of the table.

"Not in this lifetime," said J.C.

"No way," said Mule.

"I pass," said Father Tim. "I ate a gizzard in first grade, that was enough for me."

Percy frowned. "I don't get it. You're some of my best reg'lars—why should I go to sellin' somethin' y'all won't eat?"

"We're a different demographic," said J.C.

"Oh," said Percy. "So how many gizzards would go in a servin', do you think?"

"How many chicken tenders d'you put in a serving?"

"Six," said Percy. "Which is one too many for th' price."

"So, OK, as gizzards are way less meat than tenders, I'd offer fifteen, sixteen gizzards, minimum."

J.C. sopped his egg yolk with a microwave biscuit. "Be sure you batter 'em good, fry 'em crisp, an' serve with a side of dippin' sauce."

Percy looked sober for a moment, then suddenly brightened. "Fifteen gizzards, two bucks. What d'you think?"

"I think Velma's going to D.C.," said Father Tim.

A brief silence was filled with the sound of the dishwasher running full throttle behind the rear booth. Accustomed to its gyrations, the occupants of the booth no longer noticed that the wash cycle occasioned a rhythmic tremor in the floorboards.

"So how do you think your jewel thief will go over?" asked J.C.

"He's not *my* jewel thief," snapped Father Tim.

"It was your church attic he hid out in," said Percy.

"I think he'll go over just fine. He's paid his debt to society in full, but better than that, he's a redeemed man with a strong faith."

Silence.

Chewing.

Slurping.

"I hope," said Father Tim, "that you'll extend the hand of fellowship to him." There. That's all he had to say about it.

Mule nodded. "No problem. It's th' right thing to do."

More chewing.

"So how come you're not goin' to Rwanda or someplace like that?" asked Percy.

"Hoppy wouldn't allow it." Hoppy would never have considered such a thing. Father Tim knew his limitations and they were numerous.

"What about th' kids in your own backyard?

You ever thought of doin' somethin' for them?"

The fact that he'd supported the Children's Hospital in Wesley for twenty years was his own business; he never talked about it. "Tennessee *is* our own backyard." How he ever ended up with this bunch of turkeys was more than he could fathom.

"We'll miss you," said Mule, clapping him on the shoulder. "I won't hardly know what to order around here."

Father Tim laughed, suddenly forgiving. He thought he might miss them, too, though the possibility seemed a tad on the remote side.

"Here comes Hamp Floyd," said J.C. "Hide your wallet."

"What for?"

"Th' town needs a new fire truck."

"Seems like a good cause," said Father Tim. He took out his billfold and removed a ten.

"Th' town's got th' money for a standard truck, but Hamp wants a few bells an' whistles."

"Aha."

"Plus, he won't have anything to do with a red truck," said J.C.

"Seems like a fire chief would like red. Besides, what other color is there?"

"Yellow. He's holdin' out for yellow."

A *yellow* fire truck? Father Tim put the ten back in his billfold and pulled out a five.

The usually talkative Puny moved around the kitchen without once acknowledging his presence. He might have been a bump on a log as he sat at the kitchen island drinking tea.

He peered over his newspaper.

He knew that pinched brow of hers and the soulful cast of her eyes; Puny Guthrie wore her heart on her sleeve, she couldn't hide anything from him. He should ask her straight out what was going on, but then again . . . maybe he didn't want to know.

He dropped his gaze to the story about the grave sites of Union soldiers presumed to exist on Edith Mallory's sprawling ridge property above Mitford. Coot Hendrick, their unofficial mayor pro-tem and great-grandson of Mitford's founder, wanted the graves identified and available to public view, as did several preservationists in the area. Edith Mallory, secure behind a combination of electric fences and electronic gates, continued to deny access to anybody, much less what she called in a letter to the editor, "the morbid and profane."

Though the controversy between the town and Edith Mallory had dragged on for two or three years, most people didn't give a hoot either way. Who wanted to see graves? And especially Yankee graves? The legend that the soldiers were shot in cold blood by the town's founder might have gone over big a hundred years ago, but in today's world, said another letter to the editor, it was murder, plain and simple, and "nothing to be proud of."

As usual, the *Muse* printed a sidebar containing all the verses of a song said to have been composed by Mitford's founder, Hezekiah Hendrick, and believed by Coot Hendrick and his elderly mother to be proof positive that the graves could be located on the Mallory property.

Shot five yankees
a-runin' from th' war
Caught 'em in a cornfield
Sleeping by a f'ar
Now they'll not run no more, oh
They'll not run no more!

Dug five graves
With a mattock and a hoe
Buried 'em in th' ground
Before th' first snow
Now they'll not run no more, oh
They'll not run no more!

Editor's note: Mrs. Hendrick, who enjoys singing the song passed down through her family, believes the first verse may have originally said, caught 'em in **my** cornfield, adding weight to the theory that five Yankee soldiers do, indeed, lie buried on the Mallory property.

"Brouhaha!" exclaimed Father Tim.

This comment elicited no response from his longtime house help, who remained silent as a tomb as she peeled apples for a pie.

"Puny, what's on your mind?"

She turned from the sink and looked at him oddly, then burst into tears.

See there? He should have kept his big mouth shut.

Puny pulled up her apron and hid her face. "I had th' awfulest dream!"

"Tell me everything," he said. "Come and sit here." He patted the stool beside him.

"I cain't talk if I sit," she said, wiping her eyes. "Th' dream was so lifelike, I thought it was real. It's worried me to death all day."

"What did you dream?"

"It was about you. I didn't know if I should tell you. I mean, I *want* to tell you, but I don't know if I should, because it's like if I tell you, it might really happen." She drew her apron over her face again. "You were so *sick*."

"Puny, Puny, it was just a dream, don't cry, everything's fine! I'm healthy as a horse!" He got off the stool and went to her and put his arm around her solid shoulders.

"I jis' couldn't stand it if anything happened to you, you're th' only granpaw th' girls'll ever have. . . ." She blew her nose on the handkerchief he handed her.

"What was the dream about?"

"In th' dream I begged you to go to the doctor and Cynthia did, too, and you wouldn't go and you got real bad off an' . . ."

"And what?"

"An' maybe *died,* I cain't remember th' end, but it seemed like you died, Joe Joe woke me up because I was cryin'."

"Let it go from your mind, it was only a dream. You were probably sleeping on your back. I have bad dreams if I sleep on my back."

"I was sleepin' on my side, I always sleep on my side," she assured him.

"So you probably ate too late, that'll do it every time."

"No!" she said, shaking her head. "All I had was fruit salad, you cain't have bad dreams on fruit salad."

He sighed.

"I feel like this dream meant somethin'. I

think you're supposed to go to Dr. Hopper and see if you're OK."

"Well . . . ," he said, not wanting to make a big production over a dream.

"*Well* ain't good enough," she said flatly. "You need to do this for Cynthia. An' for Sissy an' Sassy!"

"OK," he said. "I'll go."

"You could pick up th' phone and make an appointment this minute."

Emma Newland made over, except with freckles. "As a matter of fact, I have an appointment coming up in . . . let's see, three days! How's that?"

She looked at him intently, red-eyed. "Father . . ."

"Yes?"

"I think th' Lord wants you to do this."

"Well, then, that settles it," he said earnestly.

"Dearest, you need a haircut."

Get a haircut. See a doctor. Was there no end to it? "It can wait awhile."

"You look like a Los Angeles film director."

"What do you know about Los Angeles film directors?"

"Television, darling. Remember television?

Film directors appear on things like Oscar night, which you and I recently watched for a full nine minutes before we fell asleep with our clothes on."

"Ah."

"So when can you do it?"

"I don't know."

"Yes, but you know the alternative. If you don't get it done professionally, that means I must do it, or Dooley." His wife raised one eyebrow and grinned.

The very thought made him weak in the knees. Both had positively butchered him once or twice before, and Puny wouldn't touch his hair with a ten-foot pole. But the last thing he wanted was to get caught in the fray between Joe Ivey and Fancy Skinner. No way would he slink in the back door of the Sweet Stuff Bakery and risk a run-in with Fancy Skinner; Fancy would curl his hair right then and there. In truth, rumor had it that she often looked down from her upstairs aerie to see who came and went to Joe Ivey, and was taking names. Emma said Fancy had seen Marcie Guthrie, to name only one, go turncoat. For a measly two bucks less, Marcie had popped in to Joe and was said to have exited the place looking like J. C. Hogan. "Let 'em *go* downstairs!" Fancy snapped, nearly burning Emma's ear off with the curling iron. "Anybody can save two dollars and spend two months wishin' they hadn't!"

"I'll run over to Wesley one of these days," he said, trying to mean it.

He was sitting on the sofa in the study when he heard Puny and his wife discussing their neighbor.

"I don't think she's the marrying kind," said Cynthia, rinsing mixed greens for a salad.

"Yes, but she's a nice-lookin' woman, seems it'd be good for her to have a husband."

"Maybe. But who on earth would it be? I mean, this is *Mitford*!"

"Watch it!" he called into the kitchen. "Mitford, after all, is where you found yours truly."

Puny giggled. "I think she's kind of soft on th' father."

"Yes, well," said his wife, "she can get over it!"

There! He was thrilled to hear this. Feeling expansive, he kicked off his loafers.

"What about the Collar Button man?" asked Puny, setting dinner plates on the island.

"I don't think *he's* the marrying kind."

"Mr. Omer," said Puny. "He has a nice, big smile."

"Omer Cunningham is a teddy bear, but not her sort. Darling, who are the bachelors in Mitford?"

"Ummm. Let's see. Avis Packard!"

"Too strange!" said his wife, rolling her eyes.

"Scott Murphy!" he called from the study.

"Timothy! Scott and Miss Pringle wouldn't be suited in the *least*. What are you *thinking*?"

"I'm not trying to make matches here, you asked me who the bachelors are. I'd like to see Scott find someone, though, if you have any ideas on the distaff side."

"Then, of course," said Cynthia, dismissing his agenda for Scott Murphy, "there's Andrew Gregory's brother-in-law, Tony, a handsome fellow, and Catholic like Miss Pringle, but quite clearly—"

"Too *young*!" declared Puny.

"This is hard." He scratched his head. "Old Man Mueller?"

"Timothy, for heaven's *sake*!"

"Remember, I'm not proposing anything, I'm only naming bachelors, as I was asked to do. Lew Boyd!" Lew had been a widower for a number of years.

His wife didn't acknowledge this contribution.

He threw up his hands, naming the only

other bachelor he could possibly think of. "Coot Hendrick!"

"You see?" Cynthia said to Puny. "There's absolutely nobody in Mitford for a nice French lady who teaches piano."

He and Cynthia were hammering down on the front and side yards of the yellow house. Mayor Gregory had poured on the coal for their annual Rose Day, advertising the event in newspapers as far away as Charlotte, Asheville, Winston-Salem, and Raleigh. Now everybody was breaking their necks to get cleaned up for the tourists just days hence. While former Mayor Esther Cunningham had despised the very word *tourist,* Andrew Gregory thought otherwise, arguing that controlled tourism was an economy that produced no factory emissions or water pollution. The merchants, while fond enough of the Cunningham reign, clearly favored the Gregory renaissance.

Though five projects had been marked off Father Tim's list, the following remained:

Add lkspr to front bds, cut wisteria off garage, grub honeyskle/ivy at steps, cultivate/mulch/spray roses, whlbarrow from H. Pringle, new hose/nzzl.

Could he finish in time? Had his list been

too ambitious? And then there was Cynthia's list, which was considerably longer than the one in his shirt pocket. He leaned on the garden spade and wiped his perspiring forehead with a worn handkerchief. "No rest for the wicked," he said.

"And th' righteous don't need none!" crowed his wife, completing a proverb favored by Uncle Billy Watson. She was squatting with a weeder, going full throttle at an infestation of wire grass in the perennial bed facing Wisteria Lane.

He heard a car brake suddenly in the street, squawking to the curb. "There she is!" a voice called.

He looked up as the driver and passenger leaped from a Buick, the motor still running, and dashed across the sidewalk to the perennial bed. Both callers wore muumuus, though of different colors, and both appeared flushed and overwrought.

"You're Cynthia Coppersmith!" exclaimed the one with a camera strapped around her neck.

"The nice man at the drugstore told us where you live," said the other, "but don't tell him we told you he told us!"

"We're your biggest fans in the whole world, we drove all the way from Albany, Georgia, just to see where you do your little cat books!"

"We hoped we'd run into you, but we never *dreamed* we'd find you out in your *yard!*"

"Oh, gosh, I'm often in my yard," said Cynthia.

"Get over there behind her, Sue Lynn, and let me take a picture!"

He noted that Sue Lynn jumped behind his wife with astonishing agility.

Click. "Sue Lynn, honey, you blinked, let me take it again." *Click.* "Oh, umm, could you move out of the picture, your arm was in that one." He moved out of the picture. *Click.*

"Now, would you take a picture of Sue Lynn and me behind Cynthia?" A camera was thrust into his hands.

"Sue Lynn, honey, take your sunglasses off, we can't see your face!"

"Oh, mercy," said his wife, clearly distressed. "I'm filthy, we really shouldn't be doing this."

He was struck by her look of dumbfounded desperation. "Ladies!" he proclaimed in his pulpit voice, "perhaps we could—"

"Just look through that little place in the middle and push down the button on the right," said the camera owner. She hunkered over Cynthia, who appeared frozen in a squat position. "We just love your little books better than anything, this is so exciting I can hardly stand it, we'll send you a copy of the pictures, we always order four-by-six glossy. Sue Lynn, honey, *move over*! It's that little button on the right! On th' *right*! There you go!"

He noted that Dooley was forking down his lasagna, itching to pick up Tommy and haul him to Wesley for a movie. The plan to eat at least one meal a day together wasn't easy to stick to, especially with a teenager, but they were all hanging in there until Dooley's move to his mother's house tomorrow night. After that, he'd be out to Meadowgate for the summer, helping Hal Owen with his veterinary practice, and they'd be heading for Tennessee.

"'Fame . . . ,'" he muttered, dribbling olive oil on a slice of bread.

"What about it?" Cynthia inquired.

"'. . . can never be a bedfellow to tranquillity,'" he said, loosely quoting Montaigne.

"And all because of little books about a cat. Who knew?" His wife looked oddly pleased.

The award business in New York and the invitation to travel around the country had been one thing, but today had been another. He'd felt strangely unnerved by the women in muumuus.

"So who's going to the movie with you?" he asked Dooley. He thought the boy looked un-

usually handsome; his bones were fitting together nicely these days.

"Tommy."

"I know about Tommy. Anybody else?"

"Jenny. And Tommy's date."

"Aha."

"Jenny," murmured his wife, arching an eyebrow. Their young neighbor in the house with
the red roof had moved in and out of Dooley's
life with some frequency over the years.

"Isn't Lace home yet?" asked Father Tim.
He'd heard Lace was visiting a roommate on
her way from school to Mitford.

Dooley shrugged.

"We'll just ring up to the Harpers and see," said
Cynthia, bolting from the table. "Excuse me!"

"Wait!" said Dooley, looking alarmed.
"Don't call. I don't want to know if she's
home."

"You don't want to know?" asked Cynthia,
clearly not concerned about being obvious.
"What could it hurt to *know*?"

With some haste, the boy folded his napkin,
a civility drilled into him at school, and stood.
"I've got to go. Thanks for dinner."

"You're welcome," said Father Tim, feeling
the tension in the air. "Lunch tomorrow,
right?"

Dooley left the kitchen without looking back. "Be there or be square!" he called over his shoulder, and was gone down the hall.

Father Tim peered at Cynthia, who had a positively wicked gleam in her eye. "You see?" she said.

"See what?"

"He's dying to know if Lace is at home!"

He sighed without meaning to. "He could have asked around town if he wanted to find out. Maybe he really doesn't want to know if she's home."

"It's not that we're trying to *force* him into anything," said his wife.

"Of course not," he said. "*Certainly* not!"

He wasn't taking Dooley to the Grill, no way. J.C. and Mule and Percy would want to know everything about school, girls, cars, grades, it was too much. Besides, Dooley did not hold the Grill in high estimation, as the menu still offered livermush and fries that were decidedly on the limp side.

He'd read somewhere that a place in Wesley was now selling wraps. He didn't know exactly what a *wrap* was, but it sounded modern and upbeat. He got the new number from information, called to find out the address, and Dooley hied them there in the Mustang with the top down.

"So what do you think?" he asked as they looked around the wrap place. There was a considerable crowd of young people with nose rings and tattoos, there was music that sounded like . . . he couldn't be certain what it sounded like, maybe like someone breathing heavily into an empty coconut shell.

"Cool," said Dooley.

"And how was the movie?" he asked as they unwrapped their wraps.

"Neat."

What had happened to the boy's vocabulary? At the stunning cost of twenty-two thousand a year, it had been reduced to that of a mynah bird. Of course, he and Cynthia had found Dooley's grades to be first-rate, so there was no complaint in that department.

"How's Jenny?"

Dooley took a huge bite. Father Tim took a huge bite; stuff from the other end of the wrap thudded into his lap.

"Great," said Dooley.

At the age of eleven, and with hardly any schooling, Dooley Barlowe had been able to speak in complete sentences. Father Tim couldn't understand this drastic decline—he couldn't blame it on one lone year at the University of Georgia; it must have taken root at that fancy school in Virginia.

"Wouldn't you, ah, like to at least say hello to Lace before you go out to Meadowgate?"

"Say hello? She doesn't want to say hello to me. The last time I called her from school, she was too busy to say hello, she never even called me back, I wish you'd quit bringing up her name all the time, Lace, Lace, Lace, I could care less." The boy's face flamed.

"Sorry," said Father Tim, meaning it.

"You just dropped lettuce in your lap," said Dooley.

"This is the coolest car in the whole town," Dooley told him on the way home. "Mitford doesn't have any really cool cars."

"Come on! There's Miss Sadie's 1958 Plymouth still sitting in the Fernbank garage. Some people would give their eyeteeth to get their hands on a car like that."

As Dooley wheeled right around the monument, Father Tim threw up his hand to Bill Sprouse, out for a walk with his dog, Sparky. Father Tim thought Sparky looked precisely like the head of a kitchen mop pulled along by a leash.

"There aren't any neat girls in Mitford, ei-ther."

According to Cynthia and Puny, there were no men; according to Dooley, there were no girls.

Father Tim felt suddenly inspired. "Let's don't go home! Let's drive to Farmer." The road to Farmer was the road Dooley had prac-ticed driving on, the road Dooley had crashed Harley's old truck on . . . it was a road of memories, it was a day that felt like summer; he wanted to savor every minute with the boy who was growing up so fast, too fast.

Dooley looked at his passenger and grinned. "Cool," he said.

They had stopped at a country store and taken their cold drinks out to a table and wooden benches under a maple tree. Father Tim relished its mentholated shade. There was even a small breeze blowing.

"I've been wanting to talk with you about something," he told Dooley. He paused a mo-ment and lifted a silent prayer. "It's about Sammy and Kenny."

"I don't want to talk about them anymore."

"But we've got to do it once and for all, we've got to find your brothers. It's been on my mind a lot, and finally I have a good idea."

"It won't work. There's no use lookin' for 'em, we'll never find 'em, it's been too long. Buck looked, you looked, and . . ."

"And what?"

"And you prayed."

"Always."

"Plus Cynthia prayed, Mama prayed, and I prayed. Even Jessie and Poo. It didn't work."

"Right. Not yet."

Dooley looked at his drink bottle. "What kind of idea?"

"If we're going to find your brothers, especially Sammy, I think we've got to find somebody else first."

"Who?"

This was the part he dreaded. "Your father."

"No," said Dooley, getting up from the bench. "No." All color drained from his face; he took several steps backward.

"He's the one who can give us leads. Sammy was with him when he was last seen. It's a chance we've got to take, son."

"I thought you wanted to be my father." Dooley had backed to the maple and stood there, defiant.

"I want to give you everything a father can give, but I can't give you any clues about Sammy like I believe your birth father can. Help me in this, Dooley."

"I hate his guts!" shouted Dooley. Tears escaped onto his freckled face. "I don't want to see him, I don't want him hanging around, bein' drunk and knockin' everybody in th' head and callin' me names."

"Yes, but—"

"He might find Mama and hurt 'er, or try to take Jessie and Poo."

"I'll be in Tennessee, but I'll manage to go to wherever he is. Or Buck—Buck will go. But you've got to help us figure out where he might be, what some of his habits were."

Dooley had less than two days left with them, and now this hard thing in the midst of the only private time they'd had together. . . .

But one couldn't wait forever to tackle hard things.

Dooley wiped his eyes with the back of his hand. "I can't remember," he said. "Besides, maybe he's dead. I hope he's dead."

"Come on. Sit down. Try to remember. Kenny is seventeen now, Sammy is fifteen, only four years older than you were when I saw you the first time." As clearly as if it had happened yesterday, Father Tim recalled the image of an eleven-year-old Dooley Barlowe, barefoot and in filthy overalls, peering in his office door. *You got anyplace I can take a dump?*

"Let's do our best, let's give it another shot," he said. "After all, life is short."

He had a terrible lump in his throat—for Sammy and Kenny, for Dooley, for the hard things of life in general.

Was he jealous of his wife's fame? He wrenched a dandelion from the damp earth and tossed it on the pile. On the other hand, could two women in muumuus be called a bona fide indication of fame? His face burned as he thought of being spoken to as if he were the yard man.

He made it a point to pray—asking for humility, for help in swallowing down his pride. At least it appeared on the surface to be pride. Was there a deeper issue? Surely he couldn't be jealous of any honor accruing to his wife's long years of hard work and dedication.

Whatever it was existed at a level deeper than jealousy. He thumped into the grass near the fence, took off his work gloves, and leaned against the pine tree. So what was really making his gut wrench?

Fear.

It was that simple.

He was afraid she'd somehow be taken from

him, swept away on a tide they couldn't antic-
ipate or control.

"How's the new book coming?" he asked as
they lay in bed. He was rubbing her neck, as
he often did when she was slaving over a drawing board. He'd long ago given up hope that
she wouldn't do this to herself anymore; no,
she loved it too much. Just as preaching had
been what he did, writing and illustrating
books was what she did, it was how she
processed her life.

"Umm. Good, dearest. More to the right,
there's an awful crick on the right."

"I need to adjust the chair at your drawing
table again."

"Would you, Timothy?"

"Of course. First thing tomorrow. Tell me
about the book."

"I'm dismayed, it won't come right. I should
have listened to myself when I said I wouldn't
do any more Violet books. I think I may put it
aside 'til we come home from Tennessee."

"No wonder you're having a problem with
it. That cat's already done everything there is
to do—been to see the Queen, learned to play
the piano, gone to the beach, stayed in a hotel

in New York, taken up French as a second language—"

"Right there! Ugh, it's sore. What did you and Dooley talk about at lunch?"

"About finding his father, to see if we can learn something about the boys. Any involvement with his father frightens him, of course. It could be like stirring a nest of hornets."

"I understand. But it's a good idea, Timothy."

"He remembered that his father had a best friend, a drinking buddy he hung out with, got in trouble with. The name came to Dooley very clearly—Shorty Justice. He lived in Holding, worked on the highway. I'm going to get Emma on it." His erstwhile secretary, who had helped locate Jessie Barlowe, liked nothing better than to spread a dragnet in cyberspace.

"I'll help you any way I can," said Cynthia. "I'll do anything."

He leaned down and kissed her shoulders, loving the feel of her living flesh. She was balm to him, she was everything he might ever want or dream of having, she was his best friend, his encourager. How had he ever bumbled along in that odd dream state of bachelorhood, thinking himself sane?

"I love you," he said.

"I love you back, sweetheart." She yawned and rolled over and put her arms around his neck. "You *are* still my sweetheart?"

He grinned. "'Until heaven and then forever!'" he said, quoting the inscription engraved on her wedding band.

CHAPTER FOUR

www.seek&find.com

Emma Newland thumped into his leather chair in the study, adjusted the needlepoint pillow behind her back, and opened her laptop.

It was her custom to arrive at the yellow house at eight-thirty every Tuesday morning, with the express purpose of inputting the latest portion of his current essay, sending various e-mails in her erstwhile employer's stead, munching tortilla chips to maintain appropriate levels of blood sugar, and tidying his desk whether he wished it tidy or not.

She considered this stint, generally four hours in length, to be her "bounden duty," having made a pact with God. She had committed to serve her helpless former priest 'til death did them part if only God would spare her the agony and aggravation of arthritis—which, at least in recorded history, had afflicted every female in her family. So far, she had suffered only a minor twinge in her right thumb, which she blamed on excessive use of the mouse.

Far be it from her former priest to mention such a thing, but he thought her eyebrows appeared singed this morning, or even missing, as if she'd failed to jump back when lighting an outdoor grill. He'd always thought her eyebrows incredibly similar to woolly worms that had grown extra-thick coats for winter. In truth, his secretary's face looked so oddly denuded that he was embarrassed.

"What're you lookin' at?" she demanded, without glancing away from the screen.

He felt like a schoolboy, caught releasing a toad in the girls' rest room. "Nothing!"

She fiddled with the thing in her lap. "So have you had your spring cold yet?"

"I don't expect to have a spring cold," he said.

"How on earth you'll escape it, I don't know . . . all that drinkin' out of th' cup with everybody and his brother and shakin' a hundred hands at th' Peace."

He didn't comment.

"Now that you don't *have* to drink out of the cup every Sunday, you ought to start dippin' your wafer, that's what I did before I went back to bein' a Baptist."

He bit his tongue.

"I guess you heard the Methodists are gettin' a woman preacher."

He didn't like it when Emma heard news before he did, especially news from the ecclesiastical realm. It was petty of him, but . . . "Well, well."

"I'm goin' to see if you've got e-mail," she said, "then we'll go lookin' for Dooley's daddy."

He swiveled around to his desk and began final revisions to the essay on Wordsworth's postulations, wondering whether he'd have to endure Emma Newland's close company even in heaven. No, surely not, as that would somehow smack of the other place. . . .

He tried to disclaim his excitement that she might indeed be able to trace Clyde Barlowe, right here in this room, today. He didn't want to get excited about a shot in the dark, though his Alabama bishop had once chastised him about that very thing.

The Right Reverend Paul Jared Sotheby had wagged his finger like a schoolmarm. "Timothy, stop this nonsense of preparing for the worst and spend your time preparing for the best!" This counsel had never been forgotten, though he was seldom able to follow it.

Emma stared at the screen, making a light whistling noise between her teeth. Pop music wasn't his strong point, but it sounded like the first two lines of "Delta Dawn," repeated ad infinitum.

"Lookit," she said, "you've got mail!"

"Really?" He leaped up and crouched over her shoulder. "Aha!" Marion Fieldwalker, his former parishioner and good friend in Whitecap Island.

"I gave her my e-mail address, bless 'er heart, so she could keep in touch."

> Dear Fr, will dash this off as well as am able, it is my first try at cyberspace.
>
> Fr Conklin has not upset us too badly. He has a fondness for parish suppers and the old hymns and is organizing a trip to the Holy Land. Sam thinks he will work out.
>
> Morris Love plays the organ each Sunday. We've never heard such a holy racket! People come from far and wide to enjoy the music & end up hearing about God's grace which is a tidy arrangement.
>
> Ella Bridgewater brings dear Captain Larkin to church most Sundays and

subs for Morris on fifth Sunday. Jeffrey Tolson is working across at the college three days and up Dorchester at the big dock two days. He is in church with Janette and the children every Sunday. Some think he will slip back into his old ways, but Sam thinks he will work out.

We miss you greatly. Otis and Marlene had a playground built behind the church and Jean Ballenger is writing a history of St. John's with a list of all the gravestone inscriptions, including Maude Boatwright's "Demure at last," which I recall was your great favorite. I will dispatch a copy as soon as the ink is dry.

Sam has a kidney infection, we would covet your prayers. You are always in ours.

Best love to you and dear Cynthia. When you left it was as if a candle flame had been snuffed out, but we are soldiering on.

He straightened up, clutching his back. "Wait!" she said. "There's more."

"My back . . . ," he said, feeling a creak in every joint.

"If you weren't too cheap to buy a printer, you wouldn't have to read your mail hangin' over my shoulder!"

Blast and double blast today's technology. He'd stood firm for years until just the other day when he'd finally sold out and let Puny teach him to work the microwave. It was a watershed moment, something he wasn't proud of, but in the space of a few heartbeats his tepid tea was steaming. Maybe he did need to buy a printer.

"Look," she said. "Your pal in Mitford, England."

"Move it this way, there's a glare on the screen." He bent closer, battling the heavy scent of My Sin that rose from his secretary like a cloud off Mount Saint Helens. "The type is too small!"

"Your back hurts, there's a glare on the screen, the type is too small. The answer is to get your own laptop, like a normal person!" She snorted. "Sit down, I'll read it to you. 'Dear Father . . .'"

She blinked and looked up. "You know, I can get you online in a heartbeat!"

"I don't *want* to be online!"

"Anytime! Just let me know."

"No way," he said, meaning it.

"Stick your head in the sand, let life pass you by," she muttered. "'Dear Father . . .'"

A sudden shower pecked at the windows. He heard his wife's radio playing in her work-room.

"'What a thumping good idea to have your Mitford and ours become sister villages. I'm sure the whole business wants a bit of pomp to make it official. I can't think what sort but I'm certain my wife Judy can make it click. She's known for pulling off the best jumble sales in the realm, and our vicar is clever at this sort of thing, as well. We'll all of us put our heads together and come up with something splendid, I'm sure. Sincere best wishes on your mission work in Tennessee, I believe that's where a considerable amount of your whisky comes from. Will keep in touch through your good sec'y. Yours sincerely, Cedric Hart, Esq.'"

"Terrific," he said. "Anything else?"

"That's it. Anything you want to send before I look for Clyde Barlowe?"

"This," he said, handing her a piece of paper on which he'd scrawled a quote for Stuart Cullen.

"You could do it yourself," she said.

"Blast it, Emma . . ."

Church architecture, she typed, *ought to be an earthly and temporal fulfillment of the Savior's own prophesy that though the voices of men be still, the rocks and stones themselves will cry out with the laud and praise and honor due unto the King of kings and the Lord of lords. Michel di Giovanni, medieval builder and designer.*

"Who to?" she asked.

"The bishop."

He watched her move the mouse around. "Done! Now. Ready if you are."

"Excellent!" He was on the edge of his seat.

"But don't get your hopes up," she said, peering over her half-glasses.

"Oh, no," he said.

"This will take a little time."

"Right."

She waved her hand at him. "So do what you have to do to your essay so I can input it before I leave."

Trying to cast the search from his mind, he created two paragraphs from one and crossed out a line that he'd formerly thought stunning. He noted by the faded type that the ribbon on his Royal manual was wearing through, a circumstance that Emma wouldn't favor in the least when transcribing.

The clock ticked, the rain pecked, the radio played Brahms. Couldn't she somehow just go to the B's and *find* it? What was taking so long?

He deleted a paragraph, transposed two lines, and capitalized Blake as in William. Thirty minutes to find one ordinary name?

"Lookit!" she exclaimed.

"What?"

"I'll be darned."

"What?"

"Well, well," she said, paying him no attention at all.

There was nothing to do but get up and look over her shoulder.

"See there?" She jabbed her finger at a list of names.

"Where?"

"Right there. Cate Turner. Idn't that Lace Turner's daddy's name?"

"Why, yes."

"There's only one Cate Turner on th' list, and he's livin' in Hope Creek, that little town close to Holding."

"Lace isn't anxious to know where her father is. Far from it. Keep looking." In truth, Lace had been legally adopted by the Harpers and had taken their surname, though most Mitfordians, out of habit, still referred to her as Lace Turner.

"Why are you in the *T*'s, anyway?" he asked, irritated. "You can't find Barlowe in the *T*'s."

"I was lookin' for Caldecott Turner, my high school sweetheart, we called him Cal."

"Emma, Emma . . ."

"I already looked in th' Barlowes."

"And?"

"And I hate to tell you, but there's no Clyde Barlowe."

"There's got to be a Clyde Barlowe. Both names are common to this area."

"I looked in all fifty states and everywhere in Canada, including Nova Scotia and the Yukon, plus—"

"But it's such a simple name. Surely—"

"See for yourself." She stood up, thrusting the laptop in his direction. "Just sit down right here and fool with it while I go to the johnny."

He backed away, grinning in spite of himself. "Oh, no, you don't! I'm not falling for your flimsy ploy to get me hooked on this miserable contraption."

Emma chuckled, a rare thing to witness. "You'll be hooked sooner or later. Might as well be sooner."

"When you come back," he said, ignoring her prediction, "I'd like you to look for a fellow named Shorty Justice."

But there was no Shorty Justice, either.

As he walked Emma to the front door, he knew he'd ask, and he knew he'd regret it.

"Ummm. Your eyebrows . . ."

"What about my eyebrows?" she snapped.

"They just look . . ." He shrugged. *"Different!"* Didn't he know that curiosity killed the cat?

"Do I ask about *your* eyebrows?"

"Well, no, but there's nothing different about mine."

"Oh, *really*? Have you looked in the mirror lately?"

She swept out the door, blowing him in the ditch.

He went at once to the downstairs powder room. Consulting the mirror, he saw there was absolutely nothing different about, much less wrong with, his eyebrows.

"Do my eyebrows look funny?" he asked Cynthia.

She studied him soberly. "No. Why?"

"Emma said I should look in the mirror at my eyebrows."

"Why would she say that?"

"I don't know. I guess because I asked about hers, they seemed . . . different."

"Oh, that! Of course, they *are* different! Which is to say she doesn't *have* any! Fancy Skinner talked Emma into thinning her eyebrows, and instead of plucking them, Fancy used a wax thing that pulled off the whole shebang."

"Oh, boy."

"When I croak, Timothy, remember my instruction. You *do* remember?"

He remembered. This instruction was hand-written and paper-clipped to his wife's will, which specified burial instead of the increasingly popular cremation. *TIMOTHY,* <u>*Do not let*</u> <u>*Fancy Skinner touch my hair!!!*</u> *Yours from above and beyond, C.*

Dooley's Wrangler was at Lew Boyd's, where Harley was working on the stick shift, which was, in fact, living up to its name and sticking.

"I'll drive you to your mom's," said Father Tim. He didn't want Dooley to leave, not at all, but of course he wouldn't mention it. . . .

"Can I have your car tonight since mine won't be ready 'til tomorrow?"

"*Can* you?"

"May I?"

Father Tim smiled, waiting.

"*Please!*"

"Yes, you may," said Father Tim, tossing him the keys.

"Thanks, Dad!"

"You're welcome."

He was touched that the boy gave him a good punch on the arm.

All the books they could possibly wish to read or refer to while in Tennessee were at last in boxes. He noticed they were virtually the same books they'd schlepped to Whitecap, with the addition of a crate of children's books.

He stood back and scratched his head. What else? Ah! He'd want the Tozer and the complete works of George Macdonald, which were upstairs, he'd forgotten about those; then there was the business about the Galsworthy. . . .

He recalled that his wife had preached him a sermon about popping into Happy Endings for any reason other than to say goodbye to Hope Winchester. The drill was that neither he nor Cynthia was permitted to add another ounce to their current shipping charges.

He hadn't promised her he wouldn't buy another book, though he did say he considered her counsel wise. That was, of course, before he realized how much he needed the Galsworthy volume. One little book! And a paperback, at that! How much could it weigh, after all? He wouldn't put it in the book crates, anyhow, he'd stuff it in his duffel bag, he'd tote it in his rolled-up pajamas. Some men chased women, some were smitten with fast cars. Big deal, he liked books.

Before going on his mission, he opened the refrigerator door and spied the cache of Cokes they kept for Dooley's comings and goings. He realized he'd been ignoring his pressing thirst, and though he shouldn't do this, the can was already open . . . probably flat, but what the heck, just a sip. He drained the contents, rinsed the can, flattened it, and tossed it in the recycle bin in the garage.

He shelled out thirteen dollars and change.

"Don't, ah, mention this," he said, confident that Hope would get his meaning.

"Of *course* not!" said Hope, offended. "I'm asked to keep all *sorts* of things confidential!"

"Really? Like what?"

She peered at him through her tortoiseshell-rim glasses and smiled. "If I told you, Father, then it wouldn't be—"

"Confidential!" he said. "Of course."

She dropped the book into a bag and handed it to him. "I suppose you know that some people are making exceedingly captious remarks about the Man in the Attic."

"I'm not surprised."

"They say his flagitious behavior will almost certainly assert itself again."

There was nothing he could say to that, nor could he help noticing that Hope looked oddly worried, a little pale. "I pray that all will be well and very well," he said. "Perhaps you'll pray about it, also."

"I don't pray."

"Aha." He tucked the bag under his arm.

"But I believe in God," she said.

"Good! God believes in you."

"So, I hope you have a really great trip, I admire you for going up there and living in the wilderness, I hope you're taking a snake kit."

"Umm, I don't think so. Well! Probably won't see you again 'til September, I hope everything—"

"Father?"

"Yes?"

"Do you have a moment?"

"Of course."

She lowered her eyes. "I think I . . . need to tell you something."

In all the years he'd known Hope Winchester, she had never confided in him.

"I wrote the Man in the Attic a letter," she whispered. "I told him Happy Endings would have a job for him when he comes."

"Why, that's wonderful!"

"You see, I thought everyone liked Mr. Gaynor for how he handled what he'd done, making his confession before your congregation and then asking you to call the police to take him away. I remember how the school-children made drawings for him while he was in jail, and all those pairs of shoes that were brought to the police station. Someone said you preached a sermon about him and called him a type of St. Paul. Now I'm not sure anymore, some people say he'd be tempted to steal again. I feel very distressed about making such a precipitate gesture. What if people refuse to come in, what if it hurts sales?"

"Have you told Helen you did this?" Though absent nine months of the year, the owner was known to be seriously interested in the details of her business.

"A few weeks ago, she told me to hire part-time help to take care of our mail order for the rare books. I know she trusts me completely, I've never let her down."

"I'm sure you haven't."

"Now I don't know what to do."

"Speaking of St. Paul, he asked us to be instant in prayer. Don't be alarmed, but I'm going to pray about this right now."

"Right *now*?" asked Hope.

He bowed his head. "Father," he said, "we're in a pickle here. Thank You for giving Hope wisdom about what to do and putting Your answer plainly on her heart. In Jesus' name, amen."

Hope looked at him quizzically. "Is that all?"

"That's it!" he said. "Just check your heart, you'll know what to do."

"Oh," she said, oddly relieved.

"And by the way, I think everyone will love George Gaynor all over again."

"Thank you, Father, thank you!"

"I'll drop you a postcard with our new address," he said. "Let me know how it goes."

❧

He stopped by the drugstore, made a beeline for the candy section, and set about examining the see-through packages of jelly beans.

"Lookin' for jelly beans for your doc?" asked Tate Smith.

"Yep."

"I think he made a pretty heavy sweep through here th' other day."

Father Tim inspected one package twice. "This looks like it has quite a few green. I'll take it."

Hoppy Harper was known to be inordinately fond of green jelly beans; he carefully picked through mixed flavors and, after robbing the bag in his favor, turned the remains over to his nurses.

"Seems like a doctor that scarfs down jelly beans idn't a very good example to his patients," said Tate. "My doc's got me plumb offa sugar, but he don't let me see what *he* eats. Doc Harper, he don't care who knows he's got a sugar jones."

Tate rang up the dollar-and-seventy-nine-cent sale. "Prob'ly eats bacon an' who knows what all."

"Link sausage!" said Father Tim.

"You playin' for th' Reds this year?" asked Tate.

Father Tim tucked the jelly beans into the bag with his book. "Can't do it this year. We're headed up to Tennessee for a while. Maybe next year."

He realized he was greatly relieved not to be playing on Mitford's star softball team. The thought of running around the bases, hitting the ball, just picking up the bat . . .

He was tired, somewhere deep in himself, in a place where he hadn't really looked before. But that didn't make sense. He was no longer a full-time priest; he wasn't sweating vestry meetings, building campaigns, or quirky parishioners; he had only occasional weddings, baptisms, or funerals to perform, and no confirmation classes to teach. He didn't even have to dash to the rest room, as he'd done at Whitecap, and jiggle the ball when someone left the toilet running.

Running! That was the solution right there. He needed to get back to his running schedule. As soon as he left Joe Ivey's barber chair, he'd head home, put Barnabas on the leash, and take a go at his old route—up Main Street, right on Lilac Road, down Church Hill, and right on Old Church Lane to Baxter Park and then home.

⌘

On the way to Joe's, he ducked into The Local and rounded up Avis, who was cutting a leg of lamb.

"Looks like a superb cut," said Father Tim.

"How do you roast your lamb?"

"Varies."

"Here's how you do it, no fail. Heat your oven to four-fifty, OK?"

"OK."

"Rub your meat with garlic and lemon, push some fresh rosemary under the skin, slap it on a rack uncovered, OK?"

"OK."

"Reduce your heat to three twenty-five, and let 'er rip 'til the internal temperature's around one seventy-five. Superb! Outstanding! Delicious! OK?"

"Got it."

"While you're at it, quarter and roast a few potatoes, and make a salad with my balsamic vinegar in th' green bottle, third row, second shelf. You want my mint jelly recipe?"

"I have one, thanks." He stood on one foot and then the other. "Avis! Any more thoughts about hiring a new driver?"

"Already hired! Starts Wednesday."

"Aha."

Avis wiped his hands on his apron. "I'd top that off with a nice merlot, is what I'd do."

In other words, thought Father Tim, the job opening was definitely closed.

❧

Joe Ivey whipped open a folded cape, draped it over Father Tim's front section, and tied it at the back of his neck.

"I hear you got a convict comin'."

"He won't be a convict when he gets here; he'll be a free man, repentant and eager to join society."

"That don't always work."

"What don't, ah, doesn't?"

"That repentance business."

"It worked for you. How long have you been dry?"

"Four years goin' on five."

"See there?"

Father Tim was dead sure he heard Fancy Skinner's high-heel shoes pecking on the floor above their heads, but he wouldn't introduce that sore subject for all the tea in China.

Joe picked up his scissors and comb.

"Just take a little off the sides," said Father Tim.

"It's fannin' out over your collar, I'm gettin' rid of this mess on your neck first."

"Cynthia said don't scalp me."

"If I had a' Indian-head nickel for every time a woman sent me that message, I'd be rich as cream an' livin' in Los Angelees."

"Why on earth would you want to live there?"

"I wouldn't, it's just th' first big town that popped to mind."

"Aha." Father Tim saw a veritable bale of hair falling to the floor.

"Where's he goin' to work at?"

"I don't know. We have a couple of possibilities."

"You wouldn't want him to be out of work."

"Of course not."

"That'd be too big a temptation."

"You're going to like this man. Remember, he made a public confession and turned himself in; he was willing to admit his mistake and spend eight years paying for it. Give him a chance."

"I don't know . . ."

"Ours is the God of the second chance, Joe."

Joe stood back and squinted at his handiwork, then handed Father Tim a mirror. "Well, there they are."

"There what are?"

"Your ears. How long has it been since you seen 'em?"

He left the barbershop and walked toward the corner of Main Street, head down. He wouldn't confide it to anyone, not even to Cynthia, but something Hope expressed had already been nagging him. Indeed, what if things didn't work out with George? Yours truly would be the one to blame. Worse, he wouldn't even be here, he'd be in Tennessee, with no way to sense the flow of things at home. Somehow, he couldn't grasp the reality of their move to Tennessee; it wouldn't stick. The boxes were packed, their clothes were ready to zip into hanging bags, but . . .

He admitted his relief that they'd failed to locate Clyde Barlowe. Indeed, it was possible that Dooley's worst fears could come true; if they found the man, the family could be at risk, it was playing with fire. Why was he messing in other people's lives, anyway, giving George Gaynor easy entry to Mitford, and actively searching for someone who'd never been anything but trouble?

When he reached the hospital four blocks away, he figured he may as well check into a room and get it over with. His feet and legs had the weight of cinder blocks; he'd literally dragged himself up the hill. He recalled that Uncle Billy had asked him to stop by this afternoon, but maybe tomorrow. . . .

"So how do you like boot camp?"

"Boot camp?"

"Your hair. What's left of it." His ever-harried doc grinned, running his fingers through his own wiry, disheveled hair, which grew in plenty. "Your glucometer reading is through the roof. Two-fifty."

His heart sank.

"You know it should be well under two hundred, around one-forty is where I'd like to see it hang."

He said nothing; he loathed this disease, he was sick of it. . . .

"I'll have Kennedy draw blood for the lab. What happened to your exercise program?"

"Let's see . . ." His mind felt positively fogged.

"Gone with the wind, is my guess." Hoppy popped a green jelly bean.

The very nerve, thought Father Tim.

"I'm ready to scuttle your trip."

"*What?*"

"Either that or I let you go on good faith,

with your absolute commitment to take care of yourself."

"Meaning . . . ?"

"Meaning you've got to get back to a strict exercise regime and watch your diet. Plus, I'm going to double your insulin."

Father Tim stared at his shoes.

"You know the higher we make your insulin the hungrier you'll get, and if you don't exercise you'll gain weight, you'll feel rotten . . . it's a vicious cycle. So it's imperative you stick with it, Father. I'm prescribing ten more units . . . every day. Every morning, every evening, no cutbacks, no slipups, and no excuses."

He nodded, numb.

"I'm worried about you, pal. There's no quick fix to diabetes."

"Right."

"Who's going to be your medical counsel in Tennessee?"

"I don't know, I haven't thought about it."

"Fortunately, you don't have to. I have an old school chum in Nashville. Call him. It's a must."

Hoppy scribbled a name on a notepad, tore off the page, and handed it to him. "I don't think you've ever realized how serious this can be, even with the dive you took a few years back."

"Maybe not. I've tried to stay with the exercise, but lately I haven't felt up to it."

"That's when you need to push yourself to do it, of course."

"Of course." Maybe he was tired because he was old. Age ought to count for something in this deal.

"Wretched thing, exercise," said his doctor. "Thank God diabetes is missing in my gene pool. Our crowd has other problems."

"Like what?"

"Prostate cancer. My father, two uncles, a cousin."

Father Tim shook his head. "Sorry," he said, meaning it. Who didn't have a cross to bear? "Tell me about Lace. Is she home from school?"

"Came in yesterday, went straight to visit Harley, said she'd try to see you and Cynthia before you go. You won't believe how gorgeous she is, Timothy. Dumbfounding."

"I'm not surprised."

"Dean's list, to boot. Olivia and I can never thank you enough for bringing us together as a family. It hasn't been easy, but she's the light of our lives."

Father Tim grinned. "I'm not the one, of course, who brought you together, but I'll pass your sentiments along in my prayers tonight. What's she up to next year?"

"University of Virginia."

"Good. Terrific."

"How's Dooley?"

"Handsome. Smart as a whip. The light of our lives."

They laughed together comfortably, the two who had prayed for Olivia Davenport to find a heart transplant. In the process of finding a heart, his good doctor had a found a wife.

In the evening, he pulled on his sweat suit, put his good dog on the leash, and ran.

It wasn't working. At the top of Church Hill, he wanted nothing more than to sit and stare down at the village. Just sit; not run, not travel to Tennessee, not even go home for dinner.

In the evening, he took his glucometer out of the box to check the number of strips he had left. He fumbled the thing, somehow, and dropped it on the floor. While searching for it in the unlit bathroom, he heard it crunch under his heel.

"Good riddance!" he said, switching on the light to do the cleanup.

CHAPTER FIVE

A Sudden Darkness

He sat at the kitchen island, pulling together a list of winter gardening chores for Harley.

Should the leaves remain on the lawn, or be raked and worked into the compost heap? There were clearly two schools of thought on the subject; he had a history of swinging back and forth between them. But why worry about it in June when Harley didn't need to know 'til the end of October?

Cynthia trotted in and climbed onto the stool beside his.

"Lace Harper called. She'll be here at four o'clock!"

"Aha! Good news."

"I've made lemonade and pimiento cheese sandwiches. We'll have afternoon tea."

"*Scratch* pimiento cheese?"

"Timothy! Is the pope a Catholic?"

Chuckling, he kissed his wife and looked at his watch. Maybe he could catch Dooley. He bounded to the phone by the sofa in the study.

"Jessie!" he said when Dooley's ten-year-old sister answered the phone.

"Hey, Father Tim."

"How are you?"

"I'm OK. Dooley gave me a whole box of candy from the drugstore, it has nuts. Do you like nuts?"

"I am nuts," he said, grinning.

"Why?"

"Because I'm going somewhere I . . . don't really want to go." He couldn't believe he'd said that.

"I have to do things I don't want to do."

"Like what, may I ask?"

"Washing dishes and homework."

"Both very popular in the category of what people don't like doing. Is Dooley around?"

"Yeah."

He heard Dooley in the background. "Say yes, *sir*!"

"Yes, sir, do you want to speak to him?"

"I do, thank you. And Jessie . . ."

"Yeah? I mean, yes, sir?"

"I've been meaning to tell you this for ages. You're a lovely girl. We're all proud of you."

She caught her breath, considered his remark, then giggled. "Thanks."

"You're welcome. See you when we get back."

"Hey," said Dooley.

"Hey, yourself! Lace Harper's dropping over at four o'clock. Cynthia made lemonade and pimiento cheese sandwiches. Want to come?"

Silence. Maybe he should throw in a plate of brownies. He could run to Sweet Stuff. . . .

"Dooley?"

"I don't know, I don't think so."

"It'll take thirty minutes, maybe an hour, it won't be a long visit."

"I don't think so."

He observed his own silence. "Well, then. I'll drive out to Meadowgate with you on Thursday morning, OK?"

"OK."

"We love you, buddy."

"Love you back."

Click.

"He's not coming," said Father Tim, feeling oddly bereft.

His barefoot wife thumped onto the sofa beside him. "Want to bet?"

❧

Perhaps he'd write an essay on the mystery of a woman's ability to know and sense things beyond a man's ken. At five 'til four, the front door opened and Dooley blew down the hall.

"Hey."

He and Cynthia offered their family greeting in unison. "Hey, yourself!"

"I forgot something."

"What?" asked Cynthia.

"My, umm, tennis shoes."

"You're wearing them."

Dooley blushed. "Oh, right. I mean, no, not these. My old ones."

"You outgrew them."

Father Tim put his arm around his wife's shoulder, hoping to distract her. She was a regular CIA agent, a storm trooper. "Cynthia . . ."

"I want them for . . . for Poo!" said Dooley.

"For Poo! What a great idea. Of *course*!"

"Of course!" said Father Tim. Quick thinking! Chalk one up for Dooley.

Dooley grinned, displaying sixteen hundred dollars' worth of recent dental work, underwritten by Miss Sadie's trust.

Handsome! thought Father Tim. Smart as a whip! The light of our lives!

His doctor was right. Lace Harper was . . . what had Hoppy said, exactly? Gorgeous. Slightly bucktoothed when he'd first encountered her stealing Miss Sadie's ferns, Lace had obviously undergone dental work of her own. However, it was her eyes that engaged him. He'd remembered them as brown, but they were, in fact, amber, a startling, clear amber that gave this young woman great presence.

Dooley tried to sprawl on the study sofa, but, finding it impossible to appear nonchalant, returned to posing as ice sculpture.

"What will you be doing this summer?" his wife asked their guest.

"My friend Alicia invited me to visit her aunt in Martha's Vineyard, but we're going to take a family trip out West."

He noted that Lace pronounced *aunt* like the Virginians, and not like Mitfordians, who comfortably used what sounded like *ant* and even *aint*.

"I love the West!" Cynthia said. "Where?"

"Hoppy's great-grandfather had a ranch in Montana, so we're going there, then we're going to explore the Oregon Trail." Lace smiled suddenly.

Father Tim thought her smile a miracle of

healing; in the early years, her countenance had reflected only anger and the weight of a terrible sadness. Further, he thought her poise was nothing to be taken lightly. Though a year younger than Dooley, she seemed wiser, more mature, more settled into her skin.

"Sounds like good medicine for my doctor," said Father Tim. In all the years he'd known the earnest practitioner, Hoppy had taken only two vacations, one of them his honeymoon.

"Olivia bought him cowboy boots."

"Aha!"

"But don't tell," said Lace. "It's a secret."

"Never!"

Though the conversation flowed smoothly enough, the tension in the room was palpable; he felt it somewhere around the region of his jaws, as if he'd clenched his teeth since their visitor arrived. There was no mistaking Lace's cool indifference toward Dooley, and Dooley's wall of defense against her.

Father Tim remembered the day Dooley had stolen Lace's old hat and she'd responded by punching him so hard in the ribs that Dooley thought a few of them broken. Now, *that* was communicating!

Cynthia passed the small sandwiches a second time. Father Tim took one, Lace declined. Dooley took two, one in each hand, then, realizing his social blunder, tried to return one to the plate, but Cynthia had passed it out of reach. He popped an entire sandwich into his mouth and sat red-faced and chewing, holding the other as if it were a hot potato.

Something must be *done*! thought Father Tim. He shot from his chair and addressed the assembly.

"Why don't we all go for a ride in my car? Dooley, you can drive!" There! That ought to do it. Dooley at the wheel of the red Mustang, the top down, the four of them without a care. . . .

"A *ride?*" queried his wife, refilling their glasses. "Whatever *for?*"

He sat as quickly as he'd stood.

"Didn't go too well, did it?" Cynthia asked. They lay in bed, holding hands.

"Depends on what we were expecting."

"We were expecting them to be friends, of course, just as they used to be."

"He told me she snubbed a phone call he made to her at school."

"Yes," she said, "but it's more than that. Because of their backgrounds, they're both terrified of feeling their feelings. Dooley can take Jenny to a movie and it doesn't mean a great deal to him, but there's something so . . . intense, so volatile in his feelings toward Lace that he simply tries to shut his feelings down."

"Deep stuff."

"Some of the stuff you dealt with when courting me."

"Really?"

"Absolutely!"

"What happened?" he asked, smiling in the dark. "How did we end up in the same bed?"

She patted his hand. "Water wears away stone."

He yawned hugely. "Whatever that means," he said.

He sat in a straight-back chair in a small, empty room with a dirt floor. It was the same cool, hard-packed floor of his grandmother's potato cellar, but there were windows through which light streamed, casting patterns at his feet.

He heard a door opening behind him; children filed into the room on either side of his chair. They came in silently, almost reverently, and settled themselves at his feet as if waiting for him to speak, to tell them a story or solve some great riddle; there were dozens of children, many more than a small room could possibly hold, but their silence made them seem fewer. The light from the open doorway fell upon their hair and illumined their faces as they looked at him, searching for something he had no ability to name or to deliver. He tried to speak, but couldn't open his mouth; he tried but could not speak—

"What is it, dearest?"

Her hand on his shoulder was the most reassuring touch he'd ever known, save that of his mother. "I keep falling asleep and waking again. Did I disturb you?"

"You were dreaming," she said. "I've been awake, too. It's the change that's coming."

It's already with us, he thought. We have disrupted something precious, something fragile. Yet they were doing what they believed God wanted. . . .

"Come," he said, taking her into his arms. They lay without talking as he stroked her cheek.

"I'm going with you to New York," he said at last.

"You don't have to, it's all right."

"No, we're going together." To arrive in Tennessee in early June and leave the middle of July didn't seem the best thing, but he was going with his wife, period. As for his lifelong fear of flying, he'd put his head down and do it, he'd reckon with it.

She kissed him tenderly. "I'll be proud to show off my husband."

He turned his head on the pillow and looked out the window to the leaves of the maple tree gleaming in the moonlight.

"Whitecap didn't seem so hard."

"We were lighthearted about going to Whitecap," she murmured. "The freedom of an island . . ."

"The wind in our hair . . ."

"Gulls wheeling above us . . ."

"The smell of salt air!" He completed their old liturgy. Whitecap had seemed inviting and open; what lay ahead now seemed closed, though he didn't know why.

"This will be our last foray," he said.

"Thank you, Timothy. We're no spring chickens."

Ah, yes. He would be sixty-nine in less than a month, looking square into the maw of The Big Seven-oh. But age had nothing, less than nothing to do with serving God. There were countless older saints who, faithful to the end, had perished on the mission field. And there were mission fields at home, right in his own backyard—hadn't he always been a proponent of the local mission field? After Tennessee, he would get down to it once and for all. He would find his niche and make his mark for

God at home, in Mitford. What with two days at the Children's Hospital in Wesley, a couple of days with Scott Murphy at Hope House, Wednesdays with Homeless Hobbes's soup kitchen, and a pulpit here and there, he'd have more than a full plate.

"Let me pray for us," he said, smoothing her hair from her forehead. The faintest scent of wisteria rose from her flesh, evanescent but consoling. He'd be able to locate his wife anywhere, even blindfolded in a crowded air terminal; her smell had become the smell of home to him, of peace and certainty.

"Lord," he said, "to You all hearts are open, all desires known, and from You no secrets are hid. We can hide nothing from You, yet something is hidden from us. Speak to us again, Father, help us discern Your direction for our lives. Are we on the path you've set for us? Have we missed the mark?"

They lay still then, hearing the ticking of the clock, and Barnabas snoring on the hall landing.

Buck Leeper dropped by the following morning on his way to the construction site in Holding. He stood at the front door holding a to-go cup of coffee, looking exhausted and apologetic.

"I figured you'd be up."

"Since five-thirty," said Father Tim. "What is it, my friend?"

"Could we sit out here and talk?"

They thumped onto the top step of the front porch.

"I had a big runaround yesterday, I thought I'd found Kenny.

"Somebody on my job said they'd seen a bunch of paintings on velvet up around Eliza-bethtown, said they were propped against a van in an empty lot, an' signed Kenny Bar-lowe."

Though the mission had clearly failed, a bolt of adrenaline surged through Father Tim.

Buck swigged the coffee. "I started to call you, but there was no time, I just jumped in th' truck an' went for it. I drove up there an' found th' van—my heart was pumpin' like a jackhammer, and then this kid came out, probably around Sammy's age. It was all I could do to keep from bustin' out cryin'."

"But?"

"But th' boy's name was Wayne, his daddy's name was Kenny Barlow, no *e*. I met his daddy, a pretty decent guy down on his luck. I bought a painting of a deer head, it's rolled up behind th' seat in th' truck."

"Well done."

"I don't know about you, but I'm ready to quit on this."

Father Tim took a deep breath. Quit. That's what he was about to do, as well. But it would do no good to quit, no good at all.

"Let's don't quit," he said. "Let's don't quit."

Buck set the cup on the step between his feet.

"A few days ago I asked Pauline to tell me everything she could remember about the boys, like if they had any birthmarks, an' th' color of their eyes."

"Good thinking."

"She couldn't remember th' color of their eyes."

There was a long silence between them.

"When she realized she couldn't remember the color . . ." Buck hunched over, his head in his hands. "It was the alcohol, of course. All those years . . ."

"Those years are behind you."

"Yeah, they are, thank God." Buck looked at him. "But you pay the consequences."

"True. But now God is in the consequences with you. Otherwise, you're in them alone, desperately alone."

Buck stood up. "Forgive me for makin' a rough start to your day, Father. Findin' a needle in a haystack ain't ever been my long suit."

The men walked to the truck together.

"I saw something on TV last night," said Father Tim. "It happened right after the Second World War when nobody had any money. A sewing machine company held a contest... whoever found the needle hidden in a haystack would win a brand-new sewing machine. There were people swarming all over that haystack, hay was flying everywhere. And guess what?"

"What?"

"The chances were one in a million, but somebody found the needle."

Buck laughed his water-boiling-in-a-kettle laugh. "Oh, yeah?"

"Yeah!" said Father Tim, beaming.

Dear Timothy:

We're elated that you and Cynthia will be arriving only a few days hence. Have done as you asked and scraped up a rug. It appears that dogs have chewed one end of it, but you can pop that end under a piece of furniture. Be it ever so humble, I'm sure you'll be pleased with your quonset hut (my lodge in the Canadian wilds wasn't half so commodious). I hope you don't mind that I mounted my moose head on your living room wall, as my own quarters (being humbler still) had no room for it. I'm living four miles away, and trust you'll let me visit the old thing when the mood strikes? Jack Farrier, a Primitive Baptist who knows these coves and firths like the back of his hand, will be taking you around on Monday following, to visit your new parish. Some areas don't have bridges, you'll be driving through creek beds, so bring your waterproofs! Spaghetti supper on arrival, courtesy of yours truly. Be assured, Timothy, that God is working in Jessup, Tennessee!

In His service, Fr Harry
p.s. Could you possibly bring mosquito netting? Enough for two Kavanaghs and one Roland ought to do the trick, Richard and Trudy are bringing their own.

He decided he wouldn't bother his wife with this latest communication from the mission field.

He opened the refrigerator and spied his lunch of freshly made chicken salad with hard-cooked eggs and celery, his favorite combination—no nuts and grapes for him, thank you. He peeled back the Saran Wrap and nabbed a carrot stick and shut the door—

lunch would wait 'til he returned from Meadowgate—he wasn't as ravenously hungry since he cut back on his insulin a few days ago. If his sugar started acting up, he'd do the ten extra units again. Which reminded him—he needed to stop at the drugstore and pick up a glucometer; it had been on his list for days. And his jogging . . . he needed to get back to it.

He was due in five minutes to meet Dooley and follow the Wrangler to Meadowgate Farm. The boy could have driven out alone, he was nearly twenty years old, for heaven's sake, but he wanted to go with him as he'd done all those years ago when he left Dooley at Meadowgate and traveled to Ireland to meet Walter and Katherine.

They found Hal and his associate, Blake Eddistoe, in emergency surgery with a border collie. After a visit on the porch with Marge and seven-year-old Rebecca Jane, he and Dooley walked to the creek, to the very place they'd said goodbye before. Dooley had been only eleven then; he remembered sitting with him on the creek bank and talking, his heart heavy. Was it so different now?

"Well, son . . . ," he said.

"I'll maybe write you or something."

"Would you? We'll write you back. And we'll call, of course. I believe it will be a good summer for both of us."

They sat on a large, smooth stone embedded in the creek bank. Dooley picked up a stick and slapped the water, precisely as Father Tim remembered him doing years ago.

"How will you get on with Blake?" There had been more than a clash or two with Hal's associate; while Dooley veered toward a more natural practice of veterinary medicine, Blake was staunchly committed to traditional treatments.

"I'll do my thing, he'll do his."

"Seems fair enough."

"He needs to keep his nose out of what I do, that's all."

"Still fair enough. But it might be good to swap ideas along the way."

Hal would keep the two in line; he was well aware of the friction between them. As Hal's own medical theories were drawn from tradition, he often sided with Blake, but Dooley's fresh perspectives intrigued the seasoned vet, and he gave the boy plenty of rein.

Dooley slapped the water with the stick. "What do you think about Sammy and Kenny?"

He would not, could not tell Dooley what

he thought. He thought that finding them may be a closed chapter. "I don't know. Buck and I will do everything we can. Just because I'm going away doesn't mean I won't think about it, pray about it, and try to come up with something."

Dooley gazed at the water. "What can I do?"

Father Tim sighed. "I don't know," he said. "I don't know." Sammy and Kenny might be two grains of sand on a beach that stretched to the horizon.

Dooley raised his head and looked at Father Tim. "*I'm* goin' to try and come up with something," he said with finality.

"Tim!"

Hal Owen waved from the front door of his clinic. "Tim! Before you go . . ."

"Yes?"

Hal walked quickly toward Father Tim. "Sorry we didn't get to visit."

"How's the collie?"

"He'll make it. He was torn up pretty badly by some dogs across the creek, but he'll be fine. Listen . . . something to think about . . ."

He didn't need another thing to think about.

"Marge and I would like to go to France

next year and take Rebecca Jane. We'd leave sometime after Christmas." Hal removed his glasses and stuck them in the pocket of his blood-stained surgical smock. "We've been invited to run the practice of a college chum for a year while they take a similar post in Italy. We were talking last night—we wondered if you and Cynthia might care to farm-sit?"

Farm-sit. He'd never sat a farm.

"You'd be fifteen minutes from Mitford in your Mustang, twenty-five if you use the pickup. Might be interesting. I know how Cynthia likes to sketch out here. Joyce Havner comes every Monday and Friday to clean house, there are two churches right down the road . . ."

"Aha."

"Dooley would be here for the summer, of course, and Blake would be around full-time to manage the practice. There wouldn't be any farmwork involved. Lewis would do the bush hogging, Sam Rayner the milking, Bo Davis the odd jobs . . . business as usual. If the notion strikes, you might take a few eggs out of the nests every morning."

"Aha!" he said again; his mind was Jell-O.

"Plus, Meadowgate would be a great place to work on those essays you mentioned!"

"I don't know, I'd have to . . ."

"Pretty soft job, all things considered."

"Right. Well . . ."

"No need to make a decision now. It's just . . . something to think about." Hal slapped him heartily on the shoulder and gave him a hug. "Take care, old friend. The Lord be with you."

"And also with you," said Father Tim, hugging back.

Though time was short, he took the long way home.

He wanted to think. He'd been in a kind of funk the last few days; a gray fog seemed present in his brain.

It came to him that he was terribly thirsty, as if something in his very soul had been deprived for a long time. . . .

Why wasn't he taking his wife on a cruise instead of hauling her to Tennessee? He envisioned a ship's passengers lined up in deck chairs, broiling like chops. No. No way. He could never do it. He and Cynthia did little to amuse themselves because there was so much he didn't like—he didn't like flying, he didn't like the thought of lining up in deck chairs, he didn't like Cynthia's occasional enthusiasm to see Spain or France or even return to Maine, the scene of their honeymoon. What had she gotten herself into? A celebrated author tied to a man as dull as dishwater and entirely self-serving.

In truth, he was too pathetic even to play golf. Didn't retired clergy have a fondness for golf? He thought so; he seemed to recall he'd heard a lot of golf talk around diocesan meetings, about how terrific it was to keep the mind alert, the body strong. Look at Stuart Cullen, for example. A golfer, and fit as any boy. Yet, in the end . . .

"Throw me in the briar patch," he muttered aloud. "Anything but golf!"

He mopped his brow with his handkerchief and cranked the air conditioner a notch higher.

It was the same unbearably tiresome nonsense he'd wrestled with for years. He didn't know how to do anything on the side of fun, didn't have a clue how to instigate it. It was Cynthia who dragged him into fun like a sack of potatoes; hadn't she come up with those famous clergy retreats, small treasuries of time to laugh, to unwind, to refresh themselves? Had he ever come up with a retreat for *her* benefit? Not that he could recall. One might question if he had a brain in his head.

But wait. She was as much a part of this trek to Tennessee as he. They had both prayed for a ministry with children, something they could do as a couple, and Cynthia had been eager and willing. It was he, however, who'd gotten the adrenaline pumping about Father Roland's deal, which, he now learned, came with a moose head in their living room, no bridges over their creeks, a rug chewed by dogs, and an infestation of mosquitoes.

Down the road, maybe Hal's idea was, indeed, something to think about. Meadowgate had always held a place in Cynthia's heart, and certainly in his. It would give them something to look forward to while in Tennessee. He mused for a moment on picnics in the Owens' meadows and long walks in the woods; on the background music of lowing cattle and crowing roosters. Best of all, they'd be with Dooley through the summer, they wouldn't have to make this wrenching disconnect. . . .

The thirst was profound, dredging up some odd anxiety he couldn't name. But right up the road was the little store he and Dooley had stopped at the other day. He wheeled into the parking area and heaved himself from the car and went inside.

"Water," he said.

"Thirty-two, thirty-three . . . Around back." Absorbed in counting money, the man at the cash register jerked his thumb toward the rear of the building.

"Around back?"

"Spigot out back. Forty, forty-five . . . Th' drink box is over there."

Drink box. He walked to it as if through high water, his legs heavy.

Coke. Pepsi. Sprite. Dr Pepper.

He couldn't drink this stuff.

But he didn't feel like going around back, either.

He dropped the change in the slot, punched in his selection, and pulled the handle. The can thumped into the dispenser. His hand trembled as he popped the top and drank, feeling the icy liquid flow down his gullet like a river of life, a benediction.

He sat on a stack of drink crates and checked his watch.

He was within two miles of Lottie Greer, Absalom Greer's elderly sister, who was still living in back of the country store built by her parents more than eighty-five years ago. He should go by and visit. It had been a long time.

The fork in the road was coming up. He had thirty seconds to make a decision.

He saw the marker, *Mitford Seven Miles, Farmer Two Miles,* and noticed how, in the well-mown V of the fork, the weeds had been left to grow up around the marker post. His father never liked to see weeds left growing around a post. . . .

He veered left; he wouldn't go to Lottie Greer's. Everything at home was now on a schedule that, if interrupted, could throw them off the mark for their early morning departure. God willing, he would visit Lottie when he came back in September. He made a vow to do it; Absalom would have wanted it.

He missed the old preacher, who had loved Miss Sadie 'til death did them part, the preacher who'd hung on to what some called "old-time religion." Indeed, there was nothing "old-time" about the truth of the gospel, it was instead a truth for all time—yesterday, today, tomorrow. Absalom Greer had never preached the fashion of the day, nor done whatever popular thing it took to fill his pews; he had preached the Word and let the chips fall where they may. He would visit Absalom's sister for this reason alone.

Speaking of visiting . . . blast! he hadn't gotten by to see Louella at Hope House. That wouldn't do, that wouldn't do *at all*. He stepped on the accelerator, hoping the sheriff's boys weren't lurking in a bush somewhere.

Louella sat by her window, gazing out to the rooftops of Mitford.

"Knock, knock!" he said, standing at the open door of Room Number One.

"Uh-oh! Look at my shameful self! I'm still in this ol' housecoat!"

"It's all right, Louella, you look beautiful in that color."

"Lord knows, I get dressed ever' day that rolls around; today I say, Louella, ain't nobody comin' that you got to impress!"

"And you were right! You don't have to impress me, I'm already impressed."

"I don' know by what!"

He leaned down and kissed her cheek. "By your stamina, your positive attitude, your fine singing voice. Want to hit a couple of verses?" He sat on the footstool near her chair. He instantly felt eight, maybe ten years old. Miss Sadie and Louella had always done that for him, made the years roll away.

"I cain't praise th' Lord in this ol' housecoat, it's nothin' but rags and patches, Miss Sadie give it to me."

"We'll just gab, then," he said.

Nurse Carter stuck her head into the room, grinning. "Y'all going to sing today?"

"No," he said. "We can't. Louella's in her housecoat."

"Oh," said Nurse Carter.

"Cynthia and I are leaving town tomorrow,"

he said. "We'll be home for a week in September." For some reason, he found it difficult to put those two sentences together.

He stood in the parking lot, trying to remember where he was and where he was going. He looked up to the roof of the front entrance and saw the angel weather vane. Of course! He was at Hope House and he was going home.

He located the red Mustang on the other side of a Bronco and got in it and drove down the long driveway to Lilac Road, turned left on Church Hill, and passed Little Mitford Creek on his right. As he approached the stop sign, he noticed that weeds were growing up around the post, and there . . .

. . . *there was his father.* His heart beat with a profound joy.

As the image of Matthew Kavanagh appeared to him, an odd and severe explosion erupted in his head, and he felt his body violently jolted into a kind of limbo, a sudden darkness.

CHAPTER SIX

The Vale

"Father?"

Dressed in dark trousers and a familiar plaid shirt, the man up ahead stood next to a road sign at the edge of a cliff. The man's right arm was lifted, as if shielding his eyes from a bright sun, though no sun shone.

His heart pounded in his breast—to think it may be his father, dead all these years and now alive and real and wearing a shirt he remembered giving him at Christmas. The brown in the plaid was extraordinarily beautiful; he'd never known that brown might have this rich and glowing life.

The man squinted in his direction, as if affronted by the interruption of an important thought.

Yes! He could see clearly now: It was his father, his young and handsome father, the very image of the picture that had sat always on his mother's dressing table in a silver frame. Tears stung his eyes. How extraordinary that he wasn't dead, that there would be another chance for them. He stood rooted to the spot, weeping unashamed.

"Who is it?" demanded his father.

"It's . . ." Who was he? He looked at his arms, his legs, his feet. He was wearing loafers he'd put on this morning, and pants he'd picked up from the cleaner's in Wesley. He felt his head, and the hair lying about his skull in a fringe. It was this that inarguably identified himself to himself.

"It's *Timothy!*"

His father knit his brow and frowned. "I don't know you!" he said, then turned and walked off the cliff's edge as though out for an evening stroll.

A voice murmured at his right ear; he felt a warm breath that cosseted his hearing and made it acute.

"O God, Light of lights, Keep us from inward darkness. Grant us so to sleep in peace, that we may arise to work according to Your will."

The voice ceased, and he waited to hear it again, desperately wished to hear it again. *Is that all?* There came a kind of whirring in his head, as if of planets turning, and then the voice warmed his ear again. "Goodnight, dearest. I love you more than life. . . ."

He could not open his mouth, it was as if he had no mouth, only ears to catch this lovely sound, this breath as warm as the tropical isles he would never visit. Nor had he eyes to see; he discovered this when he tried to open them. No mouth to speak, no eyes to see; all he could locate was his right and waiting ear.

He tried to remember what the voice had just said to him, but could not. Speak to me again! he cried from his heart. *Please!* But he heard nothing more.

The water poured in through the top of his head, as loud as a waterfall, and rushed into his neck and arms and hands and belly and legs and streamed into his feet. Immediately the wave came in again at the top of his head and flowed through him once more.

The water's journey was warm and consoling, familiar; it was as if he'd waited for this moment all his life, and now that it had come, he was at peace.

Then he was floating somewhere, weight-less, emptied of all doubt or fear, but not emp-tied of longing. More than anything, he longed for the sound of the voice at his ear, and the warm zephyr that came with it.

The birdsong was sharp and clear, the sky cloudless. He was walking along a woodland trail, carrying something on his back. He sup-posed it might be a pack, but he didn't check to see. In trying to balance the thing between the blades of his aching shoulders, he felt the weight shift wildly so that he lost his balance. He stumbled; the edge of the woodland path crumbled under his right foot and he fell to his knees, hard, and woke shouting.

Lord! Where are you?

He knew he had shouted, yet he hadn't heard his voice.

The room—was it a room?—was black, not even a street lamp shone, and the dream—was it a dream?—had been so powerful, so con-vincing, that he dared not let it go. Where are You? he repeated, whispering, urgent.

Here I am, Timothy.

He lifted his hand and reached out to Jesus, whom he couldn't see but now strongly sensed to be near him, all around him.

The tears were hot on his face. He had found the Lord from whom he'd thought himself lost, and lay back, gasping, as if he'd walked a long section of the Appalachian Trail.

Thank you! he said into the silence. Had he spoken?

" 'And yea, though I walk through the valley of the shadow of death . . .' "

There was the voice at his ear, and the soft, warm breath. *Stay! Don't go, don't leave me.*

" 'I will fear no evil, for Thou art with me, Thy rod and Thy staff, they comfort me. . . .' "

He listened, but couldn't contain the words; he forgot them the moment they were spoken.

"I love you, my darling, my dearest, my Timothy."

A fragrance suffused the air around his pillow, and he entered into it as if into a garden. It possessed a living and deeply familiar presence, and was something like . . .

. . . Home. But what was Home? He couldn't remember. His heart repeated the word, *Home, Home,* but his head couldn't fathom the meaning.

"I . . . came . . . shift . . . yes . . . it's . . . soon."

Voices. Voices interrupted by static, sounding like the radio that sat in the corner of the living room in Holly Springs, with broadcasts that left out entire words of critical war news and replaced them with air.

"Did you . . . Kennedy?"

". . . right . . . then some."

". . . twice . . . seventh leading cause . . . death."

"I . . . doctor . . . must, too."

". . . wring neck."

He grew weary of trying to piece together a puzzle that was clearly missing its most interesting pieces.

He discovered he was longing for something so finely woven into the fiber of his being that it couldn't be identified, one might as well strive to put form and feature on vapor. Longing, longing, his spirit torn with it . . .

Then he began to know. It was a gradual understanding, unfolding in him like petals opening after rain.

He held his breath, waiting for the revelation he was certain would come. When at last he could name the longing, he felt his heart lift up with a sudden, stunning joy.

He was longing for . . . his *wife*.

But he couldn't make sense of the word; his

heart appeared to know its meaning full well, but his brain refused to step up to the plate. What was "wife"? *Think, Timothy! Think!* His head felt as if a network of connections had shut down entirely and an odd rewiring were taking place.

Wife. His heart told him it meant something like comfort or solace. Yes! Wife was solace. Chocolate was candy. Candy was chocolate. Solace was wife.

Wife was also . . . He waited for the meaning to grow in his breast, then felt himself reading his heart as one might read a book to gather understanding. Wife was also wonder, his heart seemed to tell him. Yes! Wonder and pleasure and . . . *delight*!

He liked this game, he had always liked games, really, was quite good at Scrabble and practically unbeatable at something starting with . . . what did it start with? With an *M*? But he was veering off into mist again. Now that he knew he could read his heart, he wouldn't feel so alone. What else, then?

Wife was . . .

. . . *laughter!* He remembered laughter, though distantly. Laughter doeth good like a medicine! he tried to say.

He fell into a kind of sleep in which his body floated as if on waves of music. He thought it might be Beethoven's *Pastorale,* in which the crashing of the thunderstorm over the meadows would soon be heard, but the storm did not come. When he awoke, he found he'd learned yet another definition:

Wife was peace.

He felt someone caressing his hand, but couldn't open his eyes to see or his mouth to inquire who it might be. The touch was inexpressibly tender; he wanted to clasp the caress, to hold it to himself as insurance against what might come.

Wife, he said, trying to move his mouth. Wife, he had discovered in his sleep, was a place one went when one was afraid, or alone, or even senselessly happy. It was a place one wanted to be, a place one cherished . . . it was something very like Home.

"Home," he said, and heard himself speak.

"But it's what he *wants.* It's the only word he's uttered in days."

"He can't go home, it's too soon, he could be here for weeks, we don't know where this thing is going—"

"We could have help come in, surely you could find someone for us, perhaps Nurse Kennedy on her hours off." He thought the woman sounded close to tears and wanted to rise up and protect her from the other voice.

He was urinating where he lay and could do absolutely nothing to prevent it. He felt it streaming out of him and afterward was greatly relieved. He wondered why it hadn't soaked the bed beneath him. But of course he wasn't lying in a bed, he was in a hammock swung by his mother and he was wearing knickers and was barefoot and laughing, and she was singing.

Baby Bye, here's a fly,
Let us watch him you and I,
As he crawls, up the walls,
Yet he never falls.

I believe with six such legs
You and I could walk on eggs!
Spots of red dot his head
Rainbows on his back are spread.

"I'm not a baby!" he shouted, in case she had forgotten.

She laughed. "Oh, really? Is that so? I did forget for a moment, I admit, but only a very *tiny* moment!"

He thought his mother the most beautiful

woman in the world. More beautiful than the ladies in *Ladies' Home Journal,* and nine hundred thousand times more beautiful than the other ladies at church.

"I'm five!" he shouted again, flying through the air.

"You have a whole day left before you're five! I want this day to go on and on and on and on and—"

"For always?" he yelled.

"For always!" whooped his mother.

He felt secretly pleased that she wished him always to be four instead of five, though he would have hated being four forever.

O Lord, you are my portion and my cup; it is you who upholds my lot. My boundaries enclose a pleasant land; indeed, I have a goodly heritage. I will bless the Lord who gives me counsel; my heart teaches me, night after night . . .

He stood before his Sunday School class in his mother's Baptist church and recited the whole of the Sixteenth Psalm, for which he would be given a coveted gold star to wear on his lapel.

I have set the Lord always before me; because he is at my right hand I shall not fall. My heart, therefore, is glad, and my spirit rejoices; my body also shall rest in hope. . . .

You will show me the path of life; in your presence there is fullness of joy, and in your right hand are pleasures for evermore.

For evermore . . . the phrase moved him deeply and set him wondering about eternity and the souls of others. Miss Wright was smiling and nodding her head. While one part of him was twelve years old and sitting down after the recitation, another part of him, a vague and hazy part, stood filled with relief and joy that Miss Wright, whom he and everyone else loved, had not been killed in a car accident with her husband on Christmas Eve.

Well done, Timothy.

Thank you, ma'am.

His heart pounded like a jackhammer, his face blazed. He suddenly knew that tonight, possibly even before, he would pray, *Lord, show me the path of my life . . .*

Why can't we talk? he wanted to say to his father, who sat across from him at the kitchen table. But this question supposed that they had tried to talk and failed. They had never really tried to talk. He would attempt something else, then, something more straightforward and to the point. After all, what if his father died before they seized the chance?

He cleared his throat and felt the terrible fear of a man who, though poised on a diving board, cannot swim. "Let's talk . . . sir," he said.

"About what?"

His father was much older than the handsome man in the silver frame that always sat on his mother's dressing table.

"I . . . I don't know," he said, ashamed that he didn't know. Now that he had his father's attention, he remembered that he hadn't chosen a subject. "Maybe about how we could . . . communicate better."

"Communicate."

His father repeated the word, looking as he often looked—inordinately bored.

"Why do you hate me?" There it was, he'd said it. His breath failed.

"Hate you."

He gulped air. "Yes. I think you do. I don't know why." He was stricken by what he was doing, but more than that, he urgently wanted to know.

His father was stalling for time, making him suffer.

"Talk to me, Father. Tell me why."

The color had drained from his father's face. "You are impertinent, Timothy."

"No, Father, I am your son and I must know the answer." Rage flamed in him, but he resisted it. He was a man now, he had finished high school with honors, he had been accepted into a respectable and discriminating college—he would wait for the answer without asking again, and without begging or whining. He felt the heavy pounding of his heart.

"I have no idea what you're talking about, Timothy. I seldom do, in fact."

His father rose from the table and walked stiffly from the kitchen. He shut the door, which usually remained open, behind him.

He sat frozen, lest the slightest movement cause something in him to shatter.

Then there was the whisper of his mother's dress, the gray faille that sounded like dry husks of corn blown together in a breeze.

She sat in his father's chair and reached for his hand across the table. "Love your father, Timothy," she said quietly. "Pray for him."

"I can't. I've tried, but it doesn't work." He wanted it to work, if only to please her.

"It's time I told you something."

Her eyes were brown and dark. He felt he could see a kind of eternity in them.

"Your father bears many wounds."

"But it isn't right to inflict them on others; especially not on you."

"No. It isn't right. Yet, in many ways, it's no

surprise. His father treated him brutally. You know the verse from Deuteronomy."

"Lots of people have been treated brutally. Saint Paul—"

"But Saint Paul had encountered Christ, and your father shields himself against even the remotest possibility that Christ would approach him."

Through the window, he saw his father driving away.

"Timothy, your grandfather once horse-whipped your father—in front of a great number of people. It was a vicious attack that left Matthew terribly damaged in many ways. After that incident, which wasn't the first of its kind, Matthew sealed himself up like a tomb. That's how he made certain that his father could never reach him again."

He watched the black Packard make a right turn by the hedge of myrtles and disappear from view. The loss he felt was sudden and immeasurable, different from any loss he'd ever felt before.

"I'm sorry," he said at last. "But it's too easy. When he shut out his father, he shut out everyone else, too. He uses a terrible personal experience as an excuse to wound others."

"Forgive him, Timothy."

"How can I do that? I don't know how to do that."

"I'll pray for you to be able to do that," she said simply.

"Do you love him?" he asked. It was a deeply personal question. His family did not ask deeply personal questions, and today he had asked an intimate confession of both his parents.

She gazed out the window as she answered. "I thought I could soften his heart, could give him joy. I believed that love would conquer all."

"Do you still believe that?"

"Yes," she said, turning to look at him. "I still believe that. Please believe that with me."

He'd attended college for two years, then gone on to seminary, perceiving his call to the priesthood as God's way of using Timothy Kavanagh to bring his father into relationship with Jesus Christ. But his father died with a hardness of heart no mortal son could remove.

He had tried hard to believe with his mother that love would conquer all. And love had not conquered.

He felt a cool breeze on his face and heard the laughter of children.

The children appeared to be sitting on a limb of the tree above his head, for he saw feet dangling among the leaves. One small pair of feet was shod in white socks and patent leather shoes and the other feet were brown and bare.

"Father, is that you?"

"Miss Sadie! Is that you?"

"It's *us*!" More laughter. The limb moved; leaves trembled.

"What are you doing up there?"

"Playing!"

"Is Louella with you?"

"We eatin' cornbread an' milk!" Louella shouted.

"I declare," he said, shaking his head.

"Come up!" crowed Miss Sadie. "I need to talk with you about something."

"No way am I coming up there."

"Father, if you want my advice, clergy needs to climb a tree once in a while."

"Else you goes stuffy!"

"You'll have to talk to me where I stand," he said, being firm. What nonsense!

"Well, then, Father, I want you to look out for Dooley and Lace Turner."

"What do you mean, look out for them?"

"Don't let them drift apart."

"What can I do about such things?" He was

starting to feel positively huffy. "That's God's business!"

"I thought God's business was your *job!*" replied Miss Sadie.

"It is not my job to meddle in the romantic lives of people who're barely college age!"

"Oh, pshaw! What do you think I should tell him, Louella?"

"Tell 'im do the best he can."

"Do the best you can, Father. That will be enough."

"Blast!" he muttered, stomping away. He didn't like people thrashing around in trees above his head. How ridiculous.

He was a balloon shaped like a man; his right arm, his chest, his groin, his legs were being filled with a familiar substance, though he couldn't have said what it was. . . .

There was a terrible fatigue in him, as if he had toiled up mountains, mountains he had not in the least wished to climb.

Abba, Father . . .

He struggled to pray, but was disconcerted by a loud beeping noise somewhere above his head. He opened his eyes and found he could see.

He was in a dark place.

It smelled of aluminum foil, or possibly mouthwash.

A narrow column of light shone through a door that stood ajar.

Where in God's name was he? Their door wasn't on that side of the bedroom.

Cynthia!

He found he couldn't move his left hand, it hadn't yet filled up, so he examined the bed with his right. The bed was narrow, and he was alone.

He tried to roll onto his side, but found he was tethered.

"Cynthia? Cynthia!"

The beeping grew louder and the slice of light grew wider as the door opened.

"Father Kavanagh!"

"Who is it?"

Someone walked soundlessly into the room without turning on the light.

"Nurse Kennedy." She took his wrist and placed her fingers on his pulse. "Thank God," she said softly.

"Where am I?" he asked.

She did something that stopped the beeping. "You're in Mitford Hospital. Welcome home."

CHAPTER SEVEN

Grace Sufficient

"Dearest . . ."

He opened his eyes and saw Cynthia standing by the hospital bed. Though tears streamed down her cheeks, her smile was radiant.

He found he could not lift his hand to touch her, though the sight before him was the most wondrous he'd ever beheld.

He touched her with his gaze, then mutely examined her face with his eyes. Home. He was home. Whatever he had done, he would never do it again. He felt like a man who had been to a hideous war and returned at last to kiss his very doorstep.

"Timothy . . . ," she whispered, leaning down to brush her cheek against his.

"Come," he said.

She lay down in the narrow space beside him, and held him, and wept.

"Dear God, what bloody foolishness! How many times are you planning to pull this stunt?"

"What stunt?" Father Tim asked. The effort of speaking seemed monumental.

"Making yourself comatose. You did it so well the first time, you thought you'd do it all over again?" Hoppy raised his voice as if his patient had gone clinically deaf.

"Comatose?"

"For nearly forty-eight hours. I suspect it all started with delirium from severely elevated blood sugar, complicated by a concussion from whacking your head. All of which resulted in grieving your wife and upsetting half the county. . . ." Hoppy stooped and squinted at Father Tim. "What the devil did you do to yourself, anyhow?"

Get out of my face, he wanted to say; he felt nailed to the pillow by his doctor's blazing stare. "I don't remember." He had some vague recollection of going to the country with Dooley, but not much more. "How high was my sugar?"

"You don't want to know," snapped his doctor.

"How did I get a concussion?"

"You weren't wearing your seat belt."

"When can I go home?"

Hoppy walked to the window, scowling, his hands jammed into his coat pockets. "We'll take you out of ICU tomorrow, then three, four days on the floor. You'll be home Sunday, looking at a full month of recovery. To tell the truth, you'll feel rotten for six weeks."

Hoppy had the grayish pallor Father Tim had often seen in him over the years. He knew it well—it was exhaustion, plain and simple; he supposed he was the cause. . . .

"You're pretty fired up."

"Yes!" Hoppy turned from the window. "Because you don't listen. I talk, I preach, I warn, but you turn me off like I'm some know-nothing parent."

He decided to ignore this accusation. "What happened?"

"You blacked out while you were driving and hit . . ."

"Hit what?"

Hoppy raked his hand through his thatch of gray hair. "A stop sign at Little Mitford Creek. So what was it, Father? More of that infernal cake you ate last time? Or did you cut back on your insulin and try living by your own rules?"

He had cut back on his insulin, yes, but only a little. As for cake, he hadn't had any cake. Coke, maybe. Or was it cake? No, it was Coke, some glimmer of memory assured him. "Coke," he said. "I had a Coke at the country store, coming home from Meadowgate." There. His mind was back. "I thought I punched the Diet Coke button, but I guess I got the real thing. . . . I skipped lunch and then I was thirsty and—"

"I don't know," said Hoppy, shaking his head. "I just don't know." He thumped into the green vinyl chair by the bed and checked his watch. "You're a pain in the butt."

He grinned at his doctor, whose bedside manner appeared to be in drastic ill repair. "Same back."

Hoppy tried to smile. "We'll get through this," he said.

He fell asleep almost immediately after Hoppy's visit, and woke with a start.

Tennessee! What about Tennessee?

He felt around on his pillow for the nurse's bell, but the movement exhausted him and he lay panting from the effort. The phone. He could phone Cynthia and ask her; they hadn't talked about it when she rushed to the hospital this morning at two o'clock. Now it was—what time was it? No watch. No clock. How was he supposed to know anything around here? He noticed for the first time that a TV hung over his bed at a drunken slant, as if it might plummet into his face at any moment. Maybe there was a remote; he could get the time from CNN. He craned his neck and peered at the nightstand, but saw only a box of tissues and a glass of water. He decided that shouting for a nurse was out of the question—it would take more energy than he had, and worse, disturb other patients.

He would simply lie here, then, until someone came, enduring the pounding of his head and the sharp sting of the bruise where his temple had gotten banged up in that business with the sign.

He heard rain strike the windowpane, and felt strangely bereft and alone. He should be glad for the sound, glad for what a spring shower would do for the grass and the garden, his roses. But he felt no gladness. In truth, he felt almost nothing.

Was this how it would be during the long weeks ahead? And was it really his stubbornness and stupidity that had caused his wife such agony, his doctor to work overtime, and the ministry in Tennessee to go begging from the beginning?

Emma's packet arrived with his lunch, which consisted of a pint of milk, a bowl of yogurt, and something he couldn't identify— was it congealed tomato soup or aspic or . . . worse? He tore into the saltines and read his e-mails.

From: ourbackyard@aol.com

That's a fine kettle of fish, Timothy! I suppose it was the moose head that scared you off.

When you're up and about and ready to join us, I'll take it off your living room wall and hang it in your woodshed.

Forgot to mention you'll be heating with a woodstove, like the rest of us in Bear Creek Cove.

Thank God for Richard and Trudy, who arrived yesterday and have already done the work of two hale men. Youth! That's the ticket!

We discovered your roof needs a patch job, it has let a good bit of spring deluge into your sleeping quarters, which, looking on the bright side, drowned a good many of the mice.

Richard will fetch new sheathing for the roof as soon as the mud dries on the road and we can get around without miring up to our fenders.

We're all assuming you and Cynthia have four-wheel drive.

Well, old friend, hang in there and content yourself with the bald truth that God is working in Jessup, Tennessee!

Yrs, Fr Harry

P.S. A neighboring boy named Abner, as in the comic strip of yore, has come to my door looking for work, heaven knows we can use an extra hand. It makes the heart glad to see his patient industry. Around fourteen, maybe fifteen years old, can't read a word or write his name.

Pray for Abner. Keep me posted. Send money.

The eternal effervescence of Harry Roland was more than a man could take on an empty stomach. He opened the other package of crackers and downed his low-fat milk, watching the door for a sign of his wife. Four-wheel drive. Blast. Why hadn't they thought of that? Cynthia's Mazda had front-wheel drive. Wouldn't that do the trick? What could he have been thinking these last couple of months? What kind of fog had he been in, anyway?

From: hisbp@aol.com

My old friend,

I write to you as St. Paul wrote to the Hebrews.

"How can we thank God enough for you in return for all the joy that we feel before our God because of you?

"Night and day we pray most earnestly that we may see you face to face and restore whatever is lacking in your faith." (If anything be lacking, dear brother)

"Now may our God and Father himself and our Lord Jesus direct our way to you and may the Lord make you increase and abound in love . . . just as (Martha and I) abound in love for you."

I plan to come through Mitford on 28th, en route to mtg in Charlotte. Will see you then unless advised to contrary. Be encouraged.

Stuart

There was an appalling soreness in every limb, every joint; his eyes were as painful as if they'd been punched like a voting ballot. And his head—pounding like horses at a gallop. He found his left temple bandaged and supposed this had come about from crashing into the stop sign. . . .

He dropped the mail onto his blanket, exhausted.

Perhaps the yogurt would provide some strength, but he couldn't get interested in lifting the spoon to his mouth. He rang for the nurse to take his tray so there would be room for Cynthia to sit on the bed beside him. Some flame licked up at the thought of her and warmed him, and he lay back against the pillows and closed his eyes and tried to forget what he had done and where he was, and why.

His wife lay on her side next to him, her hand in his. They had been silent for some time, content merely to lie together, touching.

"We're a pair," he murmured at last. "What are you thinking?"

"I'm thanking God for you."

"What's left of me," he said, surprised at the

irony in his voice. "I'm thinking about Tennessee, how they'll have to dig deep 'til we get there. It won't help matters to start off short-handed."

"We'll think about that later."

"What about the car? Did I . . . ?"

"Let's talk about it later, dearest. We'll talk about . . . everything, later."

Hoppy blew in with a burst of energy that scattered the e-mails to the floor.

"Now I have *two* patients?"

"Multiplying like coat hangers in a closet!" crowed Cynthia, sitting up and tidying herself.

Hoppy put his hand on Cynthia's shoulder. "Have you slept?"

"Finally," she said. "But still a bit droopy."

Father Tim raised his head from the pillow. "We were just talking about Tennessee, and when we might be able to—"

"You'll have to forget Tennessee," said his doctor, folding his arms across his chest. "With your out-of-control diabetes, the last thing you need is a year in the backwoods."

"Yes, but you—"

"What if this had happened in Jessup, Father? Fourteen miles from the nearest hospital?"

Having no answer, he was silent.

"There's your answer," said Hoppy.

Hoppy had decreed that no one but Cynthia could visit him when he moved to the floor. That suited him fine. He had nothing much to say and less energy to say it with. The staff was conniving to stuff food into him at every turn. He felt like a goose in which someone sought to cultivate pâté. When the phone rang, he didn't answer it. Once, a nurse answered and announced that J. C. Hogan was on the line. He waved the proffered receiver away, spent.

Flowers poured in. Roses, tulips, even a few sprigs of ivy pulled from the yard of a former parishioner and stuck into a Mason jar. *Let this root,* said the note.

Sissy sent the heel of a potato, sprouting in a paper cup. Sassy sent an avocado seed, suspended in a jelly glass by three toothpicks, whose stupendous crop of leaves had seen better days.

Hessie Mayhew had clearly outdone herself with the offering she sent in a basket that occupied an entire corner of the room. He wanted to pore over every stem and stamen, examine the colors, muse on the fragrances, but he could not. When he occasionally glanced at it, he felt guilty that he didn't care about it in the least, and so stopped looking in that corner.

He gave it to Kennedy, who was clearly

skeptical. "I've had yards smaller than this," she said, lugging it from the room.

He discovered that he was content with the laughter of other patients' visitors along the hall. It was a kind of assurance that people's lives were going on, though his own had come to a bitter halt.

He walked down the hall once, without permission, stiff as a board, shuffling like an old person. He *was* old, of course, he was nearly seventy. When he was young, seventy had been old, hadn't it? One of his grandfathers had died at the age of seventy, and surely no one had said, *Poor Yancey, he was so young.*

He noticed that several people stared at him as he scuffed along in his slippers, as if toilet tissue might be trailing from one of the soles. At least two people, whom he'd met casually, lowered their eyes and appeared not to recognize him. He knew some of the patients, certainly, and most of the nurses—as rector of Lord's Chapel, he'd come here nearly every weekday morning for sixteen years—yet today nothing seemed familiar. He might have been a stranger in the place he'd once spent hours praying with patients and staff and reading the Word by countless bedsides.

He barely made it to the rubber plant at the elevators when Kennedy found him and hauled him back to his room as if he were a convict who'd gone over the wall.

"No wonder people die in hospitals," he muttered to the longtime head nurse. "They never let you have any fun."

I have come home.

He wrote these words on a blank page in the back of his journal, intending to say more, but discovered there was nothing else to say. It was all he had wanted and then some, just to come home.

Thinking he should date the entry, he picked up the pen and held it for moment, then put it down and looked out the window to the postage-stamp view of Baxter Park.

They should tear down the old garage and open up the view. He had no idea why they'd never thought of it before. Even the straggly hedge behind it, which belonged to the town, could be cleaned up to some extent, and dead-wood pulled out. In only a couple of days, he and Harley could get the job done, no problem. They would use the chain saw, as needed, he'd stack brush and put it out for the town chipper, and voilà! a view of Baxter Park.

"What do you think, old boy?" Barnabas jumped from the slipcovered chair by the sofa, came to him, and looked soulfully into his eyes.

He started to rise from the chair, but found he hadn't the strength or will to actually do it. The thought of pulling down the garage and cleaning up the hedge had nearly finished him.

"No more e-mails, and especially from Father Roland," he heard Cynthia tell Emma at the front door. "He needs rest."

Emma's words were muffled, but his wife's were sharp and clear, even though she lowered her voice. "No more *anything* for a while."

Emma's muffled voice, obviously cranky.

"I'm sure he wants to see you, too, but doctor's orders are doctor's orders. Call me on Monday, I'll give you a report. . . ."

The front door closed and his wife came down the hallway, his dog behind her at a trot.

Why couldn't he see Emma? Besides, he was starting to like e-mail. He didn't want to personally be online, for heaven's sake, but he liked the little sheaf of papers Emma brought every week, found them a wonder, truth be told. What about Father what's-his-name in England? What was he up to? And Father

Harry—had he received the check or had last Thursday's flood kept the mail truck out of the Cove? Since no one seemed to write regular letters anymore, how would he ever know anything? And of course there was Marion Fieldwalker . . . though just getting started at the business of e-mail, she promised to be a positive encyclopedia of news from Whitecap, a place he'd found himself missing more than once.

"Guess who's coming today, dearest." Cynthia stood behind his chair and kissed the top of his head.

"Umm." He wanted to say something bright and clever, but couldn't come up with anything.

"Dooley!" Barnabas barked at her announcement. "He'll be here at three o'clock. He was terribly worried about you, he wanted to visit the hospital, but Hoppy—"

"Blast Hoppy," he muttered.

"Hoppy is dropping in after lunch, by the way."

"Why?"

"To talk."

"Seems to me he had plenty to say at the hospital."

"He's leaving for his trip out West, and wanted to . . . go over some things with you."

"Where's Puny?"

"I've given her a few days off."

Something was up with his wife, he didn't know what. She seemed tense, distracted, worn. Perhaps it was all she'd been through; then again, perhaps it was something more.

"Uh-oh," she said, looking at the clock on his desk. "I'm off to The Local. Dooley's coming, you know what that means."

She kissed his cheek and dashed from the room, grabbing her car keys off the kitchen island. "I'll bring you a surprise!" she called over her shoulder.

No surprises, please, he thought. Anything but another surprise.

"Father . . ."

Hoppy sat in their study, looking anxious and exhausted. Any improvement Father Tim had seen in his doctor two days ago had clearly vanished. There was no small talk, no mention of the weather, which was currently sullen with rain, nor any reference to the new study, which Hoppy had never seen until today.

"You've been through a dangerous patch. It will take a while to recover your stamina."

"Yes," he said. He had the sure sense that an axe was about to fall. His wife sat with him on the sofa and held his hand. He thought she looked unwell. This whole thing had been too much. . . .

"But you're in a familiar place now, with the best nurse in the county, outside Kennedy. And I believe you're strong enough to hear what we have to tell you."

But he didn't want to hear anything more. . . .

"When you blacked out at the wheel of your car, you did hit the stop sign at Little Mitford Creek."

"If there's any damage, Rodney knows I'll take care of it."

"You also hit Bill Sprouse."

He looked at his wife, disbelieving, and saw that all color had drained from her face. Her hand tightened on his.

"And his dog, Sparky," she whispered.

Something like ice formed in his veins.

"Bill is at the hospital with several fractures and a mild concussion. His room was right down the hall from yours. I'm sorry, Father."

Everyone knew and loved First Baptist's jovial pastor, who was devoted to his dog and regularly seen walking Sparky around Mitford.

"What else?" The pounding of his heart was nearly unbearable.

"Sparky was found under the rear wheel of your car; we think he died instantly."

Lord have mercy, Christ have mercy. He put his head in his hands. "Why didn't you tell me this before?"

"We wanted to wait 'til you were stronger. Not everybody would have handled it this way, but it seemed the best thing to do."

Father Tim had a fleeting thought that this was only a terrible dream . . .

"Here's the good news. Bill is going to be all right, though he'll need several weeks to rest and heal. They're looking for someone to supply his pulpit."

. . . but no, it was a waking nightmare.

Dooley sat with him on the sofa, unspeaking. Barnabas left the slipcovered chair, came to his master, and lay down at his feet.

The clock ticked. The hand moved from 3:10 to 3:11.

"I'm sorry," Dooley said at last.

"I know," he replied.

"I would do something if I could."

"I know," he said again.

"I've been praying for you."

"Don't stop."

"No, sir. I won't."

"Bill will be all right. But his dog . . ."

"Yes, sir."

The hand passed from 3:13 to 3:14. A late June breeze poured through the open windows, bearing a scent of rain and leaf mold.

"I'd better go," said Dooley.

"I know."

The boy stood; Father Tim looked at him, stricken.

"I love you," Dooley said with courage. His voice shook.

I love you back, he thought, but could not speak.

He sat in the study as Cynthia, looking disconsolate, went up to bed. He knew he should do something to reassure her, she who had reassured him again and again. But he could not.

He took his Bible off his desk and opened it to Second Corinthians, and closed his eyes and prayed for Bill Sprouse and his wife. Afterward, he sat with the Bible in his lap for a long time, praying again.

Then he lifted the book into the warm circle of light from the lamp. Though he knew the passage by heart, he wanted to see it in print.

"'My grace is sufficient for thee,'" he read, barely whispering the words, "'for my strength is made perfect in weakness. . . .'"

CHAPTER EIGHT

Tender Mercies

Unlike the arrival of spring, which in Mitford always seemed dilatory, summer came this year precisely on time.

On the day of solstice, the weather changed as if driven by a calendar date, and temperatures rocketed into the high eighties from the previous day's low seventies.

Hessie Mayhew's deck, which was known to enjoy cool breezes from the west, became by noon a veritable broiler and Hessie an unwilling capon as she arranged flowers for a wedding at the Methodist chapel. Rescuing buckets of roses, wild larkspur, yellow heliopsis, and Madonna lilies from the perilous heat, she dumped the whole shebang in her kitchen, regretful that her screened porch was currently a storage bin with no room to skin a cat.

She absolutely despised working a wedding in a kitchen the size of a cocktail napkin, but more than that, she hated what rode in on her plant materials—caterpillars, spiders, beetles, mosquitoes, gnats, aphids, bees, inchworms, ladybugs, creatures too weird and disgusting to identify, and, depending on the season, chiggers and fleas.

Feeling rivulets of sweat streaming down her spine, she opened the refrigerator door to cool her backside and declared aloud to the Kenmore stove that this was it, this was her last year to be every Tom, Dick, and Harry's step-and-fetch-it flower arranger—she was getting out of the business once and for all and, come hell or high water, was prepared to let Social Security show her what it was made of.

And another thing. That ridiculous "Lady Spring" column, which she'd slaved over every year for ten years, was history. She'd done the first on a lark, after forcing herself to read Wordsworth and Cowper and all those other old poets who liked to hang around in the country searching for violets and stuffing their pockets with nuts. When she saw what a kick Father Tim got out of it, she did it another year, then another and another, until she was practically senseless, and all for a measly fifteen dollars a clip, which J. C. Hogan appeared to regard as a cool million before taxes.

Hessie yanked up her dress and tucked the hem into the legs of her underpants, so that she assumed, overall, the look of a mushroom turned upside down on its stem.

All these years of scrambling for her livelihood, running around like a chicken with its head cut off, and still no air conditioner, not even a window unit! And here it was, getting hotter and hotter in the mountains every blessed summer—gone were the days when people sometimes wore a sweater in August!

Hessie jabbed the rubber stopper into the drain of her kitchen sink and turned on the tap. Some people said all this weather mess was the greenhouse effect. Pretty soon the icebergs would be melting in the north and the terrible floods hurtling in this direction, which meant that, once again, the South would be taking the brunt of things.

Rankled by the doomed and unfair outcome of fuel emissions, she plunged the stems of forty-seven lilies into the tepid water. "Drink up!" she commanded.

At that moment, she realized she'd never heard a single, civilized word from Father Kavanagh about the garden basket she sent to his hospital room nearly three weeks past. She'd certainly heard straight back from Rachel Sprouse about the lovely vase of yellow roses.

She grabbed a coffee mug and smashed a worm on the countertop. What was the matter with people these days? Had common courtesy gone completely out the window? People nattered on about their sex lives 'til they were blue in the face, but there was scarcely a soul left standing who'd bother to say a simple *please* or *thank you*.

On the other hand . . .

She was stunned at the thought—had she really taken the father a basket, or had she dreamed it? Had she planned it so carefully, in every detail, that she only imagined she'd done it? To tell the truth, she couldn't remember delivering it. And no wonder—since the middle of May, she'd made so many garden baskets, slogged to the hospital so many times, and done flowers for so many weddings, that it all seemed a blur. . . .

A dull heaviness settled on her heart. Poor Father Kavanagh, with everything that had happened to him, and not a civilized word from Hessie Mayhew.

She felt like the worm she'd just sent to its reward.

❧

A few blocks south, Uncle Billy Watson carried a packet of seeds and a rusted hoe to the backyard of the town museum.

He liked the way the seeds rustled in their colorful packet. The sound encouraged him in what he was about to do. The dadjing things had cost a dollar at Dora Pugh's hardware, and he'd made such a fuss about the price, she gave him an old pack from last year's inventory, warning him they may not germinate but don't come crying to her about it.

What he was out to accomplish was a beautification plan for the town museum, since the town was too trifling to do the beautifying themselves. He would show them what a man with a little get-up-and-go could do, which ought to put the whole lot of the town crew to shame. Before long, people would be driving by and taking notice, like they did down at Preacher Kavanagh's place every summer—those pink roses blooming up the side of his wife's yellow house . . . now, that was a sight for sore eyes.

He laid the packet on the seat of a rusted metal dinette chair that had sat under the tree for several years, and considered the roots of the tree, which were exceedingly prominent. He'd better not go to digging around tree roots, Lord knows what trouble that might stir up; if he was to mess with that tree, it could end up falling on the house, and this was the side his and Rose's bedroom was on.

He moved away from the tree and into the yard, where the tall grass awaited the town crew and their mowing machines two days hence. How he would get a patch of this tall grass dug up was more than he could figure, but he was going to do it, and that was that.

He raised the hoe and gave the ground a good lick, but the hoe bounced out of his hand and landed two feet away. Uncle Billy said a word he hadn't said in a good while, then shuffled over and bent down stiffly to pick it up. "Lord have mercy," he said, wiping the sweat from his eyes.

Without returning to the original spot, he gave the ground another good lick and this time made a dent. The hoe blade turned up a smidgen of earth as red as a brick and nearly as hard. Seeing dirt gave him a feeling of confidence; he struck the ground again, but missed the opening he had just created and scored a second dent several inches from the first.

"Dadgummit!"

He was having a hard time drawing a breath, and his heart was flipping this way and that, like a fish on a creek bank.

Not to mention he was hot as a depot stove, and no wonder—he was wearing Rose's brother's old wool britches, which were not only burning him up, but itching him half to death. It was enough to make a man run around buck-naked.

He considered going to the house and changing clothes, but it was too much trouble. Besides, if he went in, Rose would start harping about this or that, and first thing you know, he'd be hauling out garbage or peeling potatoes or sharpening a knife blade that wouldn't cut butter. She might even send him to the basement for that jar of pickles Lew Boyd had brought a while back, and the thought of all those jumping spiders was enough to make his scalp prickle.

Nossir, he was going to knock this thing in the head, and by October—or was it September?—they would have a bait of yellow chrysanthemums that a man could see all the way from the town monument. It would be a help if Preacher Kavanagh would walk by with his dog, the preacher would definitely know the best way to do this job of work, but he hadn't seen the preacher in a good while, owing, he supposed, to the bad thing that had happened. He would go down the street in a day or two and tell him the two new jokes he'd learned from one of his almanacs. He would do the same for Preacher Sprouse, but there was no way in creation he could make it up that long hill to what most people called Sprouse House.

He took the hoe handle firmly between his arthritic hands, raised it as high as he was able, and whacked the ground with all his might.

By johnny, that did it. A tall stand of grass keeled over, exposing a shallow hole the size of a man's hand.

"Hallelujah!" he hollered.

He looked toward the house to see if Rose was watching. As far as he could see, which wasn't very far, she wasn't.

He decided to sit a minute and catch his breath, but the dadblame chair was halfway to China. He dropped the hoe in the grass and hobbled toward the tree, clutching his lower back, where a shooting pain bubbled up like carbonation in a soft drink.

He thumped down in the chair on the packet of seeds, wiped his forehead with his sleeve, and considered the satisfying hole he had just dug with only one whack.

How many whacks would it take to make room for a handful of seeds? How long would it take to see sprouts? Would he have to build a fence around the bloomin' things to keep the town crew from . . .

He dozed, dreaming of the creek near his boyhood cabin, the creek where he caught his first tadpole and saw his first bear and got bit by a snake. In this dream, however, there were no snakes, just his mama standing in the bend of Little Jack Creek, stooped over and washing out his school britches and humming "Redwing."

At Happy Endings Bookstore, Hope Winchester opened the front door, looked at her watch, then trotted to the rear of the shop and unlocked the back door, which led to the loading dock. She didn't care if the flies came in the back door, which had never had a screen, she would deal with it, she was absolutely craving a breath of cool air.

Cross-ventilation! Wasn't that the crux of all important southern architecture? She slid a box of paperbacks across the floor to hold the back door open and, satisfied that she might make it until the air-conditioning was repaired on Tuesday, returned to her stool by the cash register and picked up her 1913 edition of *Aunt Olive in Bohemia,* which had mistakenly been shipped with an order of rare and used books.

Hope had seen immediately that this was not

literature, it was shallow entertainment, but perhaps she should loosen up just this once and read something light and unimportant, which was precisely what most of her customers enjoyed. With the exception, course, of her good clientele from the college in Wesley or Mrs. Harper and Lace Turner and Mr. Gregory and a sprinkling of others, not to mention her favorite customer, Father Kavanagh.

She sighed, suddenly miserable at the thought of what had happened to him, and how inauspicious the whole dreadful thing had been. She wished she could do something to help, but there was nothing she could do. Two people had told her they were praying for him and suggested she might do the same, but she didn't believe in prayer, she was a lifelong friend of optimism and reason.

She had succeeded in avoiding her deepest feelings all morning, as they served only to inspire a wild swing between morbid anxiety and sheer exhilaration. Indeed, she would concentrate her energies on reading this innocuous book, keeping the shop cool, and satisfying the needs of her customers, should she have one. Whatever she did, she would make a strict and disciplined effort to keep firm control of her imagination, which had always been wayward and fitful—a problem, accord-

ing to her mother, caused by too much reading.

She glanced at her watch again, and opened
the book to Chapter Three.

It was nearly seven o'clock in the
evening, and through one of the windows
of the newly-furnished studio a shaft of
sunlight had found its way. It formed a
patch of light on the blue drugget on the
floor, and caught the corner of an oak
dresser on which the old Worcester dinner service was arranged . . .

Hope thought the imagery deft enough and
liked very much the word *drugget,* which she'd
never before seen or heard. It must surely be a
rug, but as she'd never learned anything by
guessing, she put the book down and hurried
to the dictionary on the little stand by the front
door, placed there for customers to peruse at
their leisure.

. . . a rug from India, of coarse hair with
cotton or jute . . .

She felt the breeze then, so cool and sweet
against the back of her neck that she let down
her guard and closed her eyes and found her-

self standing on a moor in England, her long, dark cape snapping in the wind and George Gaynor riding toward her on a gray steed—

"Good morning, Miss Winchester. I hope it's all right if I'm early."

She shot awake from her dream, burning with mortification and alarmed by the uncontrolled pounding of her heart. She was struck dumb before the tall, lean silhouette of George Gaynor standing in the shop door, the afternoon light shining behind him.

Hélène Pringle stood at the upstairs bedroom window in what had once served as the rectory for the Chapel of our Lord and Savior, otherwise known as Lord's Chapel.

She felt terribly perplexed and anxious—on pins and needles, really—trying to decide what might be proper.

Should she go next door and pay her respects and possibly be thought intrusive at this sensitive time? Or wait until things were back to normal and perhaps be thought cold and uncaring for not calling sooner? She had always been a worrier, and often found herself torn between complete opposites of choice and affection.

Before and after piano lessons and visits to

her mother at Hope House, she had been glued to this window, thinking she may find some clue to what was transpiring at the Kavanaghs'. But the yellow house next door might have been a sepulchre; she had seen Cynthia only once, dashing from her front door in robe and pajamas, picking up the newspaper, and running in again. Since the *Muse* was delivered on Monday and this was Saturday, it had literally been days since she'd witnessed movement. Of course, she couldn't see the new garage side of the house, where people probably came and went all the time, and certainly nothing could be seen through their upstairs windows, as they were always shuttered on the side facing her own.

Her cat, Barbizon, rubbed himself against her ankles, though she took no notice.

She couldn't bear this dreadful anxiety another moment, and certainly not another day.

How was the dear man? Was his diabetes so advanced that his life might be threatened? Was he grieved beyond telling? As someone of infinite sensitivity, and a dog lover to boot, he would have taken this thing very, very hard.

While shopping at The Local, she had questioned Avis Packard about Reverend Sprouse and learned he must endure another several weeks of bed rest, but would recover. Further,

Reverend Sprouse was stricken about the loss of his dog, but made every attempt to remain jovial and to lift the spirits of others. She hadn't the courage to inquire about Father Tim, afraid that Mr. Packard might interpret the depths of her concern as odd or extreme.

She found that she was wringing her hands, and knew she must put this thing away from her once and for all. It had jangled her nerves most dreadfully and distracted her attention from her students.

"*Ça ne va pas!*" she said aloud, scolding herself.

"Bake a loaf of bread, if you must, and leave it on their doorstep! Better still, roast a nice *poulet*!" He'd told her he enjoyed roast chicken.

Bien sûr! That solved it, then!

Since her youthful faith grew cold years ago, she regretted that she hadn't often prayed. Of course she must pray at once; she had quite neglected to do this most crucial thing for a man who had, in almost every sense, saved her life, whose tender forgiveness of the wrong she'd done him had resurrected her from a grave of bitterness and guilt.

She crossed herself quickly and looked toward the ceiling. "*Saint Père, accorde-moi, s'il te plaît, l'occasion de faire quelque chose pour ton cher émissaire, quelque chose que fera une différence!*"

She reflected a moment, then spoke the same words in English. "Holy Father, please give me the opportunity to do something for your dear emissary, something that will make a difference."

She hoped that two separate pleas might be doubly persuasive, yet had no idea at all that she'd been heard. She felt an odd relief, nonetheless, as she straightened the collar of her blouse and pinched her cheeks and walked downstairs to prepare for her next student.

In the hallway, she hesitated—was that a sound from the basement?

No, it was a car on the street. Since the Man in the Attic, as Mitfordians often called him, moved in with Mr. Welch two days ago, she thought she might hear uproarious laughter or a great deal of coming and going. In truth, she wouldn't have known another soul was down there if he hadn't come knocking on her door to introduce himself. He'd even invited her to call on him if she needed anything at all.

She had thought him attractive, or perhaps *comely* was a more precise term, and was relieved to see he was clean-shaven, which she supposed was required in prison. He had also been immensely courteous—but, of course, if he was going to get ahead in the world, he could hardly afford to be otherwise. On the whole, she had approved, confident that Father Kavanagh would not send anyone suspicious to live on his own property.

She moved toward the music room, thinking, *the man in the attic. . . .*

She mused on this odd appellation, finding it odder still that George Gaynor was now *l'homme au sous-sol.*

After a meat loaf sandwich and iced coffee for lunch, Esther Bolick lay in her plaid recliner in full repose, listening to the snores of her husband and wondering what she could do for Father Tim.

It was hard, very hard, when people couldn't—and, in today's world, *wouldn't*—eat cake. When she was coming up, families *lived* from cake to cake. A cake was a special event, it meant something. Now a homemade, baked-from-scratch cake meant next to nothing. For one thing, most young people had never experienced such a thing. All they'd ever known was bought from a store and tasted like hamster shavings, or had been emptied from a box into a bowl, stirred with low-fat milk, and shoved into an oven that nearly blew a fuse from being turned on in the first place. Such a cake could never be *your* cake, no way, it would be Betty Crocker's or Duncan Hines's cake, and the difference between yours and theirs was vast and unforgivable.

And look how people acted these days at the mere sight of a piece of cake. *Cake? Get it out of here! I'm on a diet! I don't want it in the house!*

Worse yet was the inevitable declaration: *I never touch cake!*

Never touch cake. Pathetic! The world was increasingly filled with such people, not to mention the crowd that ate cake in secret, stuffing it in their faces when nobody was looking, and claiming to nourish themselves on a diet of boiled eggs and dry toast. She knew who they were.

Father Tim was different, of course; eating cake would not merely add a measly pound or two, it would kill him dead as a doornail. Just look what he'd done to himself with a Coke, or was it a Pepsi?

Gene snorted and woke himself up. He raised his head and looked at her inquiringly. "What'd you say, Sugarfoot?"

"Go back to sleep!" she snapped, fed up with the whole notion of modern civilization.

And take biscuits—biscuits had fallen into disgrace right along with cake. Would any-body eat a biscuit anymore? No way, not on

your life. Too fattening! Too much choles-
terol! All that white flour! All that shortening!
On and on, 'til you could keel over and croak.
She'd been born in the wrong century.

She cranked her chair upright, dismounted,
and went in the kitchen and jerked open her
cabinet doors.

Nothing. There was absolutely nothing in
this house that the father could eat, except
maybe a can of salmon.

A card, then. Pitiful though it was, it was the
best she could come up with. She had waited
'til the dust settled on this awful mess before
acting, and now was the time to act; it was a
new season and a fresh beginning—Father
Tim would want to know that people didn't
hold anything against him. . . .

She went to the downstairs half bath and ran
water over a washrag and scrubbed her perspiring face and dried it, then dipped her little
finger in the lipstick tube. She had gouged stuff
out of there for so long, there was hardly a
scrap left; she'd get another tube at the drugstore when she went looking for a card. She
stretched her lips in a wide grimace and applied the dab of color with her finger. Maybe
coral this time, instead of mauve—mauve
made her look washed out.

She sighed, hoping she'd be able to find something that would make him laugh.

Over the last few days, he'd had the odd impression of a recent visit with Miss Sadie. There was some fresh, instinctive connection to her that he hadn't experienced since her death. Perhaps he'd dreamed. . . .

Father Tim sat at his desk, looking out to the space where the garage had stood. He was surprised by two extremes of feeling—he would miss seeing the moss on the roof tiles and the nest the swallows were building with daubs of mud; at the same time, the opening of the view gave him a sense of liberty he realized he'd been craving.

He watched George Gaynor toss a couple of old boards into the bed of Harley's truck, as Harley swigged Gatorade from a plastic bottle. He'd mentioned to Harley his sudden inspiration about tearing out the garage, a project they might do together when he was feeling stronger. The next thing he knew, the two men were at work, fulfilling his vision within hours of the telling.

With Harley's cleanup of the hedge, Father Tim could see into Baxter Park as if with new eyes. The labor of yesterday and today had revealed a corner of the park grounds he'd never especially noticed, including a red maple that spread its branches over summer grass that, even in today's sultry heat, appeared cool and inviting.

He felt his dog move at his feet. "Good fellow," he whispered, the lump coming again to his throat.

What would he have done if someone had . . . if the same thing had happened to Barnabas? He looked down into the dark and soulful eyes from which he'd drawn consolation for so many years, eyes that sometimes seemed a window into the depths of his own soul. Had Bill Sprouse known this mysterious and consoling connection with Sparky?

Of course . . . and it had been violently wrenched from him.

Cynthia came into the room and stood by his chair, watching George toss another board onto the truck bed.

"A blessing!" she said.

"A blessing, yes."

She leaned down and kissed the top of his head. "God is good."

"Yes," he replied. "God is good."

He heard her leave the room and wanted to turn around and watch her go, but he could not.

"Barnabas!" Cynthia called, jingling the leash. "Monument time!"

Barnabas rose slowly and trotted to the kitchen, where Cynthia snapped on the worn red leash.

"Back in ten, dearest! Then I'm dashing to the Sprouses' with a tuna casserole."

They were gone along the hall and out the front door.

He sat as if frozen. At least a month of rest, Hoppy had said; now three weeks had gone by and he hadn't recovered an ounce of strength; in truth, he couldn't even walk his dog. Perhaps he'd ask Dr. Wilson about his medication, perhaps it wasn't doing the job. He resented Hoppy's absence—he who had urged his doctor, year after year, to take a vacation.

He glanced at the open journal on his desk, and the quote from Thomas à Kempis which he'd inscribed early this morning: "Great tranquillity of heart is his who cares for neither praise nor blame."

He had no tranquillity of heart; the blame that he felt from himself and imagined from others was corrosive. He regretted, in some perverse way, that Bill Sprouse would not sue him.

"I'm not a suing man," Bill had said when they spoke on the phone. "'Dare any of you, having a matter against another, go to law before the unjust and not before the saints?' St. Paul said it, and I trust it! Then over in Luke, we're told, 'As ye would that men should do to you, do ye also to them likewise.' The Lord himself said it, and I trust it! Besides, I wouldn't want you suing me for something *I* couldn't help. You couldn't help it, brother. Let up on yourself."

"I'll be over to see you as soon as I can," he had said, mopping his eyes.

Bill had laughed. "Whichever cripple is th' first to get up an' around calls on th' other one. How's that?"

"Deal."

"God bless you, Timothy."

"And you, my friend."

You couldn't help it, Bill had said. But he could have helped it. He could have helped it by not cutting back on the insulin, by buying another glucometer and using it, by not skipping meals, by sticking to his exercise, by drinking water instead of sugar-loaded soda. . . .

But he couldn't say that to anyone, he couldn't utter the horrific truth that he had been that day like a loose cannon, that, indeed, he could have helped it.

The rabbits . . . he still thought about his little herd and how they had been seemingly well one day and dead the next, every one of them. He would never forget his father's wrath, the conviction that his son had done nothing to prevent the wasteful crime of their loss and the useless drain on the family finances.

Yes, he had noticed some listlessness in several of the does, but he hadn't known it was anything serious, he hadn't known he could . . . help it.

He watched Harley's truck pull out of view; he was headed to the dump, where, for fifteen dollars a load, a garage built more than seventy years ago would vanish from the face of the earth.

If only . . .

He realized he'd sat here like a stone for what seemed to be hours, and stood, stiff in every joint.

He wanted his wife—her softness, her breath on his cheek, her warmth, her benediction.

He went slowly up the stairs and into their room and began to turn back the bedspread. When had he ever gone to bed in the afternoon? Even when he'd had the flu a time or two, he'd toughed it out on the sofa. He wanted to stop turning back the covers, but he could not.

He undressed, noting for the first time that

he'd buckled his belt differently and that his pants were surprisingly loose-fitting. Then he hung his clothes in the closet and put on his pajamas; the whole thing seemed to take a long time.

He lay down, then, and pulled the sheet over him and waited for his wife, ashamed for her to find him like this, yet eager for her touch.

"Timothy?" she said, standing in the doorway. He couldn't see her face and read her thoughts about his lying in bed like a sluggard. He wanted desperately to please her; perhaps she would forgive him.

She came into the room and sat on the side of the bed. He was relieved to see no judgment in her eyes, only concern. "Dearest?"

"Come," he said, drawing back the sheet.

With all his heart, with all his soul, and with all his might, he wanted to reassure and gratify his wife. And yet, when she lay down beside him and embraced him, he could not.

Save me, O God; for the waters are come in unto my soul.

I sink in deep mire, where there is no standing: I am come into deep waters, where the floods overflow me.

I am weary of my crying: my throat is dried: mine eyes fail while I wait for my God. . . .

O God, thou knowest my foolishness; and my sins are not hid from thee. . . .

My prayer is unto thee, O Lord, in an acceptable time: O God, in the multitude of thy mercy hear me. . . .

Hear me, O Lord; for thy lovingkindness is good: turn unto me according to the multitude of thy tender mercies.

And hide not thy face from thy servant; for I am in trouble: hear me speedily.

Draw nigh unto my soul, and redeem it: deliver me because of mine enemies.

Thou hast known my reproach, and my shame, and my dishonour: mine adversaries are all before thee.

Pour out thine indignation upon them, and let thy wrathful anger take hold of them . . .

He sat in the pool of lamplight at three in the morning, Barnabas at his feet. He was praying the Psalms, as he'd done in times past, with the enemies of King David translated into his own enemies of fear and remorse and self-loathing, which, in their legions, had become as armies of darkness.

CHAPTER NINE

Touching God

He'd put off returning the calls of two priests who wanted to give him communion.

He'd also put off calling Dr. Wilson, but his wife had not.

Her end of the conversation could be heard through the open door of her workroom—obviously she didn't mind being overheard, though he missed some of it.

"It's dreadful . . . and he never laughs, which is so unlike him. Yes, possibly. Well, almost certainly. . . . little appetite, though I've been . . . favorite things . . . quite thin. Thank you, Doctor. What a blessing that you'll come. Yes, hardly enough energy to get out of the chair. . . ."

She came into the study and announced that Dr. Wilson would be dropping by after five o'clock.

"And since tomorrow is your birthday, dearest, I thought we might have a little party."

"No," he said. "Please. I don't want a party."

"I understand. But you'll love it, Timothy. Trust me."

He wanted to trust her.

"Depression," said Dr. Wilson. "And please don't think it's unusual after what you've been through."

Depression. The word impacted him`like a ton of bricks. He loathed the very thought of such a thing snaring him. Depression was everyone else's problem; he was clergy, he was . . .

"Depression usually stems from anger turned inward. I'm no psychologist, but I suggest you look at what the anger is about—getting to the root of it could help."

His blood surged in a kind of fury.

"We're going to change your medication, but more important, I want you to start seeing people—perhaps you could have a few friends in to visit."

"I don't want to see anyone," he snapped.

"That's all well and good, Father, but it's doctor's orders for you to have a bit of company."

That was the trouble with Wilson, he acted like he ran things when Hoppy was out of town. "Before Hoppy went tooting off to heaven knows where, it was doctor's orders that I *not* have company."

Wilson grinned. "That was then, Father. This is now."

He smelled coffee and opened his eyes.

"Happy birthday, sweetheart." His wife put the tray on the bedside table and kissed his face: his nose, his chin, the tender spot where he'd banged his head. . . .

He didn't sit up. "I'm sorry," he said. "Sorry that I can't be more . . . that I can't be . . . everything you need."

"But you are everything I need," she said. "This will pass away, Timothy, this difficult time is not for all eternity. Remember our good verse from Jeremiah, 'I know the plans I have for you, says the Lord, plans for good and not for evil, to give you a future and a hope.'"

"Yes."

"I don't understand Him, Timothy; if I did, would He be God? I believe that everything that happens must pass God's muster, and that somehow He permitted this. He is very present—and working in our lives."

"Yes."

"But sometimes you forget it?" She handed him a steaming mug.

He nodded.

"I'm praying that He will use this hard thing for good. I mean, after all, darling, look what He did for the Israelites!"

"Right." But he didn't have forty years. . . .

"You're going to have fun today!"

"Do I have to?" He couldn't believe the whine he heard in his voice; it was nauseating.

"Preacher . . ."

Bill Watson shuffled into the study. Though obviously nervous, he revealed his gold tooth in a broad smile.

"Don't git up, now." He came and stood before his former priest, bowed slightly, and shook his hand. "Happy birthday, don't you know."

"Thank you, Uncle Billy." Bill Watson's hand was as dry as a corn shuck in winter. "Sit down, my friend."

His onetime parishioner sat opposite him in

the leather wing chair. Early afternoon light from the long bay of windows dappled the old man's face.

"Rose couldn't come, she was peelin' taters f'r supper."

"Aha. How are you faring these days?"

"Fair to middlin'. I was settin' in my chair this mornin' when all of a sudden I felt somethin', don't you know."

"Like what?"

"Itchin'. Th' worst kind. What it was, I had broke out in whelks."

"Somethin you ate."

"Nossir, it's workin' a garden that done it."

"You're working a garden?" He wanted to lie down on the floor and expire. How many people had Cynthia invited? He was already exhausted.

"Mostly I'm breakin' new ground, I ain't started plantin' yet."

He racked his brain for small talk, but found nothing. He heard his wife in the kitchen, and the sound of the doorbell. Another shift coming on.

Uncle Billy cleared his throat. "I've come t' tell a joke f'r y'r birthday."

"Is that right?"

"Yessir, I've studied out two f'r you." To

keep his legs from trembling with the excitement of what he was about to do, Uncle Billy clasped his knees.

"I appreciate it," said Father Tim. He would have given anything to have squirmed out of this social event. In cahoots with Wilson, Cynthia had arranged to have a few people drop by to deliver birthday greetings; they were to be shown into the study one at a time so he wouldn't be overstimulated. He felt like a clinical experiment, they might have dolled him up in a white jacket; and all the while, Hoppy Harper was tooling along the Oregon Trail in ostrich-hide boots and couldn't care less about his patients in Mitford.

Uncle Billy straightened his tie and coughed, then got down to business.

"Wellsir! They was two fellers a-workin' on th' sawmill, don't you know, an' th' first 'un got too close to th' saw an' cut 'is ear off. Well, it fell in th' sawdust pit an' he was down there a-tryin' t' find it, don't you know. Th' other feller said, 'What're you a-doin' down there?' First 'un said, 'I cut m' ear off an' I'm a-lookin' f'r it!'

"Th' other feller jumped in th' pit, said, 'I'll he'p you!' Got down on 'is hands an' knees, went to lookin' aroun', hollered, 'Here it is, I done found it!'

"First feller, he took it an' give it th' once-over, don't you know, said, 'Keep a-lookin', mine had a pencil behind it!'"

Father Tim tried to laugh. A sound like the creaking of a gate on a rusty hinge escaped before he could choke it back. He saw the pained look on the old man's face.

"Didn' go over too good, did it?"

"I'm sorry, Uncle Billy, it's a good joke, really it is."

"No, it ain't," said Uncle Billy, obviously stricken.

Father Tim burned with shame. He knew what a desperate task Uncle Billy faced in coming up with jokes that guaranteed a laugh so as to uplift the hearer and not humiliate the teller. But what could he do? There was no laughter in him to be summoned.

"Wellsir, let me tell th' other 'un, seein' as it's studied out."

Father Tim nodded. If he could just lie down . . .

"Three preachers was settin' around talkin', don't you know. First 'un said, 'You'uns ought t' see th' bats I've got a-flyin' around in m' church attic. I've tried about ever'thing, but nothin' scares 'em off.'

"Next 'un said, 'Law, we've got hundreds of 'em livin' in our belfry. I've done had th' whole place fumigated, but cain't git rid of 'em a'tall.'

"Last 'un said, 'Shoot, I baptized ever' one of mine, made 'em members of th' church, an' ain't seen nary one since.'"

Father Tim shook his head. It was hopeless. He wanted to crawl in a hole, go out in the garden and eat worms, whatever; it was useless, he was useless. Tears sprang to his eyes.

The old man appeared mortified. "Lord help, I've done went an' made you bawl. . . ."

"No, no, that's fine, Uncle Billy, I don't know. . . . I'll make it up to you somehow. . . . I'm just not . . ."

"I ain't goin' t' take it personal, Preacher. Nossir! We're goin' t' try ag'in is what we're goin' t' do." Here was a challenge and he was determined to meet it. "You'uns jis' set right there a day or two an' I'll be back, don't you know."

Uncle Billy rose stiffly and shuffled toward the door. "I'm through with my turn, Miz Kavanagh!"

Cynthia came into the room, clearly pleased with the way things were going so far. "Uncle Billy, there's cake and ice cream in the kitchen. We'd like you to celebrate with us."

"I'll jis' carry mine home f'r Rose, an' much obliged."

"I don't know," she said, "it's awfully warm to be carrying ice cream home."

Uncle Billy pondered the import of toting ice cream from here to the town museum in ninety-degree heat. Here was another challenge and he was determined to meet it. "I'll have t' trot t' do it," he said, "but fix it up f'r me, if you don't object, Rose'll be expectin' it."

"Timothy, Emma's here to see you. Would you like another glass of water?"

Water. There was cake and ice cream in the kitchen and he was offered water. Water and Emma Newland. No wonder he'd never been much on birthdays.

"Happy Birthday!"

Emma, it seemed, had grown larger, much larger, than she'd been only a few weeks ago. Or perhaps he had grown smaller. He had a terrible urge to rise and somehow defend himself, but he sat like a rock. His dog went to Emma and sniffed her bare legs.

"He smells Snickers," she said, thumping into the leather chair and rustling a sheaf of papers. "I've been on th' Internet. . . ."

"And?" He felt interested in something for the first time today. If he couldn't have cake and ice cream, he would have e-mail.

She held up one of the papers and squinted

at it. "Listen to this, this is a good one. *'Read the Bible, it'll scare the hell out of you.'"*

There was a dull silence.

"You're not laughing," she said, accusing.

"It's not funny."

"*I* laughed," she said archly.

"Yes, well, what you just read is a very serious statement. And true, I might add. Wish I'd said it."

She shrugged. "Listen to this one. *'War Dims Hope for Peace.'"*

He stared at her.

"That's *funny*," she said, huffed.

"What is this stuff, anyway?"

"Blooper headlines. The kind J. C. Hogan writes, only better."

He sighed.

"I'll just read the whole list, maybe you'll find one you like," she said, pursing her lips. He felt oddly threatened. Why didn't his wife come in here and help him out?

"*'Police Begin Campaign to Run Down Jaywalkers.'"*

He leaned over and scratched his dog behind the ears.

"*'Drunks Get Nine Months in Violin Case.'"*

"Umm."

"*'Stolen Painting Found by Tree.'"*

"I don't get it."

"You wouldn't," she said, clearly miffed. "*'Typhoon Rips Through Cemetery; Hundreds Dead.'*

"*'Miners Refuse to Work After Death.'*

"*'If Strike Isn't Settled Quickly, It May Last Awhile.'*"

She stuffed the papers in her pocketbook and glared at him as if he were a beetle on a pin.

"So how's Harold?" he asked.

Scott Murphy came in quietly, squatted before his chair, took Father Tim's hands in his, and said, "Let me pray for you, Father."

Someone to pray for the priest!

His head was pounding, but he wouldn't say a word about it. He would ride this mule. . . .

"Who else?" he asked Cynthia.

"Just George and Harley, I'm letting them both in at once, they'll be good medicine."

"Yes," he said, brightening.

"Everyone wants to see you, they're clamoring for a visit."

"I miss the girls," he said, referring to Puny and the twins.

"So do I. They'll come on Sunday, how's that?"

He thought she looked worn, pale around the gills. It was all this messing with him, of course, day after day.

"Do you feel like seeing J. C. Hogan?"

"No." Absolutely *not*!

"I told him I'd call if you felt up to it, but he'll understand. Percy and Mule wanted to come, too, but I thought it best to wait 'til another time."

"Another time?" he snapped. "How many of these little galas are you and Wilson drumming up? I expect to be on the street any day now, I'll go see Percy myself."

"Timothy, don't be peevish." Cynthia bounded from the sofa and trotted to the kitchen, his dog behind her.

And another thing—why was everybody trying to make him laugh?

And why couldn't he just give them a good, rollicking chortle and get this ridiculous business behind him? It would put an end to their torment, for heaven's sake! He thought of the pressure they must they be under, trudging in with the awful responsibility of trying to make the preacher laugh. He could see them huddled in the yard, inquiring of the poor souls leaving the house, *Did you make him laugh? No, but we'll be back with more ammunition! He can't hold out forever!*

He was ashamed that he couldn't attain to the high summit of their hopes and affections.

George and Harley didn't appear to want anything from him. They weren't trying to make him do something he didn't want to do, or couldn't.

"Thank you," he said, as they looked through the study window to an unobstructed view of Baxter Park. "I don't know when I've ever received such a marvelous gift."

"If I'd knowed you wanted it done," said Harley, "hit'd been done a long time ago."

"*I* never knew I wanted it done 'til the other day. How's the Mustang coming?"

"Lookin' brand-new. Showroom!" Father Tim thought Harley's grin might wrap clear around his head. "George is helpin' with th' front fender, I done th' grille m'self."

"George, it seems like we're working you pretty hard right out of the box."

"Good, Father. I need it."

"How're your quarters? Is Harley's snoring too loud?"

George Gaynor smiled. "No, sir, I'm afraid I'm the one rattling the windows."

"We've got a lot to talk about. Let's have a visit soon."

"Yes, sir, I'd like that."

"What about your new job at the bookstore?"

"I'm getting the hang of it. Prison offered a lot of opportunities—one was a chance to learn the computer. I think we'll be able to move quite a few rare books via the Internet."

"If you run across a first edition of Wilberforce, keep me in mind. Let's sit, why don't we?" Was he shuffling like Uncle Billy? His legs were dead weight.

His guests took the sofa and he the chair, as his wife came in with a tray and set it on the coffee table. After serving George and Harley, she turned to him with a certain happiness. "For you, dearest."

She handed him a plate of ice cream and cake.

"But . . . ," he said, dumbfounded.

"Sugar-free! Low-fat! No sodium! The whole nine yards. I wanted it to be a surprise. Happy birthday!"

He took the plate from her, deeply moved.

Barnabas leaped into his slipcovered chair. A junco called outside the open windows. George and Harley eagerly tucked into their refreshments, as did he. Peace at last, he thought, feeling suddenly uplifted.

He and Cynthia had filled the dishwasher and turned it on when the doorbell rang.

"Ugh," she said, trooping down the hall.

"Bishop!"

"How are you, dear girl?"

Blast! He'd completely forgotten the e-mail, forgotten to tell Cynthia. . . . It hadn't crossed his mind since he left the hospital. The subsiding headache cranked up again, pounding in his left temple.

He looked at the clock above the refrigerator. Four-thirty. A fine time to go knocking on people's doors . . .

"Chuck Albright is with me," said Stuart, "I dropped him at The Local, where he's buying livermush to ship home in dry ice. Where we come from, livermush is hard to find."

"With good reason," said Father Tim, who never touched the stuff.

They sat in the study, which was flooded with afternoon light. Father Tim thought Stuart looked surprisingly older, frayed somehow.

"Do you feel like telling me everything?" asked the bishop.

He didn't want to talk about it. Surely someone had given Stuart the details; everybody knew what had happened. He plunged ahead, however, dutiful.

"I blacked out at the wheel of my car and hit Bill Sprouse, who pastors First Baptist. He was walking his dog. His dog was killed instantly. Bill had several fractures and a mild concussion." He took a deep breath. "He's going to be all right."

That was the first time he'd given anyone a synopsis, and he had made it through. His headache was blinding.

"Yes, I heard all that, and God knows, I'm sorry. What I'd really like to hear is how you are—in your soul."

"Ah. My soul." He put his hand to his forehead, speechless.

"The Eucharist, then," said Stuart. He bolted from the chair, took his home communion kit from the kitchen island, and brought it to the coffee table.

Father Tim watched his bishop open the mahogany box to reveal the small water and wine cruets, a silver chalice and paten, a Host box, and a crisply starched fair linen.

"I was reminded the other day," said Stuart,

"that when Saint John baptized Christ, he was touching God. An awesome and extraordinary thing to consider. When we receive the bread and blood, we, also, are touching God." Stuart poured the wine and drizzled a small amount of water into each glass. "I know you recognize that wondrous fact, dear brother, but sometimes it's good to be reminded."

". . . Heavenly Father, Giver of life and health, comfort and hope; please visit us with such a strong sense of Your Presence that we may trust faithfully in Your mighty strength and power, in Your wisdom vastly beyond our understanding, and in Your love which surrounds us for all eternity. At this time, we ask Your grace especially upon Timothy, that he may know Your gift of a heart made joyous and strong by faith. Bless Cynthia, too, we pray, whose eager hands and heart care for him. . . ."

As Father Tim knelt by the coffee table next to his wife, the tears began and he didn't try to check them.

"The cathedral?" He stood at the front door with Stuart, drawing upon the very dregs of his strength to inquire about the bishop's grand passion.

"That's why I'm racing out of here to Charlotte. Someone's making a gift of half a million."

"You're looking weary, my friend."

"Yes. I am that."

"You're still afraid to take a break, to rest awhile. . . ."

"I can't. The cathedral."

"Of course."

There was irony in Stuart's smile. "Besides, I'll be seventy-two soon enough, and forced to rest awhile."

The bishop kissed him on either cheek and opened the door. "You and Cynthia are ever in my prayers, Timothy. He will put things right, and don't forget it. That's what He's about, after all, putting things right."

"The Lord be with you, Stuart."

"And also with you!"

"Give Martha our love!"

"Will do!"

He watched as Stuart walked briskly to his car and climbed in.

"Father!"

Hélène Pringle darted from the side of the house and hastened up the steps to his front stoop—apparently she'd popped through the hedge—wearing blue striped oven mitts and bearing a dish covered by a tea towel.

"For you!" She thrust her offering at him with seeming joy, but how could he take it from her if oven mitts were required to handle it?

He stepped back.

Miss Pringle stepped in.

"Roast *poulet*!" she exclaimed. "With olive oil and garlic, and stuffed with currants. I so hope you—you and Cynthia—like it."

"Hélène!" His wife sailed down the hall. "What have you *done*? What smells so heavenly?"

"Roast *poulet*!" Miss Pringle exclaimed again, as if announcing royalty.

"Oh, my!" said Cynthia. "Let me just get a towel." She trotted to the bathroom at the end of the hall and was back in a flash. "Thank you very much, Hélène, I'll take it. Lovely! Won't you come in?"

"Oh, no, no indeed, I don't wish to interfere. I hope . . . that is, I heard about . . ." She paused, turning quite red. "*Merci,* Father, Cynthia, *bon appétit, au revoir*!"

She was gone down the walk, quick as a hare.

"I like her mitts," said Cynthia.

"Delicious!" He spooned the thick currant sauce over a slice of tender breast meat and nudged aside the carrots Cynthia had cooked.

"Outstanding!" He ate heartily, as if starved.

He glanced up to see his wife looking at him.

"What?" he asked.

"I haven't seen you eat like this in . . . quite a while."

"Excellent flavor! I suppose it's the currants."

"I suppose," she said.

The morning of his nativity might have begun last week or last month; indeed, it seemed an eternity since he waked to the kisses of his wife.

He rolled over in bed and tried again to position his head on the pillow so he could gain a bit of comfort and sleep. He looked at the clock face, glowing green in the dark room. Two o'clock.

His wife had given the party to cheer and encourage him, and surely underneath his exhaustion was a gladness of heart that he would feel tomorrow after he'd rested.

In all the uproar, he realized he'd forgotten

something terribly important—not only had it been his birthday, it was also the anniversary of his proposal to Cynthia. They had a tradition of celebrating that momentous occasion with his birthday, and heretofore he had always remembered. This time he'd forgotten entirely, and now it was too late.

He wondered if he really would get his strength back in the six weeks Hoppy had mentioned, or whether he was being sucked into the same quagmire that had destroyed his father.

No matter what he did these last few weeks or how hard he tried, he failed himself and everyone else. He failed to be cheerful and quick, to rise to the occasion, to look at life with thanksgiving and approval. There was a growing coldness in him, in some deep place he'd never gone before. In truth, he often felt himself sinking, out of control.

Perhaps his father had been out of control, perhaps depression had made him unable to restrain the cold severity toward his wife and son. Perhaps there was no controlling such a thing once it took root in the spirit. . . .

Then again, his father had claimed no God, no redeeming Christ, while he, the son, had claimed it all—mercy and forgiveness, uncon-

ditional love, and the capstone of the faith: salvation.

So what was his excuse?

Barnabas followed him downstairs and lay in
the soft pool of lamplight as he opened his
Bible to the second letter of Timothy.

He'd read the two epistles on almost every
birthday since his twelfth year. His mother had
instructed him in this habit, and, as a serious
youngster, he imagined the letter to have been
written across the centuries personally and directly to him, Timothy Kavanagh. He still believed this to be true in some supernatural way.

He read aloud, knowing his dog would
listen.

" '. . . continue in what you have learned
and firmly believed, knowing from whom you
learned it, and how from childhood you have
known the sacred writings that are able to in-
struct you for salvation through faith in Christ
Jesus.

" '. . . always be sober, endure suffering, do
the work of an evangelist, carry out your ministry fully . . .' "

Carry out your ministry fully. This was the
line that, every year, stopped him cold,

wondering—was he carrying out his ministry fully? A few times in his priesthood he'd actually believed that he was. Now . . . now, of course, things were different.

He could journey no further with Paul tonight. Recently, he'd become aware, however dimly, that he was looking for something in the Scriptures. He felt desperate for a specific message from God, yet he didn't know what it might be. He knew only that it would be direct, meant profoundly for him, and that he'd recognize it instantly when at last it was revealed.

He thumbed the Scriptures in reverse order to the voice of David, a voice that might have been his own:

"Hear my prayer, O Lord, and let my cry come unto thee.

"Hide not thy face from me in the day when I am in trouble; incline thine ear unto me: in the day when I call answer me speedily. For my days are consumed like smoke, and my bones are burned as an hearth.

"My heart is smitten, and withered like grass; so that I forget to eat my bread.

"By reason of the voice of my groaning my bones cleave to my skin.

"I am like a pelican of the wilderness: I am like an owl of the desert.

"I watch, and am as a sparrow alone upon the house top.

"My days are like a shadow that declineth; and I am withered like grass."

He heard a sound behind him and turned, startled.

"Timothy . . ."

"I couldn't sleep."

"Nor I."

"Forgive me for forgetting." He made a move to rise and go to her, but she came to him.

"It's all right."

"It isn't all right. I'm sorry."

She kissed him on his forehead. "What are you reading?"

"The Hundred and Second Psalm."

"Let me read to you, dearest. I know how you love that. May I?"

"Yes," he said, giving her his Bible.

She glanced at the open book. "I'll read the very next one, the Hundred and Third. Come, let's sit on the sofa where there's a breeze through the windows."

She turned on the lamp and settled into her end of the sofa. He sat beside her, thankful, realizing how happy he was to see her, to have her company.

"'Bless the Lord, O my soul: and all that is within me, bless his holy name!'"

He put his head back against the cushion and closed his eyes. His wife had a gift for reading Scripture as if it were hot off the press.

> *"Bless the Lord, O my soul, and forget not all his benefits:*
>
> *"Who forgiveth all thine iniquities; who healeth all thy diseases:*
>
> *"Who redeemeth thy life from destruction; who crowneth thee with lovingkindness and tender mercies;*
>
> *Who satisfieth thy mouth with good things; so that thy youth is renewed like the eagle's. . . .*
>
> *"As far as the east is from the west, so far hath he removed our transgressions from us.*
>
> *"For he knoweth our frame; he remembereth that we are dust. . . .*
>
> *"Bless ye the Lord, all ye his hosts; ye ministers of his that do his pleasure. . . .*
>
> *"Bless the Lord, O my soul!"*

He knew only that she covered him with the afghan, and he slept soundly until morning.

CHAPTER TEN

Up and Doing

As he turned the pages of his desk calendar, he discovered the date marked for the trip to New York.

The trip was only days away. Maybe he should call the airline and cancel; maybe they could get a refund.

But Cynthia mustn't miss this. She could go without him and he'd try and get a refund on his own ticket. There was no way under heaven that he could face a trip to New York and a high-powered social event into the bargain. But he hated that she'd have to go alone. They'd been so positive, so happy about going together. . . .

He got up and walked to the window and stared at the maple tree, unseeing.

Who could accompany his wife and look out for her and take her to the awards dinner and see her safely to and from the hotel and the airport?

The answer came at once; and at once, he knew it was right.

He was dozing on the sofa when someone knocked at the back door. Though unshaven and in the shabbiest of his sweat suits, he went to the door and opened it, eager for company.

"I come t' check on you," said Harley. "Hit's my afternoon off."

"Come in, come in! I'm glad to see you!"

"I wanted t' bring you a pan of brownies, but hit'd be outright first-degree homicide, so I brung you this. . . ."

Harley withdrew his hand from behind his back and offered a fistful of Malmaison roses from a bed at the old rectory.

Father Tim looked at them with amazement. He'd quite forgotten about his roses. . . .

"You could put 'em in a show," said Harley.

How could he have forgotten about his roses? "Sit down, Harley, sit down. I need the company, I've missed you."

He ran water into a vase he found in the cabinet and arranged the pink roses, which were just unfurling their petals. Breathtaking! He would look for the camera and take a picture. . . .

He carried them into the study and put the vase on the mantel where he could see it from the sofa. Then he thumped into the hollow he'd made in the cushion during the last weeks.

"Tell me everything," he said with interest. "How are you pushing along with George?"

"Real good. He ain't much in th' kitchen, so I cook an' he does th' washup. 'E puts 'is britches on a hanger an' keeps 'is room like he was in th' armed service. I reckon he learned that in th' penitentiary. He's tryin' t' teach me poetry, said 'e had a class in th' pen that got 'im to likin' poetry, said it helped 'im exercise 'is mind."

"Have you learned a few lines?"

"Somebody's always tryin' t' teach me somethin' I ain't in'erested in learnin'. Let's see if I can say that'n of Mr. Longfeller's." Harley propped his elbows on his knees and dropped his head into his hands. "All right, now, I'm studyin' on it." There was a long pause. "OK, here goes. 'Lives of great men all remind us we can make our lives sublime, an' departin', leave behind us, footprints on th' sands of time.'"

"Well done!"

"Let's see, they was another line or two. 'Let us then be up an' doin' with a heart f'r any fate . . . any fate . . .'" Harley looked up, defeated. "Hit's gone out of m' noggin."

Father Tim grinned. "'Still achieving, still pursuing, learn to labor and to wait.'"

"'At's it!"

"I learned that poem as a youngster. Lace would be proud of you."

"I miss that young 'un."

"What else is going on? Tell me news of the outside world!"

"Well, let's see. Ain't much t' tell. Ol' Man Mueller brought 'is rattletrap car in t'day. I got t' work on it t'morrow."

"What's wrong with it?"

"Says it won't turn right. Says it won't go in th' direction of 'is politics."

"Aha."

"Hadn't turned right in two or three weeks, 'e said."

"How did he get around?" asked Father Tim. "A man has to turn right once in a while."

"Well, gen'rally, if he was goin' t' town, he'd turn right out of 'is driveway. But since he cain't turn right, they won't nothin' t' do but put 'er in reverse, back all th' way to th' shed, go around behin' that ol' barn that fell down, an' circle around 'til he ended up beside 'is front porch—"

"Still in reverse?"

"That's what he said."

"How come he couldn't turn around in front of his house?"

"Got a cornfield right up to 'is front door an' another'n to th' left."

Father Tim shook his head as if to clear it.

"So onc't he was headed out beside 'is porch, he could turn left an' go t' town."

"If I couldn't turn right, let's see . . . how would I get to town?" A man who didn't have anything better to do than this didn't deserve anything better to do.

Harley stared fixedly at the wall, thinking. "Well, Rev'ren', you'd have t' back out of y'r garage an' turn left, that'd head you t' Church Hill, where you'd turn left ag'in. Then you'd turn left on Lilac Road an' hang a left on Main Street." He grinned broadly, revealing pink gums. "There y' go. Nothin' but left turns in that deal."

"Piece of cake," said Father Tim.

He didn't know why, exactly, but a visit from Harley always did him a world of good. In truth, he felt the courage to ask what had been on his mind daily, and what Harley would surely know.

"Harley, what are they saying on the street?"

Harley looked sober. "Sayin' it could've been a whole lot worser."

The clock ticked on the mantel.

"Nobody holds it ag'in you."

"Nobody?"

"Nossir. An' if you don't mind me sayin' so, I wisht you wouldn't hold it ag'in y'rself."

He sat silent for a moment. "I'll try, Harley. I'm going to try."

Harley nodded encouragement. "That's all a man can do," he said.

The more he thought about it, and he fervently hoped he'd never think about it again, he wondered why Old Man Mueller didn't make a U-turn beside his porch when he came home from town, which would head him in the proper direction for the next go-around.

Come to think of it, why was Old Man Mueller driving at all? Wasn't he well into his nineties? And all that backing up! Good grief. He went to the kitchen and opened the refrigerator door and stared blankly at the contents.

"Bill, it's Tim. How're you doing?"

"When th' Lord ordains, He sustains. I'm doin' all right, brother, and I hope you are."

"Yes. Bill . . . I hope it's OK for me to suggest this. . . ."

"What's that?"

It was tough to say, but he had to get it behind him. "I've been thinking that . . ." He cleared his throat and made a fresh start. "Whenever the time seems right, I'd like to buy you a dog."

"I 'preciate it, but I've never had a *bought* dog—th' Lord always sends my dogs. Except for Hoover, I believe th' Other Party sent Hoover! No, I appreciate it, Tim, but whenever it's time, my dog will come along."

He didn't know where else to go with this. It seemed there was nothing he could do for Bill Sprouse. He wanted desperately to minister to him in some way, yet Bill never seemed to need it. In truth, Bill's faith seemed stronger, his confidence surer, his hope brighter than his own.

He sat in the place he'd worn for himself on the sofa, wishing, if only for a moment, that Bill had been driving the car, and he'd been the one standing by the stop sign.

Uncle Billy Watson dragged a chrome dinette chair from the kitchen to the dining room, where stacks of newspaper stood higher than the heads of most men.

It took a while to climb onto the chair seat and stand up so he could reach the top of the stack. Because he didn't do this often, he forgot now and again what he'd hidden up there. Today he was looking for a special copy of the *Farmer's Almanac,* but hoped he might find a little cash money while he was at it. He used to hide his money under the mattress, but Rose had found out and that was the last he ever saw of two fifties and a ten he'd made from building birdhouses.

What a man had to do was feel around real gentle, because if you poked your hand in a stack too forceful, it might come down all over creation. When newspapers was stacked up, they had a way of slithering like snakes, you couldn't trust what they might do.

The town inspector had threatened to haul off the whole shebang, but he'd never gone through with it. Uncle Billy figured it must be a low-down kind of job to have, to go into people's houses and tell them what they could hang on to and what had to be hauled off.

He'd be willing to give the newspapers to a paper drive if they ever had such a thing anymore, but he hadn't heard of a paper drive in a coon's age. Nossir, now they wanted you to bundle the dadjing things up and set them on the street in a red rubber bucket. On top of that, the town give a man a blue rubber bucket for glass and a white rubber bucket for periodicals.

Red, blue, white—it was all too much to keep up with; him and Rose put everything in a grocery bag when they could think of it and

set it in a garbage can he'd found in a dumpster. That ought to be enough for a man to
lawfully do with his garbage, this side of digging a hole and burying it hisself.

He pawed around on top of the stack, trying
desperately to locate the almanac he clearly remembered putting up here. It had been full of
good jokes, about as good as any he'd seen in a
while. But if he'd left it out on a table where it
ought to be, Rose would have done Lord knows
what with it—peeled potatoes on it, or set a
cook pot on it, or cut recipes out of it. He never
knew why his wife cut out recipes when she'd
never made anything from a recipe in her life.
Heaven knows he'd made plenty of things from
recipes he remembered from his boyhood.

He had stood by his mama's table in that little cabin in the woods and watched her roll
out dough for biscuits and pies and he didn't
know what all. He'd learned to cook creasies
with fatback, and make rabbit stew, and even
use a woodstove oven to bake deer meat with
vinegar, springwater, lard, and wild onions.
You had to cover your skillet good and tight,
though, or your meat would dry out and be
tough as whitleather. . . .

He stopped trying to find the almanac and
wondered, as he usually did, how in the dickens
he'd get down from the chair. He nearly always

forgot how hard it was to climb down once he climbed up. Seem like lately his arthritis was making his limbs so stiff that when the Lord called him Home, he'd be coffin-ready.

It was a real aggravation to find a decent joke these days. Sometimes he thought he'd quit joke-telling, just put it all behind him— retire, you might say. Only thing was, he liked to hear people laugh, yes, sir, that was about as good a feeling as a man could get without it costing an arm and a leg.

Maybe he'd hid the almanac in that little pantry off of the kitchen . . .

He held on to the back of the chair and looked down.

"Go easy!" he cautioned himself aloud. The chair wobbled as he lifted his right foot off the seat and set it on the floor. Boys howdy, that done it, that sent a pain up his leg that would lay out a mule . . .

He lifted the other foot off the chair seat, set it down, and felt the solid floor beneath. That was two feet set down, and all they was to set down, thank God A'mighty!

Famed Local Arthur To Receive Award

Mitford's biggest celebrity, Ms. Cynthia Coppersmith Kavanagh, will travel to

New York City on Thursday to receive one of publishing's highest honors.

In a ceremony at the Waldurf Astoria, she will be given her second Davant Metal in recognition of her series of \% books about a white cat, Violet, who is an actual cat that lives right here in Mitford with Ms Kavanagh and her husband.

A publicity release from Ms. Kavanagh's publiser states that no other arthur has ever won the metal twice. Insiders say the Davant metal is right up there with an Oscar.

Avette Harris, head librarian at the Mitford volunteer library says, "Violet personifies today's liberated woman—she thinks for herself, isn't afraid to learn new things, and manages to get out of many interesting scrapes."

Ms. Kavanagh has been drawing and writing little stories since she was ten years old. Her first book was about a doodle bug, though it was never published. Her numerous Violet books include Violet Goes to the Country, Violet Visits the Queen and Violet Goes to School. Ms. Kavanagh also goes to school, as she reads to local students several times a year. Other book jaunts take her %^ Wesley, Holding and many surrounding comminities.

"She is our favrite arthur," says Dorene Little, who received last year's Teacher of the Year award at Mitford School. "Boys and girls alike can identify with Violet, who is more of a real person than a cat, if you ask me."

The arthur has also been invited to tour America with a literacy program called READ, along with other famous childrens book arthurs, which departs on August 5.

Ms. Kavanagh will be accompanied to New York by Dooley Russell Barlowe of Mitford, who is a rising sophmore at the Univiersity of Georgia.

"Ugh," said his wife. "Who *writes* this stuff?"

"Mostly J.C. But sometimes he hires help."

"I mean, really—*today's liberated woman*? And who are these *insiders*? And this *spelling*! The *lowliest* school computer has *spellcheck*!"

His wife was hot, and no two ways about it.

"Not to mention this picture of me. Where on *earth* did he dig it up? It's older than dirt, I'm wearing a *beehive*!"

"Here," he said, taking the newspaper from her, "why rile yourself?"

"Does he ever talk to the *subject* of his little butcher jobs? Or is all his reportage done by hearsay and rumor? I *never* wrote a book about a *doodle bug*!"

"What was it about?"

"A *lady*bug!" she said, thoroughly disgusted.

He patted her hand. "Now, now, Kavanagh."

She looked at him a moment, then fell back against the sofa cushions, hooting with laughter.

They walked to the garden bench and sat watching the moon rise over Baxter Park.

"My dear John . . . ," she said, fingering his silver tresses.

"Who's John?"

"You know, sweetheart, John the Baptist!"

He sighed. "Maybe I'll cut it myself."

"I'll do it as soon as I come home! How's that?"

"No way. I've witnessed your tonsorial skills."

"I don't want to leave you, Timothy."

"But of course you must. It's the only thing to do."

"Thank you, darling."

"I'll be fine. I *am* fine. There's nothing at all to worry about."

"Puny will be here every day, and the girls will come straight from day care in the afternoons. Dooley and I will call you in the morning, and of course we'll call you after the awards dinner. Then we'll call you the next morning and after lunch and after the play and before we leave for the airport—you'll be sick of hearing from us."

"Never!"

"Thank you for buying the theater tickets, dearest, for taking care of everything. Dooley is so excited, you'd think we're going to the moon."

"It's time we did something special for that boy. Besides, I can't think of anyone I'd rather send you off with." His heart was heavy, but he made certain his voice was light. Nearly forty years in the pulpit taught a man how to hide his personal feelings.

"Please don't be sad," she said, putting her head on his shoulder.

"Sad? How could I be sad?" He kissed her forehead. "You're the first author ever to win the Davant Medal twice!"

He wanted his wife to have a life apart from nursing him like some hothouse orchid. He really did.

"Give her your arm when you cross the street. Like this." He demonstrated.

"Why?" asked Dooley.

"Because there's a lot of traffic in New York and it's dangerous up there. Because she's a woman. And because, as a man, it's your job."

"I never heard of that job."

"You heard it here first."

Dooley grinned. "I'll take care of her, I promise."

"You've got my card. Pick a good restaurant, ask someone at the awards dinner to recommend a good place, she likes French or Italian. Call ahead and make a reservation, they're big on reservations in New York."

"OK. Cool."

"Take taxis, do whatever you need to do. Here's a hundred bucks. And be sure and tip the bellman who carries your luggage to your rooms."

"I can carry our luggage."

"They won't let you."

"But it's our luggage!"

"Yes, well, don't ask me to explain. And when the tab comes at the restaurant, tip twenty percent."

"Man!"

"Just put it on the card. And while we're on the subject, hold on to your wallet. And help Cynthia watch her pocketbook, she's been known to set it on a counter while she shops. Do you need to write any of this down?"

"No, sir."

"Good. On second thought . . ." He dug into his pocket and pulled out his wallet.

"Here's another hundred, just in case. And twenty for you."

"Wow," said Dooley, taking the bills. "I always wanted to carry this stuff around."

"One more thing. Buy flowers somewhere, they usually have flowers on the street. Give them to Cynthia."

"When?"

"Whenever you pass a flower stall. Pink roses only, no red. Or white tulips if they don't have roses."

"OK."

"A dozen. Tell her they're from me."

"Yes, sir."

"Any questions?"

"No, sir."

"Well done!"

He'd never felt so proud in his life. He could send this young man on a mission and trust him to complete it. He felt his chest literally expand as he embraced the boy who'd come into his life and changed it forever.

He stood at the garage door and watched Dooley back the Mazda onto Wisteria Lane.

"We love you!" Cynthia called.

"Love you back!"

He waved until the car disappeared from

view beyond the hedge, then hurried to the edge of the yard, where he could watch them turn left on Main Street.

He had hoped to feel better about being alone—this way, he could be as grumpy as he liked and no one would notice or care. But he felt bereft.

He opened the refrigerator door and stared inside, then shut the door without remembering what he'd seen. He walked into the study and turned on the lamp by his chair and gazed out the window to Baxter Park, noting the lowering sky. A book! Of course. That was the ticket. . . .

He took a volume from the shelf and sat in his armchair and was thankful for his good dog snoring at his feet. Then he opened the book to a random page and gazed at it for some time.

There was nothing in the book but words.

The storm reached Mitford shortly after dark. He'd taken Barnabas to the backyard as the rain began—fat, pelting drops that smarted when they hit his shirt. At ten o'clock, a full-bore electrical storm was up and running, dousing power in the village and waking him from a deep sleep.

A dazzling flash of platinum lit the room. He turned on his side and listened to the pounding of rain on the roof, and the great flume of water flushing through the downspouts.

He hadn't taken his medication for depression; he would leave it off for a few days and see what happened. It was humiliating to be taking such a thing. The only consolation was that millions of others were in the same boat; depression was common, run-of-the-mill stuff. But he'd never aspired to being run-of-the-mill; he was certain that in a few days, his energy would increase—his spirits would be stronger, his outlook brighter, and this whole miserable experience would be over.

He was clinging to the Rock, trusting it to cleft for him.

The vacuum cleaner was going full throttle, as were the washing machine, dryer, and pressure cooker. He liked to stay as far away as possible from pressure cookers; a neighbor in Holly Springs had scrubbed green beans off every surface, including the ceiling, for two weeks. But today's rumbling, hissing, churning, and roaring created a welcome cacophony in the yellow house, and he was grateful.

". . . to reach the port of heaven . . ." he inscribed in his quote journal, "we must sail sometimes with the wind and sometimes against it—but we must sail, and not drift, nor lie at anchor." Oliver Wendell Holmes had hit the nail on the head. He closed the book from which he'd gleaned the quote and gazed into the park.

He could kid himself into believing he was drifting. The truth was, he was lying at anchor.

He'd tried more than once to get back to his essays, yet had drawn a blank over and over again. He was spending time looking at the maple tree rather than pursuing the progress of what he'd titled *The Future Hour.*

As open and bright as their house might be, it was feeling like a prison. He wanted out of here. . . .

He rose suddenly and went to the back door and opened it wide. He would take the girls to Sweet Stuff as soon as they arrived. He not only needed the fresh mountain air, he needed to see people face-to-face, so that he might look into their eyes and read their judgments, if any. He had dreaded his excursion onto the street; now he was ready to get it behind him.

"Don't overdo it," Wilson had said. "Whatever energy is there will burn off quickly."

Yes, but he couldn't go on living to himself, in himself; it was sickening.

He snatched the cordless from the hook before the answering machine kicked in.

He'd hardly picked up the phone in weeks; his wife was on orders from the doctor to keep such stimulants at a minimum. However, if he was well enough to push along on his own, he was certainly entitled to answer the blasted phone. . . .

"I can't believe it!" huffed Emma.

"What can't you believe?"

"That I'm talkin' to you. I was beginnin' to wonder if you were dead or alive . . ."

"All of the above," he said.

". . . and your e-mail stackin' up over here like . . . like . . ."

Emma had never been good at analogy. "Like planes over Atlanta."

"Right! You'll never guess what's goin' on in Whitecap!"

"How fast can you get over here?" he said.

As he hung up, he was distinctly aware that he was grinning. E-mail!

Dear Father, it has been ages since your friends at Whitecap have heard a peep out of you, your good secretary e-mailed us to say you haven't been up to par.

How distressing to hear this, and please take care of yourself. Hardly a day passes that we don't speak of you at the library, where I am serving my last season as head. How quickly time passes, it has been more years than I care to remember, I think they areplotting to give me a first edition of Agatha Christie's autobiography, still in its dust jacket!

Be warned that I have not gotten the knack of writing those short e-mail messages that seem so popular with one and all. I hope you are still interested in news from our little island, as there seems to be quite a lot of it these days!

We hear a wall has been erected on the yellow line between the bait & tackle shop and Mona's. We don't know what this portends, we are hoping it is not a forecast of any more drastic action such as divorce! Do pray, as I know how much Ernie means to you.

Morris is still playing the organ each Sunday, but we haven't been able to get him to stay for the Coffee Minute afterward, Jean Ballenger has taken it upon herself to work on this. I'm not sure she's the one for the job, she may scare him off completely. I do believe that playing each Sunday has given him a kind of happiness, you should hear the praise heaped upon his head before he manages to get away in the truck with Junior and Misty, who always fetch him back and forth. Have you heard that Jr and Misty are going to have a baby? Jr is very proud, you should see how tenderly he cares for his young bride!

Jeffrey Tolson struggles with himself, I think, but is being faithful to his dear family. Janette looks wonderful. She has become a truly beautiful girl with the flowering of her marriage. Certainly she isn't forced to work so hard now that J has a steady income. Your Jonathan is full of mischief, and has stolen every heart in the parish.

Otis and Marlene have two new grandchildren and have closed up the pool at their house. Marlene says it is just until the grandchildren get older, Otis says it is for forever and a day, as a pool is nothing but nuisance and expense. He intends to have his construction people fill it with topsoil and plant palm trees therein, though I can't imagine that palms will flourish this far north—I think palmettos might be a better choice.

The Duncans have got a new rooster, which makes the neighbors complain. I think the world has gone wrong when one cannot enjoy the sound of a rooster crowing!

Fr Conklin means well, and heaven knows, he tries, but I'm not sure how he will do in the long run, if there is one.

I wish all news were good news. Sam is again going into the hospital, this time for a kidney operation. Everyone says it is nothing, not to worry, but of course I do, shame on me.

It has never been the same since you left, we would have kept you and Cynthia until the cows come home.

Give her my love and thank you for keeping us in your prayers, as we hold you faithfully in ours. I shall not rest until I hear you are feeling hale again.

Timothy, for heaven's sake, can you not give a man WORD OF YOUR CIRCUMSTANCES?

Are you dead as a door nail, or only on the downward spiral toward last rites—

which I shall be happy to come and administer if only you will ask.

We are pushing along up here in the wilderness, though frightfully short-handed. I'm wearing out a PERFECTLY GOOD pair of boots going up hill and down dale, all the while observing the most heartbreaking conditions imaginable. But we are making progress. The good Lord has brought a veritable drove of youngsters to our door, and one or two grim parents. They come out of curiosity and stay for cookies and tea and Bible stories. The flood is a particular favorite. Abner comes daily, I hope you are praying for him as I requested.

Well, brother, have you cast us utterly away? If you cannot write, for heaven's sake do the next best thing . . .

SEND MONEY!!!

Sissy unrolled the watercolor and held it before him. "See, Granpaw? This is the church, will you put it on your 'frigerator?"

"Absolutely! Well done!"

"An' this," said Sassy, "is Barnabas. I used the biggest piece of paper in th' *whole school*!"

"Terrific!" he said, admiring the watercolor of a black hulk on a red rug. "However, like your subject matter, your painting is bigger than the refrigerator."

"You could . . . umm . . . you could put it on the wall!"

"Ah, the wall."

"You have tape in your desk drawer, we saw it when we used your colored pencils."

"Let me think. . . ."

Sassy ran to the wall by his desk. "Right here, Granpaw! It would look great! You can take this other stuff down."

"I want mine on the wall, too," said Sissy, "*not* on th' 'frigerator."

Life was short.

He went to the desk drawer and got out the tape. "Consider it done!" he said.

Amazing. He'd gone from a hopeless bachelor who lived alone to a man with a dog, a son, a wife, and two grandchildren. Thinking thus, he marched down Main Street, a red-haired twin on either side, glad to be alive.

He was standing at the bakery case with the girls when he heard the door open and the *tick,*

tick, tick of heels on the tile floor. Knowing he was nailed to the wall, he turned to face the onslaught.

Fancy Skinner, in her signature uniform of hot-pink T-shirt and capri pants, arched one eyebrow and gave him a withering look. "Long time no see!"

"Fancy, how are you?"

She was smoking over his hair pretty good, he thought, ducking his head to peer into the bottom shelf of the case.

"Choc'late éclair!" said Sassy.

"Choc'late chip cookie!" crowed Sissy.

"I'm havin' a sugar-free fruit tart," Fancy informed him. "That's my favorite, it sends me over the moon, all that custard and those little slices of kiwi, I hope they have kiwi today, some days they don't have kiwi, sometimes it's just raspberries an' whatnot, thank th' *Lord* Winnie never uses *blueberries,* which I can't stand to put in my *mouth,* I don't know why, prob'ly 'cause they turn your tongue blue, even your *teeth,* an' bananas, you take bananas, I have never liked th' *texture* of bananas, I don't care if they *do* have potassium, they make me feel fat, don't bananas make you feel fat?—but you take kiwi, now, kiwi is very *tropical,* very *light* an' *refreshin'* . . ."

Actually, he hadn't thought he could have

anything. But a sugar-free fruit tart was another matter entirely. He brightened.

Winnie blew through the curtains that separated the kitchen from the bake shop. "Father! I'm so glad to see you, I could hug your neck!"

"Come and do it, then!"

Dear, good-hearted Winnie, smelling literally of sugar, spice, and everything nice, trotted from behind the bake case. "How's business?" he asked, relishing her vigorous hug.

"Booming, now that your crowd is here!"

After the girls piped their orders, he gave his. "Sugar-free fruit tart!" he said with immeasurable anticipation.

"Just one?"

"Just one."

"Good! Because that's all that's left!"

He had no intention of making eye contact with Fancy Skinner. He devoutly hoped there would never again be a necessity so dire as to force him into her chair.

"For here or to go?" asked Winnie.

"For here!" he chorused with the twins.

On her way out with a low-fat doughnut, Fancy gave his hair a final look of professional scorn. Or was it downright disgust?

"Do you think Granpaw needs a haircut?" he inquired of his counsel.

"Yessir," said Sassy. "You really do."

Sissy nodded, her mouth full.

"Well, then," he said, making short work of the tart, which had come fully loaded with kiwi.

They'd left the house less than an hour ago, and already his small spring of energy had run utterly dry. As the girls drank soda pop at Sweet Stuff, he sat in Joe Ivey's barber chair feeling raw, exposed.

"I prob'ly oughtn't t' tell y' this . . ."

Snip, snip. Joe began his labors with the hair that had grown over his customer's collar.

"So don't," suggested Father Tim.

". . . but somebody said if you was goin' to run over a preacher, you should've aimed for that clown over at Wesley Chapel."

He stiffened.

"Wadn't too funny, was it? I oughtn't to have said that."

Snip, snip.

"You're lookin' sort of down an' out. I guess this has hit you pretty hard."

Snip, snip, snip. The sound of a car horn on Main Street, footsteps above their heads, Winnie's shop door opening, his blood pressure rising.

"I don't reckon you'd like a little shooter?"

"I thought you were keeping away from that stuff," he snapped.

"I am keepin' away from it, it's settin' there for my customers."

Next time he needed a haircut, he was going to Wesley, or down to Holding . . . anywhere but here.

He glanced up to the eastern ridge above Mitford and was surprised to see the chimneys of Clear Day, Edith Mallory's rambling stone house, which boasted roughly eight thousand square feet. Apparently, some serious tree work had just been done; he'd liked it better when nothing at all could be seen of her ninety-acre property.

When he'd been rector at Lord's Chapel, she had often invited the vestry there for meetings. He was thankful to God that he was no longer forced to endure the whole miserable experience—stopping at the electronic gate box and punching in numbers that seemed to change with each meeting, then making the long, dark drive through the narrow tunnel of low-arching rhododendron. He remembered the smothered feeling he often got when coming through that tunnel, followed by a long evening of dodging her attempts to make eye contact, hang on to his arm, or remove nonexistent lint from his lapel.

Then there was the stormy night the vestry had convened about Hope House. After sending his ride home while he was in the bathroom, she'd trapped him in her library, where, after a harsh exchange, he'd spent most of the night in a club chair. Ed Coffey had claimed Edith's Town Car wouldn't start, though he'd gotten the blasted thing started well enough by daylight. Yours truly had been dropped off at the rectory just as his next-door neighbor had come out looking for her cat. He would never forget the look on Cynthia's face as he slithered out of that black Lincoln feeling humiliated and furious.

As he entered the front door with the girls, he didn't know if he could make it to the end of the hall and into the kitchen.

"Lord *help*!" cried Puny, looking shocked. "Go lay on th' sofa this minute!"

He feebly obeyed; he had no choice.

When the phone rang, he sat up, confused. Why was he on the sofa? His head throbbed wildly. It was nearly dark, with no lamp burning. He fumbled for the phone and knocked the handset to the floor. "Hold on! I'm coming!" he shouted. He went to his knees, blindly searching the rug in front of the sofa. There.

"Hello, sweetheart," he said, breathless.

"Why, Timothy!" Edith Mallory gave a husky laugh. "You must have been expecting . . . someone special.

"I won't keep you. I've just come home to Mitford from Spain and heard the terrible thing that happened to you."

"The terrible thing didn't happen to me, it happened to Bill Sprouse," he said coldly.

"Of course. Well, do let me say I hope you'll soon be well and strong and that we'll be seeing you back to normal very quickly."

He heard her exhale smoke from a cigarette.

His impulse was to fling the handset across the room. Yet he sat speechless, enduring the pounding of his head.

"I must say, Timothy, that I hold no grudge against you, none at all. I ought to *thank* you. The people I might have rented the Grill to have gone bankrupt, while Mr. Mosely's check arrives promptly every month."

"I must go," he said.

"Of *course* you must. I understand! Well, then, goodbye—"

He dropped the handset into his lap, feeling

oddly alarmed, as if a viper now lay coiled in the darkened room.

Hessie Mayhew awoke at three in the morning to the sound of . . . what in the dickens was it, anyway?

Her vintage Sears box spring creaked as she sat up in bed and listened.

Hail!

The bedroom shimmered in a dazzling flash of light, and then came a crash of thunder that shook and rattled the windows.

She clapped her hands over her eyes as if to deny this could be happening. Hail meant that every rose in her garden would be shattered, she'd be lucky to have a fistful left for the wedding at Methodist Chapel tomorrow. She'd be forced to rogue roses in other people's gardens from here to Wesley, and with a car that had tires so bald Lew Boyd said she should start writing her obituary.

Her mind was racing. Maybe Father Tim wouldn't mind if she cut what was left of his antique Malmaisons; for Pete's sake, he didn't even *live* at the rectory anymore, it was just that little bitty Frenchwoman and that cat the size of a barn, she should be *glad* to get rid of some of those roses, how many roses could one little woman *use* anyway?

Father Tim! Hessie gasped. His garden basket! Clad only in a faded toile pajama top she'd found at last year's Bane and Blessing, she bolted to the kitchen, switched on the light to the deck, and looked through the glass doors.

Mashed flat! Killed! *Totaled!* The beautiful basket with twelve herbs and five pots of miniature roses, lavender, and sweet william, all so carefully nestled into living green moss, moss which she had pulled with her own hands from her own special section of her own backyard, a gesture she extended only to very special people—*ruined*!

Hail the size of marbles jumped around on the deck and bounced against the glass doors. A blaze of lightning illumined her yard.

She turned from the awful sight and stormed into the kitchen. She wouldn't wait 'til she was sixty-five, thank you very much, she was getting out of the flower business *im-mediately*. Just as soon as she got new tires, which two big weddings and a bridal luncheon would pay for, she was out of this racket—she couldn't bear another *day* of something as frag-ile, as frail, as *puny* as flowers! She would go to work at Wal-Mart, maybe in the housewares section, or even at the front door where she would give people a shopping cart and tell them to have a nice day.

Completely disgusted and close to tears, she threw open the refrigerator door, snatched out last night's meatloaf, and gave herself permission to eat the whole thing.

The sound of a hailstorm woke him from a deep sleep.

He was lying on the sofa, with something like a rock digging into his left rib. The blasted handset. He slammed it on the hook and dragged himself upstairs, where he found Barnabas under the bed and Violet curled on Cynthia's pillow. He looked at the clock. Three in the morning, and not a word from New York. Should he call the hotel? Of course not. He wouldn't call anyone at such an hour.

He sat in the wing chair, spent though wakeful. He pulled the chain on the floor lamp next to him and took what he called his Upstairs Bible from the table. If he was going to find what he was seeking, he'd have to look, it was that simple. "Show me, Lord," he prayed aloud. "Lead me there and open my heart to Your wisdom. . . ."

The Bible lay in his lap for a long time. He had no strength to open it.

He climbed into bed and, lying on his back, listened to the clatter of hail on the roof and the baritone snore of his dog. He felt as if he'd gone back in time to his bachelor days when the place beside him was always empty. But no, he wasn't that bachelor anymore, he'd been completely changed, altered clear to his taproot. He had a wife, and day after tomorrow, she was coming home—then they'd be up and doing, with a heart for any fate.

He rolled onto his right side and punched up his pillow. He should have given Dooley another twenty.

CHAPTER ELEVEN

To Sing in the Dark

At seven A.M., he snatched the ringing phone from the hook.

"Cynthia?"

"Timothy! Are you all right?"

"Are you all right? That's the question!"

"We tried and tried to call, but the phone was busy for hours. Who on earth were you talking to?"

"Nobody. I went to sleep on the sofa and must have rolled over on the receiver."

"Pathetic! I can't leave you alone for five minutes!" He heard the relief in her laughter.

"I'm sorry, sweetheart, forgive me. Was it wonderful?"

"More than wonderful!"

"Keep talking."

"I love the hard work, and the agony of hardly ever knowing if what I'm doing is any good, and then the joy of the book being published and the children and parents liking it, and now . . . *this.*"

"Are you ten feet tall? Will you tower over your rustic husband?"

"My humility has made me small enough to put in your pocket."

"And how's Dooley treating his famous consort?"

"He's taking the tenderest care of me, opening doors, even giving me his arm when we cross the street. You should *see* this, Timothy, I can't imagine who taught him such lovely, outmoded courtesy."

"Heaven only knows."

"And he tips twenty percent! They must have a *class* in that sort of thing at the university."

"I imagine so."

"And the flowers! *Armloads* of roses and tulips! But all from you, of course. Thank you, my darling, I can't wait to see you. How are you feeling?"

"Went out yesterday. Took the girls to Sweet Stuff. Got a haircut."

"Joe Ivey?"

"Brace yourself."

"Oh, dear. How did you feel, being out and about? Was it . . . all right?"

"I felt like a chick newly hatched from the shell. What are you up to today?"

"I'm buying Dooley a suit."

"A suit?"

"Italian!"

"Have mercy, Kavanagh, he's only a youth."

"And a silk tie! He'll make the earth tremble when he walks."

He grinned. Dooley Barlowe would never be the same. . . .

"The girls here absolutely fall over themselves when they see him. I can't think how Lace has held out so long!"

"Think how long I held out," he said, "and look what happened."

"I miss my husband," she said, suddenly pensive.

"I miss my wife . . . my extravagant, generous, witty, and important wife."

"I love it when you talk like that."

"Ah, Kavanagh, what don't you love?"

"Taxis that go ninety miles an hour in midtown traffic, pantyhose that are a size too small, which one can't *know* 'til dressing for the awards dinner, and then it's too late, and, of course, age spots."

He laughed. "That about covers it."

"We'll call you tonight and again in the morning, and before you know it, we'll be home!"

"I count the hours."

When he waked this morning at six, he'd felt leaden, old. Now that he'd heard her voice, he was fit for anything.

"Father?"

"George! Come in!"

"Is this a good time? I was praying for you next door, and felt a strong conviction to do my praying over here, instead."

He opened the screen door to his tall, slender neighbor, known to all of Mitford as the Man in the Attic, and greeted him with a hug.

"Glad to see you, brother. Have a seat. Tell me how things are going in your new hometown."

"If I could tell you another time, Father? I've got twenty minutes to get to the bookstore."

"Whatever you say." Though eight years in prison had added a few lines to George Gaynor's face and his thinning hair had turned gray at the temples, Father Tim thought he'd never looked handsomer.

"Father, I understand a little of what you've

been through. I've been hesitant to ask you to let me pray for you."

"No need to hesitate with me, George. We all need prayer." He wished he could confess just how much, indeed, he needed it. . . .

After giving Barnabas a ramble around Baxter Park, he poked through the hedge to the old rectory. The hail would have made hash of his roses, and done a dandy job of hole-punching the hostas.

He wasn't especially up for visiting the scene of the crime; he still felt fragile, like nearly transparent porcelain that might shatter if jostled. He knew only that he must get on with his life, which lately seemed to have passed him by. Thanks be to God, his blood sugar had been down this morning, things appeared nearly normal, he was right on the cusp of the prophesied six weeks. Soon, all would be well and very well.

"Father! *Bonjour!*" Hélène Pringle stood on the back stoop, waving. Her cat, Barbizon, sat by her feet, looking disgruntled.

"*Bonjour,* Hélène! I hope you don't mind me lurking around your backyard?"

"Indeed not, Father. It's your backyard, you may lurk whenever you please."

"That was a terrific storm we had last night. I wanted to visit what was left of the roses. Oh, my." He looked at the leaves lying about, and the rain of petals on the dark mulch. "Not much, I'm afraid."

"My grandmother believed a bit of ill weather was good for the garden." She came down the steps, tentative yet smiling with some delight. "It's wonderful to see you out and about." She wrung her hands as she spoke, as if greeting him gave her intense anxiety. He wondered if he might try to be more affable, in hopes of putting her at ease.

"Thank you, Hélène, I was beginning to ossify."

"Ossify?" she said, perplexed.

He smiled. "Harden like bone."

"Oh!" she said. *"Oui!"*

He walked around the bed, trying to care about the devastation as fully as he might have cared a year or two ago. It took such energy to care. . . .

"Are you . . . feeling all right, Father?"

"Oh, yes. Pushing along." He sat on the bench. "If you don't mind . . ."

"Certainly not! It's your bench, after all!"

She stood on the opposite side of the bed, still wringing her hands. He realized there was nothing he could do.

"I was in Holding yesterday and saw your dear boy."

"Dooley?"

"Yes, he was coming out of the drugstore as I was going in. I don't go to Holding often, it seems such a journey."

"Yes, it is a bit of a haul. But you couldn't have seen Dooley. He's in New York."

"In New York?" She pondered this news, clearly befuddled. "But I spoke to him! Of course, he didn't reply, he appeared to be in a great hurry . . . and awfully thin and pale." She hesitated. "I wasn't going to say anything to you, but he was . . . soiled and *mal habille,* quite unlike himself. I know he's living on a farm this summer, perhaps that's why."

"Yes, well, Dooley is in New York."

"Oh, *oui, bien sûr,* you did say that." She shook her head. "I suppose this boy did look younger than Dooley, yet . . . how extraordinary."

He rose from the bench. "I'll push off, Hélène. Incidentally, the roast chicken you brought was very good, indeed. *Très* . . ."—he hesitated—*"bon! Oui, très bon!"* How hideous his French was. He had embarrassed himself and his neighbor into the bargain.

Her cheeks flushed. "It was nothing!"

"Au revoir, then!" he said, waving.

"*À bientôt,* Father! Thank you for coming, please come again!"

He shuffled home and sat on the sofa, panting. He should have the blasted sofa removed from the house, stored under lock and key, until things were a bit further along. His heart pounded.

"Water," he said, as Puny came into the room.

"You'll worry me t' my *grave!*" she said, looking distraught. She dashed to the kitchen and brought him a glass of water, which he drank down at once.

"Good. Just what the doctor ordered."

"Father . . ."

"Yes?"

"I couldn't stand it if anything happened to you." Tears rolled heedlessly down her freckled cheeks.

"Why, Puny, how amazing—I feel the very same way about you."

She laughed and wiped her eyes on her apron. "Are you all right?"

"I'm perfectly fine. It's true."

"You ain't been yourself."

"Who have I been, do you think?"

She giggled. "Somebody sad an' grouchy."

"Aha."

She looked at him, wrinkling her brow.

"Cynthia loves you more'n anything, she'd do anything f'r you, an' so would I, an' so would th' girls, they love their granpaw."

"Their granpaw loves them back."

"You cain't die," she said matter-of-factly.

"Certainly not!"

"Are you goin' to git back to your ol' self?"

"You bet."

"*Good!*" she said. "I hope you make it snappy!"

Dooley at the drugstore in Holding . . .

It dawned on him as slowly as a sunrise, when it should have hit him like a bolt of lightning.

He quickly punched the numbers on the handset and paced the floor.

"*Bonjour!*"

"Hélène, Tim Kavanagh. I hope I haven't interrupted a lesson."

"Not at all, Father. Two students are out today with summer colds. I don't have a lesson until four-thirty."

"Where is the drugstore in Holding?"

"There are two drugstores. I patronize the one on Main Street, it has a special hard candy Mother enjoys."

He'd never been on Holding's Main Street; he'd always gone to the mall on the bypass like the rest of the common horde. "Could you give me directions?"

"It's awfully hard to get to just now, they're restoring the monument to the town square and the streets are a bit . . ."—she searched for a word—"addled. In a jumble."

"Aha." He'd have to get someone to drive him; he knew he couldn't make the trip alone. He'd call Buck. On second thought, he didn't want to give false hope; and he certainly couldn't ask George, who was just getting established at the bookstore, and part time work at Lew Boyd's.

"I'm going down there if I can find someone to . . . I think it's a bit soon to make the drive myself."

"I'll drive you!"

"Oh, heavens, no, that would be asking—"

"But you're not asking," she said, clearly excited. "I'm offering! It would be a great privilege to do something for you, Father, who has done so much for me."

"Now, Hélène . . ."

"When would you wish to leave?"

He thought a moment. "Could we leave at once?"

"Je serai devant votre maison dans cinq minutes!"

"I beg your pardon?"

"I'll be there in five minutes, Father. Five minutes!"

"Thank you!" he said. But Hélène had already hung up.

Uncle Billy Watson stood before the mirrored door of the bathroom medicine cabinet and spoke aloud to his image.

"Wellsir, this feller got a parrot f'r 'is birthday, don't you know."

He glanced at the almanac he was holding, but his trembling hand caused the words to dance a jig. It was enough to give a man a headache, trying to read words that bounced around like a monkey on a mule.

"Hold still!" he commanded. He was surprised to see that his hand obeyed him. He adjusted his glasses, held the almanac closer to the light above the cabinet, and squinted at the next line.

"Hit was a full-growed parrot an' come with a mean attitude an' a manner of talkin' that was scand'lous. Seem like ever' other word or two would near about kink a man's hair.

"Course, th' feller tried t' change things, don't you know, he was all th' time sayin' polite words, playin' soft music on th' radio, anything he could think of t' try an' set a good example, but they wouldn't nothin' work."

Uncle Billy laid the almanac on the tank of the commode, squeezed his eyes shut, and repeated by memory what he'd just read aloud. He figured he'd done that part pretty good; he picked up the almanac and adjusted his glasses, which were taped across the nose bridge where, several months ago, they had broken in two.

"One day he got s' mad, he took 'at ol' bird an' shook it 'til its beak rattled. Boys, 'at fired th' parrot up, he went t' cussin' th' feller ever' whichaway, sayin' worser things than he'd been a-sayin'."

"Wellsir, th' feller grabbed 'at bird up an' stuck it in th' freezer an' *slammed th' door.* Yessir! Heard it a-squawkin,' a-kickin', a-screamin', an' I don' know what all. Then it got real still in there.

"Feller was scared he'd lost 'is parrot, so he opened th' freezer door, and dadjing if th' parrot didn't step out nice as you please, said, 'I'm mighty sorry if I offended you with my language an' all, an' I ask y'r forgiveness, don't you know. I'll sure try to correct my actions from here on out.'

"Th' feller was about t' ask what caused such a big change when th' parrot said, 'About that chicken in there—may I ask what'n th' world *it* done?'"

By johnny, that ought to work if he practiced it enough times. He just hoped it would make the preacher laugh, that was the main thing. He'd never seen a man look so low, like he could crawl under a snake's belly wearing a top hat. He'd give a dollar bill to say this joke to Rose Watson, to get somebody else's opinion, but Rose never laughed at his jokes, nossir, never did.

He noted that his right hand had begun to tremble again. He stuck it in his pocket and walked into the hall with his cane in the other hand, singing under his breath. It was the song his mother had taught him as a boy; he often mumbled or sang a few words of "Redwing" when he was happy.

Driving with Hélène Pringle made flying with Omer Cunningham resemble an Altar Guild tea party.

He shut his eyes, unable to look. Hélène was proceeding down the winding mountain road like a ball from a cannon. If his blood had been as turgid as a river bottom these past weeks, it was now pumping like oil through a derrick. To make things worse, Hélène seemed incapable of driving and speaking English at the same time. Worse still, she was precisely the height of Sadie Baxter and could barely see over the steering wheel.

"I do love these mountain roads, they make me feel so free! *Je n'ai jamais de la vie été plus heureuse nulle part ailleurs que je ne le suis ici dans ces montagnes.* I presume that's true for you, also, as you've chosen to live here so many years. *Ça par exemple! Regardez les nuages au-dessus de ce pic là!*"

"Hélène," he croaked, "could you slow down? Just a mite?" He emphasized *mite,* as he certainly didn't want to offend.

"Of course, Father, but my speedometer reads only fifty-five."

"Better take your car in and let Harley have a look, I think we're doing . . . seventy." Eighty was more like it, but he didn't want to push.

"Seventy? But this car has *never* done seventy."

He shut his eyes and prayed.

"What's he look like?" asked the pharmacist.

Father Tim reached for his wallet as Hélène explained.

"Tall, very thin. Freckles. Red hair. Quite . . . dirty."

"Here," said Father Tim, holding out a photo of Dooley. "Something like this."

The pharmacist looked disapproving. "You must be talkin' about Sammy Barlowe. We've caught him tryin' to stuff his britches with candy, but nobody's ever actually found anything on 'im."

Father Tim's heart pounded. He looked around for a chair, someplace to sit for a moment. . . ."Where does he live?"

"God only knows. Someplace with his old man, who's the worst drunk you'll ever run into. Why would you be looking for this boy? I see you're clergy."

"Yes, well, he's . . ." Father Tim paused a moment. "He's family."

The pharmacist raised his eyebrows.

"You could ask at the pool hall. Go down to the corner, cross the street, an' it's on your left."

They bolted from the drugstore, the bell jangling on the door, and went at a trot to the corner, where they waited for the light.

His breath came quickly; his head felt lighter than air. "Hélène, this could be a dead end. But you need to know how terribly, terribly important it is for us to do . . . what we're doing. Do you pray?"

"I've just begun!" she said, thrilled that this

might somehow make things more convenient for him.

"Pray, then. You may have found Dooley's kid brother."

Tears sprang to her eyes. "Oh!" she said, breathless. "Oh!"

"That definitely ain't Sammy Barlowe," said the pool hall owner. He took a long drag on the last of his cigarette, dropped it to the cement floor, and stepped on it. "This boy looks like he's livin' high on th' hog." He exhaled a considerable fume of smoke.

"Right. What I'm saying is, does Sammy look like this boy? Is there a strong resemblance?"

"Oh, yeah. I'd say so. What you need to know for?"

"I'd like to contact him."

"Has he come into big money?" The man cackled. Two other men halted their pool game and listened to the conversation.

"Nothing like that. Perhaps you can tell us where he lives."

"I cain't tell you that."

"Why not?" He hadn't careened down the mountain with Hélène Pringle, risking life and limb, to be put off so easily.

"Because it ain't nobody's business, is why not."

"I'm family," he said, as if that would change everything.

The man smirked. "You're a preacher."

"Preachers have families!" said Hélène, indignant.

"You might as well go on, I ain't tellin' you nothin'." The man walked across the room, entered a door marked *Office,* and slammed it behind him.

A radio played, drifting randomly between two country stations.

One of the pool players walked over and held out his hand. "How bad you want t' know where Sammy lives at?"

"Real bad," said Father Tim.

"Pink Shuford."

"Pink," said Father Tim, shaking hands. "Tim Kavanagh. And this is Miss Pringle."

Hélène put her hands behind her back. *"Bonjour."* Father Tim thought he heard a tremor in her voice.

"Named after m' great-granpaw, Pinckney."

"A fine old southern name."

"This here's Skin Head Bug Eye Snaggle Tooth Austin, you can call 'im Bug f'r short."

Father Tim nodded toward Bug, who blinked but didn't return the nod.

"You ever shoot any pool?" asked Pink

Shuford. His left arm was tattooed with a snake coiled from wrist to elbow.

"Once or twice. I'd appreciate knowing where we can find Sammy."

Pink walked back to the table, hunkered over it with the stick, and made a shot. The balls clicked together and rolled apart. The seven ball dropped into the corner pocket.

"I reckon you ain't played enough pool to recognize that as a mighty fine shot."

"No, I haven't," said Father Tim.

"Seven in th' corner pocket. Most places, I could've won cash money on that shot."

"What will it take for you to tell us where to find Sammy?"

"Well, let's see." Pink scratched his head and gazed at the ceiling. "Let me just see, now." The odor of stale tobacco and sour beer permeated the room; a ceiling fan oscillated over their heads.

Pink Shuford looked at Father Tim and suddenly grinned. "How about . . ."

Bug's cue ball scratched in the side pocket. Pink eyed the table, chalked his cue, bent over the rail, and returned the shot. "Eight ball in the corner pocket, eat y'r heart out," said Pink. Bug uttered a curse.

"Now," said Pink, "back to business. How about fifty bucks?"

Father Tim took out his wallet and examined the billfold. Twenty, thirty, thirty-five, -six, -seven, -eight . . . He felt a trickle of sweat along his spine. This whole scenario exuded a palpable darkness; he wanted out of here. Hélène was already backing toward the door.

"Thirty-eight," said Father Tim.

"Deal." Pink crossed to him quickly and took the money. He stuffed it in his jeans pocket. "Follow me an' Bug. I'm in th' blue Chevy truck out front."

"Perhaps you could just give us directions."

"You ain't goin' t' find it without help."

There was no turning back. "We're parked in front of the drugstore."

"A gray Dodge sedan," said Hélène, the quaver still in her voice. "How far do you think it might be to . . . where we're going?"

Pink Shuford pulled a Lucky Strike from a package in his shirt pocket. "Maybe ten, twelve miles." He lit the cigarette with a match, inhaled deeply, and grinned at Hélène. "I hope you got good shocks, lady."

Father Tim managed to beat her to the car and, racing to the driver's side, gripped the door handle. "I'll be glad to drive!"

"Oh, no, Father! There's something wrong with the brakes, I have to tap them just so or . . ."

"Or . . . what?"

"Or they don't work very well. You just get in and relax and leave the driving to me!"

Relax? *Relax?* He took out his handkerchief and wiped his brow, then got in, sat down and crossed himself. *Surround us with Your loving care,* he prayed silently. *Protect us from every danger; and bring us in safety to our journey's end; through Jesus Christ our Lord, Amen.*

Hélène started the car with a roar. "I'm so glad you're praying," she said happily.

The pickup truck didn't appear to slow down for the bend in the road. Hélène gunned the motor and they careened after it.

"Mon Dieu!" gasped Hélèn. "What haste they make. Our own speed is fifty."

Sixty! he thought, paralyzed with dread. But why worry? Didn't he believe God had a time for everybody? If so, so be it; he was ready. It's just that there were other ways he'd rather go Home, like in his sleep, with a smile on his face. . . .

He had an awful and hankering thirst. It had come upon him suddenly as they pulled away from the curb in Holding. Not only had he left the house without a bottle of water, he realized he'd utterly forgotten his morning insulin shot.

Hélène's face looked considerably pinched, not to mention white as a sheet, as his mother would have said.

"Are you . . . all right?"

"It is a very uncomfortable thing to talk about, Father. . . ."

"You can talk about it to me."

He watched her struggle with some deep truth. "I would hope to be delicate, but you see . . ."

They hauled around another curve, and were now barreling down a steep grade on a gravel road, enveloped in a flume of dust kicked up by the truck.

". . . I desperately need to . . . to . . . find a powder room!"

He thought she might burst into tears of humiliation.

"And I need to find water!" he said, equally urgent.

It didn't look hopeful. No, indeed, they were in the piney woods with no habitation in sight. In truth, he hoped they didn't meet another vehicle, as the road was fit for the passage of one car only. What had he gotten them into? He felt a sudden responsibility for Hélène Pringle, an innocent bystander. They passed a deserted house trailer.

"There's something else I should tell you," she said. "Something far worse."

"What's that?"

"Our petrol gauge reads half full, but the gauge doesn't work properly. There's really less than a quarter of a tank."

"Aha."

"We left in such haste that I forgot to look until now, but I'm sure we have enough to get back to town. . . ." her voice trailed away thinly.

Lord, have mercy. . . ."I'm sure," he said, coughing from the dust seeping into the car.

"J'en suis désolée, mon père! Pardonnez-moi. J'espère que je ne nous ai pas attiré des ennuis."

He had no idea what she was saying, but her distress was evident.

"We can turn around and go back!" he exclaimed, thinking to console her.

"Non, non! We must *not* do that! This is very crucial to your happiness, to dear Dooley's happiness! We must press on and take our chances." She turned to look at him, beseeching. "You pray, Father, and I'll drive!"

The road was a washboard; he thought his insides might be rearranged in some unrecognizable way, his liver where a kidney had been, his heart in his throat. . . .

They followed the blue truck, making a hard left turn onto an unmarked dirt road scarred with potholes; he heard the exhaust pipe scrape over one rock, then another. This was hardly better than a dry creek bed.

He realized, suddenly, that the truck had disappeared.

"Where did they get to?"

"I don't know," she said, bewildered. "But we'll catch them!"

He clapped a hand over his eyes and held on for dear life.

He didn't want to admit it, even to himself, but minutes later he was greatly relieved to find that the truck had, indeed, disappeared. Hélène slowed down and stopped for a moment, shaken. He had the odd feeling they'd gotten off light with a thirty-eight-dollar joyride.

The fatigue was like nothing he'd ever experienced; it was all the exhaustion and despair of the last weeks rolled into a single agony. He supposed he'd have to turn himself in to an institution of some sort; he could not be trusted to care for himself. Perhaps there was a kind of death wish in him that he'd never routed out, that he'd held back from God and never let Him touch.

On their way home, they had stopped to go

to the rest room, get gas, and take nourishment. He sat in the car at the service station like an invalid, while Hélène pumped gas, bought drinks and two bags of Fritos, and ministered to his pathetic needs. It was desperately humiliating, but he could do nothing about it. As they sped up the mountain, he guzzled bottled water and feebly consumed the Fritos.

He came into his kitchen, out of breath and dazed, and reached for the countertop of the island. As the wave of fatigue rolled over him, he felt like a sinking swimmer whose foot had just touched an undertow. He inhaled deeply and shook his head, panicked; then it passed and he was safe again, holding on to the countertop and looking into the eyes of his dog.

He let Barnabas into the yard without a leash, something he rarely did, and thanked God that his faithful companion obeyed his master's every command.

Now he could administer his evening shot and drag himself to bed—that's all he wanted, nothing more: nothing.

He was sleeping when the phone rang; he fumbled it to his ear.

"Hello?"

"Ah, Timothy, so glad you're there, it's Edith."

Edith! Was this a dream?

"When we spoke last evening, I said I *ought* to thank you, and then, silly me, I forgot to actually *do* it! So, thank you, Timothy, *thank* you. God uses everything for good, don't you think? But I mustn't keep you. Blessings to you and Cynthia and that dear boy you took in. Toodles!"

He was dumbfounded all over again, but more than that, he felt molested, plain and simple. Why would Edith Mallory never leave him alone? Why did she endlessly insinuate herself into his life? He hated this business of phoning him up like some old school chum, and fervently hoped it would never happen again. Perhaps it wouldn't; she had thanked him, after all, for whatever aberrant reason she might have had, and that should be enough.

He hoped to God it would be enough.

The talk with Cynthia hadn't gone well; she'd heard his fatigue and wanted to know everything, but he'd been afraid to tell her everything.

He knew that hiding the raw details from his wife, or any wife, did not bode well for future outcomes. But he couldn't explain it all; it was too exhausting, too complicated, too . . . he thought the whole afternoon vaguely dreamlike, as if it had never happened. He'd been to another world with the intent of accomplishing a grand mission, and had come home humbled and defeated. Why even speak of it?

At the foot of the bed, Barnabas scratched furiously, causing the mattress to throb like a great, arhythmic heartbeat.

Still awake at three in the morning, Father Tim lay in the dark room and looked out the window to darkness. The heavens were overcast, obscuring a nearly full moon, and the street lamp had been knocked winding two weeks ago by a careless driver.

Who was to say that Cynthia wouldn't give up on him? In truth, he was wearing down while she was gearing up. How long could a bright, successful, beautiful woman be patient with a man who had no passion in him anywhere? His wife was all about passion, passion for whatever she was doing, for whatever lay ahead. At the beginning, she'd declared him charming and romantic—perhaps now she was changing her mind. But he couldn't bear such thoughts, it was blasphemy to think these vile things.

"Are you there, Lord? Sometimes I can't sense Your Presence, I have to go on faith alone. You want us to walk by faith, You tell us so . . . don't we go on faith that the sun will set, the moon will rise, our breath will come in and go out again, our hearts will beat? Give me faith, Lord, to know Your Presence as surely as I know the beating of my own heart. I've felt so far from You. . . ."

He remembered Miss Sadie's story of falling into the abandoned well, of her terror as she cried out, unheard, in the dark summer night, unable to move—she said she'd known for the first time the deep meaning of the prayers she had learned by rote. "It was the darkness," Miss Sadie had told him, "that was the worst."

The tears were hot on his face. His own life seemed overwhelmed by darkness these last weeks; there had been the bright and shining possibility, then had come the crushing darkness. Something flickered in his memory. "Song birds," he whispered. "Song birds, yes . . . are taught to sing in the dark."

That was a line from Oswald Chambers, from the book he'd kept by his bedside for many years. But he couldn't bear switching on the lamp to read it; his eyes had been feeling weak and even painful. He turned on his side and opened the drawer of the nightstand and took out the flashlight. Then he pulled Cynthia's pillow atop his own and shone the flashlight on the open book.

He thumbed through the worn and familiar pages. There! Page forty-five, the reading for February fourteenth. . . .

At times God puts us through the discipline of darkness to teach us to heed Him. Song birds are taught to sing in the dark, and we are put into the shadow of God's hand until we learn to hear Him. . . . Watch where God puts you into darkness, and when you are there keep your mouth shut. Are you in the dark just now in your circumstances, or in your life with God? Then remain quiet. . . . When you are in the dark, listen, and God will give you a very precious message for someone else when you get into the light.

The flashlight slid onto the bed beside him as he fell asleep, but his hand resolutely gripped the book until dawn.

CHAPTER TWELVE

Where the Heart Is

Uncle Billy Watson decided he was fed up with trying to learn jokes from a book. A man had to study out a little bitty part in print as fine as frog hair, then close his eyes and say it out loud 'til he got it right, then study out the next dadblame part, and so on and so on, 'til the whole works was so mixed up in his head he didn't hardly know hisself if it was funny. He hadn't laughed one time over that parrot joke, so why did he think he could get the preacher to laugh?

"Where are you headed?" demanded his wife.

"Out t' m' dadjing garden!" he said, stomping to the door.

"This soup's cooked and ready to eat!"

"Hit's too hot f'r soup!" he said, mad as a

hornet about things in general. "A man oughtn't t' have t' eat soup when th' weather's ninety degrees in th' shade!"

"A man ought to eat what's offered and be glad to get it!"

He thought Rose Watson was the meanest-looking woman he ever laid eyes on, the way she crossed her arms and glared down on him like he was two feet tall. He sometimes figured they wadn't nothing at all wrong with his wife. She was smart as a whip and twice as tough; her sickness was just something she used to get attention and worry a man to death.

"No rest f'r th' wicked an' th' righteous don't need none," he said under his breath. He let the screen door slam behind him, even if slamming doors wasn't allowed in his house, and went down the back steps with his cane.

For all he cared, she could holler at him 'til she was blue in the face, he was going out to his little patch and set in a chair and watch his sprouts grow. He'd make up his own joke, by johnny—a man who'd lived eighty-some years ought to have enough dadblame sense to make up his own joke.

They lay facing each other in bed; the moon had risen, bright and full, illuminating the room.

"It was good for you to get away," he said, tracing the outline of her ear with his finger-tips.

"Yes. It was. But it's better for me to be home."

"Do you really mean it?"

"I really mean it."

He kissed her, lingering.

"I think you're glad I'm home."

"Amen!"

She smiled. "Home is where the heart is."

She put her palm against his cheek and kissed him back; he felt the slow, steady tide rising in him.

He wasn't as old and feeble as he'd thought. No, indeed, he wasn't old and feeble at all.

Hope Winchester sat on the stool behind the cash register at Happy Endings, not daring to lift her eyes from the book she was reading. She couldn't make heads nor tails of the words; they seemed to mush together in a kind of typographical quagmire. What a snare she'd gotten herself into; she was exerting every effort to appear absorbed in *Jim the Boy*, which the *New York Times* had raved over, but her mind was riveted on the mailroom.

It was nearly unbearable that the door to the

mailroom, just a few feet from the register, was partially open; occasionally she saw him walk to the stacks and take a book from the shelf. She thought his hands mesmerizing—long, tapered fingers that seemed to hold things with sensitivity and purpose.

She tried to forget that he'd used those same fingers to unscrew the oil pan from a car and steal a friend's jewels, which, as it turned out, had been stolen from a British museum. But that was over, that was past; he had suffered his punishment, and was nice as anything and very serious and kind and loved books as much as she did.

She thought she might have borne his nearness with more equanimity if he had not loved books, or if he were not so very handsome. She had never been around handsome men, and the fact that one was working in the next room and speaking her name and occasionally bringing her coffee in the mornings was . . . she tried to find words for what it was. It was something like painful, even excruciating to have him so near and to feel such an avalanche of emotion and be completely unable to laugh and talk and go about one's life normally, instead of sitting on a stool, frozen with longing and fear and pretense, trying to read words that would not penetrate her brain.

"Miss Winchester?"

George Gaynor stood at the open door, only feet away, smiling. He was wearing a denim shirt the color of his eyes; she could barely speak. "Yes?"

"I wonder if you would show me how to enter this order—it's different from all the others."

She wanted to die on the spot and get it over with, and not suffer so cruelly.

"Of course," she said, slipping off the stool. The book crashed to the floor and she stooped to pick it up. She looked at him as she laid it on the counter and saw that he was smiling.

"You know how things have gone the last couple of years," he told Buck on the phone. "We've had a lot of disappointments. Maybe we shouldn't say anything yet to Pauline and the kids . . . or to Dooley . . . but Sammy is in Holding."

He heard the sharp intake of breath.

"What're the circumstances?"

"He's living with his father, I don't know where. I had someone drive me down the mountain and we were led on a wild goose chase."

"I'll stop by tomorrow night on my way home, if that's all right. I've got to take Poo and Jessie to a ball game tonight, I promised."

"I have a big event planned tomorrow night. How about in the morning—maybe the Grill—could you be there at, say, eight-thirty?"

"I'll be there," said Buck.

For a man who had once scared the living daylights out of him, not to mention made him plenty mad, Buck Leeper now offered a kind of consolation. If there was anybody he'd want in his corner when facing down Clyde Barlowe, it was Buck Leeper.

He should tell his wife the news about Sammy. But it took too much energy to start at the beginning and explain everything. He would wait. He was feeling stronger today than in a very long time, but every activity cost him dearly in strength—bringing in the paper, talking to Harley, walking his dog to the corner, the slightest thing. He would tell her after he and Buck had talked, when they had put together a plan. After all, she was good with plans. He could run it by her and get her input, that had always proved to be a good thing.

"Tim, it's your brother in th' Lord!"

"Bill!"

"You'll never guess what's happened!"

"No, sir, I couldn't. What is it?"

"Th' Lord has sent me a dog."

"You don't mean it. . . ."

"He was mighty quick about it, I wasn't lookin' for one so soon, but this is it, this is th' one. I want you to see 'im, Tim, he's a laugh a minute! Are you gettin' out yet?"

"I got out for a haircut and a little . . . drive. I want to come up for a visit. When would be a good time?"

"Anytime is a good time. Just come on."

"Have you named him?"

"Buddy."

"Buddy. Good name. I'm sure he'll live up to it."

"He walks sideways."

"That takes some doing. What age, do you think?"

"Five, maybe six years old. One of th' congregation found 'im in a ditch, no tags, bones stickin' out. I talked to Sparky about it last night, Sparky says it's OK, said to let 'im have . . ."—Bill's voice broke, but only for a moment—"to let 'im have his bed over in th' corner of our bedroom."

"I'm thrilled for you, Bill."

"Are you doin' all right?"

"God is faithful, I'm coming along," said Father Tim. "How about you, my friend?"

"Can't complain!"

"Well, if you can't complain, nobody can. Why don't I bring you and Rachel some fruit tarts?"

"Nossir, Hoppy's got me off sugar."

"He's got everybody off sugar. These deals are sugar-free."

"Bring 'em on, then, brother," said Bill Sprouse, laughing.

Father Tim felt the weight lifting from his shoulders, moving off his chest. Bill Sprouse had a dog! Bill Sprouse was laughing! God was faithful, indeed.

When he took the tarts up the hill tomorrow, he'd throw in a box of dog treats.

He didn't think he'd ever driven to the Grill before; he'd always walked, no matter what the weather.

Feeling like one of the modern-day common horde, he backed the Mustang out of the garage in order to drive two blocks. He was saving the energy it would take to walk, saving it for her.

"I ain't believin' my eyes." Percy wiped his hands on the towel he kept tucked in his belt and trotted to the rear booth. "I thought you'd dropped offa th' face of th' earth."

"Back again and better than ever. It's great to see you, buddyroe. Where's Velma?"

"In th' rest room, takin' curlers out of 'er hair."

"Aha."

"I ain't poached a egg since th' last time you was in here."

"We'll see if you've lost your touch! I'll have two poached on whole wheat, the usual." He slid his coffee cup to Percy, who filled it.

"You're trouble," said Percy, feigning aggravation, but clearly pleased. "Want you a little bacon on th' side? A dish of grits?"

"Cantaloupe. I've been craving a good cantaloupe."

"Sliced or cubed?"

"I've got a choice?"

"Naw, I was jis' kiddin,' all we got is sliced."

"All I want is sliced," said Father Tim, grinning.

"I got somethin' in th' back with your name on it. Come in yesterday, UPS."

"Right. I'll get it before I go. Thought I'd hang with Mule and J.C. awhile, then meet Buck Leeper here around eight-thirty."

"Yeah, well, th' Turkey Club ain't been the same with you gone."

"The Turkey Club?"

"That's Velma's name for th' reg'lars in the rear booth."

"Descriptive. So what's the latest scandal and gossip? What have I missed?"

J.C. slid into the booth with his bulging, un-zippered briefcase. "All scandal and gossip has been duly recorded in th' *Mitford Muse*. If I didn't report it, it didn't happen." The editor shoved a copy of the newspaper across the table. "Hot off the press, all th' news that's fit to print, you heard it here first. That'll be fifty cents."

"Fifty cents?" said Father Tim.

"Paper's gone up, ink's gone up, distribu-tion's gone up. . . ."

Percy filled J.C.'s cup, frowning. "Quality's gone down. . . ."

"A man has to make a living," said J.C. He dragged a rumpled handkerchief from his jacket pocket, unfurled it, and mopped his brow.

"Ten cents' worth of news for half a dollar is what *that* deal is.'

"While you're preaching," snapped J.C., "let me have a quarter's worth of sausage biscuit for a dollar, with a twenty-cent side of hash browns for a dollar seventy-five."

"Turkey," muttered Percy, legging it to the grill.

"So look at th' front page," said J.C.

There was his wife, nearly as large as life, with a shot of the Davant Medal used as an inset. The picture definitely did not do her justice, no, indeed, heads would roll at her publishing house for sending out this particular photo. . . .

"Read th' headline," said J.C. "I wrote that, I always write th' big stuff, I don't farm out th' big stuff."

" '*Prestigious Davant Metal Bestowed on Local Author.*' "

"I had trouble with the headline," confessed the editor.

"No kidding."

"Yeah, I didn't know whether to say *local* or *world-famous*. I thought *local* was more . . ."

"Sells more papers," said Father Tim, trying to be helpful.

"Then I thought *bestowed* kind of a big word for a small town newspaper. . . ."

"Right."

"But I figured that learnin' a new word could be educational."

"Good thinking." Why should he be the one to point out the *spelling* in the much-talked-about headline?

"Lookit, I put in there about the invitation for her to tour the country on that literacy deal. It was in th' letter her publisher sent down."

"Very thorough story. But she won't be going on the tour."

"Let me slide in here and drink a little coffee b'fore th' roof caves in!" Mule Skinner thumped down beside Father Tim.

"Why is the roof caving in?" asked J.C.

"Because th' father's here, blockhead."

"Oh," said J.C.

Though he'd been out of the picture for only a few weeks, Father Tim felt it might have been a few years; these guys looked . . . different, somehow. It would take a while for the new to wear off and the old to kick in again.

"So what's it goin' to be?" Percy called from the grill, where he was working bacon, sausage, and hash browns.

"The usual!" said Mule.

"What th' dickens is that?" Percy wanted to know. "You ain't ordered th' same thing twice in twenty years!"

"Give me a break. Just last week I ordered eggs over light twice in a row."

"So that's your order, eggs over light?"

"I didn't say that was my order, I said—"

Velma blew out of the rest room. "Let me get in here! I'll yank 'is order out of 'im."

J.C. put his head in his hands. "Just once, man, heaven knows, just once . . ."

"Just once what?"

"Just once, *order and get it over with.*"

"Right!" said Velma, gripping her order pad. "And make it snappy."

"Over light or not?" demanded J.C.

"Over light, for Pete's sake! White toast! Hold th' butter! Grape jelly! Orange juice! Hash browns!"

There was a stunned silence.

"There, dadgummit!" Mule looked triumphant. "I hope y'all are satisfied."

"I cain't believe it!" said Velma. "This'll be one for th' hist'ry books. Now—what was it you said after orange juice?"

Mule shrugged. "I don't know."

"You don't know what you said?"

"I wadn't listenin'."

"Hash browns," said J.C. "He said hash browns."

"Yeah, but maybe I should have grits. With butter! Why not? Butter on the grits, but no butter on the toast."

"Bring 'im hash browns," said J.C.

Velma gazed briefly at the ceiling, ripped the order off the pad, stuck it on the spindle at the counter, and stumped to the next booth.

"Man!" said J.C., mopping his face.

Mule turned to Father Tim and grinned broadly. "So, buddyroe, welcome back."

"Thanks. Glad to be back. Looks like nothing's changed."

"Same ol', same ol'," said Mule.

Father Tim was certain that Mule had glanced at him in an odd way. In truth, he might as well take the bull by the horns and deal straight up with what people were thinking about the accident. His heart hammered as he asked, not really wanting to know.

"So, what are you thinking?"

"Thinkin'?" asked Mule. "I'm not thinkin' anything."

"Par for the course," said J.C.

Father Tim smelled the bacon frying, he heard the rattle of the window air conditioner, he saw Percy slicing the cantaloupe. . . .

He wedged his back into the corner of the booth as he'd done for nearly two decades; the place where the green, painted wood converged felt a lot like home.

"Maybe we should turn it over to the authorities, let Social Services be the go-between."

"With three marriages an' a drinkin' problem, I've had all the go-between I can choke down," said Buck. "Sometimes I think we should let sleepin' dogs lie. Jessic was a baby when the kids were split up, she doesn't remember Sammy or Kenny, and Poo hardly remembers them, either. Things are settled with us, runnin' pretty smooth." Buck looked at the tabletop, then at Father Tim. "But there's no way we can't try an' pull this family back together. No way."

"If it all works out, you'd want Sammy to live with you?"

"We'd want to give him the option," said Buck.

"The boy could have serious behavior problems."

"We understand that. It would mean a lot just to know he's all right—and if he wants to live with us, if we could get it through th' courts . . . we'll give it our best shot."

"When I went to Holding the other day, I did it without thinking. I don't know what I hoped to accomplish, perhaps it was just to see him, to remind him of his brothers and sisters, to look over the circumstances—maybe he wouldn't have been home, or maybe it would have set his father off in some way that—"

"Let's just find him, then take it from there. We've both got a pretty good idea how he's livin', an' as far th' courts go, it wouldn't stack up against th' home we could give him."

"You're doing a fine job with Jessie and Poo."

"It's been good tryin' to be their daddy, I couldn't ever have kids . . . an' when you think about th' road I've been down, that's prob'ly th' best. I try to do right by Dooley, too, but I know he looks on you as his dad an' I'd never want to mess with that."

"The first time I saw him is etched in my memory like an engraving—a little redheaded guy with freckles, mad at the world, old before his time. It hasn't been easy, but it's been rich . . . and I'm thankful."

"I admit I'm real uneasy about what could come of this. . . ."

"Dooley's afraid it could be a powder keg."

"But I've been prayin' about findin' th' boys since we got married. So has Pauline. And I know you're prayin'."

"Have been, will be."

"So . . ." Buck finished his coffee and set the cup down firmly. "Why don't you an' me plan a time to run down th' mountain? I'd like to start from scratch with Pink Shuford an' 'is buddy."

"Father Tim!"

He turned and saw Father Talbot trotting toward him from Happy Endings, in his running gear.

"Wait up!"

It wasn't easy, thought Father Tim, to have been succeeded at Lord's Chapel by a man who, though only a few years younger, had all his hair, ran daily, worked out, used a rowing machine, and wore top-of-the-line Nikes.

"Henry! Glad to see you!" And he was glad.

"Just going down to the office to ring you," said Henry Talbot, huffing. "You're looking terrific, very trim and fit!"

In truth, he was so drained that he was headed home instead of to Sweet Stuff for fruit tarts. "Pushing along very well, thanks. How are you and Mary getting on?"

"Planning our trip to the Bahamas for ten days, a surprise anniversary gift from our kids. I'm hoping you can supply for me at Lord's Chapel next month. The, ah, let's see . . ." Henry Talbot fetched a small planner from the pocket of his running shorts, and flipped the pages. "The eighth and fifteenth. It would make a lot of people happy, I daresay."

Lord's Chapel! Something like fear pierced his heart. Was he rusty? Was he up to it?

"Yes!" he said. "I'd like nothing better."

Hessie Mayhew dodged into the handkerchief garden between the Collar Button and the Sweet Stuff Bakery and stood, frozen, by a bed of dahlias, hoping Father Tim would not spot her as he passed.

She clutched a brass vase chock-full of multiflora roses that she'd just cut from her arbor and was taking to the office building next door to Sweet Stuff. It was a forty-dollar arrangement and worth every dime, but she suddenly felt like a common criminal. To think of all he'd been through, and now, at last, he was out and about, no doubt to pay tribute to those who'd sent food and flowers through the long weeks, while the absence of a single, solitary word from Hessie Mayhew pained him like a sore and festering thumb. . . .

"Good morning, Hessie!"

She turned, humiliated, and looked into his beaming face.

"It's great to see you, Hessie! How are you?"

Unthinking, she hastily closed the distance between them and thrust the vase of roses into his hands.

"There!" she blurted, sloshing water onto his shirtsleeve. Appalled at her grossly inept presentation, she turned and fled along the sidewalk.

Since he was standing at the door of Sweet Stuff, he decided to go in. It would, at the very least, be a place to sit for a few minutes before he began the long trek home. The vase of flowers seemed to weigh more than he would have thought. He went inside, thumped the vase onto a table, and sat.

"Water," he said to Winnie, who gave him a concerned look.

"Where's your car, darling?"

"Ah," he said. "My car."

"Yes. You know, the red Mustang with the rag top, the leather seats, the—"

"Oh, *that* car." Blast! "Parked in front of the Grill."

He thrust the vase into her hands. "There!" he said, not knowing what else to say.

"Oh, my! Lovely!"

"Happy birthday!" he said, recovering his wits.

She set the vase on the coffee table before the sofa. "Perfect! What a wonderful shade of pink! Thank you, dearest!" She plucked a small envelope from among the roses and smiled. "Let's see what tender sentiment you've in-scribed to me."

He lifted his hands helplessly. He hadn't seen an envelope!

She withdrew a small card and peered at it.

"'Happy retirement, Mildred. . . ,'" she read aloud.

"'Old bookkeepers never die, they just nickel and dime the rest of us to death.' Timothy, what on *earth*?"

"Joke," he said feebly. However, as the joke was on him, he told her the truth and was vastly relieved when she howled with laughter.

He lay across the bed, remembering what else he'd forgotten—the fruit tarts, the promised visit to Bill and Rachel. . . .

Voices floated up from downstairs. Three o'clock. He must have fallen asleep after lunch. He was slightly disoriented; the morning had seemed an entire day in itself. Maybe he should see Hoppy tomorrow—but no, tomorrow was full. . . .

He sat up on the side of the bed and gazed at the floor, unseeing.

"Timothy?"

"Yes?"

Cynthia stood in the doorway; the blanched look on her face alarmed him.

"Harley just brought this over." She walked to the bed and handed him a sheet of paper.

"'For labor and parts,'" he read aloud, "'one hundred and sixty-eight dollars.'"

"For Miss Pringle's car. Harley said you told him to repair the brakes and gas gauge and that you'd pay the bill."

The tone of her voice made his heart beat heavily. "Come and sit down," he said.

"I'm perfectly fine standing up. He said you noticed her car needed work when she . . . drove you down the mountain while I was away."

He hadn't told his wife everything. He had postponed the truth.

He would definitely be paying for this unfortunate mistake.

The pain he'd experienced over the last terrible weeks had been a dull pain. This suffering was sharp and hard. He looked at the closed door of her workroom; he had seldom ever seen this door closed. . . .

In both cases, he'd hurt someone through selfish neglect. The accident had occurred because he'd neglected to follow doctor's orders; he'd hurt his wife by neglecting to share the simple truth of what he'd done. Hélène Pringle had made a gesture of sacrifice for him, and in return, he'd tried to do something he knew she needed and couldn't easily afford. It hadn't occurred to him that this act of gratitude might be a breach of Cynthia's trust.

It was as if the earth had disappeared beneath him, and he was falling through a space both vast and cold.

Words cannot express the sorrow I feel for having . . .

He put the pen down and stared into Baxter Park.

This was his wife's birthday, the day he was to take her into this very park for a picnic and give her the gift he'd planned so carefully all those months ago. They could not utterly lose this day, it was too important; indeed, it was crucial. One must not lose the day that belongs so especially to a loved one; birthdays must not be tossed about by every ill wind that blows. . . .

He looked at his watch. Four forty-five. He had thirty minutes to throw himself on her mercy and get this show on the road.

"Here y' go," said Avis Packard, wearing an apron imprinted with the green Local logo. Father Tim stood at the front door and held out his arms to receive the picnic basket, packed to the brim. "Tell me what you think, maybe I'll offer this as a reg'lar deal, maybe have a banner printed . . . *First-Class Picnics, Fresh Daily,* what d'you think?"

"I think it'll work," he said, backing away from the door. Avis was a talker and he didn't have all day. . . .

"A nice touch for honeymoons, anniversaries, or just takin' th' ol' buggy for a spin on th' Parkway, pull off to an overlook with your honey, roll out this basket, an' . . ." Avis rubbed his hands together, grinning.

"You're a marketing genius," said Father Tim, closing the door to within an inch of the jamb. "Thanks for the personal delivery. Put it on my tab."

"Th' goat cheese is from France," said Avis, peering through the crack, "not th' valley. I thought for your special occasion you'd want th' French."

"Right. Thanks a million." He closed the door.

Avis knocked.

He opened the door.

"Your champagne . . ."

"What about it?"

"It's from Champagne, France, th' real thing, you said do whatever it takes. An' oh, yeah, happy . . . what is it? Anniversary?"

"Birthday," he said. "Got to run."

"I'm havin' a birthday next week, guess how old—"

"Catch you later," he said, closing the door.

"Cynthia," he implored, standing at the door to her workroom. "I have something important to say."

She opened the door and looked at him, calm, unruffled.

"Will you come out to our garden bench?" he asked.

He gave her his arm. As she took it, his heart leaped with gratitude.

"When I asked you to marry me," he said, "I failed to do all that you deserved."

He stood before her, ashamed and naked in his regret.

"When I asked you to marry me, I went down on one knee. My very soul knew it wasn't enough, but in those days, I didn't heed my soul the way you've taught me to do. I heed it now."

He sank to one knee, then the other, and took her hands in both of his.

"Forgive me, please, for shutting you out. I was going to tell you everything, I vow that I was."

He saw a certain light return to her eyes, the light he had lived by, the light he could not bear to lose.

"Hélène remarked that she'd seen Dooley at the drugstore in Holding, and something in me knew it might be one of the boys. I didn't have the strength to drive down the mountain, and she offered to take me. It was the most urgent thing I'd done in a long time, I had to go, I wanted to see whether it might be . . ." He swallowed down a lump. "We've all waited so long, and prayed so fervently . . ."

"Yes," she said.

"And so we went, and it was a wild goose chase and Hélène's car had very bad brakes, I tell you I was scared out of my wits the way she careened around the curves. . . ."

She looked at him, silent.

"And her gas gauge wasn't working, we might have run out of gas in the middle of nowhere . . . believe me, this was nowhere."

"I believe you," she said quietly.

"There is absolutely nothing between Hélène Pringle and myself except a mutual respect. Having her mother at Hope House is a considerable expense, I daresay she couldn't afford the work on her car—I didn't think twice about asking Harley to do it, she'd gone out of her way for me. I feel certain she helped us find Sammy." He looked at her, imploring. "She's a kind neighbor, nothing more."

"Yes," she said.

"Do you believe that?"

"I have always believed that, and ever shall. I don't mind so much that you went down the mountain with another woman, or even that you footed the bill to have her crankcase greased—"

"Her brakes, it was her *brakes*."

"Brakes, then! What I mind very, very much, indeed, is that you didn't tell me. And such good news that you've found Sammy . . . but nothing, not a word to me. I'm more than a little sensitive, Timothy. Remember that I was married to someone who enjoyed the company of other women, and in the end, he chose them over me."

The leaves of the dogwood by the bench murmured in a light breeze.

"These last weeks haven't been easy, you've been so silent and dark, so unlike yourself. It has frightened me terribly to see you this way, to feel you might be moving away from me, drifting toward some other purpose—"

"Never!" he said, stricken that she would think this.

She patted the bench beside her. "Come and sit, darling."

His legs were beginning to notice what he'd done; they were as numb as tinned mackerel. "Not until I get what I'm down here for."

"And what is that?"

"Your forgiveness."

He was the blind beggar, he was the lame man at the pool called Beautiful, he was the woman with the issue of blood. . . .

She gazed at him fondly, then leaned over and kissed his forehead. "There, dearest. I'm sorry I fretted so. I love you with all my heart."

"I love you back with all of mine."

"Of course I forgive you," she said.

He looked into her eyes and found what he was seeking. "Happy birthday, sweetheart."

She laughed, and stood, and held out her hands to him. He grasped them, noting that he couldn't have gotten up without her help.

They had dined, they had toasted her nativity, they had lolled on the quilt in Baxter Park like rustics.

"Hurry," he said, "before we lose the light. . . ."

He took the box from under the park bench and handed it over; it was wrapped in blue paper and tied with raffia he'd found on her potting table.

She placed it in her lap, beaming.

"I ordered it months ago, it was made just for you." He could hardly wait to see her face. He was nearly bursting with anticipation and relief.

She tore the paper off—his wife was not one to iron and save wrapping paper—and twined the raffia in her hair, laughing. She lifted the lid of the box that enclosed her gift, and found another box. Her initials, inlaid into the warm olive wood in brass, gleamed in the twilight.

She was hushed and silent.

"Look inside," he said, touching her shoulder.

She lifted the hinged lid and saw fat pastel sticks fitted into the box, row upon row—indigo, violet, ultramarine, cobalt, yellow ocher, vermilion, carmine, purple, and all the hues in between.

"Timothy . . ." His chipper and talkative wife could barely speak.

"The box is from Italy. It was made by Roberto's close friend, Marcello, from olive wood. Roberto included something wonderful in this little compartment. Lift the pull."

She lifted the small brass pull and peered inside the Lilliputian box within the box.

"Seven   of   his   grandfather   Leonardo's

pastelli," he said. "Leonardo was the boy who helped paint the angel ceiling at Fernbank when Miss Sadie was a child. Roberto sends these with love."

He found his wife's tears of joy an odd pleasure, rather than the fright they'd been during their courtship. "There," he said, holding her in his arms. "You once said you'd like to try pastels. . . ."

"You are the dearest man I've ever known, there is none dearer than thee."

"Regrettably, I'm vastly handicapped by selfishness. Now, there's a gift I'd like you to give me."

She looked at him and smoothed the hair over his left ear. "Anything, Timothy."

"I want you to go on the literacy tour." There. He'd said it, and his heart did not wrench. In truth, as the words came out of his mouth, a certain peace flooded in.

Uncle Billy Watson stood at the bathroom mirror, raking his bushy gray eyebrows with his wife's pocket comb, and faced the terrible truth.

He couldn't make up a joke if his life depended on it.

Every time he tried, he fell off to sleep and woke up with a blooming crick in his neck. If he couldn't find a joke over at the Grill today, it looked like the preacher was going to have to make his own self laugh.

Puny had brought the girls this morning, as she was working only a half day. He was sitting in the study with his prayer book when Sassy came in and thumped down beside him.

She nestled into the crook of his right arm. "What's wrong, Granpaw?"

"Wrong? Is something wrong?"

"You're sad. Is it 'cause Miss Cynthy's goin' off on a trip around th' world?"

"No, no. Not around the world. Around the country."

"That's th' same thing."

"Yes," he said. "Yes. You're right."

He was at Sweet Stuff soon after it opened, to buy a half dozen fruit tarts. Then he walked to his car and zoomed up the steep hill to the Sprouse place, where, his nerves alarmed by the prospect of what lay ahead, he had a cup of coffee with Bill and Rachel, prayed with Bill, laughed his head off at Sparky's replacement, and felt immeasurably better when he said goodbye an hour later.

The hall was illumined only by a gray light from windows on the street front. Father Tim walked with Buck Leeper to the pool table.

"Mr. Shuford, I believe you have something that belongs to me."

Pink Shuford didn't look up; he knifed himself over the rim of the table and studied a shot. "What's that?"

"Thirty-eight dollars."

"Make me laugh, Preacher. Can I help it your broke-down car couldn't keep up?"

"Right," said Bug Austin from the other end of the table.

"You lost us, which was clearly your intention."

"Law help, Bug, you recall how we had to hold back to keep 'em behind us?"

Buck moved within inches of Pink Shuford and stood, silent, until Pink looked up.

"I don't understand why we have to discuss this particular issue," said Buck. "Father Kavanagh paid you to do something you didn't do. You can give 'im his money back, or you can lead us to Sammy Barlowe. Take your pick."

Buck Leeper was a big man, a very big man. His whole physique spoke of physical power; Father Tim saw that Pink Shuford noted this fact.

"Clyde Barlowe, he's got some bad dogs back in there, ain't he, Bug?"

"Bad dogs don't mess with me," said Buck.

Pink turned away and chalked his cue.

"I can see you and your friend here have all day. . . ." Buck nonchalantly rolled up one shirtsleeve, then the other. "But we don't."

Pink Shuford appeared distinctly pained. "If you ever say I run you out there, I'll say you lied. Where you parked at?"

"Right behind your truck, ready to roll," said Buck. "By the way, you wouldn't want to pull th' same trick again."

"Right," said Pink. "No problem."

Father Tim felt a definite surge of adrenaline. While bad dogs might not mess with Buck, they'd sure messed with him a time or two; at the age of nine, he'd been badly bitten on the ankle. However, with God in control and Buck Leeper second in command, he figured the odds were definitely improved over his last trip down the mountain.

CHAPTER THIRTEEN

Sammy

They followed the truck along a state highway, then veered left onto a gravel lane that ran by the wayside pulpit of Shady Grove Chapel.

Don't wait for six strong men to take you to church.

Father Tim uncapped a bottle of water and peered at the landscape. "This is a different road," he said as they made a hard right.

"It better be the right road," said Buck. "If Shuford don't deliver this time, I'll wrap that tattoo around 'is neck."

Father Tim took a swig of water with one hand and with the other gripped the handle above the passenger door. Pink Shuford was moving, no two ways about it, and Buck was hammering down on the blue truck's rear bumper. In the absence of air-conditioning, the windows of Buck's red pickup were cranked open and they were taking on the dust of Creation.

The gravel track was now running beside a shallow river. Its banks rose steeply from a streambed that was randomly paved with large boulders; gnarled vines knit an intricate web among the trees.

"Spooky," said Buck.

"How far have we come from town?"

"Twelve miles. By th' way, don't worry, I won't wrap Shuford's tattoo around 'is neck." Buck grinned. "But he don't know that I won't."

They saw an abandoned farm building with a collapsed roof, then a derelict house overgrown with honeysuckle; at the end of a rutted drive, a dog sat by an open mailbox, panting. Father Tim could no longer ignore the headache that had started in the pool hall. It throbbed in his temples like a hammer.

The blue truck braked so suddenly that Buck swerved off the road. He leaned out the window and shouted, "What's th' deal?"

Pink Shuford made a U-turn, heading his truck the way they'd come in. Bug sat in the cab as Pink got out, chewing a tooth-pick.

"That's it over yonder." Pink gestured toward a house trailer set back from the opposite bank of the river. Two pairs of pants hung on a clothesline between the house and a nearly empty woodshed. A chicken scratched in the dust.

Father Tim and Buck got out of the truck. "How do we know that's it?" asked Buck.

"You asked me to bring you out here, that's what I done. I ain't got papers t' prove whose house it is."

"Is Barlowe home? I don't see a car."

"They ain't got a car."

"How does the boy get to town from out here?" asked Father Tim.

"Hitches a ride with Lon Burtie, whatever."

"Does he go to school?"

Pink shrugged. "I don't keep up with 'is personal life."

"Does he go to town often?"

"A good bit."

"What does he do at the pool hall?"

"Shoots pool."

"He's underage."

"That ain't my problem."

Buck shaded his eyes and looked across the

river. "I don't see anybody over there," he said to Pink.

"So? Somebody bein' there wadn't in th' deal."

"How does Clyde Barlowe make a livin'?"

"He don't make a livin', he gets a check from th' gov'ment, plus Sammy's a sharp little pool shooter, he wins enough to help out with a few rations, 'is daddy's liquor, whatever. Course, he don't win nothin' offa me." Pink grinned, hanging his thumbs in the loops of his jeans.

"Where's th' bridge?"

"A little ways down an' make a right. It's a hangin' bridge, you cain't take a vehicle on it."

Someone appeared in the doorway of the house. The distance was great enough that Father Tim couldn't distinguish much more than a blue shirt.

"That's Clyde right yonder," said Pink. "We can see him better'n he can see us, he's blind in one eye. Can't hear too good, neither." Pink spit the toothpick on the ground. "That toothpick ain't gittin' it. Any chance of bummin' a cigarette?"

"I quit that foolishness," said Buck.

"So, look, if y'all got what you come after, me an' Bug are headed back t' town." Pink extended his hand, palm up. "I don't reckon you'd like to buy a man an' 'is buddy a cold beer."

"Nope," said Buck, "I wouldn't. Thanks for the ride."

"Seem like f'r runnin' y'all out this way twice, thirty-eight dollars ain't much, you'd of paid more for a cab."

"When you took th' father on a wild goose chase, I figure you were on your way home, anyway, so that's no charge. Today'll be twenty-four miles round trip at thirty-four-point-five cents a mile gover'ment allowance, which amounts to eight dollars an' change. This leaves thirty bucks for an hour of your time. I call that good money."

Pink's laugh was raucous. "You're a pretty cool dude, maybe I'll shoot you a game one of these days. By th' way, Preacher, you don't believe 'at ol' mess about God bein' real, do you?"

"I know He's real."

"How d'you know?"

"I was talking to Him this morning."

Pink took a step back, laughed again, and walked quickly to the blue truck. He got in, gunned the motor, let out the clutch, and scratched off, the tires digging into the red clay of the riverbank.

They watched the truck disappear around a

bend, then turned, silent, and gazed across the river.

"You lookin' for clean jokes or th' other kind?" the truck driver asked Uncle Billy. He lifted the top off his burger and removed the sliced tomato, added pickles and a dollop of fries, shook ketchup over the revision, re-placed the top of the bun, and mashed down the whole caboodle.

"Clean," said Uncle Billy. "That's all th' kind I tell. Besides, they're f'r a preacher."

"They's some preachers as like th' other kind."

"Not this preacher," said the old man.

"I got your wife jokes, your in-law jokes, your schoolteacher jokes . . ." The driver took a generous bite of his burger. "Then there's your preacher jokes, which might be a good idea, under th' circumstances."

Uncle Billy was dumbfounded at his good fortune. All he'd done was climb on a stool at the Grill, strike up a conversation with a trucker making a run to Greensboro, and look here . . .

"Plus I got your doctor jokes, your lawyer jokes, your cabdriver jokes . . ."

"I'll be et f'r a tater," said Uncle Billy. "I

don't hardly know where to start at." He thought the good Lord must somehow be in on this.

"I got a old-maid joke that's pretty funny."

"Hit's clean, is it?"

"Clean," said the driver, hammering down on his burger.

"Wellsir!" Uncle Billy felt light-headed. All these years scrambling around for jokes, and right here at a feller's elbow set the Joke King hisself. This called for a celebration.

He felt carefully in his left pants pocket and located the twenty, then looked up and caught Percy's eye. "I'll take a order of chicken fingers with y'r honey mustard dip!" he called in a loud voice. It had a been a long time since he'd set on a stool and ordered like a man.

"An' give me a Pepsi-Cola with that!"

Hope Winchester jumped as if a shot had been fired.

"Excuse me, Miss Winchester . . ."

She turned quickly and blurted, "Call me Hope!"

"Hope," he said, smiling. He stooped and picked up the book he'd just dropped. "*Gray's Anatomy,* no harm done."

She hadn't meant to say what she'd just said,

she'd planned to say it when they were convers-
ing quietly about poetry or even the nuances of
mail order. "The thirteenth edition before the
revision?" She strained to appear casual.

"Yes. I'll be more careful."

"I find you very careful, Mr. Gaynor, you
handle books as if they were infants."

"Please call me George. No one has called
me Mr. Gaynor since I taught economics."

"George." Saying his given name seemed
alarmingly intimate. She colored deeply and
turned away, reaching for the book lying open
beside the register. Her aim was awkward, and
the book crashed to the floor.

She was humiliated. She had twice dropped
a book in front of him, and of course he had
just dropped a book. . . . Was there some epi-
demic of the nervous system passing through
Mitford?

He walked over and picked it up and handed
it to her. "Thank you," she whispered.

She knew she could no longer bear the
crushing fear and attraction she felt, and the
terrible conflict between the two.

Hessie Mayhew parked in the no parking
zone at Mitford Hospital and took the eleva-

tor to the second-floor nurses' station. Her cargo was destined for Minnie Louder, who had just undergone a kidney operation and turned eighty-four, all in the same day.

She gave the basket a last once-over, critiquing the simple harmony of periwinkle, cinnamon fern, moss from which a tiny red mushroom was growing, and a real bird's nest that she'd plucked from a pot of ivy after the wrens had flown.

"Oh!" said Nurse Kennedy. "Beautiful! You've done it again, Hessie!"

"It could use more color," Hessie said sternly.

"Oh, nonsense, you're too hard on yourself! But of course nothing measures up to the basket you gave Father Tim when he was with us."

"The basket . . ."

"Yes, it was just glorious, and as big as Johnson County!" Nurse Kennedy would never have confessed that Father Tim had given the basket to her, and that she'd planted everything in it around her birdbath.

Hessie thumped the basket down at the nurses' station. "Minnie Louder, Two-oh-six!" she proclaimed in a loud voice.

Then, mad as a wet hen, she turned and hot-footed it to the elevator.

"Don't move," said Father Tim. The pounding of his heart nearly took his breath away. "Look there."

They watched the tall, barefoot boy come along the riverbed, walking on boulders that inlaid the stream.

Sunshine filtered through the canopy of trees overhanging the water; as he stepped into a patch of light, Sammy Barlowe's hair blazed like a coronet of fire.

They had walked to the bridge, crossed over, and come along a path by a pine wood to their left. They paused when they approached the clearing where the Barlowe trailer sat on an underpinning of concrete blocks.

A dog limped toward them with its tail between its legs. Father Tim judged it to be a member of the hound family; he could easily have counted its ribs.

"If that's a bad dog, I'll eat a billy goat," said Buck.

Father Tim reached into his shirt pocket and withdrew the rest of the granola bar his wife had sent on this mission. He unwrapped it and laid it by the root of a white oak at the edge of the yard. "Good fellow!" he said as the dog devoured it and sniffed for crumbs.

"Are you ready?" asked Buck.

"Ready. And praying there won't be any guns in this encounter." He was also praying that his headache would ease off. It was the worst he could remember.

"A man with a dog like that prob'ly don't keep a gun."

"I'd stop right there if I was you."

Both men jumped, startled by the voice from the shadow of the woods. Peering into the pine grove, they saw the boy standing by a large outcropping of rock.

"We're looking for Sammy Barlowe," Buck said.

"You ain't g-goin' t' find 'im. He's done m-moved off t' Statesville an' ain't comin' back."

Father Tim looked into the face of a younger Dooley Barlowe, and knew he must make an effort to keep his voice calm. "But you're Sammy, of course."

"No, I ain't! An' you better git out of here right now, this is p-private property."

The dog sniffed Father Tim's pant legs. "We've come to talk with you about your brothers and little sister."

Sammy uttered Dooley's once-favorite four-letter word. "I ain't got no brothers an' sisters."

Had Pink led them on another wild goose chase? No. This was Dooley Barlowe's blood kin, freckles and all; nothing in him doubted it.

"Jessie doesn't remember you," said Buck, "but Poo does, and Dooley. They really want to see you."

"I'm goin' t' b-bash y'r heads in if you don't git on." Sammy picked up a stick and brandished it.

"You remember Dooley," said Father Tim. "He took care of you that time you were so sick with the flu, he gave you his best jacket to wear to school and put a dollar in the pocket. You remember." He was piecing together fragments of stories Dooley had told him. They didn't amount to much, but it was the best he could do.

He walked closer to the patch of woods, to the narrow path that led into the cool, chiaroscuro shade. Even from this distance, he saw the anger and fear in the boy's eyes; he thought he also saw something else—a kind of hope or longing. "And Dooley was saying how—"

"Come another step an' you'll fall in a nest of rattlers big as y'r arm!"

"Right," said Buck, "and Jessie was sayin'

how if she could see her brother, Sammy, she'd give him all the money she's saved and make him scrambled eggs every mornin'. Jessie makes fine scrambled eggs."

"I've got a shotgun hid under this rock. I'll blow y'r brains out if you don't git back where you c-come from."

"She likes to crumble up livermush in her scrambled eggs," said Buck, "the same as your granddaddy Russell Jacks likes to do."

"We've got pictures to show you," said Father Tim, reaching into his jacket pocket. Sammy's confusion was visible; he appeared ready to turn and run. Instead, he stood his ground as if frozen.

"Sometimes," said Buck, "Jessie sets a place at the table for you. She turned ten years old last week."

They were walking into the woods now, toward the rock, toward the boy with the blanched and stricken face.

Without looking at each other or exchanging a word, the two men knew they had to show Sammy these pictures; it was crucial. Father Tim wondered if there might really be a shotgun, but something in him doubted it. He felt a kind of eagerness about walking into the wood; it had to be done. He smiled at Sammy, though it was Dooley he saw in this thin boy with the scar on his cheek and the lank red hair pulled into a ponytail.

He stood aside to let Buck walk ahead of him on the narrow path, and reminded himself to keep talking. "Dooley dreams about you, Sammy. He saved his first bicycle for you. . . ."

Sammy didn't move; he was listening now. He was trying not to, Father Tim observed, but he was listening, waiting, letting them come in. Buck drew the pictures from his pocket. Father Tim did the same. *Be with us, Lord, send Your Holy Spirit. . . .*

As they approached the rock, he looked directly into Sammy's eyes. The joy this gave him was indescribable; he wanted to throw his arms around the boy and shout, but restrained any show of feeling. They were walking on eggs. *Stay calm, stay cool.* He laid the pictures on the rock, silent; Buck followed suit, fanning the snapshots like a hand of cards. They had run the bases; they were nearly home.

"That's Poo, he's eleven," said Buck, keeping his voice casual. "His school picture, he made an A in geography, I never even knew where Idaho was when I was in school. This is him with his new bat, he can hit a softball all th' way to Tennessee. . . . An' this is him on his bike. . . ."

Buck breathed deeply, as if he'd held his breath for a long time. "And this is Jessie . . . her last school picture . . . she's ten."

Father Tim felt the hard knot in his throat; this was a type of miracle and he was standing in the midst of it. He pointed to a picture of Dooley and Cynthia sitting on the front steps of the yellow house. "This is Dooley," he said, "he's nineteen."

Father Tim watched Sammy Barlowe resist the depth and power of his feelings. Sammy was doing what Dooley had always done, hardening his face into a mask, a stone; only his eyes betrayed the depth of his longing to examine the images spread before him.

Sammy stepped back from the rock. "You'uns better git out of here. When my p-paw sees you hangin' around, you'll be skinned."

Buck grinned. "It'd take a while to skin me. He prob'ly don't have time to complete th' job."

Father Tim realized his adrenaline had been pumping hard all morning; exhaustion was sweeping through him in a wave. His vision suddenly blurred, then cleared. In that moment, the exhaustion vanished, taking his headache with it.

"Ahh," he said aloud, amazed and grateful. The place where they stood became abruptly vivid; he hadn't looked about him until now. It was wondrously cool in this light-and-shade-dappled copse; indeed, they were standing in a garden.

"Lady slipper!" said Father Tim. "And by heaven, look there! Jack-in-the-pulpit." Though the blossom had gone, he recognized the leaves.

"Stay on th' path!" commanded the boy. "W-watch where you're steppin'."

"Of course. I'm sorry. And there's trillium, a whole grove! Is the bloom white or pink?"

Sammy hesitated a long moment. "W-w-white," he said.

Father Tim heard water rushing along the nearby riverbed, the first time he'd heard it since they crossed the bridge "These lovely things surely didn't grow here in the same patch?"

"I dug some in th' woods over yonder."

In a space hardly bigger than Cynthia's work-room, and carpeted with black loam and leaf mold, was a remarkable variety of wild plants— tall ferns with furred fiddleheads, a colony of silvery Dutchman's-pipe that lit the woods floor like small candles, a grove of mayapple. . . .

Father Tim squatted down and peered beneath the leaves of a plant where rows of onyx berries hung like necklaces.

"Solomon's seal?" he asked, looking up at Sammy.

"It's common," said Sammy. "Not diff'rent like some of th' others, but it g-grows good and gives cover to th' jacks."

"And these pink lady slippers," said Father Tim. "I've never seen so many in one place."

"They was already growin' in here, in a bunch, it give me th' idea to"—Sammy glanced around—"d-do this."

"Is that a yellow slipper over there?"

"Yeah, they's five kinds of slipper. This is th' only yeller I ever found. They's a yeller an' white, too, but Lon Burtie says it don't grow excep' out West som'ers."

"What a blessing to see all this," said Father Tim, smiling up at the boy. "A blessing." Sammy's grandfather, Russell Jacks, had been the finest gardener Lord's Chapel had ever hired. . . ."I believe the slipper is in the orchid family." He was feeling like a new man, light of spirit, the headache vanished.

"Lon Burtie was in a jungle in Nam where he seen plenty of orchids. He says they's two million kinds of orchids."

"And that purplish leaf? Let's see, I can't think of the name . . ."

"Galax. I didn't dig that, it was already g-growin' over there, but I've got t' take s-some of it out, it's forceful."

Father Tim squatted for a moment more, then stood, his knees creaking like rusted gates. Something had just happened in here, quite a lot had happened. . . .

"This is a private place, isn't it, Sammy?"

The boy lowered his eyes and shrugged.

"Thanks for letting us come in."

"Yeah," said Buck, clearing his throat. "Thanks."

"Let me say that last 'un back t' make sure I learned it right."

"Take your time," said the trucker, who had just ordered apple pie à la mode. "This is a easy run, nothin' perishable like last week when I was haulin' cantaloupes to Pennsylvania."

Uncle Billy cleared his throat. "Woman went to th' new doc, don't you know, he was s' young he was hardly a-shavin'. Wellsir, she was in there a couple of minutes when all at once't she busted out a-hollerin' an' run down th' hall."

Uncle Billy paused.

"You got it," said the trucker. "Keep goin'."

"Wellsir, a doc that was a good bit older

took off after 'er, said, 'What's th' problem?' an' she told 'im. Th' ol' doc went back to th' young doc, said, 'What's th' dadjing matter with you? Miz Perry is sixty-five a-goin' on sixty-six with four growed chil'ren and seven grans—an' you told 'er she was a-goin' t' have a *young 'un?*"

"New doc grinned, don't you know, said, 'Cured 'er hiccups, didn't it?' "

Uncle Billy knew when a joke hadn't gone over, and this one hadn't gone over—not even with the person he'd gotten it from in the first place.

The trucker gazed thoughtfully at his reflection in the chrome napkin dispenser. "Seem like it was funny when I heard it th' first time, but now it might be what you call . . ." He shrugged.

"Flat," said Uncle Billy, feeling the same way himself.

"I'd advise you to axe it," said the trucker, digging into his apple pie. "Start off with your two guys on a bench, slide in with your cab-driver joke, and land you a one-two punch with th' ol' maids."

Uncle Billy wished he had some kind of guarantee this particular lineup would work.

CHAPTER FOURTEEN

Waiting for Wings

As families around Mitford waked and stirred, more than a few wondered what last night's violent storm might have done to the valley corn crop. Second only in importance to the town's Independence Day parade was the season's first delivery of Silver Queen corn, expected to arrive any moment at The Local.

After hearing a weather bulletin, Neese Simmons and his wife and four children had picked corn until two o'clock in the morning before the storm broke over the valley at three a.m. Working by torch and flashlight, they loaded their hasty harvest in the farm truck and backed it into the barn in the nick of time. From three until seven, the storm dumped five inches of precipitation into the valley below Mitford, washing out large crops of potatoes, cantaloupes, and strawberries, all destined for sale at The Local. This devastation caused the Simmons family to worry whether their prayers for rain had been too fervent. Neese told his wife, Vada, that he would make a point of discussing it with their preacher to see whether any of the blame for crop loss might, in fact, lie squarely on the shoulders of the Simmonses.

"Hush an' go to sleep," she said, patting his hand. "Th' Lord knows what He's doin'."

"Will you ride up with me t'morrow?" he asked.

"If I'm not too give out," she said.

On the way to the airport, Father Tim passed Neese and Vada Simmons driving into Mitford as he and Cynthia drove out. Both parties threw up a hand in greeting.

"There's our corn," said Father Tim. It would be a big day in Mitford. By one o'clock, every ear would be emptied from the bins on Main Street, and by six o'clock, the lot of it would be boiling on village stoves, his own included.

But his wife wouldn't be here to enjoy it with him. For two weeks, she would be touring the world—and he was the one who'd encouraged her to do it.

The truth was, she needed a chance to relish

the fruits of her labors, to see the rapt faces of the children for whom she'd written and painted with such passion for so many years. And there was a further truth, one they hadn't talked about, one that he'd hidden in his heart so carefully he hardly knew it himself—he needed time.

Time for what? To somehow get his act together, to work on his essays, and pitch in with George and Harley to build bookcases in the hallway and maybe a cabinet for her illustrations. Just a little time, that's all he needed, and he would once again be himself.

For weeks on end, he'd been a swimmer sinking to the pond bottom, with his brave wife struggling to pull him ashore. He'd been a heaviness to her, though she'd never said it; indeed, she may not even have known it. But he'd known it, for he'd seen it in her face and heard it in her voice. If he were half the man he'd like to be, they'd be driving to the airport on their way to Venice or Tuscany, or one of those other places she might love to go . . . even their honeymoon cottage in Maine, for heaven's sake. But he was not that man, and there was no use thinking he would one day become that man. He was the worst bump on a log ever given breath.

He swallowed until the knot in his throat disappeared. "I'm not going to cry," he said, taking her hand.

The tears were streaming down her cheeks, though they were scarcely beyond the town limits.

"Thank you, dearest. I'm so sorry I'll miss your sermons."

"Rats in a poke!" he said, quoting one of her favorite epithets. "You've heard me preach a hundred times and I hope you'll hear me preach a hundred more. I'll save you my notes . . . if I use any."

She looked at him, smiling. "Promise me something."

"Anything," he said.

"Don't put butter on your corn."

No butter on his corn!

"Use olive oil, it's better for your health."

"No rest for th' wicked," he sighed.

She squeezed his hand and laughed through the tears. "An' th' righteous don't need none!"

His house was not a tomb nor a crypt, after all. The very light may have gone from it, but Puny Bradshaw Guthrie, his appointed guardian and watchdog, was doing her mightiest to make it shine. Dooley was coming to lunch and they were having a feast fit for royals—nay, for the heavenly hosts.

"Alleluia!" he declared to Puny, who wiped her face with her apron as she stood at the stove. Not even the air-conditioning could spare them from the furnace produced by roiling steam, sizzling grease, and the divine tumult of preparation in general.

Their house help, a.k.a. his nonlegally adopted daughter, was frying chicken, making potato salad with scallions, bacon, and sour cream, cooking fresh cranberries with shavings of ginger root and orange peel, simmering a pot of creamed corn, deviling eggs with homemade mayonnaise, and rolling out biscuits on the countertop. A pitcher of sweet tea stood at the ready, covered with one end of a tea towel; his grandmother's heavy glass pitcher, filled with unsweetened tea, was covered by the other end. A three-layer coconut cake, set square in the center of the kitchen island, reigned over the room next to a small vase of early, apple-green hydrangea blossoms.

Excited as a child, he went to the downstairs powder room and tested his sugar.

The banquet being prepared for Dooley Barlowe had none of the criminal restrictions required by the diabetic. Thus, lunch would be filled with land mines that he must circumnavigate as best he could. Even so, a man could die with happiness on a day like this and have nothing at all to regret.

He'd discussed it in detail with Cynthia, and they'd agreed: Go straight to the point—but only after the cake.

"So, what do you think?"

"Good!" said Dooley, looking up and grinning. "Really good. The icing's great."

"Tell Puny."

"Yes, sir, I will."

"Remember when you first came to bunk with me, and Puny dunked you in the tub?"

Dooley grinned. "I remember."

"She had to chase you around the house a time or two."

"I chased her back."

Father Tim laughed, aware that simply watching Dooley eat cake today would be among his happiest memories.

Dooley licked the icing off his fork. "I'd like to stay with you and Cynthia next summer."

Something like joy surged in him. "We'd love nothing better, but be warned—it's pretty dull around here."

"That's OK."

It seemed eons since Dooley had lived in their house, clattered up and down the stairs, sat at their table. They were silent for a moment. "How are things at Meadowgate? Still wanting to be a vet?"

"Yes, sir!" The acclamation was immediate and fervent. "We did a uterine torsion procedure on a llama yesterday."

"A llama!"

"There's a llama farm in Wilson Creek."

"What's a uterine torsion procedure?"

"Sometimes a llama, even a cow, will have a twisted, or torsed, uterus. That means the fetus can't pass through the birth canal. Doc Owen says most fetuses are in the left horn of the uterus—"

"Left horn?"

"The lamoid uterus has two horns. Doc Owen says most u.t.'s are twisted in a clockwise direction, so the left horn flips over the right horn. It's really hard on the llama, and we had to work fast, so Doc Owen decided to do a plank in the flank."

"A what?"

"We used a two-by-five board, put it into the flank of the llama, and Doc Owen told me to kneel on the plank, right over the flank area. Then we used ropes looped around the front and hind legs and rolled her over. See, what we wanted to do is hold the fetus and uterus in place with the plank and roll her to kind of catch up to the uterus. That solved the whole thing."

"It did?"

"Yes, sir. Her cria is really beautiful."

He was stunned by this piece of completely incomprehensible information. Dooley Barlowe must be a genius.

"You're a genius!" he said, gushing, proud, moved.

"No, I ain't, I mean aren't." Dooley turned red. "Doc Owen is."

He didn't know when such seeming nonsense had made him so happy. "I'm so proud of you I could bust!"

Dooley studied the geranium in a pot on the table.

"So how's the social life out there in the sticks?"

He loved to see his boy grin from ear to ear.

"Not bad, I take it."

"No, sir."

"Aha."

"I'm going out with Reba Sanders."

"Really? Who is Reba Sanders?"

"A girl."

"Glad to hear it."

"Her dad's a farmer, they have four hundred head of cattle. Angus crossed with Hereford. Her mom teaches fifth grade."

Maybe he should tell Dooley that the Harpers were coming home in a couple of days—wouldn't he like to know how Lace liked the Oregon Trail? Probably not.

Dooley hammered down on the remainder of his cake. "She's cool."

"Reba?"

"Yes, sir. The Jeep needs some work. Hal thinks it's the carburetor."

"After lunch, we'll run over to the station and let Harley take a look. Why don't you take a look with him? It's good to know what's going on with your vehicle." He was a fine one to talk; he'd never peered under a car hood in his life, except to scratch his head momentarily before slamming the thing down again.

His heart was full, and so was the boy's. He sensed the quiet happiness between them; yet he was about to change all that. Surely it couldn't hurt to postpone his announcement a few minutes— let the boy's meal digest, for heaven's sake.

"So. Tell me more about Reba."

"Tall."

Lace was tall, if he was looking for tall.

Dooley thought a moment. "Her hair's kind of brown—or maybe blond."

"Good. Anything else?"

"Umm. I can't think of anything."

Getting quality information out of Dooley Barlowe was right up there with squeezing blood from a turnip.

"What are her interests?"

"Motorcycles."

"Motorcycles." What could he possibly say to that? He pushed ahead. "In . . . what *way,* exactly, is she interested in motorcycles?"

"She rebuilds sport bikes to make money for college next year. Right now she's working on a Suzuki GSXR 1100. When she gets through, it'll do a hundred and sixty, just like it came out of the crate." Dooley looked at his empty cake plate. "Man! I'm killed!"

"I'm only half killed, but we'd both better hug Puny's neck."

Dooley cackled. "I ain't huggin' her neck."

"I like it when you say *ain't.*"

"I can't believe you said that. You used to hate it when I said ain't."

"I know. I only like it because you never say it anymore."

"Let's go see Harley, we can take ol' Barnabas."

His stomach was literally churning over what he'd just learned about Reba Sanders. While he had dreaded delivering a blow to Dooley, Dooley had delivered one to him. *A hundred and sixty miles an hour?* Nonetheless, he couldn't put it off any longer.

"I have something to tell you, son. We found Sammy."

Dooley's fork clattered to the table and bounced to the floor.

"He's living with your father, he's blind in one eye and has lost part of his hearing." Why had he said that, what did it have to do with anything? Perhaps it would make Clyde Barlowe seem less threatening.

"Who's blind?" Dooley asked, hoarse.

"Your father."

"He's not my father!" Dooley shouted.

He would not tack to the left or the right, he would sail directly into the storm. "They're living about twelve miles east of Holding. Buck and I have seen Sammy and talked with him. He's fine, he looks a lot like you, he wants to see his brothers and little sister." Sammy hadn't said that, but Father Tim had read it clearly in his eyes; thus it wasn't a lie. "I thought we could talk about it, work out how you'd like to handle it."

Dooley turned from the table and faced the stove, stricken.

The boy's conflicts would have to do primarily with his father, but Father Tim remembered a lesser issue: Dooley had said he would find Sammy and Kenny, he would do something that would be miraculous, magical. Instead, it had been done for him. He wished Dooley could have found his brother, but it had been ordained otherwise—Sammy had been found by a Frenchwoman who, as an infant, had been deserted by her own father.

The very thought made him pace the study like something caged. He was itching to preach a sermon, but he knew better.

At six-thirty, he called Meadowgate Farm and was relieved that Dooley answered.

"Hey, buddy."

"Hey back."

"Are you wearing a helmet?"

"Right now?"

"When you ride a motorcycle."

"Yeah."

"Every time, no excuses?" He knew country roads, and the lure of breaking a few rules.

"Yes, sir," Dooley said over a burst of background laughter.

"Good. I'm counting on it." He paused to let that pronouncement sink in.

"Don't worry," said Dooley.

Music to his ears. "Is Meadowgate having a party?" he asked, trying to sound nonchalant.

"Reba came over for supper, we're having spaghetti. Miz Owen says tell you thanks for what you sent. Got to go."

I give him into Your hands, Lord, he prayed as

he hung up. *Send Your angels with him, to keep him from every harm.* He pondered a moment. *And bless him, please, with wisdom and discretion in all that he does, through Christ our Lord, Amen.*

While he was at it, he figured he'd better pray for Reba Sanders, too.

At seven o'clock, he was rustling up a partial reprise of lunch, and found he wasn't even remotely tempted by the sweetened tea; thank heaven he'd learned a little sense in this life. For safety's sake, he'd packed Dooley off to Meadowgate with the rest of the cake.

"Preacher?"

Startled, he turned around from the kitchen island to see Uncle Billy peering through the screen door. "Are you'un's havin' y'r supper?"

"Getting ready to, Uncle Billy. Come in here and have it with me."

"Don't mind if I do," said the old man.

Father Tim was shocked to see his friend—some inner illumination had gone from him, like sap tapped from a tree. "How did you get way down here?"

"Harley seen me a-comin' down th' street an' picked me up. I like t' never climbed in 'is truck, hit seemed tall as th' Wesley bank buildin'. I'd as soon walked."

"You're out of breath, my friend. I'll carry you home."

"I'd be beholden."

"How are you?"

"I ain't been too good."

Father Tim helped the old man to the island.

"Can you swing up here on this stool?"

"Let me git ahold of you." Uncle Billy set his foot on a rung, then grabbed Father Tim's shoulder with one hand and pushed on his cane with the other. "Aye, law!" he exclaimed as he hauled himself up and thumped onto the stool. He couldn't help but wonder why an important man like the preacher didn't have a table and chairs like the rest of Creation.

"Glad to see you, Uncle Billy. I hope you don't object to leftovers."

"Nossir, I like leftovers, as we don't usually have none. A man stays s' hungry on Rose's provisions, they ain't nothin' t' leave over, don't you know."

Father Tim ducked to the refrigerator and pulled out the platter of chicken and the bowls of potato salad and cranberry sauce, and displayed them proudly. "And there's fresh corn to boot. Puny cut it off the cob and creamed it, it's sweet as sugar. Let me heat you a bowlful."

"That'd be good," said the old man. "I hate t' trouble you."

"No trouble at all!" In truth, he was thrilled to do something for somebody after weeks of being as useless as moss on a stump.

He poured a hearty portion of corn into a bowl, assembled a few leftover biscuits, and zapped the whole caboodle in the microwave. He'd gotten to be a pro at microwaving; it was a liberation he never dreamed he'd enjoy.

As he served two plates and got out the flatware, he eyed the old man from the corner of his eye. Something was wrong. "Uncle Billy, you're not your old self. I'm going to ask a blessing on our supper, then I'd like you to tell me what's what."

Uncle Billy clasped his hands under his chin and bowed his head. His left hand was doing its best to keep his right hand from trembling.

"Father, thank You for sending this dear friend to our table, it's an honor to have his company. Lord, we ask You for Bill Watson's strength: strength of spirit, strength of mind, strength of purpose, strength of body. May You shower him with Your mighty, yet tender grace, and give him hope and health all the days of his long and obedient life. We pray You'd heap yet another blessing on Puny for preparing what You've faithfully provided, and ask, also, that You make us ever mindful of the needs of others. In Jesus' name, Amen."

"A–men!"

He set the bowl of corn and a plate of hot biscuits in front of his guest. "Piping hot! Have at it, Uncle Billy, and here's the butter."

"Yessir, I will, an' I hope they ain't too much salt in y'r corn, doc said stay offa salt."

"You're in good hands. We don't use much salt around here."

"When we're done, I've got a joke drummed up f'r you."

"Great!" he said. *"Great!"* And he'd laugh if it killed him.

Uncle Billy picked at his supper; then, with what Father Tim's mother had called "a coming appetite," he worked up momentum and laid his bowl and plate thoroughly bare.

The old man grinned. "I've eat 'til I'm about t' bust!"

"And I'm bustin' to hear your joke."

"They's three in all. Hit's took a good bit of time t' collect th' dadjing things."

"I understand. Sermons can come hard, too."

"Are you glad you ain't a-preachin' steady n'more?"

"I'll be preaching next Sunday—right down the street. And the Sunday following, as well. I hope you and Miss Rose will be there."

"If we're able."

"Tell me how you're feeling. What does Hoppy say?"

"One of them pills he give me made me swimmy-headed, so I ain't a-takin' 'em n'more."

"I don't know who's the worse patient, you or me."

"He says my heart ain't a-pumpin' right, makes me weak as pond water."

"You can't stop taking your medication, Uncle Billy, this is serious business." He heard the sternness in his voice. "Maybe it's time for you and Miss Rose to move to Hope House." He knew the reaction he'd get, but it wouldn't hurt to bring it up again.

"Nossir, we ain't a-goin' up there, you couldn't drag Rose out of 'er brother's place with a team of mules. What with m' arthur a-botherin' me an' m' heart a-givin' out, I'd as soon go on home to th' Lord if it won't f'r leavin' Rose."

Father Tim sighed.

"They's not a soul a-livin' that'd put up with 'er, don't you know."

He would call Dr. Wilson tomorrow and find out the whole story. Right now they'd better cheer up before both their chins were dragging on the floor.

"How's your garden coming along?"

"Hit ain't. They didn't nothin' come up from them seeds Dora give me. I got one little sprout is all, an' a rabbit eat that."

"Let's go sit in the study, Uncle Billy, I'll help you down."

With Father Tim's assistance, the old man aimed his feet at the floor and slid from the stool. "By johnny!" he exclaimed, as the mission was accomplished.

"Wellsir . . .," said Uncle Billy. The first joke had gone over better than he expected. Now came the preacher joke, which he reckoned had a fair chance due to the subject matter. Standing by the coffee table, which seemed a central location, he took a deep breath and leaned on his three-pronged cane.

"A preacher died, don't you know, an' was a-waitin' in line at th' Pearly Gates. Ahead of 'im is a feller in blue jeans, a leather jacket, an' a tattoo on 'is arm. Saint Pete says to th' feller with th' tattoo, says, 'Who are you, so I'll know whether t' let you in th' Kingdom of Heaven?'

"Feller says, 'I'm Tom Such an' Such, I drove a taxicab in New York City.'

"Saint Pete looks at th' list, says, 'Take this silk robe an' gold staff an' enter th' Kingdom of Heaven!' Then he hollers, 'Next!'

"Th' preacher steps up, sticks out 'is chest, says, 'I'm th' Rev'rend Jimmy Lee Tapscott, pastor of First Baptist Church f'r forty-three years.'

"Saint Pete looks at 'is list, don't you know, says, 'Take this flour-sack robe an' hick'ry stick an' enter th' Kingdom of Heaven.'

"Preacher says, 'Wait a dadjing minute! That man was a taxicab driver an' he gits a silk robe an' a gold staff?'

"Saint Pete says, 'When you preached, people slept. When he drove, people prayed.'"

Father Tim threw back his head and hooted with laughter. Then he clapped his hands and slapped his leg a few times, still laughing. Uncle Billy had never seen such carrying on. Why didn't the preacher save something back for the last joke?

"Hold on!" he said. "I got another'n t' go."

"Right," said Father Tim. "That was a keeper."

"You can use that'n in church, won't cost you a red cent."

Uncle Billy felt his heart pumping, which was, in his opinion, a good sign. He straightened up a moment and rested his back, then leaned again on his cane as if hunkering into a strong wind. This was the big one and he wanted it to go as slick as grease.

"Wellsir, three ol' sisters was a-livin' together, don't you know. Th' least 'un was eighty-two, th' middle 'un was ninety-some, an' th' oldest 'un was way on up in age. One day th' oldest 'un run a tub of water. She put one foot in th' water, started a-thinkin', hollered downstairs to 'er sisters, said, 'Am I a-gittin' *in* th' tub or *out* of th' tub?'

"Th' middle sister, she started up th' stairs t' he'p out, don't you know, then thought a minute. Yelled to 'er baby sister, said, 'Was I a-goin' *up* th' stairs or a-comin' *down*?'

"Th' baby sister, she was settin' in th' kitchen havin' a cup of coffee, said, 'Guess I'll have t' go up yonder an' he'p out . . . boys, I hope I never git that forgetful, knock on wood!'

"Went t' knockin' on th' table, don't you know, then jumped up an' hollered, 'I'll be there soon as I see who's at th' door!' "

Uncle Billy couldn't help but grin at the preacher, who was not only laughing, but wiping his eyes into the bargain. The old man took it to be his proudest moment. He'd had laughs before; he reckoned anybody could get a laugh now and again if he worked hard enough, but crying. . . . that was another deal, it was what every joke teller hoped for. His heart was hammering and his knees were weak. He sat down, hard, in the preacher's leather chair and heard something he hadn't heard in a good while—

It was the sound of his own self laughing.

After Father Tim dropped his friend at the town museum and walked him to the door, he drove home and parked in the garage. As he switched off the engine, the exhaustion switched on. It came suddenly, in a wave that left him feeble and shaken. But for Barnabas needing a walk, he would have sat in the car 'til Kingdom come. Would this snare to his soul never end?

He would force himself to walk his good dog to the monument. It was a known fact that both dogs and diabetics required exercise.

Barnabas was slower this evening than his master, which was something Father Tim didn't enjoy noting. His dog wouldn't be with him forever; a man might mourn the loss of four or five best friends in a lifetime—but he mustn't think of that now.

The fireflies were coming out as they walked through town. At the monument he stood transfixed in the grassy circle and watched the minuscule lights dancing above the hedge. One briefly illumined the ear of his dog, others sparkled among the branches of trees across the

street. He should go home and find a Mason jar
and punch holes in the lid and catch a handful
and turn the lights out in his room and, with
Barnabas lying on the foot of the bed, watch
them flicker and gleam like stars. Later, of
course, he would open the window and let
them go, just as he'd done as a boy. . . .

He was leaving the circle through the opening in the hedge when a car approached. It was
Edith Mallory's black Lincoln Town Car, a
new model that gleamed and glittered under
the light of the street lamps. Driving slowly, it
cruised by the monument and turned right
onto Lilac Road.

Barnabas growled, low in his throat. When
Father Tim reached down to pat his head, he felt
the hair bristling on the back of his dog's neck.

At nine o'clock, he sat in his darkened bedroom, listening to Barnabas snore.

He wondered whether he should have taken
the job at the Children's Hospital. Several years
after retirement, he was still trying to figure out
what God wanted of him. How much more
could he, much less God Almighty, stand of his
boundless and incessant navel-gazing? Was this a
blasted midlife crisis, delayed by thirty years?

Drifting toward some other purpose, Cynthia had said. What other purpose? He seemed to have no purpose at all, much less an other purpose. With the Children's Hospital, he'd be able to work his own hours, contact the existing donors, nearly all of whom he liked immensely, and build a list of new contacts— there were a number of people he'd never contacted in the western diocese. . . .

The last time he'd spoken with John Brewster, the position hadn't been filled. What harm could it do to call John and inquire about the lay of the land?

But did he really, in the deepest part of his spirit, want the job? Or was he trying to fill time with his own agenda for good works, unwilling to wait on the Lord's agenda?

He remembered a story, heard from the Wesley pulpit. A young boy found a cocoon, and seeing how hard the insect struggled inside, split the cocoon with his camp knife, thinking to let it escape. Instead, the nascent butterfly died. A butterfly collector told him that it's the struggle within the cocoon that gives strength to the butterfly and enables its wings to grow and develop. Only then can it emerge and go free.

Was he trapped in this confused and unspeakable state, waiting for his wings?

"Lord," he prayed aloud, "I'd like to have this position if it be Your will."

He would brush his teeth and call John.

But the position was filled.

"And in the nick of time!" said the hospital administrator.

What could he say? His prayer had been answered.

"We just discovered that the foundation of the entire building needs to be underpinned. When this old place was built in 1901, they just started laying brick on grade. What with the runoff from the mountain behind us, the brick is deteriorating and the foundation's bowed, which explains the cracks in the interior plaster."

"Not good."

"When I saw the estimate, I nearly ran down the hall and jumped in a bed."

"What are we talking about here?" asked Father Tim.

"Close to three-quarters of a million."

"You've got a good man coming in?"

"A good woman. I was going to call and tell you the news in a day or two. She's perfect for the job, Tim, absolutely perfect, she's the one we've been praying for."

When he hung up, he felt glad for John, and for the hospital he'd supported for more than twenty years. Yet he couldn't help but remember that John had once called him the absolutely perfect person for the job. . . .

He sat in the wing chair, sensing again that God had something for him, some wisdom that would flash upon his heart like lightning and illumine the dark. He read in the Psalms, then felt inclined toward the Gospel of John. Every truth was there, what more could a man possibly wish for or want? But he wasn't finding the yet-unknown truth meant profoundly for him, the truth he'd recognize instantly when at last it was revealed.

He placed the book on the table and closed his eyes and prayed the prayer that never failed. Whether or not he found the longed-for wisdom, whether or not he redeemed his joy, this prayer would cover him in sickness and in health, in sorrow and in celebration, in success and, yes, even in utter failure.

His wife was in Boston; tomorrow, the contingent would debark for Chicago, then head for points west, including Los Angeles. The other authors had arrived safely, they'd just finished dinner, and Miniver Tarleton was everything Cynthia had hoped the legendary, eighty-something author/illustrator/role model might be. His wife was clearly exuberant, and he wouldn't begrudge her a moment of this sojourn.

He couldn't, however, resist tossing in a nagging fear, if only to hear her denounce it. "I hope," he said, "you won't fall too hard for all this big-city glamour."

"Timothy! I could never live in a city, big *or* small! You know that, darling."

"I know that," he said, soothed.

"In fact, I think we should take Hal and Marge up on their farm-sitting offer next year."

"Would you really like that?"

"I'd love it!"

"Speaking of next year, Dooley says he wants to spend the summer with us."

"Perfect!" she said. "At Meadowgate, we could all be together in a place he loves."

"You could write a book about Violet going to the country."

"I already wrote that book, dearest. *Ages* ago! Besides, I'm not going to write any book at all next year!"

Whenever his wife said she wasn't going to

write a book, that was when a book started pouring forth.

"I'll be a farm wife, instead. Go barefoot, pick meadow flowers, gather eggs, churn butter . . ." She paused, thinking. "Drive a tractor!"

"Cynthia, Cynthia . . ."

"Life is short, Timothy!"

"Driving a tractor could make it shorter still," he said, being the family worrywart.

"What does Dooley want to do about Sammy?"

"He's thinking about it."

"He'll make the right decision."

"Yes," he said. "Pauline doesn't want to make a move 'til Dooley settles it in his own heart. Poo and Jessie don't know yet."

"I'm praying, dearest, and I believe all will be well and very well. Now off to bed with both of us. Check your sugar, watch your diet, get some rest, mind Puny, and don't forget your eye doctor's appointment."

"Consider it done," he said. "May His angels attend you every step of the way."

"Timothy . . ."

"Yes?"

Happy sigh. "You're the love of my life."

"Same back!" he exclaimed. "By the way,

have you heard the one about the three old sisters who . . ."

"Timothy? I apologize for the lateness of the hour—"

Edith Mallory.

Instinctively, he flung the handset across the room and heard it crash against the wall and clatter to the floor.

Long before Puny arrived, he was up and about, having a single cup of coffee, then, on his doctor's advice, switching over to herb tea. Herb tea! He never thought he'd live to see the day.

"Right," Hoppy had said, "and if you don't shape up, you won't live to see the day."

"Very funny."

"Laughter doeth good like a medicine, pal."

He shook his head as he poured boiling water over the tea bag. Using a white jacket and stethoscope as free license, Hoppy Harper was getting away with murder.

He was setting the kettle on the stove when the phone rang. Hoping it was Cynthia, he answered at once.

"Timothy, if you hang up, you'll completely miss the wonderful idea I've had, something that should be very close to your heart."

He tried to speak, but couldn't.

"Please don't stress yourself so when I ring, I'm only trying to do something worthwhile for the community. Wasn't it you who once pestered me about that very thing? Hmmm?"

"Don't call here again," he said, trying to keep his voice even.

"Not ever, ever again?"

He heard the sharp intake of breath as she inhaled smoke from her brown cigarette. "Precisely!" he said, slamming the phone onto the hook.

He stood at the kitchen island and took a deep breath. Then another. In only moments, he was feeling calm again, even confident; he had at last taken control.

Yet he noted that his hand trembled as he lifted the mug.

"Please!" he told Puny, who was washing yellow squash at the sink. "Take the day off! I'm fine, you don't have to be my nursemaid."

"I'm not takin' th' day off."

"Puny, why do you have such trouble obeying orders from your employer?"

"When it comes to lookin' after you, I take orders from Cynthia. She said I was to come ever' day and look after you, an' that's what I'm doin'."

"You could spend the day with your children."

"I am spendin' th' day with my children. They've gone to the drugstore an' they'll be right back."

"The house is clean, the wash is done, my shirts are ironed . . ."

"But your lunch idn't cooked yet, or your supper."

"I could have lunch at the Grill."

"Father . . ."

"Yes, Puny?"

She turned from the sink, exasperated. "I'm goin' to say to you what Joe Joe says to me when I ask 'im to git up in th' middle of th' night and bring me a bowl of ice cream with sweet pickles."

"So what does he say?"

" '*Git over it!*' "

"Fine," he said. He took his sermon notebook from the island and turned to walk down the hall. He stopped at the door.

"Wait a minute. Ice cream and *pickles*?"

"Yes, sir."

"You mean . . . ?"

He'd never seen her freckled face more beautiful, more radiant.

"Yessir. You're goin' to be a granpaw ag'in."

CHAPTER FIFTEEN

In This Mountain

George Gaynor gazed east from the Lord's Chapel bell tower to the green hills bordering Mitford.

"X marks the spot," he said. "My soul was saved as I stood in this very place."

Father Tim crossed himself, moved by the memory of George Gaynor coming down from the church attic one Sunday morning more than eight years ago. Standing barefoot in front of a stunned congregation, he confessed his theft of the jewels, the long months of hiding in the church attic, and his new-found faith in Jesus Christ.

"Sometimes I think it was the singing," said George. Tears coursed down his cheeks; he wiped his eyes with his shirtsleeve. "Still bawling, Father, when I think of it."

"It's the Holy Spirit keeping your heart soft."

"But of course it was more than the singing. I remember stealing your Bible. . . ."

Father Tim chuckled. "I turned the place upside down looking for it."

"It took several days to make the decision to open it. I was convinced that if I opened it, something powerful would happen, something . . . out of my control."

"Yes!"

"Finally, I began reading in the Gospel of John, which was the best of all places to begin. As I moved through the chapters, I was intrigued, also, by what you'd written in the margins. What had Christ done for you? What difference had He made in your life, in the part of your life that no one sees, that maybe doesn't show from the pulpit?

"I tried to find your heart in what you'd written privately, perhaps to see whether you would slip, somehow, and expose it all as a sham."

"Did you hope to find it all a sham?"

George sat on the deep stone sill of the bell tower window. "Yes, sir, I did. It would have saved me the trouble of surrendering anything to God. Wretch that I was, I was clinging to my wretchedness."

"Don't we all, at some time or other?" He'd felt the sordidness of clinging to his own wretchedness these past weeks, seemingly unable to surrender anything.

"I read all the Gospels, but kept going back to John, where I studied what Jesus had to say with deep concentration. I began memorizing verses, thinking this was nothing more than a way to pass the time. Then a verse in the fifteenth chapter began to . . ." George hesitated.

"Began to . . . ?"

"Torment me, in a way. 'If ye abide in me, and my words abide in you, ye shall ask what ye will and it shall be done unto you.' I realized that I had no idea what to ask God for. I especially had no belief that God, if He were real, would be interested in entertaining whatever request I might cobble together."

A light breeze traveled through the tower.

"It was a kind of intellectual nightmare, a wrestling match between logic and longing, if you will. I wanted to ask Him for something, but couldn't believe He was really open to being asked.

"Then one day Pete Jamison walked in downstairs and I heard someone yell, 'Are you up there?'"

George looked at Father Tim, grinning.

The two men burst into laughter as if sharing a family joke.

"It scared me out of my wits," said George. "I thought, who is this idiot asking if I'm up here—does he think I'm going to yell down and say, *Sure, come on up and enjoy the view*? I thought it might be the feds, but couldn't figure out why they were being so polite."

They laughed together again, relishing the comfort of their bond, the familiarity of a story that had passed into Mitford legend.

"And then I heard you speak to Pete, and I listened to what you said as if my life depended on it. Of course, my life did depend on it.

"You said the question isn't whether He's up there, but whether He's down here. I realized then that I'd begun to experience His presence down here, and that His words were somehow beginning to abide in me.

"When you asked Pete to recite the prayer with you, I had no idea what you were going to say, but I knew it would contain all that I ever wanted to ask Him for.

"That's why, when Pete prayed the prayer of salvation, I prayed it with him."

"Two for one."

"That prayer, that moment, changed everything."

"Alleluia!" Father Tim said softly.

They gazed from the windows, silent for a time. Someone was riding a blue bicycle along the opposite sidewalk. A car driving on Church Hill wheeled into the driveway leading to Fernbank.

"Please forgive me if I overstep," said George, turning to Father Tim. "I sense you may be . . . wrestling with something yourself."

He hated to think that others could sense it. His cheeks burned. "Perhaps as much in recent weeks as ever before in my life." He knew, however, that he was safe with George. He didn't have to pretend to be perfect because he was a priest. "I try to wait for Him to make the darkness light, then grow afraid and try to create the light on my own."

"Something you'd written in a margin," said George, "I can't remember where . . . 'The significant, life-forming times are the dull, in-between times.' A pretty simple statement, but profound if we think it through. I used to believe the life-forming times were the times on the mountain, the great hurrahs . . ."

"The glad hosannas . . ."

"Your buddy, Oswald Chambers—you know I read him avidly in prison—said something like, 'The height of the mountaintop is measured by the drab drudgery of the valley.' He went on to say it's in the sphere of humiliation that we find our true worth to God, that there's where our faithfulness is revealed."

"I'm ashamed to confess it, but I thought I knew my true worth to God, I thought my faithfulness had long ago been revealed to Him. I didn't think He'd . . . require anything more." There. He'd said it.

"Perhaps you should be glad He's requiring more. It seems to me He doesn't ask more of just everybody."

Father Tim took his handkerchief from his pocket and wiped his eyes and blew his nose. "Bless you," he said. "Thanks."

"Thanks for asking me to come along today. I made something a few weeks ago. This is the perfect time. . . ."

George withdrew a small paper bag from his jacket pocket and removed a wooden cross.

"You made this?"

"Yes, sir. Harley had a few sticks of cherry wood lying around. Cherry is hard as granite, but I managed to whittle it into shape and then rubbed it with wax."

Morning light streamed onto the polished cross. A piece of twine was looped through a hole at the top.

"See this nail, Father?" George pointed to a rusted nail between two of the tower windows.

"Ah!" He'd never seen it before, but then he hadn't often dawdled around up here. . . .

"I used to study that nail as if it were a great philosophical conundrum. Why was it there? What purpose could it possibly serve? Who had put it there, taking the trouble to fix it so neatly in the mortar between the stones? I never forgot this nail."

George looped the twine around the nail, tied the cross to it, then stood back. "In this mountain," he said, "the hand of the Lord rested on me. . . ."

The wooden cross hung against the stone wall between the windows. On either side, the view of the high, green hills rolled away to summer clouds in a dome of blue sky.

George turned and placed his hands on the shoulders of his friend. "In this mountain, may the hand of the Lord rest always upon you, my brother. You remember the last thing you said to me when I left here eight years ago?"

"I do."

"'They that sow in tears shall reap in joy; He that goeth forth and weepeth, bearing precious seed, shall doubtless come again with rejoicing, bringing his sheaves with him.'"

Father Tim smiled. "You did come again with rejoicing."

"And so will you, Father, so will you."

Before leaving, they noted with pleasure that the cross appeared to have hung there a very long time.

❧

Father Tim picked up a rough draft of Sunday's pew bulletin from the Lord's Chapel office and asked for a correction of two typos. Then, mission accomplished, the two men stepped out into the warm August afternoon.

At the end of the short walkway to the street, George hesitated. "There's something I need to tell you."

"Tell away!" He felt lighter; his flesh seemed less dense and burdened.

"A customer was pumping gas the other day at Lew's and recognized Harley as someone he'd done time with."

"Ah." Not good.

"He was from West Virginia, so he had nothing to lose around here by saying he'd been in prison, he broadcast it all over the station. Harley was devastated.

"Now Lew has two ex-cons on his hands and people are talking. Since we're living in your house, you may want to know what they're saying."

"What are they saying?" The lightness

of spirit he felt only moments ago had fled, and something like dread came rushing in.

After jogging for two miles along the flat road to Farmer—uphill to Church Hill was out of the question—he went home and called Hoppy. His doctor was with a patient, but the receptionist took his number.

He changed clothes and went to the kitchen and opened the refrigerator door. Starving. But he'd eaten already. He took two carrot sticks from the crisper. Blast this disease to the ends of the earth, he wanted a burger, lightly charred on an outdoor grill, with mayo and sweet pickle relish, a slab of Vidalia onion, and a thick slice of a valley-grown Big Boy with plenty of salt and pepper, all on a homemade sourdough bun with a side of coleslaw. He went to his study and kicked the footstool in front of his leather chair.

There was no more putting it off, no more pacing the floor, and no more holding on to even the faintest hope that Sunday's sermon would drop from the sky into his lap.

Could he do it? Could he preach in his old church and bring something worthwhile to the service? He couldn't kid himself or God, either—he felt jittery about it, unnerved. He needed someone to preach *him* a sermon.

"'I can do all things through Christ who strengthens me!'" he shouted aloud from Philippians 4:13.

"Is that merely a few things, Timothy, or is it actually all things?" he demanded of himself as he walked to and fro in the light-filled study. He was ravenous.

"*All* things!" he thundered in his pulpit voice.

There. That should do it.

He thumped into his desk chair and stared at the Royal manual he'd foraged from the corner of the room where it had sat for an age under its dust cover, then opened the drawer, took out a sheet of paper, and rolled it into the typewriter.

So far, so good.

He took up his Bible, already turned to the passages in Hebrews that he'd studied again last night. Thank God for this chapter, one of the grandest in the whole of Scripture. Its powerful reminder had saved his neck and that of legions of others more than once.

In truth, the eleventh chapter of Hebrews was a sermon in itself, requiring no feeble exegesis from him, a tired and re-tired country parson—but it was exegesis folks wanted and exegesis they would have. . . .

He answered the insistent phone, forgetting he'd planned to turn the ringer down and switch on the answering machine.

"Father? It's Betty Craig."

"Betty!" The wonderful nurse who cared for Dooley's grandfather in her cottage up the way. "Did we forget Russell's livermush delivery this week?"

"No, sir, it's not that."

He knew at once.

"Mr. Jacks passed this morning at eight-thirty."

"I'm sorry, Betty." This was a blow. It would be a greater blow, however, to Dooley, to Pauline, and the children—and even to Betty Craig, who had learned to love the former Lord's Chapel sexton who made the church grounds a showplace for many years.

"He always said he wanted you to do his funeral."

"Yes."

"He sat on the side of th' bed this mornin' an' just stared at the wall, I saw him when I went down th' hall. 'Betty,' he said, 'can you come here a minute?' an' I went in an' . . ."

He prayed silently as she wept.

"An' he said, 'Betty, you've been a daughter

to me.'" She sobbed into the phone. "I can't talk now, Father, can you come?"

"I'm on my way."

He and Russell had been friends for twenty years and in recent times, except for the interim at Whitecap, he'd toted Russell his liver-mush every week or two. He'd always stayed awhile to sit in the rocker, or walk with Russell to the small garden he'd proudly installed for his "keeper."

"See there, that's m' keeper!" the old man once said of Betty. "God rest 'er soul!"

Now Russell's soul was at rest. And he must be the one to break the news.

He drove to Meadowgate, where Dooley was disinfecting the kennels. They sought the shade of a maple tree behind the barn.

"I feel really bad I didn't go see him more." Dooley rubbed his eyes, then with evident shame and sorrow said, "I could've."

Father Tim went looking for Pauline at Hope House, and found her in the dining room setting tables for the evening meal.

Pauline dropped her head; tears escaped

along her cheeks. "I'm sorry," she whispered. "So sorry I didn't visit Daddy more'n I did."

Regret. As his own heart could attest, the world seemed filled with it.

❦

"Law *help*!" said Puny. "I'd th'ow that phone out th' *winder* if I was you!"

He was helping Pauline with the funeral arrangements; a young couple had called for counseling; he was wanted down at the church to advise the sexton where to plant four white azalea bushes that had to be moved for a water line repair. . . .

"It's jis' like it used t' be!" said his house help.

Yes, he thought. It is! And to tell the truth, he rather liked it. In fact, he liked it immensely.

❦

Harley came to the door at four-thirty on his way home from Lew Boyd's.

Father Tim had seldom seen Harley without his toothless grin.

"I cain't even tell you how sorry I am," Harley said, hanging his head. "I hate f'r Dooley t' know it worser'n anybody. Lace, she knowed, but hit didn't matter t' her."

"Harley," he said, "it doesn't matter to me, either."

Harley looked at him, wordless.

"You and George have paid your debt, it's over, it's all in the past."

"Seem like th' worst thing is me'n George bein' in your house, like you might be . . . collectin' criminals."

Father Tim laughed.

"Seem like it might he'p a little if one of us was t' move som'ers else."

"Don't think about it. This will blow over. You and George come walk with me to church on Sunday, I could use the support."

There went Harley's grin again, meeting behind his head.

Hoppy rang after five o'clock. "Bill Watson has congestive heart failure. There's no cure, but medication can help relieve the symptoms."

"He's off his medication," said Father Tim, feeling like a turncoat.

"When we hang up, I'll give him a call and preach him a sermon."

"Have at it!" He wasn't eager to conduct another funeral service.

"Now," said Hoppy, "how are you doing?"

"Doing fine." He hadn't keeled over, so he

must be doing fine. "How was the Oregon Trail?"

Hoppy completely ignored this thoughtful inquiry.

"You're taking your shots twice a day?"

"Absolutely."

"No cornbread?"

"Not a crumb."

"Exercise?"

"Three times a week, two miles on the road to Farmer."

"What about the antidepressant?"

Silence. He could not tell a lie.

"I want to see you tomorrow. Speak to Jean about working you in."

"Can't do it! I have a funeral."

"Funerals don't last all day, pal. I'll tell you about the trail when I see you tomorrow."

Blast.

⟋

He was dozing on the sofa when the phone rang.

"Father, how you doin'? It's Lew Boyd."

"Lew!" He was addled from sleep, but conscious enough to sit up straight and take a deep breath. This was the call he'd been dreading.

"There's somethin' I been meanin' to talk to you about."

"Yes, Lew, I know, and it's very unfortunate. I'm sorry."

There was a startled silence. "You are?"

"Yes. I regret it deeply, and hope it doesn't hurt business in any way."

"Hurt business? How could it hurt business?"

"I've been concerned it could scare some of your customers away."

"I don't see how," said Lew, sounding completely bewildered. "All I'm tryin' to do is git married."

"Married!" Good heavens, he'd just shouted. His dog leaped off the rug, barking.

"When I won a pickle contest back in high school, she kissed me."

"That'll do it every time!"

"I didn't enter kosher dills that year, I entered gherkins."

"Aha."

"Her name's Earlene."

"Earlene! I'll say . . ."

"You know Juanita's been gone six years."

"That a long time."

"Almost seven."

He couldn't seem to figure out where this was headed. "Is there something I can do to . . . help?"

"See, Earlene lives in Tennessee an'

me'n her, well, it's about to half kill me runnin' up an' down th' road in my ol' pickup. I'm no spring chicken, you know what I mean?"

"Indeed I do."

"So, what it is, I'd like you to marry us."

"Ah! Well! Goodness. Congratulations!"

"But we can't tell nobody for a while yet. It has t' be secret."

"Why is that?"

"Her mama's real bad off with heart trouble. It wouldn't do to tell 'er, we want to go real easy on breakin' this to 'er; see, Earlene's been takin' care of 'er mama more'n ten years, since her daddy died."

"I see. When were you thinking?"

"Sometime next week."

"Next *week*?"

"It'd have t' be a Tuesday or Wednesday," said Lew, apologetic. "Those are th' only days she could get off from th' flour company. She used to be a librarian, but th' flour company offered a benefit package you wouldn't believe."

"This is great news, of course. However, I can't perform the ceremony until I've counseled with you and Earlene." Older marriage prospects seldom cared for this idea, so he emphasized its consequence. "That's very important; it's practically canon law."

"Cannon law?"

"Also, there would be a waiting period of thirty days."

His caller was clearly flabbergasted.

"May I ask why you'd like me to marry you?" Lew was a Baptist, no two ways about it.

"Well, see, Bill Sprouse is still laid up. An' since I been workin' on your vehicles f'r twenty years or such, I thought it'd be a good way to say I 'preciate your business."

When Lew rang off, Father Tim lay on the sofa, dizzied by the prospect of what lay ahead.

How would he get it all done? He didn't know. One thing he did know was that he needed help, he needed . . .

He was loath to even think it, but truth be told, he needed Emma Newland.

He clapped his hand to his forehead and uttered a piteous sound, loosely akin to a moan.

Though his startled dog sat bolt upright, he declined to bark.

He was afraid to answer the phone. Let the machine take it . . .

Beep. "Father! It's Olivia. We're back home

in Mitford, and we'd love to see you. I hear Cynthia's traveling, and—"

He grabbed the receiver from the hook. "Olivia! Welcome home!"

"There you are, Father! How lovely to hear your voice! Will you come to dinner tonight? Everything we're having is good for us. I know it's short notice, but do say yes!"

"Yes!"

"Lace brought you something, I mustn't say what, you may faint! It was her idea, I had nothing whatever to do with this scheme."

Lace *brought* him something? He was grinning from ear to ear.

"She also wants to show you her new car—it isn't really new, of course, still I'm mortally envious! And I'm sure Hoppy would like to have a look at his patient—though you'll be the one making the house call."

He dressed for dinner, and had a few minutes to scan his sermon notes when the phone rang.

Cynthia wouldn't call 'til late evening; he'd let the machine pick up.

"Tim, Bill Sprouse, you got to hear this. Buddy, tell th' father how many Persons in th' Holy Trinity."

Hard by the receiver, Buddy barked three times.

"Good fella! Now, how many Testaments in th' Bible?"

Two barks.

"Amen! Now tell 'im how many true Gods."

One bark.

"Brother, did you ever hear th' beat of that?"

Hooting with laughter, Father Tim snatched the receiver from the hook.

"Ask Buddy if he'd like to preach for me on Sunday."

"Sorry, but he won't be able—he's supplyin' over in Farmer."

Father Tim couldn't remember the last time he'd laughed from the heart instead of the head.

"I wanted to tell you I'm up an' hobblin' around," said Bill.

"Thanks be to God!"

"Buddy an' I'll be out on th' street first thing you know, evangelizin' the neighborhood."

All the way to the Harpers, he held on to the sound of happiness in the voice of Bill Sprouse.

The mint-condition, fern-green BMW 325 coupe was parked in the drive, bathed in the glow of a gas-lit lamp.

"*Man!*" said Father Tim, speaking for Dooley as well as for himself.

Lace stood before him with the wrapped box, radiant.

"Would you like to guess? You could shake it!"

"I can't imagine . . . ," he said, feeling like a kid at Christmas. He took the deep, square box and shook it. Muffled knocking about of something heavy. "Umm . . ." He would love to make this beautiful girl laugh with a clever guess or two, but blood could not be squeezed from a turnip.

"Bellows for the fireplace?" he asked, completely pathetic.

"No, Father! Guess again!"

Hoppy sat in an easy chair, one long leg crossed over the other, wearing his much-talked-about cowboy boots and grinning from ear to ear.

"Perhaps you could give him a clue!" said Olivia.

"You'll be head over heels about these!" Lace crowed. He thought it marvelous the way her amber eyes danced and shone.

He shook the box again. The pressure was on. It could be books. . . .

"Books!"

"You're warm!" she said. "Change one letter!"

In the easy chair, Hoppy couldn't seem to remove the foolish grin from his face as he conspicuously jiggled his foot.

Aha! Could it be? "No way," said Father Tim, laughing. "No way are these *boots*!"

Lace jumped up and down. "You guessed it! You did it! Now you can open the box!"

Hand-tooled. With heels. Sharp as a tack.

Boots.

"Do you like them?" Lace waited, expectant, as he trotted around the living room to a minuscule thunder of applause.

Being a loafer man for roughly the whole of his existence, he was a tad nonplussed. Boots, like capers and eggplant, might be an acquired taste. On the other hand, they seemed to fit, they definitely made him taller. . . .

"He's thinking about it," said Hoppy, "like I had to do."

"I believe I've thought it through," said their guest. "It's entirely possible that in the not-too-distant future, I may well be . . . head over heels!"

That they all gave him a congratulatory hug was a welcome bonus.

Lace studied the car owner's manual; Hoppy returned to the hospital to check on a patient; Father Tim and Olivia walked out to the terrace and stood at the railing. In the cool night air of August, there was an ephemeral scent of fall.

"Father, Lace's gift is meant to thank you, if only a little, for all you've done for her. When she saw how thrilled Hoppy was with his present, she wanted to give you that delight, also. She bought them with her own money."

"All the more appreciated!"

"We know a pair of boots can't express everything we feel. I hope you aren't offended."

"*Offended?* Good heavens, I'm flattered beyond words."

"Without you, I almost certainly wouldn't be standing here on this wonderful evening, and who can say where Lace might be? Thank you, dear friend."

"Don't thank me," he said. "It was altogether the leading of the Holy Spirit." He patted Olivia's hand with true fondness. "Lace looks wonderful; tell me how she's doing, what's happening in her heart."

"I wonder if the anger will ever go away. But even worse is the fear—she lived with it for so many years, I still see it in the way she holds her shoulders. It's softening, yes, but a kind of around-the-clock alertness to danger seems just beneath the surface.

"I remember walking in the woods with my father, I was perhaps nine or ten. He showed me a special tree near the river. Long years ago, someone had struck a blow with an axe, leaving the blade in the tree. Daddy showed me how the trunk of the tree had grown around it 'til only a little of the blade was left showing.

"Lace's fear and anger are an old axe blade, buried deep."

"Her faith. How has that helped?"

"It's helped greatly. Yet I think she may believe what too many of humankind believe— that it's really our own raw determination which sees us through. The power of God's grace isn't fully realized in her yet, she's still young."

"I'll pray that it be fully realized," he said. Indeed, as he moved each day down the list of souls for whom he prayed without ceasing, Lace Turner was nearly always next after Dooley Barlowe. "I know it's premature, but Cynthia and I have hoped that one day . . ." He found he couldn't say it, after all; it seemed foolish when spoken aloud.

"That one day they'll form a truce?"

"Well, yes."

"Hoppy and I think about that, too. We love Dooley, and I believe Lace cares for him. But the odds seem short for them, don't you think? Lace can be critical and cold, and very suspicious of love."

"So can Dooley."

Olivia looked beyond the trees to the twilit mountain beyond. "Regarding any future . . . truce . . . there's one thing we can be certain about."

"And what is that?"

She turned and looked at him, smiling.

"That time will tell," she said.

Olivia's mortal envy of that BMW, he thought on the way home, would be nothing compared to Dooley Barlowe's raging jealousy. Suddenly Dooley's seven-year-old Jeep would be prehistoric, ready for the Smithsonian's permanent collection.

If Dooley had the million and a quarter Miss Sadie left him in her will, what he'd choose to drive would be different, indeed. Just how different was, of course, the point.

He had memorized that entire portion of Miss Sadie's letter, which was delivered to him only days after her death.

As you know, I have given a lot of money to human institutions, and I would like to give something to a human individual for a change.

I have prayed about this and so has Louella and God has given us the go ahead.

I am leaving Mama's money to Dooley.

We think he has what it takes to be somebody. You know that Papa was never educated, and look what he became with no help at all. And Willard—look what he made of himself without any help from another soul.

Father, having no help can be a good thing.

As he recalled the letter, word for word, he could hear Miss Sadie as if she were at his very elbow. . . .

But having help can be even better—if the character is strong. I believe you are helping Dooley develop the kind of character that will go far in this world, and so the money is his when he reaches the age of twenty one.

(I am old fashioned and believe that eighteen is far too young to receive an inheritance.)

I have put one and a quarter million dollars where it will grow, and have made provisions to complete his preparatory education. When he is eighteen, the income from the trust will help send him through college.

I am depending on you never to mention this to him until he is old enough to bear it with dignity. I am also depending on you to stick with him, Father, through thick and thin, just as you've done all along.

Cynthia loved the questions her young readers asked; though having a grand time, she was keenly missing her husband; life on the road had its downside; and how was Violet handling her prolonged absence?

"Well enough," said Father Tim. "She's lying in my lap."

Violet seldom acknowledged his presence until her mistress left the house. At once, she glommed on to him, raveling his sweater sleeves, giving his pants a generous coating of white hair. . . .

"The little flirt! Have you put the top down since I left?"

"Umm, no."

"Please put it down, dearest. Summer will be over before we know it, and our glasses freezing to our noses."

"I will, I promise." Even in absentia, Cynthia was trying to help him have fun. "You'll never guess what Lace brought me from Oregon."

"Cowboy boots!" she crowed.

"How did you know?"

"She called me from the trail, I'm the one who gave her your shoe size."

Wives knew everything. Except on the rarest occasion, it was almost impossible to surprise a wife.

He pondered his own axe blade. Over the years, time and time again, he would forgive his father, then the bitterness would seep back into his soul like a toxin. Often, it lingered and did its damage for months before he came awake to the Enemy's ruse, whereupon he forgave Matthew Kavanagh yet again.

Without faith, his soul may not have survived the blade. But like the tree, God had enabled him to grow, and even flourish, around it.

He got into his pajamas, weary beyond telling, and knelt beside the bed and thanked God for survival, for overcoming, for grace. He remembered Sammy and Kenny and Dooley and Jessie and Poo, and all those whom the blade had struck. . . .

Cynthia would be home in ten days, he mused as he climbed into bed, and Dooley would leave for school in twelve. He missed Dooley already.

The summer break had come and nearly

gone, with only the briefest interludes of hanging out, being together. And virtually all the interludes had contained some hard issue.

He reminded himself that things would be different next summer.

Yes, God willing, things would be different next summer.

With this thought, which delivered a certain peace, he drifted to sleep, breathing the faint scent of wisteria from the pillow he held in his arms.

Next door, Hélène Pringle stood at her bedroom window and watched the Kavanaghs' second floor go dark.

She had wanted to take a loaf of her homemade bread to her neighbors, but heard in The Local that Cynthia was on a worldwide tour, or was it a whirlwind tour? Whatever sort of tour it might be, she was away, and it would not be appropriate to carry food to the father in his wife's absence.

She was relieved, really. It seemed to her that giving food bore the marks of sympathy, and surely he had grown tired of sympathy for what happened months ago, and which was, she hoped, forgiven and forgotten by all.

Of course, he continued to look *épuisé*. She

based this opinion on his pale face and slow step as he walked by the rectory with those little red-haired girls whom he claimed as grandchildren.

She heard the wind chime caroling on the porch below, and was pleased with the sound. Harley and Mr. Gaynor had been very kind to give her a hand with hanging it—in fact, they'd helped her with a great many things around the house and yard. She'd been terribly surprised to learn, just yesterday, that Harley had also been incarcerated. It did seem odd, of course, to have two former prisoners living downstairs, but if the father approved and thought it all right, so did she. Perhaps one of the father's ministries was to help such people get a new lease on life, just as he'd helped her to do.

Hélène leaned her forehead against the windowpane. Indeed, if the father had pressed charges against her for . . . she could not bear to use the word *stealing* . . . for removing the bronze angel from his mantelpiece, she, also, might have been incarcerated

She sighed deeply, then turned and went to the bathroom to brush her teeth. She occasionally recalled that this had been the father's bed and bath for many years, a thought that always drew her closer to him in spirit.

She had, some time ago, come to terms with the fact that she loved him, but not with passion. *Non!*

She loved him very gratefully for all he had done for her, for the fact that he had brought her back to herself and saved her from destruction. He insisted it was the work of the Holy Spirit, and she sensed that this may be accurate, that there truly had been a greater force than the father himself who rescued her from the deep.

She was pleased that she'd again formed the habit of praying, something she hadn't done since her grandmother died. As she'd prayed during recent weeks, she tried to picture God as a large man with a flowing white beard, sitting on a throne and holding what, on closer inspection, appeared to be a pitchfork. She later recognized this to be a likeness of Neptune seen in a childhood book, and thus abandoned the image at once.

She moved along, then, to a God striding through heavenly gardens, wearing shimmering robes that billowed as He walked; He was also wearing sandals, though she restrained herself from looking at his toes. This God, however, had seemed so deep in thought that He noticed her not at all, and thus she turned from the image in some despair.

As it seemed unconscionable to pray to vapor, she sought to form another likeness, but failed utterly. She prayed on, nonetheless, keeping it short. And then one evening, quite to her own surprise, she stopped trying to figure out what God looked like.

God was God, she concluded. It no longer mattered what He looked like.

In truth, trying to assess what He looked like had been terribly distracting and in the end had kept her from the business of praying with ardor and absorption. Currently, she felt that if God wished to reveal Himself to her, He would do so in His own time, and in a way that she couldn't begin to imagine.

Meanwhile, she decided to approach Him as if He were sitting on the other side of a drapery, distinctly near but unseen.

She removed her old blue robe and hung it over a chair, then knelt on the rug by her bed and crossed herself. Tonight she would pray in English. After all, if she was going to live as an American citizen, which she'd recently become, she felt it her bounden duty to make a greater effort to speak in the national tongue of her country.

"Dear God, Thank you for the students you have given into my hand, and for my life in Mitford. Please bless the father to recover completely from his . . . *malheurs,* and to live a long life in which he will be helpful to many others as he has been to me. I should like to be a good neighbor, God, if you would kindly fashion me so. Rescue young Sammy Barlowe from his plight, so that he might live a good and useful life—I can't think who said it, but I've been told You have a plan for each of us. Perhaps You would let me know, somehow, if this might be true for . . . Hélène Pringle?"

She caught her breath and wondered whether this might be everything she had to say.

"And do take care of all those at Hope House, especially Mother.

"That's all, I believe." She waited a moment, then whispered, *"Bon nuit."*

She wondered if she should mention something about Jesus, God's Son.

However, she knew hardly anything about Jesus, except as He appeared in the arms of the Blessed Mother, first as a babe and again as a grown man taken bleeding from the cross.

She got into bed and lay on her right side and closed her eyes, hearing only the sound of Barbizon's light snoring from his rug by the door.

Soon, like almost everyone else in Mitford, Hélène Pringle slept.

CHAPTER SIXTEEN

Gizzards Today

His sugar was nearly normal, his weight good, his cholesterol low. But Hoppy wanted him back on the antidepressant.

"I don't want to take it," said Father Tim. "I want to ride this thing out, it has to have an end. I'm . . . dealing with it."

Hoppy shrugged. "OK."

"What do you mean, 'OK'?"

"Don't take it. Ride it out. And if it starts riding you, resume the medication."

There was nothing like a long vacation to relax an uncompromising doctor.

"You've had every lecture in my arsenal," said Hoppy. "Every plea, every warning."

Hoppy popped a couple of green jelly beans. "See me in three weeks."

They laughed. They shook hands. They compared boots.

Then, feeling like a prisoner with a reprieve, he was out of there.

He awoke Sunday morning and waited for the fatigue to hit.

He was wearied of bounding out of bed ahead of it, only to have it snare him by the time he reached the kitchen. He would wait for it, settle into it, and get up slowly; this was a big day.

The processional at the eleven o'clock was thrilling. He hadn't remembered Lord's Chapel being so strikingly beautiful, nor the choir so gifted and accomplished.

From the altar, he looked eagerly into faces he'd never seen before, and was heartily encouraged by the familiar—Hoppy, Olivia, and Lace, three rows back on the gospel side; Buck, Pauline, and the Barlowe clan across from them on the epistle side, with Dooley in his school tie and blazer. Just there, Harley and George, his cheerleaders at both the early and late services . . . Emma and Harold Newland, the Bolicks, Hal and Marge Owen. . . .

For the second time that morning, he acclaimed the opening words with true joy.

"Blessed be God: Father, Son, and Holy Spirit!"

"And blessed be His kingdom," responded the congregation, "now and forever. Amen!"

He had expected his heart to hammer with a certain anxiety as he stood before the majority of his old flock; instead, there was an empowering peace.

In the churchyard, he visited with Dooley and the Owen family.

"Did you see Doc Harper's new Beemer?" asked Dooley. *"Man!"*

"That's not Doc Harper's new Beemer," said Father Tim.

"He was showing it to somebody just a few minutes ago."

"That's Lace Harper's Beemer."

He saw in Dooley's face a fleeting moment of shock, outrage, and then . . . something like humiliation.

In the afternoon, they stood under a tent at the town graveyard as the coffin was lowered into the pit. Russell hadn't wished to be cremated, though it meant giving up the privilege of lying at rest in the Lord's Chapel Prayer Garden he'd created with his own hands.

Jessie sobbed quietly as Poo sought to comfort her; Dooley was stoic. Father Tim believed he knew Pauline's heart in this—busy rebuilding her life as a working mother and wife, she had largely neglected her father and left the nurturing to Betty Craig. But guilt would not prove useful. . . .

He put his arm around Pauline and held her as she wept against his shoulder.

"We've made a decision about Sammy," Buck told him.

"Yes, sir," said Dooley. "I want to go see him with you and Buck."

"Wonderful."

"We're standing together now as a family," Buck declared. "Nobody ever has to stand alone again."

"If something bad happens . . ." said Pauline.

". . . we'll handle it," said Buck.

As the Lord's Chapel bells tolled nine o'clock on Monday morning, Emma Newland arrived at his front door, her laptop in one hand and a bulging file folder in the other.

"I practically had to ring the bell with my *chin*," she said, glowering at him over her glasses.

He opened the screen door and threw his arms wide to give her a hug. Suddenly remembering that hardly anyone ever hugged Emma Newland, he brought his hands together in enthusiastic applause.

"Glad to see you!" he exclaimed.

"You could've seen me a whole lot sooner," she said, stomping into the hall, "if it wasn't for people protectin' you like th' Dalai Lama."

Remember, he told himself—I asked for this.

She thumped into his chair in the study. "Here's your e-mail from that money-grubbin' Father Roland! All he ever says is send money for this, send money for that! Does he think it grows on *trees* down here? He's worse than a Baptist.

"If I were you, I'd let 'im tough it out up there in th' boondocks, he asked for it, it was his big idea! You'd better thank God on bended knee that you missed th' flood that swept your quonset hut into a creek and sent it bobbin' downstream like a cork. That'd be a fine thing to wake up to in th' middle of th' night.

"He said somebody named Abner jumped in an' managed to save a moose head, he didn't say what a moose was doin' in Tennessee, I thought they mainly came from Alaska.

"An' here's th' deal from Mitford, England—we're gettin' close to bein' Sister Cities or whatever, I guess you'll have to call it Sister Villages, bein' as their Mitford only has five hundred people and us a thousand an' thirty-three at last count. I hope you don't have to fly over there for any ceremony, you're green around th' gills an' skinny as a rail! I'm glad your wife can't see you right now, she'd be on the next plane."

She sniffed the air. "Is Puny cookin' anything for you to eat around here? I should've brought th' rest of last night's pork roast, I did it with raspberry preserves instead of mushroom soup. Harold ate 'til he fell!" She adjusted her glasses and peered at him. "What you need is some good red meat!"

Emma Newland, he thought, made Fancy Skinner look mute as a doorknob. In the moment of blessed silence that prevailed as Emma booted her computer, he heard Puny switch on the vacuum cleaner in the upstairs hallway.

"You did a good job at church yesterday, Esther Bolick said it was just like you'd never left, except you look older. I told her it wasn't fair to compare you to Father Talbot, who bleaches his teeth and maybe even wears . . . I shouldn't say it."

"Shouldn't say what?"

"A hairpiece. Some people say his hair is, you know . . ."

He sighed, rubbing his forehead. He felt a headache coming on, or was it only Emma?

"I guess you saw that Hoppy's back from wanderin' all over creation while people suffered an' died back home, an' have you heard what he bought Lace? A car that costs as much as some people's houses. When I was her age, I didn't have a car, I was lucky to have money to ride th' bus, I hope they don't let th' poor girl get above her raisin'."

"Lace Harper didn't have any raising to get above."

"Oh, well, you know what I mean. You take Dooley . . ."

"And the car is a used car."

"Anyway, you take Dooley—there he is ridin' around in that old Jeep with rust on th' fenders, which, if you ask me, is more like it. I didn't see you trottin' out to buy him a car that cost th' national debt."

He read while this blather went in one ear and out the other. Emma's enforced separation from him had made her mad as a hornet, to say the least. As he'd learned from long years of experience, the only thing to do was let her talk 'til she was thoroughly cleansed and could go to work and get something *done,* for heaven's sake. On the rug by the hearth, his dog heaved a huge sigh. His own sentiments, exactly.

"An' I guess you heard what people are sayin' about Harley and th' Man in th' Attic—"

He looked up from his e-mail. "He's not the Man in the Attic."

"You know what I mean."

"His name is George, and I trust him completely, as I do Harley. And no, I'm not collecting criminals who'll loose themselves on the town to wreak havoc. Who's saying such things anyway?" If she knew so much, maybe she knew the source of this wild rumor-mongering.

She shrugged. "Don't ask me."

"I am asking you. Who's saying this? Where did you hear it?"

"At The Local."

"Who said it?"

"Somebody . . . ," she said, throwing up her hands and looking pained.

"Next time you see Somebody, tell them these men paid their debt to society and are now making every effort to contribute to it."

"Oh, all right," she said. "It was Ed Coffey. I didn't want to say his name, since I know how you feel about that witch he works for."

Edith Mallory. Alive and well and spewing her venom.

He'd just written and delivered a sermon and now it was time to write another. A priest whose name he couldn't remember had nailed it: "It's like having a baby on Sunday and waking up pregnant on Monday."

He ran along the road toward Farmer, with Barnabas loping behind.

He wanted Sunday's message to count for something. Otherwise, why bother?

"Your words for Your people," he huffed aloud.

"Hey, buddy."

"Hey, yourself."

"Is this a good time?"

"I'm just gettin' ready to feed the horses."

"There's no way to know whether Sammy will be home, but we could take a shot at it tomorrow morning. That's a good time for Buck and me. What about you?"

"Yes, sir."

"Can you meet me at the Grill at eight o'clock? We'll have breakfast and connect with Buck on the way down the mountain."

A long pause. "I'll be there."

He heard the apprehension in the boy's voice, and went to his chair in the study and prayed again about tomorrow's mission. "And while I'm at it, Father, please . . . show me how to put an end to this darkness, or if You choose to let it go on, give me a brighter spirit to endure it." He was whining. He hated whining.

"Father! John Brewster here."

"John, how's it coming? I'll be over next week to see the children. I've missed my visits."

"We'll be glad to have you, as always. I've got great news!"

"Shoot."

"We've had a call from an anonymous donor. They want to give us a check for twenty-five thousand dollars."

"Great! You can use it."

"There are a couple of strings attached."

"The usual," he said.

"They want you to conduct services at a private chapel over in Kinloch, somewhere on the lake."

"Me? Why me?"

"I don't have all the details, the check will be

delivered with the info as soon as they know whether you'll do it."

"What's the timeline for the service?"

"Next Sunday evening at six o'clock. You know how much twenty-five thousand would mean to us right now, Tim."

"Yes, I do know. But why not Stuart Cullen?" The sum of twenty-five thousand bucks didn't equate to a country priest, it equated to a big-city bishop.

"You're the one they requested, said they'd heard you preach a couple of times."

"Do you know the identity of this anonymous donor?"

"I don't. That was the other string. Maybe you've heard that Kinloch is currently without a priest. Looks like this is something the donor wants to do for the parish, but doesn't want to be recognized for it."

"What sort of service? What's the occasion?"

"I'll tell you more when I know more, probably by tomorrow morning. You'll do it, then?"

He hesitated.

Did he have the stamina to perform two services at Lord's Chapel, make the nearly four-hour round-trip drive to celebrate and preach in Kinloch, then meet Cynthia's plane the following morning? But that wasn't the point. The point was twenty-five thousand dollars for a cause with an urgent need, a cause he'd passionately believed in and supported for more than two decades. . . .

"Consider it done," he said.

He was relieved to hear from John Brewster as he was going out the door to meet Dooley for breakfast.

"Got the check!" said the hardworking administrator. This was a big day in John's book; currently, thirteen seriously ill or handicapped children were counting on his skills. "Of course, I can't cash it 'til you do the service. By the way, there's no special occasion, they just want a good, all-around worship service."

"Who signed the check? Where did it come from?"

"Signed by . . . let's see, Jonathan Ferguson, out of a Schwab account in Miami."

His heart literally skipped a beat.

Edith Mallory, of course, had a home in Miami. But then, so did a couple million other people.

"It arrived by courier service about ten minutes ago, they knew I'd be in early this morning. I never realized we had a courier service in these hills." John laughed, heady with the up-draft of unexpected financial support. "Thanks, Father, this is great, thanks a million."

Besides, thought Father Tim, Edith would never let twenty-five thousand dollars go so easily, and for so little in kind. She craved honor, glory, fame, and praise, which the low-profile Children's Hospital rarely bestowed, save in an inexpensive annual printout of donor names. No, this had nothing of her stamp on it.

He released his breath in a long sigh.

He was in the booth at ten 'til eight.

Though ready for the trip to the trailer, and believing in the best, he was trying to prepare himself for the worst.

"How're the gizzards doing?" he asked Percy.

"Big," said Percy. "Really big."

"It's th' sauce," said Velma.

"I like your sign." Father Tim nodded toward the hand-lettered broadside taped to the back of the cash register.

Gizzards Today.
Now with Velma's
Homemade
Dipping Sauce.

Someone had tried to illustrate the broadside with pencil sketches of gizzards. Not a good idea.

"What we're findin,'" said Percy, "is Velma's dippin' sauce is great with a whole bunch of menu items."

"Burgers!" said Velma.

"Fries!" said Percy.

"You name it," Velma concluded. "Even turnip greens."

"Aha!"

"Th' fire chief puts it on 'is eggs, you ought to order your eggs scrambled this mornin', goes great on scrambled eggs."

"It's a little too early for dippin' sauce," said Father Tim, feeling queasy.

Velma gave him the once-over. "Variety is th' spice of life."

"Right," he said. "But not before eight o'clock."

🐚

Dooley was tight-lipped, as he idled his spoon in a bowl of Cheerios. Father Tim felt quiet himself—who knew what the day would bring?

Dooley looked up suddenly. "How come Doc Harper bought her a BMW?"

"It's in mint condition, he got it for a great

price, and it's said to be one of the safest cars out there."

"It was a stupid move."

"A stupid move?"

"Nobody in college needs a hot car like that, it makes her look like a snob, a real show-off."

"I don't believe Lace is a show-off."

Dooley didn't respond. The look Father Tim saw on his face was familiar; he'd seen it when he and the boy first met. Dooley was seething inside.

"Talk to me," said Father Tim. "What's going on?"

"My Jeep looks like crap. I don't have the money to get the rust spots fixed or have it painted. I hate driving it."

"You never mentioned that 'til Lace got the . . . coupe." He wanted to avoid using the name *BMW* entirely; it seemed to have some spell-binding power that *coupe* or *car* lacked.

I have put one and a quarter million dollars where it will grow, and have made provisions to complete his preparatory education. When he is eighteen, the income from the trust will help send him through college.

I am depending on you never to mention this to him until he is old enough to bear it with dignity.

Dooley's voice was cold. "I don't want to talk about it."

"Then let's don't," said Father Tim.

🌀

The air had cooled; along the riverbanks it was fresh and sweet, with none of the broiling humidity of August.

Buck steered the red pickup down a road that Father Tim now found familiar, and made the turn by the wayside pulpit.

Fear knocked, faith answered.

No one was there.

Buck pulled at his chin with his left hand, deep in thought. Dooley was as frozen as park statuary; Father Tim knew that, in his father, the boy would face a thousand demons.

As for himself, he tried sitting loose. He had prayed the prayer that never failed and was trusting the One to whom he'd prayed it.

There was nothing more he could do. Nothing.

🌀

Frail and shirtless, Clyde Barlowe squinted through the torn screen door.

"They ain't no Sammy livin' here."

"I'm Tim Kavanagh from Mitford." The dog sniffed his pant leg.

"Buck Leeper," said Buck.

"And this," said Father Tim, "is Dooley. Dooley Barlowe."

The barefoot, unshaven man peered closely at Dooley, then uttered an oath.

"When's Sammy due back?" Buck demanded.

Clyde Barlowe's left eye gazed at them, blank. "I don't keep up with nobody named Sammy. Y'all better split before I git my dogs on you, I keep some bad dogs out back."

Father Tim recoiled at the flume of breath that issued like a sour vapor through the screen.

"Look here, Barlowe . . ." Buck stepped closer to the door.

"M' name ain't Barlowe, it's Jaybird Johnson. Ever'body calls me Jaybird, that's th' name on m' my gov'ment checks. Cain't nobody prove I ain't Jaybird. Now git offa my place, an' stay off." Clyde Barlowe stepped back, grabbed the door, and slammed it hard.

Dooley jumped from the top step and ducked around the corner of the trailer by a propane tank. He returned moments later, shame-faced, wiping his mouth with the back of his hand.

"Puked," he mumbled.

They waited a half hour near the entrance to the shade garden, speaking very little. Perhaps he would come . . .

For a time, the dog stood at a distance, then ambled over and lay at Dooley's feet, its tail beating the dust.

"Let's wait a few more minutes," said Dooley.

They were walking toward the bridge more than an hour later when Dooley stopped and looked back at the trailer.

"He's not . . ." There was a long pause.

"He's not what?" Father Tim asked.

"He's not tall anymore."

Hope Winchester knew what people were saying about George Gaynor.

Not that it was anything incredibly serious, but she despised the snide remarks made here and there, and the skeptical glances.

It seemed very clear—as long as he'd been the Man in the Attic, he'd been glamorous, mysterious, exotic. He'd descended the church stairs looking like a rock star with his long, flowing hair, then made his dramatic confession in front of the entire congregation, afterward asking Father Tim to call the police to take him away. Not a few witnesses of this breathtaking event thought it a thrilling scenario for a movie; several found it a shame that Harrison Ford was too old for the part.

She remembered vividly the day the FBI arrived in Mitford in their black cars with dark windows that no one could see through—nearly everybody in town had stood on Main Street to wave goodbye to a confessed criminal who'd endeared himself to their hearts for all eternity.

But of course it hadn't been for all eternity.

Now the Man in the Attic was real and actual, a flesh-and-blood human being working in their bookstore and living with another convict just down the street. At least two customers had insinuated that for all they knew, George Gaynor and Harley Welch spent their nights plotting shadowy deeds while innocent people lay sleeping. They thought it unwise of Father Tim, who did so many things right, to get this one thing so very wrong. The least he could do, someone suggested, was separate the two. The owner of Chelsea Tea Shop, who considered Harley a good sort, said that being in prison for running liquor wasn't all that bad, really, but consider what a criminal *did* in prison—he learned bad things from other criminals, so that what he knew going in was horribly multiplied when he came out, did anyone *get the point*?

Helen, the bookstore owner, hadn't said a word about their new employee, but then, she lived in Florida for nine months of the year and all she looked at was the bottom line. In truth, the first several weeks of George Gaynor's employment had been quite evident in the bottom line—people had swarmed in to see him, people like Emma Newland, who had never read a book in her life, as far as Hope could determine, and Esther Bolick, who had purchased a copy of *Bathroom Trivia, Volume I* for her husband who, Esther didn't mind confiding, was constipated due to his current medication for a brain tumor.

Scott Murphy, the chaplain at Hope House, had come in at least twice. Once he'd stepped into the mailroom with George and she thought she heard Scott call him "brother" and heard them praying together, which didn't please her at all; maybe Scott knew this, because on the way out, he bought a copy of *The Clean Joke Book* in paperback. "For the residents at Hope House," he said, smiling. She'd heard that Scott Murphy had those elderly people dancing, writing their life stories, and working in the garden. She knew

he had two Jack Russells which he used somehow in his work.

Hope had been frankly relieved when the
common horde had gotten their fill of George
Gaynor and made room for people who actually
loved and read books, which, in the scheme of
things, seemed a dwindling and precious few.

In any case, the owner had for years trusted
Hope Winchester to get it right, and so far,
Hope believed, she had gotten it right.

And now this.

She was wringing her hands in the mailroom when George came in with a large box
for UPS. He set it down and looked at her,
smiling. She realized she was wringing
her hands, but couldn't seem to stop, she
could not will herself to stop. It was hugely
embarrassing to be caught in so many awkward
circumstances—talking too much, laughing
too loudly, dropping books, calling Henry
James 'James Henry'; she had even stopped using big words unnecessarily.

"You're concerned about something," he said.

She hated the direct way he stated things,
stripping away convention and getting to the
very marrow of meaning. If only she had
courage, she would fire him at once, just to be
rid of the volatile feelings she suffered in his
presence.

But she'd never fired anyone; and, until George Gaynor, she'd never hired anyone, either. All she had ever wished to do was sit on the stool and order books, read, and satisfy customers like Father Tim, who often wanted the unique, the hard-to-find, the out-of-print. She had never wished to be *management*.

"Yes!" she said. "I mean, no. *No!* Not at all."

"Are you concerned about what people are saying?"

"What . . . exactly . . . are they saying?"

"Some feel uncomfortable because Harley and I—"

"Oh, *that!*" she said, her voice hoarse. Then, without warning, she burst into tears. The tears seemed to explode from her, as one might suddenly be seized by a violent cough, and she realized she was sobbing.

She had every intention of running into the bathroom and locking the door, but instead thumped down on the box of books he'd just carried in, and put her head in her hands, and wept without caring what he thought.

They were making the turn by the wayside pulpit when they noticed the faded green pickup truck moving toward them.

Though his vision wasn't the best, Father

Tim saw the hair through the windshield and knew at once.

"Dooley," he said with a lump in his throat, "it's your brother."

"Ho!" yelled Buck, throwing up his hand at the driver.

Lon Burtie made the turn and braked his vehicle as he pulled alongside. He peered cautiously at the occupants of the red truck. "How're y'all?"

"Good," said Buck. "Sammy, we've brought your brother, Dooley, to see you."

Father Tim opened the passenger door and got out. Dooley sat for a moment as if paralyzed, the color drained from his face. Then he moved over and got out, also, and walked around to the front of the truck as if in a dream.

Sammy jumped down from the green truck and stood by the door, waiting, his eyes wide and frightened.

No one spoke. Lon Burtie cut off the ignition and sat with his right wrist on the steering wheel. Buck turned off his ignition.

Dooley stood for a long moment, leaning against the hood. Then he drew himself up and walked to the front of the green truck.

"Hey," whispered Dooley, looking at his brother.

Sammy nodded, but could not speak.

CHAPTER SEVENTEEN

A Coal Yet Burning

He'd expected to pay a price for yesterday's journey. Yet it hadn't exhausted him in the least.

After bounding with Barnabas to the monument, he legged homeward with schoolboy eagerness, changed into something comfortable, brewed a cup of tea, and sat down to his long-neglected essay.

He found it as mute as marble.

What had he meant by all that scribbling, anyway? Another man might have penned it; he'd never known something from his own hand to be so alien in meaning and purpose.

He dumped the pages into the wastebasket, removed the legal tablet from his desk drawer, and took up the pen his wife had given him. Then, filled with conviction, he went at it— head down, as into the wind.

Surviving . . . the . . . Blade, he wrote.

Had he turned a corner, somehow, and survived the blade of these last ghastly months? Was it over? Had God brought him out into the light, or was there darkness yet to come?

But he mustn't try to second-guess God. He had no idea at all what was yet to come—no one ever knew, of course. St. Francis de Sales had spoken ably to that: "Do not look forward to what may happen tomorrow; the same everlasting Father who cares for you today will take care of you tomorrow and every day. Either He will shield you from suffering, or He will give you unfailing strength to bear it."

He bent over the tablet, writing furiously, his tea going cold in the cup. . . .

A cramp in his right hand brought him awake to the sight of the maple tree in the park; to the sound of his dog snoring; to the realization that Violet was wrapping herself around his leg, leaving a pelt of white fur in her wake.

Thanks be to God.

He was alive, he was writing, he was working! He had vanished into another realm for . . . how long?

He checked his watch. Two hours. Two hours in which his feeble frame had sat without aching or remorse, two hours in which he'd taken a kind of winged flight and unburdened his heart, able to say what he had to say without looking back. It was the mountaintop after a long trek through a parched valley.

He got up and went to the back stoop and inhaled the afternoon air, seeing the hedge in some crisp, clear way he hadn't seen it in a very long time. He put his head back and closed his eyes, giving thanks. For two blessed hours, he had been a river without a dam, a colt without a fence.

He would relish the moment, and not expect the worst to befall him for relishing it.

" 'And now in age I bud again!' " he recited aloud from George Herbert. " 'After so many deaths I live and write, I once more smell the dew and rain, /And relish versing: O my only Light, /It cannot be That I am he /On whom Thy tempests fell all night!' "

Suddenly self-conscious, he turned and hurried inside to the phone, where he kept the list of places he might reach Cynthia.

He wanted her to know that he'd written the first draft of an essay he actually liked, that he had found in himself a coal yet burning. Even if his new freedom couldn't be counted on to last, he wanted to savor this pinprick of joy and share it.

Hélène Pringle was placing an African violet on the radiator shelf by the dining room window when she looked up and saw her neighbor.

Father Kavanagh was standing on his back stoop in what appeared to be drawstring pajamas, speaking aloud and lifting his hands in what could be described as a priestly gesture. She saw on his face an odd look—something like bliss, she thought.

A shiver of happiness seized her, as if she'd just witnessed a kind of omen she'd been looking for without realizing it.

He sat in the wing chair in their bedroom, missing his wife—her countenance, her whiffling snore on the neighboring pillow, her softness of spirit, her unaffected eagerness, her warm flesh.

He missed the way she took over when he needed her to take over and the way she stepped back when he needed to make decisions, or even mistakes, on his own. He'd done the right thing by insisting she go; he despised the mewling infant he'd been for weeks on end, and was learning he could do without her if push came to shove.

He stood up and stretched and placed his glasses on the night table. In a sense, her going away had allowed him to really come home.

He patted the foot of the bed; Barnabas leaped to his place at once. Then he knelt and prayed for his wife, traveling to places he would never see, flying in planes he would never board—in her was a vast store of courage and adventuring that he would never possess.

He crawled into bed, thinking that one day he would make up to her the long weeks she'd pampered and protected him. He would do something wonderful for her, something that required a true sacrifice on his part, not just any old thing that was easily tossed off.

Perhaps he would take her somewhere . . . somewhere she had always wanted to go.

The idea that suddenly occurred to him was electric, bringing him fully awake and sentient. He would take her to his ancestral homeland, that great, green, mysterious land out of whose loins his paternal line had found its way to America—to Pennsylvania and Kentucky and Mississippi and Mitford.

The excitement he felt over this idea was startling. It surpassed even the joy he felt about the meeting at Lon Burtie's house two days hence, the meeting in which Dooley, Jessie, and Poo would visit their brother, as God continued to restore to the Barlowes the days the locusts had eaten.

He took notes as John Brewster gave him the scoop.

. . . r. on Tamblin Rd at serv station 1 mi and r. on Springlake Dr—park in lot next to lake, Mary Fisher wl drive me to private chapel, Rite I arrive 5 p.m. MF @ 972/604-7832

The roads to Kinloch were winding—it would be more than an hour and a half each direction.

He rang Mary Fisher twice but got an answering machine with a digital voice recording that declined to take a message.

He gazed into the mirror of his old walnut dresser, turning his head this way and that. He definitely needed a little shearing for the events of Sunday.

He hoofed to Joe Ivey's minuscule shop at the rear of Sweet Stuff. *Closed,* read the sign.

He went around to Main Street and opened

the door to the bakery—one of his favorite things to do. In truth, just opening the door was enough for him; he'd learned to relish the aroma without craving an entire tray of glazed donuts.

He rang the bell on the bake case. "Winnie! Are you there?"

"Yessir," she said, coming through the curtains, wiping her hands on a paper towel. "But I just got here a minute ago, I've been at th' hospital, I guess you heard about Joe." She looked red-eyed and worn.

"No! What?"

"He's got this." She pulled a scrap of paper from her apron pocket and handed it to him.

"Hemochromatosis," he read aloud.

"It's inherited. It's too much iron collectin' in th' blood, an' it's caused . . . it's caused . . . Look on th' back of that paper."

He turned the slip of paper over. "Cirrhosis. Ah."

"Dr. Harper said he'd always worried Joe would get cirrhosis from drinkin' brandy, and here he got it from too much iron in 'is system!"

Ironic in the true sense of the word, he thought. "What can I do?"

"He's been real weak an' run-down lately, but we thought it was all th' ruckus with that woman upstairs. Th' hair business in this town has turned into another Desert Storm because of her. I could take a *whippin'* for lettin' Fancy Skinner sign a lease for two miserable years—and do her dirty work right over our *heads*!"

He'd never seen Winnie so distraught, except for the time Edith Mallory's henchmen tried to force Winnie to sell the bakery.

"What can I do?" he asked again.

"Pray!" she said, sounding urgent.

He stood on the sidewalk at the foot of the stairs, looking up.

There was no way he could deliver himself into the hands of Fancy Skinner, even if her haircuts were the only game in town. No way. He was not hauling up those stairs and into that pink room that looked like the interior of an ulcerated stomach. No, indeed! No, no, no, a thousand times no.

He turned and trotted home, put the top down on the Mustang, and roared to Wesley, where, for twelve bucks, he got a decent haircut, albeit with a slightly spiked look, reminding himself all the while that beggars couldn't be choosers.

In the tiny rest room of Happy Endings Bookstore, Hope Winchester washed down an aspirin with a Coke Classic, something her mother had always done to settle her nerves.

She was going to be calm today, she was not going to study George Gaynor's profile when she thought he wasn't looking, and she definitely wasn't going to compare him with literary figures like Lord Byron or even the fictitious Heathcliff. She was going to be aloof, poised, complete.

Hessie Mayhew stood on her deck, drinking a second cup of coffee with hazelnut Coffee-mate and eyeing the lawn chair blown by a recent wind to the railing.

It was the only chair in a collection of seven with its woven plastic seat still intact. She had been in a quandary about her aging lawn chairs for several years. At times she considered setting them on the street for the Annual Town RoundUp. At other times, she was determined to haul them down the mountain to get the seats rewoven. A note on her refrigerator read, *DO NOW!!! Take chairs to Wesley.* By loose calculation, the note was five years old.

That's the way life worked. It raced by. Write a note, look up, and five years had galloped past. While volunteering at the library, she'd studied the old poets in order to write her annual "Lady Spring" column. Old poets had a lot to say about the passage of time, not the least of which was Robert Herrick. "Gather ye rosebuds while ye may," he wrote, "Old time it is a-flying."

She hadn't gathered many rosebuds lately. All she'd done was work, work, work. The summer had worn her out, and here was fall staring her in the face with three weddings in Wesley, an ECW fund-raiser at Lord's Chapel, a missionary dinner at the Methodists' . . .

Lord knows, missionary dinners didn't pay anything, they would expect her to practically give them fourteen arrangements. Well, then she'd use leaves—fall color should be great this year because the nights had been cold for weeks, she'd worn a sweater to bed more than once. And of course there were nuts and berries. There were always nuts and berries.

She took a sip of coffee and eyed the chair. Why didn't she sit down in the blooming thing? Why didn't she ever sit down? Her grandmother had never sat down, her mother had never sat down, and the gene had clearly passed to her. Refusing to give herself time to think about it further, she thumped into the chair, sighing deeply.

Heaven help her for being raised Baptist. The Baptists hardly ever sat down, unlike the

Presbyterians, of which she was now one, who *occasionally* sat down. Episcopalians were another matter; they appeared to sit down whenever they wanted to.

The trouble with sitting down, of course, is that it made you feel guilty. She pondered this. Maybe what she needed to do was get up and go inside and grab her yellow tablet and bring it out here and, while sitting down, make a list of things to do.

But if she got up and went inside, she would never come back.

She stayed put, deciding to follow an instruction she'd seen on bumper stickers out the kazoo: *Take time to smell the roses!* Ha! It didn't take an old poet to come up with that notion.

Hessie scooted the chair back and put her feet up on the railing.

Then she took them down.

She wasn't the sort to put her feet up on a railing.

Well, then, maybe just one foot.

She put her right foot up, let it rest there a moment, then took it down. One foot on the railing made her back feel like it was going out.

In order to make use of the time, maybe she should meditate. She'd heard of meditating, but didn't know what you were supposed to think while you did it. Maybe you didn't think anything, maybe you just sat there.

What a horrible thought!

She was about to jump out of her skin when suddenly she had an idea.

Last Sunday, her preacher asked everyone to go over in their minds who they needed to forgive. He was always giving them something to do: List how many times you pray this week! Make a list of all the times God answers your prayers! Give someone a smile! Think of who you need to forgive—and then forgive them! She never paid attention to these injunctions; it was too much like homework, which she'd never cared for, either.

But maybe she'd do just this one thing.

She took a deep breath and closed her eyes. Polly Morris!

Hessie didn't see how in the world she could forgive Polly Morris.

She considered the whole incident from start to finish. How could *anybody* have taken apart every single centerpiece that she, Hessie Mayhew, had made for the Mitford Country Club Azalea Ball at a discount—at a *discount*!—and put them back together again in a totally different way that was *ugly as mud*? It was a slap in the face! Polly Morris, as everyone knew, didn't have a life, which gave her all the time in the world to mess with other people's lives from here to kingdom come!

Hessie felt her blood pressure pounding in her temples. Starting from the chair, she splashed coffee in her lap. "Dadgummit!" she shouted. A bird flew out of a bush by the railing.

Enough of this sitting-down nonsense! Let other people sit down and waste time!

Hessie trotted to the kitchen, mopped the front of her khaki pants with a dish towel, and poured another cup of coffee. Then she snatched her tablet off the breakfast table and scrawled the words, *Throw out deck chairs TODAY!!!*

"The Enemy will not let you rest!" her preacher had said. "He doesn't want you to forgive anybody, he wants you to hold all that bitterness and anger inside 'til it turns to sickness and ill health!"

Clutching the mug, she threw open the sliding doors and raced back to the chair; sitting down was working her to death.

She would try one more time, and if that didn't get results, she was out of here. She had the back porch to clean off, the chairs to dump in the basement 'til the next RoundUp, groceries to buy, a tire to be retreaded. Unlike some people she could think of, *she* had a life that couldn't be lived on her rear end.

She closed her eyes and listened to the rasping call of a bird in the maple tree. A squirrel clucked near the creek.

Father Tim. Now, there was somebody she needed to forgive. When she delivered that garden basket to the hospital, the poor man had been in a *coma,* for heaven's sake. Or just *out* of one, or in any case, *sick. Very* sick. He couldn't have written a thank-you note if his life depended on it. But Cynthia could have. Yes, indeed, what kind of preacher's wife couldn't write a simple thank-you note or make a phone call?

But maybe Cynthia had been so distraught over her husband that she couldn't think of writing thank-you notes. Hessie understood that. Of course! It had been an oversight.

Then Hessie remembered the basket itself and how much it had cost, even wholesale. She thought of the miniature roses and all the other wonderful items she'd tucked into it, not to mention *acres* of moss from her own special, private place in her own backyard.

"Lord," she said aloud, "You're goin' to have to help me do this!"

She set her coffee mug on the rail and gripped the arms of the lawn chair.

"I forgive Cynthia!"

There.

She took a deep breath. "And Father Tim, in case hc had anything to do with it!"

She felt better at once.

"You'll never guess who's in the slammer," said J.C.

Father Tim stirred his tea. "Old Man Mueller ran the red light one time too many?"

"Ed Coffey found Coot Hendrick stumblin' around in th' yard up at Edith Mallory's, lookin' for that Yankee grave."

"Oh, boy."

"And Coot with an honorary appointment to th' town council," said Mule. "I hate it when politicians break th' law."

Percy refilled the coffee cups. "Beats me why anybody'd want to go lookin' for a grave full of Yankees in th' first place."

"Idn't that th' truth!" Velma stood at the counter, wrapping fork and knife combos with paper napkins. "Nobody'll pay cash money to look at th' bloomin' thing if he finds it."

"He wants to find th' grave because 'is great-granddaddy shot th' Yankees, and it's town history," said Mule.

Percy snorted. "Let sleepin' dogs lie is what I say."

"Look," said Father Tim, "if his ancestor

shot and killed the enemy, he wouldn't have given them the honor of a marked grave. Marking a grave is a type of tribute, so this grave wouldn't be marked. Therefore, how could Coot hope to find it?"

"Right!" J.C. forked an entire sausage link into his mouth.

"He told me he'll just *know,*" said Mule. "But how come he didn't go lookin' before th' Witch set up housekeepin' on th' ridge?"

"Because," said Percy, "when she bought that parcel twenty years ago, Coot didn't give a katy about town history." Percy counted himself among the few who knew what was what in the early days of Mitford; the turkeys in this booth had all come from someplace else. "He was more into chasin' women."

"I don't even want to *think* about what women Coot *Hen*drick was chasin'." J.C. pulled out his handkerchief and mopped his forehead.

"As I recall," said Percy, "he was chasin' Emeline Poovey from over at Blackberry."

"I thought all Pooveys live in Poovey's Grove," said Mule.

"Th' crowd over at Blackberry splintered off from th' Poovey's Grove Pooveys."

"So if he was chasin' her, did he catch her?"

"Emeline married that big bootlegger that

robbed Th' Local when Avis's daddy first had it. Sauce Harris was 'is name, he burrowed hisself into a dumpload of roastin' ears, somebody backed th' truck up to th' storeroom in th' rear an' dumped th' corn, then locked th' storeroom doors and drove off. Sauce got into th' grocery, eat a smoked ham, guzzled three quarts of chocolate milk, an' cleaned out th' safe behind th' butcher case. Busted through a window and run off with two thousand smackers."

Father Tim gave his whole wheat toast a light buttering. "That was a lot of money back then."

"That's a lot of money *today,* buddyroe."

"Right. How did they catch him?"

"Emeline turned him in. Th' county was about half dry for four years."

"So how long do you think Coot's in for?"

"He'll be out on bail late today," said J.C. "That reminds me, I've got an interview set up in"—J.C. checked his watch—"thirty minutes."

"Who with?"

J.C. surveyed the table with a smug dignity reserved exclusively for the press. "Edith Mallory."

"*What?*" Percy set the empty coffeepot on the table, hard. "You're talkin' to that low-life, money-grubbin'—"

"Hold on!" yelled Velma, who was setting up the adjoining booth. She grabbed her husband by the arm and dragged him to the grill, where she planted him like a chrysanthemum.

"Now hush up!" she snapped to J.C. "I've told you before, don't talk about that woman in our place, it makes 'is heart act up. If you got to talk about that woman, step outside and do it on th' dadblamed *street*."

"She means business," said Father Tim, lowering his head in case anything started flying.

"I'm a *journalist*!" J.C. yelled in the general direction of the grill. "I can't confine my inquiry to the upstanding, kindhearted, and lovable; it's my duty to dig down, get at the truth wherever it exists, and report it to the readers—whether some people like it or not!"

"Preach it, brother!" said Mule under his breath. He'd never much cared for Velma Mosley, who, just for meanness and only last week, had served him a side of slaw made with pickles when she knew for a fact that he despised pickles.

Father Tim was surprised to see Ed Coffey out and about in broad daylight. Though often observed chauffeuring Edith Mallory, Ed otherwise kept a low profile in Mitford—some said Ed drove his employer to Wesley, where all grocery shopping and other errands were done. Yet here was Ed Coffey in the produce aisle of The Local, only a couple of feet ahead.

When Father Tim first came to Lord's Chapel, he'd often seen Ed at the Grill. Everyone agreed he'd been a decent enough fellow, born and raised just down the road, until Edith and Pat Mallory hired him. Soon after Pat dropped dead of a heart attack and tumbled down his hall stairs, the town saw a change in Ed. He became furtive, sullen, and short-tempered, as if Edith's toxic nature had somehow contaminated him.

Father Tim started to turn his cart around and head in the other direction, but stopped abruptly. No, he wouldn't go the other way. He rolled his cart alongside the man who, on a warm August morning, was wearing a black raincoat and the billed cap he sported in his role as chauffeur.

"Good morning, Ed."

Ed Coffey turned, startled.

"I hear you're mongering some pretty negative stuff about Harley Welch and George Gaynor." Emma Newland might be a lot of things, but she was no liar.

Ed's face flushed with anger. "I don't know what you're talkin' about, I don't know anybody named Gaynor."

"If you did know this particular Gaynor, I

believe you'd find him to be upright, law-abiding, and a contribution to our community. As for Harley Welch, he, too, has paid his debt to society and proves daily to be a kind and responsible citizen. I pray you'll find it in your heart to think twice . . . before misrepresenting these men again."

"Where do you come off, tellin' me what to do about somebody I never heard of? Preachers think they know it all—goin' around actin' high an' mighty, tellin' innocent people how to live."

Father Tim walked away, pushing his cart toward the seafood case. Ed Coffey, it appeared, did not take kindly to reprimand.

"Fresh salmon!" he told Avis Packard. "That's what I was hoping. But of course your seafood comes in on Thursday, and if I buy it on Thursday, I'd have to freeze it 'til Monday."

"For ten bucks I can have a couple pounds flown in fresh on Monday, right off th' boat. Should get here late afternoon."

No one in the whole of Mitford would pay hard-earned money to have salmon shipped in. But his wife loved fresh salmon, and this was no time to compromise. Not for ten bucks, anyway.

"Book it!" he said, grinning.

"You understand th' ten bucks is just for shippin'. Salmon's extra."

"Right."

"OK!" Avis rubbed his hands together with undisguised enthusiasm. "I've got just the recipe!"

Some were born to preach, others born to shop, and not a few, it seemed, born to meddle. Avis was born to advocate the culinary arts. Father Tim took a notepad and pen from his jacket pocket. "Shoot!"

"Salmon roulade!" announced Avis. "Tasty, low-fat, and good for diabetes."

"Just what the doctor ordered!" said Father Tim, feeling good about life in general.

After putting the groceries away, he made a quick swing up the hill to the hospital, where he prayed with Joe Ivey. Then he visited the Sprouses, where he dropped off dog treats, delivered a pot of chives for Rachel's kitchen window, prayed with Bill, and was able to witness, firsthand, Buddy's Bible quiz. Afterward, he hustled to Hope House, where he sat on the footstool and provided rough harmony for Louella's rendition of "Bread of Life," after which he took the elevator to the dining room and found Pauline.

"How do you feel about tomorrow?"

"It's all right," she said. "I don't blame Sammy for not wantin' to see me. I understand."

"You do?"

"Yessir, I think I do. Just look at th' miracles God has worked in our family. But I'm countin' on Him for two more. Do you think that's askin' too much?"

He saw the scar on her cheek from the terrible burn. "Never! Saint Paul reminds us that God is able to do super-abundantly, over and above all that we ask or think. But it may take time."

"Yes," she said. "I know."

He hugged her, wordless. Pauline was the one whom God had chosen to give Dooley Barlowe to the world, to him; he was extra thankful for that gift.

It was a conundrum.

As technological advances increased to make people's lives easier, life became increasingly difficult, i.e., faster, more frantic, more complicated and demanding, all due, in his opinion, to technological advances.

Nonetheless, he could hardly wait to get hold of his e-mail.

"*Everybody's* online," said Emma, giving him a look that would stop a clock.

"Good for them!" he said, more determined than ever to go against the grain.

Timothy, for heaven's sake+*

this is a new keyboard /I am doing my best9

have not hearD from you in a coon's age. Get cracking.

abner expert at building things—a bookcase for my hut and a dog house for Willie who has adopted the lot of us. tHe children come daily, their number grows We are having a show of their art based on Bible stories and charging one dollar admission which goes to the local food bank/I hope you'll be willing to triple what we raise, in return you will receive a vibrant depiction of Noah and the Flood. oR would you rather have Jonah And the Whale?

(*U

Hope you've mended,, too bad your medic won't allow you into the boondocks, it would do you good and help you, too. Richard backed the Jeep into the front corner of my hut yesterday a/

.m. as I was having morning prayer. The underpin was knocked out which sent the corner dipping—all books and furnishings on the northwest side slid/ flew/careened to the south east side, piling on top of yours truly. I am uninjured, but justifiably appalled at Richard's driving skills. We have heaved the thing back onto its pin, a monstrous job.

attendance growing at all churches, we break bread together on Sunday in a parish-wide dinner on the grounds. Pray for us.

your sec'y says you abhor anything to do with computers, be a good fellow and join us in the twenty-first century . . . if you were online we could have daily chinwags. Great fun@

will let you know amount raised Tues next, will look for yr check returnmail, best greetings to yr lovely consort. Fr Roland

PS Elly is a seven year old girl who yesterday asked if my collar keeps away fleas and ticks. Look what you're missing!!

PPS Thanx for the $$, it wasn't half enough but we shall manage.

Thank you, Father, for asking Emma to keep in touch, I urge you to start e-mailing, you will enjoy it ever so much!

The wall between Mona's and Ernie's has been partially removed and turned into a kind of waist-high divider with pots of artificial plants sitting on top. This is being generally looked upon as good news. All I know is that Ernie is more himself again.

Sam's health is improving daily. Thank you for your prayers, we could not do without them. It helps so much to know that a dear friend takes our concerns to the Lord, sometimes Sam and I believe we can actually feel the prayers lifted for us, and ask God to bless those praying!

Will let you know when Misty's baby arrives, it won't be long now. Junior is beside himself.

More good news! Morris stayed for coffee and cake last Sunday, but only a few minutes, it is a great triumph for Jean Ballenger who has always believed it could happen. We are planning a most ambitious Christmas program around our organ music. Morris is composing something special, and people will be coming from across. Oh, how I wish we could get you to join us!

I think we can safely say the Tolsons will make it—Jeffrey is what we call a changed man in every degree! Clearly, it is the work of the Lord (he says you had a long talk that night on the beach).

We beg you to take care of yourself! Please give our fondest greetings to Cynthia. Any time you can get away for a visit, you may have our guestroom and all the love our hearts hold for you both. Sam sends his best. Marion

Hope Winchester climbed the wooden stepladder and, poised on the third rung, cleaned the topmost interior of the bookstore display window with a solution of vinegar and water.

She had considered asking George Gaynor to do the job, since he was so much taller and wouldn't have to stand on tiptoe as she was doing. But she couldn't ask a Ph.D. to perform a menial task like washing windows.

She was careful not to splash any of the smelly solution onto the display below, which featured stacks of *Foggy Mountain Breakdown* by Sharyn McCrumb, and other books set in the southern highlands. So far, the third annual Mountain Month at Happy Endings had enjoyed only mild success, even in view of the ten percent discount for every book containing the word *mountain* in its title. People could get ten percent off anything, anywhere, she concluded. She proposed that next year they offer fifteen percent. In her opinion, fifteen percent was when people started to pay attention.

She raised the squirt bottle with her right hand and fired the solution toward the window, then turned slightly to wipe it down with the paper towel in her left hand.

It seemed as if she were falling in slow motion, like a feather, or perhaps some great hand held her gently, guiding her down and breaking her fall to the floor of the display window, where she landed on an arrangement of Charles Frazier's *Cold Mountain* in paperback.

"I declare!" said the Woolen Shop's Minnie Lomax, who was on her way to the post office. "That is the most *interesting* window display. Very modern. A mannequin lying on books." She knew Hope Winchester liked to try different things; she had once put a fake cat on a footstool, which caused half the population to stand in front of the window waiting for the cat to move. Though impressively lifelike, it never did, of course, which made some people feel foolish.

Adjusting her bifocals and walking on, Minnie deemed the current display "too New

York for this town!" a criticism she proclaimed aloud, albeit to herself, as she waited for the light to change.

"Hope!"

She saw George Gaynor bending over her, instructing her to do something.

"Hope!" he said again, looking anxious.

Why should she hope any longer? She was an old maid who would never marry, who made clumsy, foolish mistakes in front of handsome men, and who had fallen off a ladder. She was so disgusted with herself that she didn't even try to move or get up. She felt no pain, only a certain breathlessness, as if the wind had gone out of her altogether. She wanted nothing more than to lie here, to close her eyes and somehow get the whole thing over with. She was mildly disappointed that she hadn't died in the fall.

"Are you hurt?"

"I don't know," she whispered.

"I've had some medical training. I'm going to lift you very gently. Easy, now."

His face was close to hers. What if she had bad breath? She drew her head away sharply.

"Have I hurt you?"

"No!"

He raised her to a sitting position. "There. How does that feel?"

"Wonderful!" she said, without meaning to. "That is, *fine*! Just fine, thank you." She supposed she would have to get up now, and go on with her life; she couldn't just lie in the window with a gaggle of small children staring at her. She spied Miss Tomlinson waving at her with one hand, while holding on to a string grasped by each of her kindergarten students.

Are . . . you . . . all right? mouthed Miss Tomlinson.

Yes, Hope mouthed back.

"How does your back feel?" asked George.

"Good! Great! I'm just a little . . . addled, I think."

"Shall I help you stand?"

She nodded.

His long, slender fingers touched hers, and then his hands gripped her own and were pulling her up, up, up . . .

When she came to her feet, she felt strong and tall—easily as tall as George Gaynor.

"There!" he said, smiling. "Thank God you weren't hurt."

"I was only standing on the third rung," she said, dazzled suddenly by an extraordinary happiness.

CHAPTER EIGHTEEN

Looking Alike

"I bet I know why Sammy don't want to see Mama."

"Why?"

"'Cause he hates her for givin' him away."

Jessie announced her opinion to Poo, who sat between herself and Dooley in the backseat of the Mustang on their way down the mountain.

"But Mama says our daddy run off with 'im."

"Yeah, but Mama didn't run after our daddy to get Sammy back."

"Oh," said Poo.

Jessie took a comb from her plastic purse and pulled it through her long hair. "Me an' Sammy were lost."

"But now you're found," said Dooley.

"I wadn't ever lost," said Poo. "I was always with Mama."

Jessie frowned. "Because you're her pet."

"I ain't her pet, she likes us all th' same."

"No, she don't."

"Doesn't," said Dooley, clenching his jaw.

"Yeah, she does, 'cause you're th' only one she didn't give away or let somebody run off with."

"She loves us all th' same," said Poo. "Exactly th' same."

Jessie dug into her purse and pulled out a compact. "I wonder if Sammy looks like us."

"He does!" Father Tim peered into the rearview mirror at the talkative and opinionated Jessie, the peacemaking Poo, and Dooley, who looked unseeing out the window. "When Miss Pringle saw Sammy, she thought he was Dooley."

Dooley shot a brief but irritable glance into the rearview mirror. Clearly he didn't agree that the boy with a ponytail might be confused with himself.

Jessie sat forward and questioned the front seat. "Do y'all think me an' Poo an' Dooley look alike?"

"Peas in a pod," said Father Tim.

Buck laughed. "The only way I can tell you from Poo, is Poo don't wear a skirt to school."

"How can you tell Poo from Dooley?"

"Dooley's a couple heads taller," said Buck.

Jessie sat back, surveyed herself in the mirror of the compact, then studied her younger brother. "Poo is much, much uglier than me," she announced.

"You're a big, fat dope," said Poo.

Lon Burtie's place was a 1950s Amoco station set on a slab of cracked asphalt.

Lon greeted them at the door. "It ain't much," he said, extending his hand. "But come on in, an' welcome."

They entered a small, concrete-floored room with a wall of empty shelves. A vintage snack-vending machine stood in the corner.

"Y'all come on back, I don't live up here in th' front."

"I'm scared," Jessie whispered to Buck.

He took her hand. "What's there to be scared about?"

"I don't know, but I'm shakin', so I must be scared."

"You're excited," said her stepfather. "There's a difference."

Jessie looked sober. "Maybe sometimes," she said, "but not every time."

When they entered the room, Sammy sat in

a chair opposite a television set. He stood instantly, looking anxious.

"Better turn this thing off," said Lon. He walked to the table next to Sammy and picked up the remote. The screen went black and Lon nodded to the group. "Y'all sit down. This is where I hang out, it was th' grease rack back when Amoco had it."

Sammy cleared his throat. "H-h-hey," he said.

Jessie burst into tears, clinging to Buck's arm.

Buck's hand was gentle on her shoulder, guiding her toward Sammy. "You an' Poo come say hey to your brother."

Sammy moved stiffly toward them; Father Tim watched the scene unfold in a kind of slow motion.

Jessie approached Sammy with caution, as did Poo. The room was strangely quiet. Dooley remained by the door, his face tense.

Suddenly Poo sprinted toward Sammy, arms outstretched, sobbing. "Hey, Sammy! Hey, Sammy!"

Poo and Jessie reached their brother at the same time, where some awkward connection of feet knocked Sammy to the floor. The three went down in a pile, Jessie shrieking with excitement.

Father Tim watched Dooley go to his

brother and hold out his hands and help him to his feet. They looked at each other for a moment, then embraced, silent and weeping.

"I'm goin' to cook for you, Sammy!" Jessie pulled on Sammy's T-shirt. "Every mornin' before school, I'll cook you eggs an' you can have all th' money I been savin'."

"I got a new baseball bat, Sammy, it's th' best bat you ever seen, you can use it if you want to."

Lon Burtie wiped his eyes on his bare arm.

Buck drew a bandanna from his jeans pocket.

Father Tim turned and looked away, his heart nearly bursting with joy and sorrow intermingled.

"Sammy wants to show us his garden, may I take the car?"

"How far is it?"

"A couple of miles."

"What about . . . ?" He didn't want to say *your father.*

"He's not there, he won't be there all day."

"Good." Father Tim reached into his pocket and handed the key to Dooley. He had never before seen the boy's face so radiant. The power of love was transforming; God had known that all along.

"I learned to drink this stuff in Nam," Lon said as he poured tea into three mugs.

"They wouldn't take me." Buck looked at the floor, then up again. "What branch?"

"Army. I was a machine gunner's mate, E-4. We flew Hueys in and out of th' war zone, a big 'copter that transported men and artillery."

In a moment of uncomfortable silence, the only sound came from two fans moving the close, humid air.

"I thought I might never get over bein' there, but I had to, it was eatin' me alive. The stuff goin' down in Nam was hard enough to deal with . . . then we came home and had to deal with what was goin' down in here." He made a fist and hit his head with a quick, ironic gesture.

"I'm sorry," Father Tim said.

"Yeah, well, I can talk about it a little now. Only thing is, there's not many to talk to 'cept Sammy." Lon grinned. "He's a good boy, I'm glad you found 'im. But you don't want to cross 'im, he's got 'is daddy's temper."

Buck blew on his steaming tea. "We don't know how to go about this, exactly, we're tryin' not to step in anything. I don't know if he might like to, you know, come live with us."

Lon shrugged. "Sammy feels responsible for

'is daddy, he does everything but wipe 'is rear end. Buys 'is liquor, puts food on th' table, hoofs to town when I can't take 'im, washes th' bedsheets his old man pukes on. Clyde Barlowe is one sorry sonofagun. For a fact, about as sorry as they come."

"We assume it's true about Barlowe bein' gone today. I wouldn't want th' kids to get in any trouble."

"It's all right, he hightailed it up to Virginia with Cate Turner, one of his drinkin' buddies."

Cate Turner. Lace Harper's father. Father Tim was glad there'd never be any reason to mention this to her. "When will he get back, do you know?" Maybe they could take Sammy up the mountain for a day. . . .

"He'll get back tonight, they go across th' state line to buy lottery tickets. He'll come home blasted out of his gourd and stay that way for four or five days."

"He needs help," said Buck. "I was bad to drink myself."

"Us ol' liquor heads, you line us up, we'd go around th' world more'n a few times."

"What can we do?" asked Buck. "For now? For th' short haul?"

Lon shook his head. "I don't know what to tell you. I offered Sammy a place over here, but he wouldn't leave Clyde."

"We don't want to force anything," said Buck. "But . . ."

"If you ran this deal through a social service agency, you could get Sammy out. The question is, would he be willin' to go?"

"What's this Jaybird Johnson business?" asked Father Tim.

"I think Clyde prob'ly stole somebody's ID, I don't have all th' details on that."

"How much schooling has Sammy had, do you have any idea?"

"I've known him since he was around seven, eight years old. Not much schoolin', I can tell you for sure. He don't like sittin' in a classroom, they've held 'im back two grades. But he's got a keen mind, very keen. You saw his garden, he took to doin' that like a pig takes to slop, it's natural to him. On th' other hand, he can shoot the hair off any pool player you want to name. That's natural, too; it's an odd combination. I believe he could do 'most anything he set his mind to, but stayin' around here, he'll never amount to nothin'." Lon shrugged. "I don't much care to stay around here myself, but . . ."

"But what?" asked Father Tim.

Lon gave a short, cackling laugh. "But I ain't plannin' to amount to nothin', so why bother to leave?"

"An old preacher in Mississippi once said,

'God don't make junk.' I'm sure you amount to more than you let on." Father Tim smiled. "You have a trade?"

"I paint houses. I got a truck, a couple of ladders, I keep busy. Th' whole deal is to show up on time, do your work, stay sober, an' clean up after yourself."

"Good plan."

"You might say my sideline keeps me goin'."

"What's that?" asked Buck.

"While th' kids are over at Clyde's, I'd like to show you—I don't get much of a chance to, you know, show it to anybody."

"Please!" said Father Tim. "Lead on."

Lon took them across the large, sparsely furnished room to a door.

"This was th' head."

"That's OK," said Buck, "I don't need to go. How 'bout you, Father?"

"*Was* th' head," said Lon. Father Tim thought their graying, fiftyish host was a surprisingly handsome man when he smiled. Lon opened the door and stood back.

Father Tim drew in his breath. "Good heavens!"

Buck removed his ball cap. "Man!"

"This is my garden. Walk in."

The room was fairly sizable. Where toilet stalls had been, the walls on three sides were lined with shelves containing potted orchids of varying colors and petal shapes. Orchids also sat in pots on shelves above a washbasin, and clung to a wire screen, their roots trailing into the air. A rattan blind was raised over a small window admitting light from the south.

"Some of these plants are pretty old, I bought 'em after I came back from Da Nang. This'n right here, it's *Paphiopedilum delenatii,* I brought it out of Nam in a duffel bag, wrapped bare root in my underwear. For a long time people thought it was extinct, it would've been worth ten, fifteen thousand bucks back then."

Buck whistled softly.

"It'd probably bring about as much today, but I wouldn't part with it, no way."

"Are they all out of Nam?"

"They come from all over. These here originated in th' Philippines, this one in India, over there, th' dark pink, that's a South American variety."

"Marvelous!" said Father Tim.

"It's good an' humid down here by th' river, they like that."

"How'd you get started doin' this?" Buck wanted to know.

"Th' whole thing started with a man named . . ."—Lon cleared his throat, suddenly moved—"Tran van Hoi. We met in the mountains, where he lived with his family in a little hut. He was the enemy, accordin' to th' U.S., but he was . . . the best friend I ever had."

Lon wiped his eyes with the heel of his hand, unashamed. "I took most of my R and R time in th' jungle, just lookin' at th' beauty. I was never afraid of th' jungle, I grew up in th' woods around here before it was timbered off and strip-malled. Tran taught me about orchids, they say there's twenty-five hundred different kinds just in Nam."

"Words fail," said Father Tim.

"Yeah, well, I wish everybody who pulled time over there could have somethin' like this. It's what's kept me from losin' it completely. See these halogen deals I installed? Th' light fakes 'em out, they don't have a clue they're growin' in a Amoco station outside of Holding, North Ca'lina."

Lon grinned. "You might say electricity's my only vice since I laid off weed an' alcohol."

"This is great," said Buck. "Just great!"

"A day of miracles!" said Father Tim.

Four miracles down, and one—at least—to go.

Hope Winchester sat on the stool at the cash register, a book closed in her lap, and tried to understand what had happened when she fell.

She had gone down in a state of perplexity and anguish, and had been lifted up in a state of . . . it was important to find just the right word . . . in a state of happiness. She had always been leery of that word, and avoided using it. But happiness seemed to be what she had experienced—happiness and liberty.

Liberty!

She had never felt free in her life, until after the fall. To put it another way, she had gone down bearing a heavy weight and come up light and diaphanous, like the wings of a moth.

Even her mother had noticed something different when they talked on the phone the other day. Her mother, who was in constant pain, seemed to forget the pain for a change and concentrate on her daughter, a hundred miles to the north. "You sound good," her mother said. "You sound different." And then, at the end, she said, "You must be happy. I hope you'll get on the bus and come let your sister and me see you looking happy."

Though she was sitting in the way she usually sat on this odd and disagreeable stool—tight in the shoulders and along her spine, having nothing to lean her back upon—in her mind she was dancing, her face to the sun.

"That's a beautiful smile you're wearing today," said George, coming in from the mailroom.

"Thank you," she said. She noticed that she didn't roll herself into a ball inside, nor was her heart racing. She'd said thank you in the most natural way in the world, which was part of the miracle of transformation she'd just been contemplating.

"By the way, if you ever need help for any reason, you can call me at Miss Pringle's. I know you had trouble with the plumbing the other evening."

"I appreciate it. I do." The toilet had run over just as she was getting ready to lock up, and a plumber had to be summoned from Wesley.

"Coffee this morning?"

"Yes!" she said, still smiling. She didn't try to pay him, for he would never take it. "I'd love coffee."

"The usual way," he said. It was not a question.

"Yes." Her eyes met his, and she felt no fear, no fear at all. She didn't shrink or recoil or wish to hide her head beneath the sales counter. "Thank you."

"Back in ten." Now he was smiling, too. "Hold down the fort," he said, closing the door behind him.

She slid from the stool and walked to the center of the room to bask in the pale rectangle of light that shone through the glass-paneled door. She still felt stiff and sore from the fall, but stretched her arms and arched her back, in the manner of Margaret Ann, the bookshop cat, who was slumbering in the Gardening section. It was all she could do to restrain herself from dancing, though she knew nothing at all about dancing, had never danced, nor ever before wished to.

She remembered the story of a man who'd suffered a blow to the head and, shortly afterward, sat down and played Chopin and Beethoven, though he'd never had a lesson, much less been exposed to a piano. Then there was the ten-year-old boy who, after a fall down the stairs, suddenly became a genius at math. Even though she hadn't injured her head, had something like that happened to her?

She should read about this phenomenon, of course, and turned toward the shelf where such a book might possibly be found. But . . . she stopped and considered: she didn't want to read a book. Not at all. She didn't even want to pore over the dictionary and learn the word, if there was one, for what seemed to have happened to her.

What, then, did she want?

A light flickered in her eyes. She wanted to feel her new feelings. One by one.

&

He'd come back from his trip down the mountain elated and exhausted at once.

But "old time it was a–flying," and he had to get cracking with his sermon notes.

Unfortunately, a ringing phone was always a temptation when he was working on a sermon. . . . It blew the weight of responsibility away, if only for a fraction of . . .

"Hello!"

"Father Tim, Lew Boyd."

"Lew! I hadn't heard back from you, did you change your mind?"

"Oh, no. Wouldn't do that. Thing is, we, ah . . ."

"Yes?"

"We run off to South Carolina and done it with th' justice of th' peace."

"Ah!"

"See, me an' Earlene ain't exactly spring chickens."

"Right."

"So we already knew all th' stuff you aimed to talk to us about."

"Aha."

"So we didn't see no use to waste your time . . ."

"No waste at all."

". . . or ours, you know—we didn't want to waste ours, neither."

"Don't blame you a bit."

"You don't?"

"Certainly not! Congratulations!"

"Remember, you can't tell nobody."

"I remember."

"Not a soul."

"Got it."

"You come on by th' station, I'll give you a free wash and sweep you out."

"That's mighty good of you, Lew, you don't have to do that."

"I *aim* t' do that! You come on by."

"Thank you kindly. I wanted to say I was sorry about the news regarding Harley. I knew it, of course, but . . ."

"I ain't goin' to worry about it. I took a little heat when George pitched in to help on weekends, an' I'll take a little over this, but they're two of th' hardest-workin' fellers you ever seen. Most of th' help I've had th' last few years has been so triflin' it's criminal . . . in a manner of speakin'."

"Well, then! When do we get to meet Earlene?"

"She's goin' to stick with her job another year to, you know, get her retirement benefits an' all, then she'll be movin' to Mitford."

"A long-distance marriage. I hear that's the going thing these days."

"I'm puttin' a new engine in my Dodge Ram, an' replacin' th' carburetor."

"That'll do it."

"Remember not to tell nobody."

"Right."

"We're plannin' to stay low-key 'til, you know, we get things straightened out."

"Aha."

"Well, you come on over in a day or two and get your wash job."

"I will, Lew, and thank you. We'd like to have you and Earlene over when things settle down."

"We 'preciate it, Father."

"May God bless your marriage to be a long and happy one!"

"We 'preciate it."

He was grinning when he hung up. He had rather a fondness for late-blooming romances.

They had found Sammy Barlowe; Bill Sprouse was preaching at First Baptist on Sunday; and as for himself, his weight was steady, his sugar hovering around normal, and he had his own preaching to do.

He should have been shouting for joy. Instead, he felt the old darkness moving upon him.

At four o'clock, he pulled on his running clothes and laced up his shoes. Exercise doesn't take energy, he lectured himself, it gives energy, everybody knows that.

Barnabas came and stood by his knee, looking soulfully into his eyes. His was a profound dog, always had been. He put his arm around the large head, its dark coat now shot through with silver, and whispered, "You, my friend, are the best of the best." He held his dog's head close to his beating heart. There had never been, nor ever would be, a more boon companion than this.

"God be with you," he said, hoarse.

He wandered down to the kitchen and opened the refrigerator and saw that Puny had left his dinner covered with foil, ready to be reheated. He peered under the foil.

Chicken-something, carrot-something, spinach-something. He was sure it would look more appetizing when hot, though he could have eaten the whole thing on the spot. He devoured a spoonful of peanut butter, instead, smiling to see that Puny had placed the *Anglican Digest* by his plate on the kitchen island, to keep him company at supper.

Instead of heading toward Farmer, he decided they'd run north on Main Street, hook a right, cross over Little Mitford Creek, hook another right, then take a left up to the hospital. Afterward, they'd run down Old Church Lane and across Baxter Park. This would give them better than a mile and a quarter, which was, after all, better than nothing. When Cynthia got home and things were back to normal, he'd make up for this week's short time.

Cynthia . . .

He stood on his front steps, holding the red leash. He missed his wife. No wonder he was feeling blue. He had tried to keep himself from knowing this. . . .

He experienced a sudden wave of emotion, something like the "sinking feeling" his mother used to talk about, and shrugged it off. His sugar was fine, he'd just checked it, and he'd drunk plenty of water—it was time to get on with it.

They trotted down the steps and along the walk and out to the street. Another beautiful August day in the mountains—but dry. Dry as tinder. The little rain they'd had was hardly enough to make a showing on the gauge. Harley had watered the roses with the soaking hose eight times, by Father Tim's count, and the perennial beds were looking none too hale. In truth, the *Mitford Muse* had warned of a forthcoming Water Watch.

"Okay, old fellow," he said, as they broke into a light run.

❧

He huffed by the Woolen Shop and nearly steamrolled a woman coming out with a shopping bag.

"Excuse me, I'm sorry, I should look where I'm going—"

"No harm done in the least! Are you Father Tim?"

"Yes ma'am!"

She extended her hand, smiling. "Millie Tipton from Methodist Chapel."

By George, she was wearing a collar. . . .

"Reverend Tipton! Glad to meet you at last. Welcome to Mitford." He'd have to bake her a pie, and be quick about it; she'd been in town several weeks.

"I'm proud to be here. I was hoping we might have coffee sometime. Even though you're retired, I understand you're still quite a force in Mitford. Everyone loves you."

His face flushed. A former bishop had warned him never to completely trust a man loved by everyone. "Not everyone!" he insisted. "Perhaps you'll join us one morning at the Grill, if you can bear the company of an aging clergyman, a grouchy newspaper editor, and a . . . a realtor." He decided his buddy Mule defied description.

"A microcosm of the world social order!" she said, laughing. "I hear the Turkey Club meets around eight o'clock most mornings?"

"Alas, there are no secrets in Mitford!" he said.

Joe Ivey seemed pale, withered.

"They's somethin' else wrong, they don't know what. They're runnin' tests enough t' cave in th' whole Medicare system."

"Sorry you're down, buddy, but you'll get up again."

"I hate t' turn th' haircut trade in this town over to that blankety-blank woman."

"She'll be swamped, all right, you've built up a good business. But you haven't turned it over yet."

"When Winnie rented 'er that space, Winnie seen it as a kind of hair emporium that would serve all y'r hair needs in one place— upstairs for a perm an' rinse an' whatnot, downstairs t' my chair for a cut an' maybe a shave. But nossir, Miz Fancy Pants got so she wanted th' whole dern shebang." Joe looked him in the eye. "I'm tryin' not t' hate 'er guts."

"That's the ticket. Keep trying! Ask God to help you."

Joe sighed deeply. "You know th' trouble with th' barberin' trade?"

"What's that?"

"Nobody wants to do it n'more. Too much standin' on your feet all day."

"I hear you."

"Varicose veins, lower back pain, bunions, I don't know what all. That's why I run off t' Graceland that time t' do security."

"And God used that time in your life. Just think—at Graceland, you gave up drinking."

Joe closed his eyes; a faint smile appeared on his face.

"You did give it up?"

Joe opened his eyes and burst into laughter. He laughed 'til he coughed. "Before God, I did, but I like to see you *fret* about whether I done it or not."

"You scoundrel," said the priest. "Let me pray for you."

While he was on the hill, maybe he could work in a quick visit to Hope House—give Louella a kiss, swing by to see Pauline, catch up with his old friend Scott Murphy. . . .

But no. He didn't have it in him.

"Home," he said to Barnabas.

They loped down Old Church Lane and

hung a right into the cool, green shade of Baxter Park. Why did he so often forget about Baxter Park and its sweet, hidden beauty? It was time to bring his wife here again for a picnic, maybe in early October when the sugar maples were turning.

"Hello, Father!"

Barnabas came to a screeching halt, his hair bristling, as Lace Turner appeared with a brown Labrador puppy on a leash. Barnabas stood, stiff and suspicious, uttering a low growl.

"This is Guber!" said Lace, struggling to keep the leaping puppy at a proper distance.

"Goober?" What kind of name was that for a beautiful young woman's dog?

"For *gubernatorial.* Hoppy says he looks gubernatorial, like our governor."

"By George, he does! How are you, my dear?"

"Great! Look, Barnabas is getting friendly."

His dog's tail was now wagging, albeit with a dash of caution. The puppy was barking to beat the band, and eager to get at the black behemoth on the red leash.

"Think we could sit down and visit a minute?" asked Father Tim.

"I don't think it would be a good idea," she said, smiling. "But—we could try!"

She picked up her puppy and sat with it in

her lap on one end of a park bench. He thumped down beside her.

"Ahh," he said. "This is a treat!" Barnabas sprawled in the grass, his eyes alert to the puppy. "Are you excited about the University of Virginia?"

"Yes, sir. It's beautiful there."

"I visited as a young seminarian. I remember they don't call their campus a campus."

"Yes," she said. "It's called 'the grounds.'"

"You'll do well. And if you ever need prayer—for anything, at any time, please give me a call. Will you remember that?"

"Yes, sir. I will."

"I wore my boots the other day."

"Are they comfortable?"

"Very! Thanks again. One of the most thoughtful gifts I ever received."

She smiled and nodded, pleased.

"When are you off?"

"Monday."

"That's when Dooley leaves, as well."

She lowered her eyes and kissed the top of Guber's velveteen head.

"We've found Dooley's brother Sammy," he said.

He heard her quick intake of breath.

"They've had a visit, we're hopeful about the future."

She continued to nuzzle the head of her puppy, silent.

"I'm sorry for the times Dooley has treated you rudely."

She looked up at him; there was a flicker of sorrow in her amber eyes.

"He told me you once declined to return his call. I think that . . . hurt him, somehow." He was meddling, of course. Preachers couldn't seem to help themselves when it came to meddling.

"Why should I return his call, when he would only act arrogant and cold towards me?"

"That's a good question. I don't think he wants to act arrogant and cold towards you."

"If he doesn't want to, then he should stop doing it." The anger he saw in her eyes might have been as ancient as the pyramids.

"Yes. I agree. He should. And Lace . . ."

"Yes, sir?"

"I believe he will."

He didn't know whether she heard him—or believed him.

"Look," said Lace. "Guber is asleep."

"You may leave early, if you'd like."

They were packing most of the gardening books into boxes; except for a couple of storms, the season in Mitford had been too dry for much enthusiasm in the garden. Hope hated returns—all that work to write a book, and then, in the end, if it didn't sell, off it went to a book graveyard.

"That's OK, I'd rather stick around."

"You were here late yesterday, it would be fine for you to leave early." She didn't think people on a small salary should be required to work overtime, free.

"Most people know the shop closes at six. It wouldn't look right for me to be taking my ease at four-thirty."

She thought his eyes as blue as the sea. "Why not?"

"I don't want to cause any unnecessary talk or suspicion, because it all falls back on good people like you and Father Tim. If, God forbid, anything went wrong in town, a lot of eyes would turn to me—or to Harley. It's just the way things are."

"Things shouldn't be that way."

"Yes, but it's the way things are."

She saw the resolve in him. "Yes," she said. "Well."

She'd had few friends in her life, and had never once been friends with a man. But the feeling with George was different now; ever since the fall, it had been different. It was a nice, comfortable feeling.

"How's your mother?" he asked.

"A little better. But not much. I think I should go see her in September."

"You seem to be doing fine since your fall."

"I feel wonderful, really. It's hard to express, I've been trying to understand it. But something happened when I fell. Something . . . lovely."

"I'm glad. I've been praying for you."

She supposed that was what Christians did—they prayed for people. But she didn't want them praying for her; it seemed an invasion of her privacy.

"You really needn't bother to pray for me, I don't believe in it." Something of the old, cold reserve returned and chilled her heart.

"You don't need to believe in it for me to pray for you. And it's no bother, it's a blessing."

"Oh," she said, looking at him. She supposed he was still handsome, but she didn't see that now. What she was seeing, more and more, was his kindness.

"Since the fall," he said, smiling, "you seem to be living up to your name."

"Yes." She mused on this with wonder. "I think that's true. I never really believed in my name. Hope seemed very . . . alien. I thought I should have been a Janet or a Peggy."

"I think Hope is right for you."

"Thank you." A lovely warmth flooded her

heart; tears sprang to her eyes. It was as if she'd been given her name for the first time, in a kind of baptism. "I remember when you looked down at me in the window—you said, *'Hope!'* as if it were a command. I didn't associate the word with my name; instead, it was something you were urging me to do."

"*Hope* is a verb," he said, "as well as a noun."

They were sitting on the floor now instead of squatting, the open boxes between them.

"Where are your parents?" she asked. "Do they know you're in Mitford?"

"My parents were killed in a plane crash fifteen years ago. I was in the plane, also."

"Oh." She couldn't imagine such horror. "I'm sorry."

"I was pinned in the cockpit for three days, in freezing temperatures. Broken legs, fractured skull."

She shook her head, wordless.

"I made a deal with God then, but I didn't keep my end of the bargain."

"Are you . . . keeping your end of the bargain now?"

He smiled. "I'm trying."

"Do you like it in Mitford?"

"Very much."

"I don't think I ever quite understood how you came here, why you picked Mitford."

"I didn't pick Mitford, God did. I thought I was driving without purpose or direction. Mitford seemed no more than a random choice for a place to hide from the feds. Now I know that God led me here and put me in the attic of Lord's Chapel, specifically, so that when Father Tim prayed the prayer of salvation in the nave, I would be there—at that precise moment in time—to pray it, too."

"Couldn't it have happened anywhere?"

"Possibly. But I don't think so. I think this was my place, and that was my time."

"What sort of prayer is the prayer of salvation?" She had once read it in the letters-to-the-editor column of the *Muse,* but had no recollection of the words.

"It's simple. Very simple."

"But you don't seem a simple person. What made you think it true or profound?"

"The Holy Spirit spoke to my heart, and I knew it to be true."

She felt a slight shiver along her spine. The Holy Spirit. Speaking! "And it changed your life," she said. It wasn't a question; everyone in Mitford knew that some sort of prayer had changed the life of a man who turned himself in to face eight years of punishment.

"Yes."

She didn't relish the thought of asking him

to recite the prayer, if, indeed, he could; it would seem awkward. But she wished to know its content; it was natural that she wished to know, she was a curious person.

She was debating this when the bell jangled on the door and three Mitford School teachers breezed in, chattering happily. Hope knew they'd stopped by the bakery before coming to the bookstore; their clothes brought in a carefree scent of cinnamon and chocolate.

He spoke with Cynthia at eight-thirty; she was missing him, too.

"You miss me, I miss you. Bookends!" she said, calling the two of them by an affectionate name she'd contrived during their courtship.

"But I'm glad I encouraged you to go."

"You didn't encourage me at all, you insisted! But thanks for making me do it, Timothy, it's been a wonderful experience—exhausting, but wonderful."

"It was good for me to send you away."

"Why, dearest?"

"Because I'd grown afraid of losing you. Somehow, by sending you away, I lost the fear of losing you."

"Why were you afraid?"

"Your success. . . . I wondered if it would overshadow what we had."

"Nothing can do that, Timothy. And you can never, ever lose me, I refuse to be lost."

"I love you, Kavanagh." He was in the mood to be mushy with his wife. Life was short! "Madly."

"I love you madly back!"

"I'll have a surprise or two for you." Salmon roulade was all he'd come up with so far, but surely he could think of something else.

"I love surprises," she said, happy. "Now hurry to bed, sweetheart. You sound bushed."

He read the evening office and was hurrying to bed, minding his wife.

Somehow, the day had seemed a hundred years long. It might have been another age and time when he'd driven with Buck and the children down the mountain and witnessed their joy. Even Dooley, who usually chose his words carefully, had talked nonstop going home—what they'd all do when they got together with Sammy again, how they might talk him into coming to Mitford for his first visit, how he would buy Sammy a really great pair of tennis shoes, plus he'd give him a lot of stuff he no longer wore. . . .

Jessie was determined to give Sammy her savings, which amounted to more than forty dollars; Poo would probably hang on to his new bat, but would give his brother his catcher's mitt and teach him to play softball; he was incredulous that Sammy didn't know how to play softball. . . .

He couldn't let the day end without talking to his boy.

"Hey," he said, when Dooley came to the phone.

"Hey, yourself!"

He heard the happiness in Dooley's voice.

"Just wanted to call and say how glad I am for today."

"Yes, sir. Me, too. I hate to go back Monday."

"I know. When you come home for Thanksgiving, maybe we can get Sammy to come, too." He felt an unexpected knot in his throat.

"He's got bad teeth."

"Yes."

"Maybe somehow we could get his teeth fixed, like Miss Sadie left money to fix mine."

"We can probably work that out." What a great idea. "Can you spare the time to swing by on Monday, on your way to Georgia? I should have Cynthia home a few minutes after twelve. You can have lunch with us, fill up on Puny's macaroni and cheese."

"OK. Great."

"Terrific."

"You know when you were asking me what Reba Sanders is like?"

"Yes."

"I forgot to tell you something."

"Ah."

"She's beautiful. Really beautiful."

"I'd like to meet her sometime. Which reminds me—I saw someone beautiful today."

"Who?"

"Lace Harper."

Silence.

"Don't hold her car against her, son. She's worth more than that. Far more. Remember the day Barnabas got hit? God enabled you to save his life. But you couldn't have done it without Lace.

"Remember how she pitched in?" He was filled with emotion at the memory of his stricken dog, lying helpless in the street and bleeding from a wound in the chest cavity as his master stood by, more helpless still. Dooley had known exactly what to do, while Lace, leaning only on courage and raw instinct, assisted him as if trained.

"I feel the greatest gratitude and pride toward you both."

"Yes, sir."

Dooley had heard him; he felt the arrow hit its mark.

So, maybe he was meddling, but he felt good about it. One thing he would not do is tell Dooley about Guber. He remembered Dooley once saying how much he wanted a brown Lab. Dooley might hear about the puppy from someone else, but no, indeed, he would not hear it from yours truly.

Uncle Billy Watson lay in his bed at the rear of the Mitford town museum, next to his wife of more than a half century.

He heard her snoring, and could plainly see the glow of the street lamp through the window, yet in some way he couldn't figure, he wasn't lying in his bed at all.

He was standing barefooted by the train track in a bright cove of Turncoat Mountain, listening for the whistle and watching the hawks soar and dip on unseen waves of thermal.

Yesterday he'd stood by the track in the very same place, and waited for the log train to come roaring through, blasting cinders and noise, power and heat on its way to Mortimer, fourteen miles south.

The train wouldn't even slow down here, nossir, this wasn't even a wide place in the road, but something wonderful could happen anyhow, something nearly about as good as the train grinding to a stop and the conductor leaning out the window and hollering, "Want a ride, Little Billy?"

His uncle, who helped the conductor, had several times in the past throwed him a packet from the train—though nothing in the past had ever matched the plain wonder of the little tin box that landed in his hands yesterday.

He remembered the first time his uncle throwed something out the train window. It was a note weighted with a small stone and tied with twine. According to what his mama read off to him, the note said:

> *Little Billy, I see you standin by the trak ever day wavin & think of your mama and how I haint seen my baby sister in two year. one day ill get off in mortimer & walk back to visit yall. be a good boy help your mama. yrs truly uncle joe.*

One time it was hard candy wrapped in a handkerchief that was none too clean.

Another time it was a pair of work shoes—but they was way yonder too little. He'd worn them anyhow, they'd near about crippled both feet, then passed them on to Maisie. His little sister had wore the shoes all day and slept in them at night, even though they was about two years this side of a good fit.

It was always a happy time standing there by the track, even if his uncle wasn't on the train, or if he maybe waved and didn't throw nothing down; it didn't matter. It made him swimmy-headed just to stand there and let that blast of heat run by him, scorching his bones and rattling his teeth 'til he sometimes hollered for pure joy.

Whatever was throwed out, he never messed with it right there by the track. He as good as shut his eyes and run all the way home about three mile, before he'd let it enter his mind what he was toting.

Like the time he got shoes, he knowed they was shoes, the fact of them being shoes went straight to his heart and made it beat like a hammer striking, but he kept his mind plumb closed to the fact they was shoes 'til he got down to their little log house by the creek. That way, him and his mama and Maisie could all be surprised at the same time.

"What's that you're a-totin'?" asked his mama.

He'd set the shoes on the table and his mama give a little gasp, and then tears gushed out of her eyes. He didn't say nothing and she didn't say nothing, either. She just sat down and looked at the shoes like they was a bag of pure gold.

"Well," she finally said, smiling at him. "Let's see do they fit."

But they didn't fit. He shoved his bare, callused feet into the shoes like he'd seen his mama stuff ground pork into a casing. It was all he could do to get them in there and tie up the strings.

"They might fit Maisie," she said.

"No ma'am, please, I want t' wear these shoes, they was give to me."

"Go on, then," she said.

One time Uncle Joe had throwed out a little paper sack with a duck call in it. You blowed in one end and out the other end come a sound like a wild duck calling its mate. He studied whether to keep it or sell it, he could've sold it if he'd walked to Mortimer, but Uncle Joe might have got wind of it getting sold and got his feelings hurt so he kept it and carried it in his pocket for a long time, always blowing on it whenever the notion struck. It had been a treat better than candy; then he'd lost it jumping over a creek.

He remembered one Christmas him and Maisie got presents in a stocking. It was one of his pap's old stockings with holes ever' which-away, it was hanging on a nail over the fireplace.

They had never had a Christmas stocking

before, and he nearly wet hisself for pure happiness. But when it come right down to it, they wasn't nothing in it to speak of.

Not one thing could match what Uncle Joe had throwed out of the train. Nossir. In the stocking was two oranges that got eat right up, and four little hard candies, two apiece, that they sucked on awhile, then took out of their mouth and laid up on the mantel to last another day, and a little doll for Maisie made out of corn shucks.

When he failed to carry on over the goods in the stocking, his pap said, "I'll be et f'r a tater if you ain't spiled rotten."

And he reckoned he was. Anybody who'd already got shoes and duck calls and all, they was bound to be spiled rotten.

The train whistle sounded faintly from the north. It would be coming around by the old riverbed. . . .

With his left hand, he patted his britches pocket to make sure the tin box was still there, and it was. His right hand held tight to what he'd worked on last night.

He had laid on the floor in front of the last of the little cook fire, to get the light, and with his mama helping him, managed to write a single line on a piece of paper his pap had brought him from the lumber company.

Writing just one line had taken what seemed like hours; he had erased again and again and again.

"*Joe's* got a *e* on th' end," said his mama. "Looky, this is a *e,* you can make a *e* if I can!" She signed the *e* in the air, and he copied it on the paper.

"Don't wear your pencil down too far," his mama said. "Hit's your drawin' pencil."

"That's OK, I won't need this 'un n'more, I'll give this 'un to Maisie."

"That drawin' you do, hit's not mortal," said his mama. "Hit's from th' good Lord."

"Looky here, is this *e* any good?"

"Hit is!" She clapped her hands together, and then a worried look come on her face. "I reckon I ought t' send you off t' school one day, where they can learn you to read an' write."

"No ma'am," he said, "I ain't a-goin' t' no school, I can learn m'self to read an' write."

It was bitter out by the track, but he was glad for no wind a-blowing. His bare feet stung with the cold, and he pulled his pap's old coat around him good and tight. Then all of a sudden he heard the whistle getting louder. Here it come!

He hoped to the good Lord he could do this right. Everything in him wanted it to land smack-dab in Uncle Joe's outstretched hands. What if it landed under the train and was grinded to bits? He prayed out loud for God in heaven to help him get the job done and not let old Scratch mess things up.

The train drew closer, *clacketyclackclackety-clack*.

If he ever got on that train, he knowed he'd never come back even if he did love his mama better than anything on earth and Maisie, too, and sometimes his pap.

Here it come, now, it had rounded the bend, and he seen Uncle Joe a-leaning out the window and waving. He waved back.

He'd never give Uncle Joe a dadjing thing before. Until yesterday, it had never entered his mind to do anything but wave.

His heart hammered. The train was nearly on him.

He drawed his arm back and throwed the best he could. The folded note, weighted with a stone and tied with a frayed apron sash, sailed up and up, over and over. . . .

Deer uncle joe . . .

The passage of the note, with the apron string fluttering on the air, seemed to take a long time . . .

it is th best thing i ever got . . .

. . . before it started falling down to where it

was going, and then it landed—smack-dab in Uncle Joe's hands. . . .

Yrs truly billy

He didn't have time to stand there patting hisself on the back, nossir.

He whipped that little tin box out of his britches pocket and the folded piece of paper out of his other britches pocket and set down on the rail, which was warm from the grinding of the great iron wheels, and balanced the box on his knee and opened it and took out one of the brand-new pencils he'd sharped with his mama's butcher knife and began to draw the caboose of the train, in quick, sure, flying strokes, until the image on the paper became real to him, as real as the train that had just hurtled by, taking his breath away.

When the phone rang at two o'clock in the morning, Father Tim sat up in bed, anxious.

"Hello?"

"Is this th' preacher?"

Rose Watson—he would know her voice anywhere. "Yes! What is it?"

"Get over here quick!" she squawked. "Bill Watson's passed!"

CHAPTER NINETEEN

A Day in Thy Courts

But Bill Watson had not passed.

After calling 911 and rushing to the Porter place to meet the ambulance, Father Tim found Uncle Billy semiconscious and Miss Rose hysterical.

"Dead as a doornail!" squawked the old woman.

"His heart is *still beating*!" he shouted.

"Still eating? Of course he was still eating, I suppose you think I starved him to death!"

"Oh, for *Pete's sake*!" he thundered.

"A piece of *cake*? You want a piece of cake at a time like this?" Her voice rose by several decibels. *"You'll not get a piece of cake out of me!"*

Thank heaven for that, he thought, hearing sirens race north along Main Street.

He rode in the ambulance with Uncle Billy, holding his hand and praying all the way, unmindful of how he'd get home from the hospital.

Nurse Kennedy, who was working the night shift, volunteered to drive him as soon as her break time came around.

It was four in the morning when he walked in the back door, arousing his dog, who had been waiting. He slumped into a chair in the study, too weary to navigate the stairs, then realized he'd failed to have Kennedy drive him to his car.

At four-thirty, he stumped upstairs, furious with himself and everybody else.

When the phone rang at six o'clock, he rolled over in bed and grabbed the blasted thing from the hook.

"Who's there?" He surprised himself by answering with his father's phone salutation.

"Good morning, Father Tim, it's Beverly Hobgood."

"Beverly Hobgood, Beverly Hobgood . . ." He had no idea.

"Bishop's secretary!"

"Oh, yes! Of course!"

"I knew you were an early riser. . . ."

"Absolutely." His head was pounding.

"I'm calling to ask you to pray for Bishop, I know he would covet your prayers."

"What is it?"

"Chest pains, very severe. He'll go for testing today."

No need to spend all that money to find out the cause, he wanted to say—it's stress, pure and simple. "Yes, I will pray. Certainly! Faithfully! And I'll ask others to pray."

"He depends on you!" she said, her voice breaking.

"And I depend on him."

When he hung up, he began to count the casualties. Joe Ivey, Uncle Billy, his bishop. . . .

He lay back against the pillows and stared at the ceiling.

Why in heaven's name didn't Stuart retire? Now that he'd gotten the ball rolling, let someone else build the cathedral!

But what good would it do his bishop to retire? Get a load of the fix yours truly was in—stress here, stress there, stress everywhere. If things kept going like this, he'd be looking for a way to retire from *being* retired.

Tomorrow was a big day, a huge day, what with two morning services, the lakeside service, and a four-hour round trip that, but for the large donation to the Children's Hospital, he would never in this lifetime have agreed to do.

As usual through the years, he couldn't rest until the sermon was finished and he felt a certain peace about it. Yet, no matter what he did, it wouldn't come together in the way he'd thought it might; the premise was strong, even powerful, but he couldn't make the pieces add up.

Strung out! he thought. That vernacular seemed to describe with considerable eloquence the way he was feeling.

After the morning office, he knelt to pray but found his mind wandering like an untethered goat. He wanted to call his wife and ask her to intercede for him, but that would alarm her. Besides, what was he thinking? She *was* praying for him; she did so faithfully.

"Dear God," he said aloud.

He remained on his knees in a kind of fog, finding he couldn't get beyond that pitiful supplication.

He was priest-in-charge, he thought as he had breakfast at the kitchen island, but without any help to lean on. The deacon had been called away to a family funeral, and the church's current senior warden was not, in his opinion, the one to visit Uncle Billy and pray with him.

Surely he himself could squeeze out a simple visit up the hill—one final effort and then home to seclude himself, take the phone off the hook, and delve the meaning of this thing he needed to communicate.

But no. He couldn't do it. The very thought of trotting down Main Street to his car and driving up the hill to the hospital . . . and Miss Rose would, of course, need a ride to visit her husband . . . maybe Hessie Mayhew, maybe Esther Bolick, though they'd never forgive him for asking . . .

He finished his poached eggs, took two aspirin, and went to his desk, glad that Puny wouldn't be in today.

"I preached as never sure to preach again, and as a dying man to dying men," Richard Baxter had written in the seventeenth century. That's how he wanted to preach. Every time may be the last time! Just as important, however, he wanted to preach with energy and enthusiasm as if for the first time. Well, he knew what he meant by all that. . . .

Scott Murphy. The idea came out of the blue.

"Of course, Father," said the Hope House chaplain. "I'll be glad to go pray with him. Anything else while I'm there?"

"Joe Ivey. Room Two-fourteen. If you could . . ."

"No problem at all."

"I owe you," he said, relieved.

"Consider yourself indebted to the Lord, if you will, but not to me. The truth is, I'm forever in your debt."

"How's that?"

"For bringing me to Mitford. Remember how you hired me before I interviewed with Miss Sadie?"

He grinned. "Yes, that was a great presumption on my part, but completely instigated by the Holy Spirit. So consider yourself indebted to Him, if you will, but not to me."

"Stalemate!" said Scott, laughing.

He spent the day in a kind of daze, walking his dog to the monument, opening and closing the refrigerator door, reading Emily Dickinson, Spurgeon, Whitefield. He read with absorption, grasping their meaning for long moments, then losing it and beginning again.

He kept his sermon notebook at his side, waiting. . . .

At two o'clock in the morning, he realized he'd fallen asleep in his chair in the study, and found his notebook on the floor. He regretted waking. There seemed a film over the lamplit room, as if he were wearing sunglasses. It had nothing to do with his eyes and everything to do with his spirit. He felt at the end of himself.

Perhaps he should have gone forward with the medication for depression. The film, the darkness seemed always hovering nearby; if it disappeared for a time, it came back. He felt again a moment of panic—what if he were succumbing, as his father did, to the thing that brought down his marriage, brought down his business, ruined his health?

But he mustn't dwell on that. He must dwell on the message, for the message still hadn't come right.

He'd be forced to drum up something from days of yore, some antiquity that might be dredged from sermon notes stored in the study cabinet.

But he didn't have what it might take even to dredge.

"Lord," he said, "speak to me, please. I can't go on like this. Speak to me in a way I can understand clearly. I've read Your word, I've sought Your counsel, I've whined, I've groveled, I've despaired, I've pled—and I've waited. And through it all, Lord, You've been so strangely silent."

He sat for a time, in a kind of misery he

couldn't define; wordless, trying to listen, his mind drifting. Then at last he drew a deep breath and sat up straighter, determined.

"I will not let You go until You bless me!" he said, startled by his voice in the silent room.

He took his Bible from beside his chair and opened it at random.

Stop seeking what you want to hear, Timothy, and listen to what I have to tell you.

He felt no supernatural jolt; it happened simply. God had just spoken to his heart with great tenderness, as He'd done only a few times in his life before; it produced in him an utter calm.

"Yes," he said. "Thank you. Thank you."

Where the book had fallen open in his lap, he began to read with expectation and certainty.

He found the passage only moments later. Instantly, he knew: He'd discovered at last what God had held in reserve—expressly for him, expressly for now, and expressly for tomorrow morning.

The peace flowed in like a river.

Though he'd known for decades that the exhortation was there in First Thessalonians, and had even preached on it a time or two, it came to him now as if it were new, not ancient, wisdom. It came to him with the utterly effulgent certainty that this Scripture was his, and he might seize upon it as upon a bright sword that would help him pierce . . .

. . . pierce what?

The darkness.

The time to begin was now.

"Thank You," he whispered, "for this time of darkness."

"You up, brother?"

"Bill! Good morning! You're preaching today, and I'm praying for you!"

"I don't mind tellin' you I've got butterflies. How about you?"

"Running on fumes, not enough sleep. But God is faithful; this morning He gave me something I've needed for a long time."

"You might say He's done th' same for me, that's why I'm callin'. He laid it on my heart last night that I was to thank you."

"Thank me?"

"You know that stop sign . . ."

"I do."

"He's been showin' me that I was to take that stop sign as a sign to stop. Before I got stopped by th' stop sign, you might say, I was runnin' around in circles like a chicken with its head cut off. I'd been so busy workin' for Him that I'd fallen out of relationship with Him! These weeks have been long, but they've been good. I've had wonderful times of fellowship with th' Holy Spirit, an' time with Rachel that we haven't had in years. An' to cap it all off, He's brought me Buddy."

"Coals to Newcastle."

"To tell th' truth, I feel brand-new. And I just wanted to thank you, Tim, for lettin' th' Lord use you, as bad as it all seemed to be for both of us."

In the space of a few hours, he had twice been succored.

"Thank you," he said, hard-pressed to speak. "Thank you."

Esther Bolick settled into the worn oak pew with a certain satisfaction.

This was where she and Gene always sat, unless some thoughtless parishioner nabbed their spot before they could get to it. You'd think people would respect the place you'd chosen and been faithful to for twenty-three years, but no, some people didn't care where you sat, much less where they sat. One Sunday they'd plop down next to the choir stall in the rear and another Sunday they'd turn up in the first row, gospel side.

She'd occupied this same spot since way before Father Tim came. It was like home. The minute she sat down, she was as rooted as a turnip, which, in times like these, she considered a blessing.

She opened her pew bulletin and squinted at the order of service. Oh, law, there was that communion hymn she could never get right to save her life! Minnie Lomax from the Collar Button used to sit beside her and Gene every Sunday morning 'til the fateful day when, singing her brains out, she, Esther Big Mouth Bolick, had squawked for all to hear, "When I fall on my face with my knees to the rising sun, / Oh, Lord have mercy on me. . . ."

The next Sunday, Minnie had gone across the aisle, where she remained to this day. Esther decided to keep her trap shut during hymn 325.

She was pleased that she and Gene were fifteen minutes early. Being early gave her time to collect her wits, which had been blown on the wind all week like bedsheets on a clothesline.

Thank the Lord, Father Tim was back again. Two Sundays in a row! She tried to keep her opinion to herself about why she was so glad to have him back, but the truth was, she'd never warmed up to Father Talbot, though she'd been impressed to start with.

You take Father Tim—he was a big hugger and hand-shaker, even a kisser. He'd whopped her one on the cheek when she and Gene had their first grandbaby, and given her a hug into the bargain.

But you take Father Talbot. If you started to hug him, he jumped back a foot, probably because you might mess up his hair. Or was it a wig? Nobody knew for certain, but his hair always looked perfect, like it was never slept in.

And another thing. It seemed like Father Talbot had this relationship with God that he didn't want to share. Somehow, it was just him and God, with nothing dribbling out on his parishioners. On the other hand, he was smart as a whip, using words she'd never heard before in her life. Plus, his sermons were like the front page of the newspaper. Unfortunately, she had already read the newspaper by the time she got to church and so occasionally took a nap while he preached.

Somebody said he'd gone to Harvard. Or was it University of Michigan? She could never remember which. The story was, he'd come out of college as a stockbroker. According to Hessie Mayhew, who knew all about the Episcopalians even though she belonged to the Presbyterians, he did stockbroking 'til he was forty, then got called and went to seminary.

Maybe his late start was the problem. She wondered how his wife liked him jumping from one job to another.

Anyway, it was a blessing to have Father Tim again, she didn't know why they couldn't let him attend his old church—what an aggravation it must be to tool over to Wesley every Sunday! The problem, of course, was that ridiculous church law saying the old priest couldn't hang around because everybody would run to him and leave the new priest out on a limb.

There went the bells chiming! Since childhood, that had been one of her favorite things about church. Then the organ cranked up the prelude. Though she had no idea what music it was, she knew it was something Father Tim liked, Richard often played it in the old days. . . .

It was easy to think, if only for a moment, that nothing had changed—except, of course, that Father Talbot had talked the vestry into having the carpet yanked up so the choir would have better acoustics. *Un*believable! Walk down the aisle on a snowy Sunday morning with your boots melting snow on that slick wood floor, and *blam!* down you could go, ending up in the hospital with a broken hip and a blood clot racing to your heart. Or was it your brain?

She would never in a hundred years understand church politics.

Hélène Pringle stepped from the bright, warm sunlight into the cool, sweet shadow of the narthex.

Before she quite recovered from the small shock to her senses, someone thrust a copy of the pew bulletin into her hand and gave her a surprised, albeit warm, greeting, which, to her regret, she returned in French.

She was trembling slightly, with both fear of the unknown and a deep, childlike excitement.

The service would be different from the services her grandmother had forced her, for a brief period, to attend in that great, cold church built of stone. She'd hardly ever understood anything the priest had said, for the echo made his voice sound tremulous and metallic, as if it were coming from the walls and not from a man. The acoustics, however, had done wondrous things for the voices of the choir; she remembered the goose bumps she felt as a nine-year-old; they prickled along her spine and made her hair feel as if it were standing.

She was afraid she wouldn't know what to say or do in this morning's service, though someone had declared that Episcopal and Catholic liturgies weren't so vastly different, in the end. Of course, the whole Episcopal thing had come about in the first place because of Henry the Eighth, who'd been a vain and vulgar man, to say the least. She wondered that anyone would admit to being part of something he'd established. But she sensed the moment she awoke this morning that she had to be here, and so she had arisen and dressed, asking the unseen Being on the other side of the drapery to help her select attire that wouldn't stand out or offend.

She suspected there would be a lot of kneeling and jostling about, which led her to choose the very back row, on the side by the stained-glass window of the Sermon on the Mount, where she tried to shrink herself as small as she possibly could, so no one would notice she was there.

> *"How lovely is thy dwelling place,*
> *O Lord of hosts, to me!*
> *My thirsty soul desires and longs*
> *Within thy courts to be;*
> *My very heart and flesh cry out,*
>
> *O living God, for thee.*
> *Beside thine altars, gracious Lord,*
> *The swallows find a nest;*
> *How happy they who dwell with thee*
> *And praise thee without rest,*

And happy they whose hearts are set
Upon the pilgrim's quest.

They who go through the desert vale
Will find it filled with springs,
And they shall climb from height to height
Till Zion's temple rings
With praise to thee, in glory throned
Lord God, great King of kings.

One day within thy courts excels
A thousand spent away;
How happy they who keep thy laws
Nor from thy precepts stray,
For thou shalt surely bless all those
Who live the words they pray."

Hope Winchester entered the church as the pipe organ began the prelude, and looked around anxiously for a place to sit. There was only one person in the rear pew on the left.

Thinking the rear pew a good choice, she slid in quickly, noting that Hélène Pringle occupied the other end. She nodded to Miss Pringle, who had bought note cards at Happy Endings just last week.

She consulted her pew bulletin, turned in the prayer book to page 355, and hugged the open book to her chest. She'd been inside

Lord's Chapel only twice before, and was feeling utterly naked, as if she were raw and exposed altogether. She hoped she wouldn't make a fool of herself, and especially hoped that George wasn't sitting where he could see her in case she did. She only knew that it was important to be here this morning, though she wasn't sure why.

Perhaps, she thought, it was because she'd given up being a noun, and was being transformed into a verb.

"In the name of the Father, and of the Son, and of the Holy Spirit, amen," he said, crossing himself.

"I wrestled with this morning's message as Jacob wrestled with the angel, until at last I said to God, 'I will not let You go until You bless me.'

"I had prayed and labored over a sermon, the title of which is listed in your bulletin and which no longer has anything to do with what I have to say to you this morning, nor does it delve the meaning of today's Propers.

"What I'd hoped to say was something we all need to know and ponder in our lives, but the message would not come together, it would not profess the deeper truth I felt God wanted me to convey.

"And the reason it would not is simple:

"I was writing the wrong sermon.

"Then . . . at the final hour, when hope was dim and my heart bruised with the sense of failure, God blessed me with a completely different message—a sermon expressly for this service, this day, this people."

Father Tim smiled. "The trouble is, he gave me only four words.

"I was reminded, then, of Winston Churchill, how he was called to deliver the convocation address at his old school—where, by the way, he had not done well, his headmaster had predicted nothing but failure for Churchill. He was called to give the address and he stood to the podium and there was an enormous swell of excitement among the pupils and faculty that here was a great man of history, a great man of letters and discourse, about to tell them how to go forward in their lives.

"Mr. Churchill leaned over the podium, looked his audience in the eye, and here, according to legend, is what he said; this is the entire text of his address that day:

"'Young men, nevah, nevah, nevah give up.'

"Then he sat down. That was his message.

Seven words. In truth, if he had said more, those seven words might not have had the power to penetrate so deeply, nor counsel so wisely.

"Last night, alone in my study, God gave me four words that Saint Paul wrote in his second letter to the church at Thessalonica. Four words that can help us enter into obedience, trust, and closer communion with God Himself, made known through Jesus Christ.

"Here are the four words. I pray you will inscribe them on your heart."

Hope Winchester sat forward in the pew.

"In everything . . . give thanks."

Father Tim paused and looked at those gathered before him. At Emma Newland . . . Gene Bolick . . . Dooley Barlowe . . . Pauline Leeper . . . Hope   Winchester . . . Hélène Pringle. Around the nave his eyes gazed, drawing them close.

"In *everything,* give thanks. That's all. That's this morning's message.

"If you believe as I do that Scripture is the inspired Word of God, then we see this not as a random thought or an oddly clever idea of His servant, Paul, but as a loving command issued through the great apostle.

"Generally, Christians understand that giving thanks is good and right.

"Though we don't do it often enough, it's easy to have a grateful heart for food and shelter, love and hope, health and peace. But what about the hard stuff, the stuff that darkens your world and wounds you to the quick? Just what is this *everything* business?

"It's the hook. It's the key. *Everything* is the word on which this whole powerful command stands and has its being.

"Please don't misunderstand; the word *thanks* is crucial. But a deeper spiritual truth, I believe, lies in giving thanks in . . . everything.

"In loss of all kinds. In illness. In depression. In grief. In failure. And, of course, in health and peace, success and happiness. In everything.

"There'll be times when you wonder how you can possibly thank Him for something that turns your life upside down; certainly there will be such times for me. Let us, then, at times like these, give thanks *on faith alone . . .* obedient, trusting, hoping, believing.

"Perhaps you remember the young boy who was kidnapped and beaten and thrown into prison, yet rose up as Joseph the King, ruler of nations, able to say to his brothers, with a spirit of forgiveness, 'You thought evil against me, but God meant it for good, that many lives

might be spared.' Better still, remember our
Lord and Savior Jesus Christ, who suffered ag-
onies we can't begin to imagine, fulfilling
God's will that you and I might have everlasting life.

"Some of us have been in trying circumstances these last months. Unsettling.
Unremitting. Even, we sometimes think, unbearable. Dear God, we pray, stop this! Fix
that! Bless us—and step on it!

"I admit to you that although I often thank
God for my blessings, even the smallest, I
haven't thanked Him for my afflictions.

"I know the fifth chapter of First Thessalonians pretty well, yet it just hadn't occurred to
me to actually take Him up on this notion. I've
been too busy begging Him to lead me out of
the valley and onto the mountaintop. After
all, I have work to do, I have things to
accomplish . . . alas, I am the White Rabbit
everlastingly running down the hole like the
rest of the common horde.

"I want to tell you that I started thanking
Him last night—this morning at two o'clock,
to be precise—for something that grieves me
deeply. And I'm committed to continue
thanking Him in this hard thing, no matter
how desperate it might become, and I'm going

to begin looking for the good in it. Whether God caused it or permitted it, we can rest assured—there is great good in it.

"Why have I decided to take these four words as a personal commission? Here's the entire eighteenth verse:

"'In everything, give thanks . . . for this is the will of God in Christ Jesus concerning you.'

"His will concerning you. His will concerning me.

"This thing which I've taken as a commission intrigues me. I want to see where it goes, where it leads. I pray you'll be called to do the same. And please, tell me where it leads you. Let me hear what happens when you respond to what I believe is a powerful and challenging, though deceptively simple, command of God.

"Let's look once more at the four words God is saying to us . . . by looking at what our obedience to them will say to God.

"Our obedience will say, 'Father, I don't know why You're causing, or allowing, this hard thing to happen, but I'm going to give thanks in it because You ask me to. I'm going to trust You to have a purpose for it that I can't know and may never know. Bottom line, You're God—and that's good enough for me.'

"What if you had to allow one of your teenagers to experience a hard thing, and she said, 'Mom, I don't really understand why you're letting this happen, but you're my mom and I trust you and that's good enough for me'?"

He looked around the congregation. "Ah, well," he said, "probably not the best example."

Laughter.

"But you get the idea.

"There are, of course, many more words in the first letter to the Thessalonians. Here are just a few:

" 'Pray without ceasing.'

" 'Abstain from all appearance of evil.'

" 'Quench not the Spirit.'

"These words, too, contain holy counsel and absolute truth.

"But the words which God chose for this day, this service, this pastor, and this people, were just four. Yes, do the other things I command you to do, He says, but mark these."

He gazed upon his former flock with great tenderness.

"Mark these."

Hélène Pringle realized she had been holding her breath for what seemed a very long time.

"When we go out into this golden morning and meet in our beautiful churchyard, let those who will, follow yet another loving command from Paul's letter. 'Greet the brethren with an holy kiss!'

"Amen."

Miss Pringle exhaled; and then, with the congregation, gave the response.

"Amen!"

Hélène Pringle went quickly out the side door of the church and along the street to the corner of Main and Wisteria, where she stopped for a moment and looked back.

She hadn't wanted anyone to kiss her, not at all, that was the trouble with Americans, they required a lot of touching. Yes, of course, the French greeted each other with a kiss—a kiss on both cheeks, for that matter—but it meant nothing in particular. It seemed to her that the holy kiss the father spoke about might actually mean something, though she wasn't sure what.

She trembled slightly, and wondered what on earth was grieving the father so deeply. Then she turned and hastened up Wisteria Lane toward the old rectory, where Barbizon would be wanting his liver snacks.

❦

Hope Winchester had gotten over feeling naked and now felt fully clothed, able to stand in the sunshine and talk with several of her customers, as young people passed trays of cookies and lemonade in paper cups.

"Why, bless your heart!" said Esther Bolick. "Look who's here!"

"Will wonders never cease?" A choir member who collected Penguin Classics gave her a hug.

Though Hope didn't see George, Harley Welch bobbed his head in her direction and offered a shy grin.

She was turning to go down the walk when the chaplain from Hope House, standing with a group on the church walk, suddenly swung around and jabbed her in the ribs with his elbow.

"Ouch!" she said.

"Miss Winchester! I'm so sorry."

He looked sincerely distressed.

"It's all right," she said. "Really."

Scott Murphy turned and picked a small, cream-colored hydrangea blossom from the bush next to the church walk. He smiled congenially, ducked his head in a modest bow, and handed the bloom to her. "Forgive me!"

Having no idea what to do with it, she tucked it into the small chignon she'd been wearing these days.

"There you go!" he said, looking pleased.

She thought the chaplain, whom she'd seen only twice, and both times in blue jeans, looked very grown-up in a tie.

For someone whose life consisted of little more than going to the bookshop and home again, she found church a dizzying whirl of laughter, music, cookies, pealing bells, new ideas, children playing on the lawn, and people who were generally swarming like bees in a hive.

Father Tim walked over and gave her a kiss on the cheek.

She touched her cheek and smiled. "A holy kiss!"

"Yes. We're happy to see you, Hope."

Hope! Once again, her name sounded brand-new.

CHAPTER TWENTY

In Everything

After a quick lunch, he rang the number in Kinloch. No answer.

"Barnabas!"

Barnabas crawled from under the hall table and stretched. Then he trotted to the study and sat down, looking steadily at Father Tim.

"How would you like to get out of Dodge?"

The Great Wagging of the Tail began.

"Meet new squirrels! See new sights! Broaden your horizons!"

The wagging accelerated.

The crowd in Kinloch would surely have a corner where he could tether his dog to a table leg, or perhaps some intrepid youth would dog-sit him in a rear pew.

He went to the study and thumped onto the sofa for a thirty-minute nap. Then he got up and changed clothes, foraged in his desk drawer for his handwritten directions, rounded up a dog bowl and bottles of water for the car, and set a dish of tinned liver on the floor by the refrigerator.

"Violet," he said, "you're on your own."

He felt wonderful, he felt eager.

He felt ready for anything.

They were well out of Mitford and heading north, north where the rain had obviously come with greater regularity and the hills were still green with summer.

"How about a little Wordsworth?" he asked his dog, who, in the passenger seat, rode belted in and looking straight ahead.

No response. He supposed Barnabas had heard enough of Wordsworth over the years.

"Longfellow, then!"

Barnabas flicked his left ear.

"Let's see." He'd have to dig deep for Longfellow, it had been a while. . . .

"I'm noodling my noggin," he explained to his companion.

Ah, but it was good to be off and away, with no one to mind what a country priest might say to his best friend.

He pulled the steep grade to Kinloch, listening to a country music station. "What's made Milwaukee famous has made a fool out of me...."

Feeling expansive, he considered a few things he'd like to do now that the weight seemed to have lifted off his chest, off his heart.

First, he'd like to visit Homeless Hobbes in his new digs. Also, he wanted to build a latticework fence around their garbage cans, take the twins to a movie in Wesley, and... definitely!... make Mississippi barbecue for George and Harley.

What else? He was going to finish the book of essays if it killed him.

Driving up the side of a mountain on a dazzling afternoon made life's possibilities seem bright and endless.

A car was waiting for him in the parking lot, the sort of car that suggested Kinloch was a comfortable parish. Settled by Scots in the late eighteenth century, Kinloch was now known as a venerable stronghold of ample cottages built in the twenties by Florida money and passed down through succeeding generations.

Given its lush and manicured banks, even the lake appeared well-heeled.

"Father Kavanagh! Welcome!"

Stout, gray-haired, and lively, Mary Fisher gave him a bone-crushing handshake, then snatched the hanging vestments from his hand and hung them in the car. As Barnabas relieved himself at the water's edge, she opened the passenger door and all but lifted him onto the seat. "I was told to take good care of you!" she shouted, obviously a dash hard-of-hearing.

"Wait! My dog . . ."

"Dog? What dog?" Mary Fisher turned to look as Barnabas galloped up to the astonished woman and thumped down at her feet, panting.

"Good Lord!" she gasped, crashing backward against the car.

"It's a bit out of the ordinary, I admit, but I hoped that someone might—"

"Nobody said anything about a dog!"

"True, true. I failed to mention it. But he'll be no trouble. And look! I washed him! He's clean as a pin!" He maneuvered his dog onto the backseat as Mary Fisher grumbled her way to the driver's side, where she leaped behind the wheel, put the car in reverse, and backed up at dizzying speed.

"The lake . . . ," he muttered.

"What about it?" she bawled.

She had nearly backed into it, that's what about it. He figured this experience would make riding with Hélène Pringle look like a Lord's Chapel coffee hour.

He turned and peered at his dog, clinging to the leather for dear life as Mary Fisher floored the accelerator and they lurched ahead.

"So what are you preachin' on today?"

"Ah . . ." He gripped the handle above the passenger door as his driver made a sudden right-hand turn and hauled up a narrow lane carved into the side of a steep hill. His sermon topic fled all conscious memory.

"How many are we expecting?" he asked.

"What's that?"

"How many are we expecting?" he boomed in his pulpit voice.

"God only knows!"

Flying around a curve, it appeared likely they would meet the panel truck head-on, but Mary Fisher deftly whipped around it. He would have considered leaping out, but it was a considerable drop into the gorge, with no guardrails in sight. Weren't there laws about guardrails? Perhaps he'd walk back to the parking lot after the service.

He looked at his watch. Seven minutes after five. His visit to Kinloch felt protracted before it had hardly begun.

"See over there?" His driver slung her arm in front of his face and pointed toward a large house topping a mountain ridge. "That's where we're headed."

"Good to know," he said, as she rounded a curve.

Seeing a straight stretch before them, Mary Fisher hammered down on the accelerator. Clearly she had driven professionally. The Grand Prix, perhaps, or maybe only Talladega.

"Here you go!" she said, wheeling at last into a gravel drive and jumping out.

"Is the chapel nearby?" he asked as she opened his door.

"What's that?"

"The chapel. Is it nearby?"

"Right, this is goodbye! You won't see me 'til I haul you down after the service." She opened the rear door and Barnabas spilled out like so much molasses. "Nobody said anything about a dog!" she reminded him.

"Right. Sorry. Really." He snatched his vestments himself.

❧

Mary Fisher had ushered him into a bedroom where he might change before going on to the chapel. Though it was clearly a home, and an unusually handsome one at that, no one was around. Everyone was at the chapel, he supposed, setting things up.

Barnabas sprawled in a corner, definitely out of sorts from the winding drive up the mountain. In truth, the priest wasn't feeling so well, either. Robed and wearing his stole, he walked up the hall, looking for a kitchen. He'd left the dog bowl and water in his car, and they could both use a good, long drink. Why wasn't someone around to see to things? It was a little . . . he searched for a word . . . eerie, somehow.

He found a bowl, and hoping nobody would mind—it was only stoneware, not porcelain, he reassured himself—filled it at the kitchen sink. As he did so, he noticed a familiar but indefinable smell in the room. He stood motionless for a moment, trying to name it, but found he couldn't.

After drinking a glass of water, he hurried to the bedroom with the water bowl.

He supposed he should set the bowl on a towel, Barnabas's water-lapping style had a way of distributing heavy precip over a large area; better still, he'd set it on the tiled floor of a small sitting room adjoining the bedroom, and mop up afterward with his handkerchief.

Of course he shouldn't have brought Barnabas, it had been a foolish, last-minute notion and a desire for company. Now here he was, dirtying people's bowls. He was mildly disgusted with himself. Retirement, of course, was the culprit. Unless one kept one's hand in, things seemed to slide downhill.

Barnabas drank with great thirst and crashed onto the sitting room floor for a nap.

Five-thirty. Why didn't someone come for him? And there was the smell again. What was it about that smell? Though faint, it repulsed him. He flexed his right hand, feeling the stiffness from gripping the car handle.

He paced the room, anxious, before realizing what he needed.

He needed prayer.

Dropping to his knees by a striped wing chair, he crossed himself. "Almighty and eternal God," he prayed aloud, "so draw our hearts to Thee, so guide our minds, so fill our imaginations, so control our wills, that we may be wholly Thine, utterly dedicated unto Thee; and then use us, we pray Thee, as Thou wilt, and always to Thy glory and the welfare of Thy people, through our Lord and Savior Jesus Christ."

There. Better! Much better. He rose and peered through the window, where he saw only a bank covered with rhododendron. Where was the lake for this so-called lakeside service? Five thirty-two.

He turned, startled by his dog's deep growl.

"Good afternoon, Father."

Ed Coffey closed the door to the sitting room and looked at him, unsmiling. "Making yourself at home, I see."

His heart pounded into his throat. "What are you doing here?"

"I'm just checking this door," said Ed. He heard the lock click, and Barnabas barking on the other side.

"No!" he shouted, racing across the room. "Wait!"

Ed Coffey stepped quickly through an adjoining door as Edith Mallory stepped in.

"Timothy!" she said, closing the door behind her. "How good of you to come."

He stood rooted to the spot, his breath short. "What do you mean by this?"

She smiled. "I paid a generous sum for you to come here. Therefore, I'm entitled to your company." She shrugged. "That's all."

She walked across the room and sat on the love seat by the window. "Do sit down, Timothy."

"I will do no such thing." He went to the sitting room door and jiggled the knob.

"Barnabas! Are you there?" Silence. He turned quickly to the other door, frantic.

"It's locked, Timothy." Edith lifted the lid of a box next to the love seat and withdrew one of the long, dark Tiparillos she was known to smoke. She held it between her fingers before lighting it. "Ed will open it just after six-thirty. I've bought an hour of your time and I expect to have an hour of your time."

She smiled in a manner he'd always thought ghastly.

"Consider me your congregation," she said.

"Is Barnabas still in the other room?"

"Of course not. You're far too courteous to disturb your congregation with the barking of a dog."

"Edith, believe me, believe me . . ." He would throttle her with his own hands, he would.

"Believe you in what way?" She flicked a silver lighter. The end of her Tiparillo glowed; she inhaled deeply.

There! That was the sickly sweet smell he hadn't been able to identify.

"If anything at all happens to my dog, I shall take every measure under heaven to see you brought down."

"Umm," she said, smiling again. "You're far more attractive when you're angry; I always thought so."

"You are a wicked and unkind woman, Edith."

"You've said worse about me in the past."

"Everything I've ever said about you I've said to your face."

"Speaking of my face, you may notice that I've had a little . . . touch-up here and there. Do you like it?"

"No cosmetic procedure is capable of disguising a cruel spirit."

"Oh, please. You're in your usual high-and-mighty clerical mode, I see. Look around you, Timothy. Do you like this house? I bought it recently, already furnished with exquisite antiques. And what do you think of this rug? It's Aubusson, of course, early Federal period. I know how you love beautiful things, it's a shame you've never been able to afford them. All this might have been yours, once, along with many other comforts I'm able to offer. But you fancied yourself too proud. You know what is said about pride, of course."

She patted the cushion beside her. "Come, Timothy. Come preach to me and save my soul."

"I cannot save your soul. That is strictly the business of the Holy Spirit."

"Then come and pray for me, dear Timothy."

"Don't taunt me, Edith. And don't blaspheme God with your insincere remarks."

"But I'm not at all insincere, I mean it truly. You've never prayed for me, just the two of us.

I've always had to share you with hordes of people. You went 'round to everyone but me, Timothy, for more than sixteen years." She made a pout and looked at him with the large, gold eyes he'd always likened to those of a lynx painted on velvet.

Since Pat Mallory died, she had done everything in her power to seduce and harass him; he would never have dreamed of praying with her alone. "I've often prayed for you, Edith. And often I had no desire at all to do it."

"Do you think God answers prayer that isn't prayed sincerely?"

"It was prayed sincerely. For years I've prayed you might turn from your coldness of heart and hurtful indiscretions, and surrender your life to Him. I don't have to feel warm and fuzzy to pray that prayer for you, I pray it with my will alone, in accordance with the will of God that you abandon your soul to the One Who created you, the One Who died for you, and the only One Who is capable of truly loving you."

She inhaled and let the smoke out slowly. "I've always found it hard to believe that God would love someone who doesn't love Him."

"That's the way humans think. God is different. He loves us no matter what."

"Timothy, there's no way you'll get me to believe that. Ever."

"You're right. There's no way I can get you to believe that. The Holy Spirit, however, can get you to believe that, if He so chooses."

He walked across the room to her. "Now tell me. What exactly is the nature of this charade?" He stood at the love seat, cold with anger. "Why are you holding me in a locked room? What are your intentions?" He swallowed down the fear. He could always break through a window. . . .

"My intentions? I was forced to give away an additional twenty-five thousand dollars to keep the U.S. Treasury from being miffed with me. I called you in hopes we could come up with a plan, but you hung up on me.

"When you did that, I thought, how delicious to give money away and have some fun doing it! It's quite a compliment, Timothy. I could have offered the hospital a piddling five thousand and given the remainder elsewhere. You would have come, of course, for a piddling five thousand. Shame on you, that's why you'll never amount to anything when it comes down to it. You should thank heaven for your wife, who amounts to so much more in the world's view." She looked at him through narrowed eyes and inhaled again.

"By the way," she said, "if you tell anyone

the room was locked, I shall deny it and say you made improper advances toward me."

"What would you have me do, Edith?" He could not commit murder. He could not and would not. But he relished the thought for the briefest moment. His mouth tasted of bile.

"I'd have you deliver what you were paid to deliver."

"A sermon? A full liturgy?"

"For twenty-five thousand dollars, Timothy, I should think a full liturgy would be in order. Wouldn't you?"

"There are two problems with that. One is that I have no communion set with which to administer the Holy Eucharist. The other is that something crucial is required of the soul who presents himself to the Host. You must be earnestly willing to repent of your sins."

She threw up her hands in mock helplessness. "Then it's simple. We skip the communion! I must say, you look charming in that stole. Isn't it the one Pat and I gave you years ago?"

"It is not."

"Well, then, do begin." She drew another Tiparillo from the box and flicked the lighter. The tip glowed as she inhaled.

He stood dumbstruck, praying the prayer that never failed. What did God want of him in this thing? What could He possibly have intended by bringing him face-to-face with Edith Mallory in a locked room? It was a dream, a nightmare.

His knees, he realized, had begun to shake. He sat down at once in the armchair next to the love seat.

"I'll give you your hour, Edith. Happily. There's a little girl at the hospital right now, four years old, I think—her leg was broken by her uncle because she tried to run away from his abuse. Another child was born with a hole in his heart and is facing his third medical procedure. I could go on. The point is, if such an hour as this can spare these children even a moment of suffering—"

"You gag me, Timothy, with your preacher talk. Will you never *weary* of such pap?"

"Never."

"You're not alone, you know, in wanting to serve God. I want to serve God, too."

"Yes, of course, but only in an advisory capacity."

She furrowed her brow. "What do you mean?"

"Never mind."

"You're rude. You were always rude to me, Timothy. I find no excuse for it. Nor would God." She pouted again, drawing her mouth down at the corners.

"Would you care to put your cigarette out?"

"I wouldn't care to."

He stood. "Let us begin." His knees trembled, still. "Blessed be God; Father, Son, and Holy Spirit."

He waited for her response. "Will you respond?"

"And blessed be His kingdom," she said, snappish, "now and forever. Amen."

"Almighty God, to You all hearts are open, all desires known, and from you no secrets are hid. . . ." He didn't know how he could get through this; it was a travesty. All he wanted was for God to get him out of this preposterous mess. He sat down again, humbled and desperate, without any poise left in him.

"Give me a moment," he said. The message of the morning service, which seemed days in the past, suddenly came to him with the complete conviction with which he'd preached it. *In everything . . .*

"Oh, forget that stuff you learned from a book! I never wanted you to do a full liturgy, anyway, I could never remember all those tiresome responses. All I wanted is for you to talk to me, Timothy, to . . . to hold me."

She leaned forward on the love seat. "You're a human being, you have feeling and passion like everyone else. Are you so frightened of your passion, Timothy?"

As she placed her hand on his knee, he recoiled visibly, but didn't get up and move away. Instead, fighting down the nausea, he thanked God for putting him in this room, at this time, for whatever reason He might have.

Be with me, Lord, forsake me not. I'm going to fly into the face of this thing.

He removed her hand from his knee and took it in his. He was trembling inside as he did it, but his hand was steady, without the palsy of fear.

"Let's begin by doing what you asked. Let me pray for you, Edith." Her hand felt small and cold in his, like the claw of a bird, the palm surprisingly callous. He felt her flinch, but she didn't withdraw her hand—the beating of her pulse throbbed against his own.

He bowed his head. "Father."

But he could do no more than call His name. "Abba!" he whispered. *Help me!*

Christ went up into the mountain; He opened His mouth and taught them . . . *But I say unto you, Love your enemies, bless them that curse you, do good to them that hate you, and pray for them which despitefully use you. . . .*

"Bless your child Edith with the reality of your Presence," he prayed, and was suddenly mute again.

He was forcing himself to intercede for her; it was stop and start, like a mule pulling a sled through deep mire. He quit striving, then, and gave himself up; he could not haul the weight of this thing alone.

"By the power of Your Holy Spirit, so move in her heart and her life that she cannot ignore or turn away from Your love for her. Go, Lord, into that black night where no belief dwells, where no candle burns, where no solace can be found, and kindle Your love in Edith Mallory in a mighty and victorious way.

"Pour out Your love upon her, Lord, love that no human being can or will ever be able to give, pour it out upon her with such tenderness that she cannot turn away, with such mercy that she cannot deny Your grace.

"Fill her heart with certainty—with the confidence and certainty that You made Edith Mallory for Yourself, that You might take delight in her life . . . and in her service. Yes, thank You, Lord, for the countless thousands of dollars she's poured into the work of Your kingdom, for whatever reasons she may have had." Right or wrong, a good deal of Edith Mallory's money had counted for good over the years, and he would not be her judge.

He was gripping her hand now; as he had gripped the handle above the passenger door, he was holding on to her as if she might be taken from him by force.

"Thank you, Father, for this extraordinary time in Your presence, for holding us captive in the circle of Your love and Your grace. With all my heart, I petition You for the soul of this woman, that she might be called to repent and become Your child for all eternity."

Beads of sweat had broken out on his forehead, though the room was cool.

"Through Christ our Lord," he whispered. "Amen."

He raised his head slowly, feeling an enormous relief.

Tears had left a smear of mascara on her face; she withdrew her hand from his. "I despise you," she said. "I despise you utterly."

"Why?"

"Because you believe."

She took a handkerchief from her suit pocket and pressed it against her eyes. "I think for the first time I actually believe that you believe."

"Why do you despise me for that?"

"Because I would like to believe, and cannot."

"Why can you not?"

"Because none of it makes sense to me."

"Good!" he said.

"What do you mean, good?"

"Faith isn't about making sense. Faith is faith."

"Foolishness!" she said.

"Chesterton put it far better. He said, 'Faith

means believing the unbelievable, or it is no virtue at all.'"

"Enough of such blather! I don't know why I did this ridiculous thing." She tapped the ashes from her Tiparillo, impatient.

"Who are you, Edith? I met you nearly twenty years ago, yet I know almost nothing about you. Who were your parents? What was your life like when—"

Her laughter was hoarse. "I've never paid twenty-five thousand dollars an hour to be analyzed, especially by a country priest, and I don't intend to start now. I'm sure you learned a great deal about me from my husband, though he was devoted to twisting the truth. He loved saying how he frequented that grease pit you call the Grill, in order to be out of my presence."

He'd known as much. Pat Mallory often spoke maliciously of his wife.

"I cared nothing for my husband because I quickly learned he could be beaten down. A man who can be beaten down is no man at all. That's one reason I've been intrigued by you over the years, Timothy—it's difficult to beat you down."

"If God be for me, who can be against me?"

She stiffened. "Can't you have a simple conversation without dragging God into it? I abhor piety. It's something clergy in particular should strive to avoid."

"This is going nowhere."

"Perhaps you'd be titillated by a bit of local Mitford gossip. I'm selling Clear Day. I always hated Mitford, Mitford was Pat's idea. All of you think yourselves above me, I've scarcely received a decent welcome there in years." She angrily stubbed her Tiparillo in an ashtray.

"You tried to rig a mayoral election, you tried to throw a family out of their rightful lease—"

"I'm sick of this nonsense. Go home!" She rose from the love seat, so near to him that he couldn't get up from the chair. "In the end, what misery it always brings to be in your company. It wasn't worth it, not twenty-five thousand, not twenty, not five."

She strode to the door, where she turned, her expression pained and bitter. "Your hour is up. Collect your dog outside."

"Edith."

Her hand was on the knob "What?"

"I have a request."

She looked at him, frozen.

"Tell Mary Fisher I'd like to drive the car to the parking lot. If this isn't agreeable, I'll walk down."

She burst suddenly into laughter. Still laughing, she opened the door, then slammed it behind her.

CHAPTER TWENTY-ONE

Salmon Roulade

"Father Tim?"

"Yes!"

"I'm sorry to call you so early, this is Jeanine Stroup at th' hospital, I'm new and don't know everybody yet. Mr. Bill Watson's askin' for th' preacher. Would you by any chance be th' one, somebody said it was probably you."

"Yes, ma'am, I think it's probably me. Has he taken a bad turn?"

"Nossir, he's pretty lively."

"Wonderful! Well, look . . . how about eight o'clock?"

"Oh, good! I'll go down the hall right now and tell him."

"Can he have a doughnut?"

"A doughnut? I don't know."

"Plain, of course," he said. "No jelly."

"Why don't you bring one, and if he can't have it, I'll eat it."

"Jeanine," he said, "I think you'll go far."

"Emma! Tim Kavanagh." He didn't have to apologize for calling; Emma got up so early, it was hard to beat her out of bed. "Got a minute?"

"Shoot."

"I need some jokes off the Internet."

"*Jokes off the Internet?* You, who don't want anything to *do* with the Internet, absolutely, positively *leave you alone* about the Internet, you want *jokes off the Internet*?"

"Right," he said. "Clean jokes."

"That's hard," she said. "Trust me."

"If anybody can do it, you can."

"Flattery will get you nowhere. I'm going to teach you how to get online, once and for all."

"Now, Emma . . ."

"It'll take thirty minutes, max. I'll even run over to Wesley with you to buy a computer. We'll go Tuesday morning. You can't keep doin' this."

She was right. "You're right!"

"I'm *right*? Has my *hearin'* gone bad? Do I

need to get fitted for a Magic Ear while we're at th' *mall*?"

"No, dadgummit, you heard me—you're right. I can't keep calling you to do these things for me, I'm a grown man."

She was speechless.

"So get me some jokes," he said. "By seven o'clock."

"Seven o'clock this *morning*?"

"That's right."

"Consider it done!" she said, quoting her erstwhile employer.

Uncle Billy opened his eyes. "I'll be et f'r a tater if it ain't th' preacher," he whispered.

Father Tim swallowed hard. "Uncle Billy . . ."

The old man lifted his hand and Father Tim took it. Dry as a corn husk, cool as marble. Father Tim sought to warm it with his own. "How are you feeling?"

"Rough as a cob."

"Didn't take your medication."

"Nossir, hit was makin' me feeble."

"They say mean people live longer. You've got to mind Dr. Harper and get mean about it."

"Rose, she's mean enough f'r th' both of us." Uncle Billy's eyes twinkled, but only a little.

"I brought you a doughnut. Nurse Herman says you can have it."

"Put it over yonder," said Uncle Billy.

Father Tim had never seen Uncle Billy so sick he couldn't eat a doughnut. He felt the lump in his throat. Though he didn't relish the thought of rooting the old woman out of her childhood home, he would now make every effort to get them moved to Hope House.

"Are you strong enough to hear a joke, Uncle Billy?" He had studied this one out, along with a backup. He hoped with all his heart that he could make Uncle Billy laugh.

"Yessir. I'm about t' give up joke-tellin', maybe I can turn th' job over t' you."

"That's a mantle I can't wear, my friend. Too much responsibility."

"For a fact."

"Okay, here goes. Are you sure you feel like hearing a joke?"

"If hit's any good, I do, if hit ain't any good, I don't."

The pressure was on.

He wet his lips. He cleared his throat.

"Two men were sitting on a bench arguing about their devotion to their faith. First one says, 'I bet five dollars you don't even know the Lord's Prayer.' The other one says, 'I do, too—now I lay me down to sleep, I pray the

Lord my soul to keep.' First one says, 'Dadgummit, here's your five dollars, I didn't think you knew it!'"

Uncle Billy gazed at him at a long time, then shook his head. "Law, law."

"You don't like it." He felt mildly stricken.

"They won't nothin' to it."

"I've got another one!"

"Let's hear it," said Uncle Billy, not sounding very enthusiastic.

"OK. Here goes. A man was digging a hole in his backyard when his neighbor came up and said, 'What are you doing?' He said, 'I'm digging a hole to bury my dog—'"

"Wait a minute!" said Uncle Billy. "Is this th' one where th' neighbor says, 'What's that other hole f'r over yonder,' an' th' feller said, 'That was m' first hole, hit was too small'?"

"Yessir, that's it."

"I heard that dadjing thing when I was fourteen year old."

"Ah," said Father Tim.

"If you're goin' to go t' joke-tellin', you got t' do better'n that by a long shot."

"Yes, sir."

"You cain't tell jist any ol' thing that comes along."

"No, sir."

"You got to wait f'r th' right one; sometimes

you got t' wait a long time, hit's like shootin' ducks."

"I never shot a duck."

"See what I'm sayin'?"

He left the hospital determined to make Bill Watson laugh. Uncle Billy was being stubborn as a mule simply because he was Mitford's certified Joke King. But he'd find a good one somehow, somewhere, just wait.

In the meantime, he had to race to the airport and pick up his wife . . .

"Good morning, Father!" said Nurse Herman.

. . . then return to Mitford to collect his fresh salmon, and rush home to have lunch with his boy. A shower of blessings!

"Herman, this is the day the Lord has made . . ."

"Yes, sir!"

". . . let us rejoice and be glad in it!"

"Proverbs?"

"Psalm One hundred and eighteen!"

Nurse Herman was pleased to see that Father Tim had definitely recovered his health and good spirits.

Dear Editor:

The term Yankee has an underlying hostile meaning in the south. It doesn't just designate where the person is from as much as it calls that person a jerk. I myself personally am from the north and don't appreciate being called a Yankee. I suggest that when you write about the unfortunate multipile murder now lost to history, you use the term Union soldiers out of respect. Another thing, why do people say so and so is from *up* north? Of course north is up, just like south is down.

As for me, I prefer to be known as someone from the great city of Boston. Go, Socks.

Sincerely yours,

Richard Crandon, POLITICALLY CORRECT AND PROUD OF IT!!

Hendrick Attorney Says Client Will Enjoy Victory in the End

Once again, Mrs. Edith Mallory, a longtime Mitford resident of more than twenty years, has refused to speak with the *Mitford Muse/* Her attorney could not be reached for coment.

Johnson Cutliff,e the attorney for Coot Hendrick, local resident and great great grandson of Mitford's founder, said that Mr. Hendrick would appear in court in mid to late October. Mr. Cutliffe reports that Mr. Hendrick, who was recently released on $500 bond for trespassing on the Mallory property, will plead guilty.

"Mr. Hendrick ought not to have broken the law and gone looking for the gravesights on private property," he said. "But there are larger issues involved here and I believe my client will enjoy victory in the end."

Mr. Hendrick's elderly mother, Mrs. Marshall Hendrick, has offered to sing the song composed by her grea-tgrea-tgrand-father at the court trial.

The song indicates that her ancestor Hezekiah Hendrick, killed five Yankee soldiers and buried them on the property which was once the sight of our founder's humble cabin and which now is known as Clear Day and belongs to Mrs. Mallor.

Mrs. Hendrick told the *Mitford Muse* that she will also sing the song for any local organization or group who cares to hear it.

For more information on getting Mrs. Hendrick to sing for your club or group, call 555-6240 at the town office and ask for Mildred. Sign up and bring your tape recorder! Please note that Mrs. Hendrick needs wheelchair access.

He was as nervous as a schoolboy. It had been two weeks by the calendar, but two years by other calculations.

He dressed himself with special care, agonizing over his hair, which he thought wouldn't please her—once again, it looked like a chrysanthemum, and no help for it. He slicked it down, then decided this made him appear too formal. He fluffed it up. No way; he looked as if he'd just rolled out of bed.

"Puny," he said, as she busied herself making macaroni and cheese, not to mention chocolate cake, "I've got an hour to get down the mountain to the airport. Look at my hair. What can you do with it?"

She studied him carefully. "Turn around," she said.

He turned around.

"Nothin'."

"Nothing what?"

"There's nothin' I can do with it."

"Oh," he said.

☙

Of all things, he thought, of *all things!* When he saw his wife step off the small commuter plane from Charlotte, tears sprang to his eyes.

Though he was profoundly embarrassed, she thought his tears wonderful and shed a few of her own for good measure.

They sat for a moment in the parking lot, holding hands.

"Hey," he said.

"Hey, yourself."

During the first leg of their drive up the mountain, she told him everything—the great enthusiasm of the school audiences, how she climbed on a horse in Montana, but only to have her picture taken, the funny thing that happened on the way to San Francisco, her renewed inspiration for the Violet books, her complete and utter exhaustion. . . .

During the second leg of their drive, he told her everything—the visit to Lon Burtie's, the chance meeting with Millie Tipton, Bill Sprouse's welcome phone call, the sermon on Sunday, the trip to Kinloch.

Though the latter made her furious, to say the least, he would never again keep anything from her.

If he'd learned nothing else, he'd learned that.

"Really good," Dooley said.

Puny grinned. "Thanks, sport!" Getting a compliment out of Dooley Barlowe was something to write home about.

Father Tim pushed his chair back from the kitchen table. "Let's go sit on the porch."

"You and Dooley?" asked Cynthia.

"All of us, the whole caboodle."

Why didn't people use their porches anymore? Occasionally he heard of a porch revival in which a few pioneering souls were seen sitting on theirs, but the trend quickly passed.

Father Tim and Cynthia thumped onto a bench; Dooley sat on the bench facing them.

"I've got to get out of here in . . ."—Dooley looked at his watch—"ten minutes."

"Got your shaving kit?" asked Father Tim. Heaven knows, he'd left it behind on two occasions and they had to hustle it to Georgia, two-day air.

"Yes, sir."

"What Cynthia gave you?"

"Right here." Dooley patted his jeans pocket. A hundred-dollar bill.

"What I gave you?"

"Same place." Another hundred. "Thanks again."

"You stopped by Lew's."

"Yes, sir. Gas, oil, air in the tires."

"And macaroni and cheese into the bargain," said Father Tim, happy for this boy, this moment. "Not a bad day's work."

"Don't forget the chocolate cake," said Dooley, indicating the paper bag beside him on the bench. "It'll be history before I hit Spartanburg."

Father Tim thought Dooley Barlowe looked a prince in his University of Georgia T-shirt and pressed khakis. He missed the freckles, however. "I've been meaning to ask—what's become of your freckles? I see only three or four, max."

Dooley shrugged. "I don't know. They just started disappearing."

"Shaved them off!" declared Cynthia, who appeared to know. "Please don't worry about anything; we'll try and see Sammy next week, and keep you posted about Thanksgiving."

"We believe it's all going to work out," said Father Tim.

"Oh, look!"

Cynthia stood and waved to Lace Turner, who was coming along the sidewalk at a trot, with Guber pulling hard on the leash.

"Let's go say hello!" Father Tim hurried down the steps.

Dooley was stone-faced as Cynthia grabbed his arm. "Come on, you big lug."

They trooped to the sidewalk, where Cynthia gave Lace a fond embrace. Father Tim followed suit as a taciturn Dooley stood by.

"Hi, everybody!" said Lace, "This is Guber. For *gubernatorial.*"

Father Tim found Lace Turner a sight for sore eyes—her smile was lighting up the street.

"Olivia and I are driving to Virginia in a couple of hours, I had to give Guber a long walk first." She stooped and stroked her puppy's head. "I hate to leave him."

Guber wriggled from under her hand and executed a couple of high leaps aimed at Dooley's chest.

"No, Guber! Down!" Lace tried controlling the puppy with the leash. "Down!"

"Hey," Dooley said to Guber.

"No, Guber!"

As Lace scooped the puppy into her arms, Father Tim glanced at Dooley, who was gazing at Guber's mistress.

"I'm glad you found your brother," said Lace. "Thanks."

In Dooley's blue eyes, Father Tim recognized desire, tenderness, dejection . . . hope. He turned quickly away, oddly ashamed to have seen the soul of his boy so utterly exposed.

He knew he would never have to worry about Reba Sanders. No, indeed. Not at all.

❧

"Timothy, she's done this before, surely you remember the time you came home looking like you'd been in a cat fight, trapped all night in that woman's house, miles from any living soul . . ."

"Roughly a mile and a half. Yes."

". . . and now she's done it again. Locking you in a room like that! What will she do next? I won't have it, I won't *have it!*

"And that horrid henchman of hers, slinking

around Mitford like some cat with a mouthful of feathers. Laundry! Laundry! Dry cleaning!"

She was flinging the contents of her suitcase into piles on the carpet.

"I never liked that woman, not for one second, why doesn't she leave Mitford alone? She was never one of us, anyway, always so high and mighty and arrogant and prideful, as if we're vermin to be trodden underfoot, and chasing my husband like a snake with her fangs dripping venom—"

"Calm down, Kavanagh. Come and sit a minute." He pulled her onto his lap in the wing chair. "It's OK. She's selling Clear Day, she says she despises Mitford. I believe we've seen the last of her." He searched his heart to know whether he truly believed this.

"But how can you say that? This was a low and malevolent trick. There's bound to be some other malicious deceit up her sleeve, something far more dangerous than being locked with her in a room for an hour, though I can hardly think of anything worse than being *imprisoned* with that lawless and unrepentant witch on a broom!"

What could he say?

"Can't we sue? Can't we do something? Must we be two hapless victims waiting for the next strike?"

"The thing in Kinloch worked out in the end. It's nothing to sue over—what a turmoil that would cause."

"Timothy, I can't sit on your lap all day like a child, I have things to *do!*"

She tumbled off his lap and went back to her suitcase. "Laundry! Laundry! Dry cleaning! Medicine cabinet!"

Pajamas, panty hose, a skirt, a pillbox—the air was alive with the contents of her suitcase.

He slipped down to the kitchen.

"What's goin' on upstairs?" asked Puny. "It sounds like Mr. Sherman advancin' through Atlanta."

"You're close," he said.

"Timothy! Your bishop here!"

"Stuart! What does your doctor say? What's the problem?"

"Stress! The scourge of the postmodern horde. All the tests were great, actually, but my doctor insists on a new regime—diet, exercise, and rest. In any case, I have less than one short year to raise the rest of the capital, and I'm still determined to go into this project debt-free."

"Can't someone else move and shake the cathedral project?"

"Absolutely not! Would you turn your

fondest dream over to someone else? Besides, if people are going to give money, they want to be asked by the guy in the pointed hat."

"Stuart, Stuart . . ."

"Martha's using a new cookbook, I'm walking every day and seeing the grandchildren on Tuesdays. I'm going to be fine. Now. You know this is the poorest diocese in the state. I need serious capital, Timothy."

Father Roland, Bishop Cullen . . . was there no end to it?

"You have to know some bigwigs I don't know," said Stuart, "or maybe someone lost to the records of the diocesan filing cabinet. Lord's Chapel always had its share of Florida money. Help me out here, brother—tell me again the name of that woman who was such a pest."

"Edith Mallory. I have no idea how to phone her—she has a home in Florida and a new place in Kinloch."

"Pat Mallory's widow, right?"

"Right."

"We can find her. Anybody else?"

"I can't think of anyone else. Shouldn't you be taking it easy for a while?"

"I am taking it easy. I'm supposed to lie down, every day at three o'clock."

Father Tim consulted his watch. "It's ten after three, go lie down, for Pete's sake."

"I am lying down."

"You call this lying down? This is fund-raising, this is nudging and nagging, this is work!"

"The first three million came easy enough, but the last three is a stretch, it's like squeezing blood from a turnip."

"You're talking to a turnip right now, which shows how your prospects have dwindled. I'll speak with Cynthia and we'll send a check."

"Any idea how much?"

"Not until I've talked with Cynthia. Remember the sermon you preached us before we married? The one on marital finances?"

Stuart chuckled. "You're a hard man."

"Worse has been said."

"When are you coming my way?" asked Stuart. "I'd like to see your face."

"Soon, brother, soon. I'll come and let you drag me over that wind-whipped cow pasture again."

"I'd like nothing better. I want you to see the plans; it will be wonderful, my friend, wonderful! There'll be nothing else like it in the whole of America. God will be honored in our log cathedral; I have every confidence He'll be pleased."

"Are people warming to the idea?"

"Oh, yes! Most are beginning to understand that a cathedral is a center for liturgical life, a space for music and worship and prayer and coming together. I believe the popish image is slowly, I repeat slowly, wearing away, and there's growing excitement about the choir school."

"You're faithfully in my prayers, Stuart."

"As you are in mine. And look—when you come, bring Cynthia. I'd like to see her beautiful face into the bargain."

"She's a treasure."

"I knew it before you did!"

"Always hogging the credit. Just like a bishop."

They laughed together, at ease. Few things in life were more consoling than an old friendship in which all the hair, as in the story of the velveteen rabbit, had been rubbed off.

Happy Endings' rare book business was definitely growing, as Hope could see by last month's sales records. She would e-mail everything to the owner by the end of the day, and would look for Helen's usual single-word e-mail reply of *Bravo!* to a strong bottom line. In this case, Hope thought she could count on a rare double bravo, considering that the dismal Mountain Month promotion had not impacted overall sales.

She went to the room where George was working at the computer.

"We had a great month!" she said as he glanced up. "You're doing a wonderful job."

She thought he appeared stricken, somehow, by this declaration. She had noticed for days that he was unusually quiet, even distant.

"Thank you," he said. He stood and looked at her in a way he had never looked at her before. "There's something I need to tell you."

She stepped back, as if fearing a blow, then sat down in the rickety chair she'd once dragged to Happy Endings from the Collar Button Dumpster.

"I'm going to be leaving," he said.

Leaving? She tried to speak the word aloud, but could not.

"I wanted to wait until after your bookkeeping was done. I know how you dislike doing it."

"Leaving," she said.

"I'm going back to prison."

Tears welled in her eyes, she who had never wept until these last weeks. "I don't understand."

"I've known for some time that my coming here wasn't what I was supposed to do. Let me put it another way: I was supposed to come to Mitford, it was vitally important for me to come, but I can't stay. I didn't know that in the beginning, but as I came to know it and pray about it, God put a call on my heart to go back into the prison system, into ministry."

"Ahhh," she said.

"I can never thank you enough for giving me a job and trusting me to handle it."

She shrugged. "It was nothing."

"I can never thank you enough for the way you stood up for me when people made snide remarks. You have great character, Hope, and I'm grateful."

She had always thought character something old-fashioned, out of a book, something no one seemed to bother having anymore, but if it meant so much to George . . .

"Thank you," she said.

"I'll be sorry to leave."

"Oh," she said, hearing a disgusting bit of whine in her voice.

"I'm going to Connecticut—first there's a training program, then I'll be working in ministry at a federal penitentiary.

"In the eight years I served time, I saw men who had no hope come to trust in the one true hope. I saw families rebuilt and lives changed in ways no one could have dreamed—but not every life.

"I remember the nine o'clock lockdown, we had five minutes to get to our cells. For a lot of inmates, this was payback time—a time when the dark night of the soul devoured them alive, while I went into my cell with a Brother, a Friend, a Confidant. No matter how tough it got, I had that consolation, that power—I had everything, I could make it."

She let her breath out in a long, slow, unconscious sigh.

"With God's help, I'll be serving as assistant chaplain—if I can get through the red tape."

"You can do it, George! If He's going to help you, He can certainly do something about the red tape."

"There you go, living up to your name." He laughed, tears shining in his eyes. "I'll be here for two more weeks, if you'll have me. I'll show you how I've been handling your Internet sales, and help out any way I can. Of course, you can't manage the store and the rare book business, too. I'm praying God will send the right person."

"I think . . ." She drew a deep breath.

"What do you think?"

"I want to tell you something." She was afraid to tell him, but it was important. "I thought I was . . ." This was hard, and embarrassing.

"I thought I was falling in love with you, and then . . . I don't know what happened, it had something to do with really falling and landing on all those books, because after that I realized how much I value you as a friend. I knew that, more than anything, I was grateful for your kindness to me." She drew a deep breath again and smiled as he sat on the edge of the desk and looked at her, seeming relieved about this, about everything.

"I felt comfortable with you after the fall, I wasn't afraid anymore. I want to tell you again how I'll never forget the way you spoke my name when I was lying in the window."

She saw the way his eyes looked into hers as she spoke, saw some joy in them that moved her.

"I truly have begun to hope," she said. "I feel there's something more for me, for my life. I can't explain it, I don't know what it is. But I do know that I'm glad for you, George. I think I can honestly say I'm happy you'll be leaving."

He moved from the desk, pulled his chair close to hers, and sat down, leaning forward.

"Did you know your name is everywhere in the Bible?"

"No," she said. "I don't read the Bible. I tried once because it's said to be great literature, but Mr. Wordsworth and Miss Austen seemed more accessible. And Mr. Wodehouse was loads more fun."

He laughed a little; she was consoled by the sound of it.

"Then you couldn't know that He's called the God of hope."

She felt an odd excitement, something like a child might feel. . . .

"In the letter to the Romans, Paul wrote, 'Now the God of hope fill you with all joy and peace in believing, that you may abound in hope, through the power of the Holy Spirit.'"

"Abound . . . ," she said, liking the word.

"I trust that one day you'll come to believe, and that He'll fill you with joy and peace in your believing. That's how your hope will come to abound, to grow a thousand times over. I pray for that daily."

"But I don't want you to pray for me, re-member?"

"I know." He rolled his chair back to the computer. "By the way, I'd appreciate it if you wouldn't say anything to Father Tim until I see him on Wednesday."

"I promise. Does Harley know?"

"I told him last night."

She nodded and turned to leave the room.

"Hope?"

"Yes?"

"It occurs to me that I've also seen a building named after you."

"Really?" she said, laughing.

"Hope House. Have you ever been up to Hope House?"

"Never!"

"Over their door, engraved in limestone, you'll find this: 'Let thy mercy, O Lord, be upon us, according as we . . . hope in thee.'" His grin was warmly ironic.

"I'll be darned," she said, grinning back. "We'd better get to work, or next month we won't have any sales at all to report."

The rolls were coming out of the oven when the phone rang. "Hello!" he said, decked out in a matched pair of oven mitts.

"Father! It's Marion Fieldwalker, I have news that deserves better than e-mail!"

"I'm all ears."

"Junior and Misty have a baby boy! Four o'clock this afternoon!"

"Thanks be to God!"

"You'll never guess its name!"

"Jedediah?" Nobody seemed to used the "iahs" these days.

"It's Timothy! Named after your own good self."

He was dumbfounded. No one had ever been named after him, as far as he knew.

"Great news, Marion! Give them my congratulations, we'll send a gift right away."

After hanging up the phone, he turned to his dog. "Junior and Misty Bryson, you remember them, they had a baby boy!" Barnabas cocked his head to one side. "Named Timothy," he said proudly. "After me."

He took off the mitts and raced to the bottom of the stairs.

"Cynthia! Junior and Misty had a baby boy."

"Lovely!" she said, appearing at the top of the stairs in a chenille robe she confessed to have owned since Watergate.

"Dinner's ready. His name is Timothy."

"Timothy! My favorite!"

"Named after me."

"Congratulations, dearest, what an honor." She blew him a kiss. "Would you mind if I come down in this old robe you hate with a passion?"

"Of course not. If I had time, I'd get into that old robe of mine you hate with a passion."

"Timothy Bryson," he said to himself as he went to the kitchen to serve their plates. "Timothy Bryson! A fine name."

His travel-worn wife was devouring the salmon roulade as if she hadn't eaten in weeks.

"Heavenly!" she murmured. "Divine!"

"Thank you." His cheeks grew warm with pleasure. "I got the recipe from Avis."

"Perfection!"

He'd nearly forgotten her boundless enthusiasm, it was wondrous to have it again, he'd been barren without her. . . .

She peered at him over the vase of late-blooming roses. "It's no wonder women chase after you, Timothy."

"Now, Kavanagh . . ."

"It's true. You're handsome, charming, thoughtful, sensitive—and you can *cook*! The very combination every woman dreams of. However . . ." She patted her mouth with her starched napkin and went after another forkful of wild rice. "Do remember this. . . ."

"Yes?"

"You're mine."

He laughed.

"All mine."

"Amen," he said.

"Totally, completely, absolutely mine, just like it says in the marriage service."

"I vowed so once, I vow so again."

"So watch it, buster."

"Consider it done," he said, grinning like an idiot. He loved it when she talked like that.

CHAPTER TWENTY-TWO

Even to the Dust

"Does it have to be used in the lap?"

"Of course not! I use mine in my lap because there's nowhere else to put it when I work in your study. What a question!"

Emma rolled her eyes as if he were the dunce of the millennium. The computer salesman stared at the ceiling as if counting the acoustic tiles.

Why did he have to do this, anyway? He'd rather go out in the yard and eat worms.

He walked to Winnie Ivey Kendall's house, formerly Oliva Harper's mother's house, and more recently the house where Miss Sadie and

Louella had lived before Miss Sadie died. Musical chairs!

He'd been here to a hat party, he'd visited Olivia in that terrible hour before her heart transplant, he'd come to see Miss Sadie the day she hung up her car keys, and now he was paying a call on Winnie's brother, also his retired barber. Indeed, there was an ever-changing drama behind every door on which a priest knocked.

Joe Ivey opened the door, unshaven, barefoot, and in his pajamas.

"Just dropping by to get a little taken off the sides," said Father Tim.

Joe didn't find this humorous.

"I won't stay but a minute, just wanted to see how you're pushing along."

Joe hobbled to the sofa, where a pillow and blankets awaited. He lay down, leaving his caller to shift for himself. "I'm makin' it."

Father Tim thumped into a worn, silk-covered chair once belonging to Olivia's deceased mother. "Hoppy says you're going to do just fine if you stick to what he tells you. And there, my friend, is the rub."

"What rub?"

"Sticking to what the doctor tells you."

Joe grunted, pulling the cover under his chin.

"And just think what lies ahead!"

"What lies ahead?" asked Joe, suspicious.

"You're retired now, you can go fishing!"

"I never fished in my life an' I don't expect t' start now."

"Aha. So, what will you do?"

"Cross-stitch," said Joe.

"*Cross-stitch?* That beats all I ever heard. In fact, maybe I didn't hear right. . . ."

"Men do needlework, too, you know." Joe looked more than a little ticked.

"Yes, but it's the last thing I'd ever dream would interest you."

"So what'd you think might in'erest me?"

"I don't know; I never thought about it. Maybe . . . greeting customers at Wal-Mart in Wesley?"

Joe looked menacing. "You got t' be kiddin' me."

"It pays well, you get to meet a lot of nice people."

"I've met all th' nice people I ever want t' meet," said Joe. "I don't need t' meet n'more nice people."

Being a priest was hard. You had to try and make sick people feel better, even when they had no intention of feeling better.

He talked to the Hope House administrator; all rooms were full. Though Mr. Berman was the eldest of the residents, he'd made it clear that he had no intention of going anywhere anytime soon, and the resident whom they thought last week might be dying had rallied and was planning her ninetieth birthday party. However, given Miss Rose's link to Miss Sadie, the administrator would do what she could as soon as a room came open.

Why was he always messing in other people's business? He had never understood this lifelong compulsion, especially as it often landed him in trouble.

He phoned Betty Craig.

"Betty, now that Russell's gone—"

"Don't even say it, Father. I been hopin' you wouldn't call, I know what you want me to do."

"What do I want you to do?"

"You want me to look after Miss Rose Watson, and maybe Uncle Billy, too, if he makes it."

"Oh, he's going to make it, all right. What I propose is—"

"It gives me th' shivers just to *think* of lookin' after Miss Rose."

"I understand, Betty, but consider this— you're the best one there is."

"No, sir, don't try to sweet-talk me, I'm the *only* one there is, outside of Hope House."

"Right. But you are the best, Betty. Look what you did for Russell Jacks—softened his disposition, lengthened his life . . ."

"Shortened mine. . . ."

"Betty, what if you go to the town museum twice a day, once in the morning and again in the afternoon, that's all? I'm not asking you to take anybody into your home like we did with Russell."

"Twice a day?"

"That's all, 'til we can get something open at Hope House. Uncle Billy needs to be watched; he might go off his medication, and I expect Miss Rose is none too regular with her own."

Betty sighed.

"Maybe you could look after their meals twice a day, while you're at it. We'll get someone to come in and clean."

Betty was thinking. . . .

"I suppose I wouldn't be a good Christian if I turned you down," she said.

"If you turn me down, it wouldn't necessarily have anything to do with whether you're a Christian, good or otherwise."

Betty was thinking some more.

"What if I pray about it and call you back, Father? How would that be?"

"I think that's one of the wisest answers anyone has given me about anything in a long time," he said.

"Dry, ain't it?"

"The worst I can remember in some years. Kindly fill it up, and sweep me out if the offer still holds." Father Tim slid from behind the wheel and located a paper towel to clean his windshields.

"I'm about to give up on this sweepin' out business," said Lew.

"Why's that?"

"Age. Age and drivin' t' Tennessee ever' weekend. I'm feelin' about six cookies short of a dozen."

"I've been wondering—how can you keep Earlene a secret in this town? Hasn't anybody guessed you've got a sweetheart up the road?"

"No, sir, I tell 'em I'm visitin' my old aunt."

"You have an old aunt in Tennessee?"

"Yes, sir, I do. Th' one that taught me pickle-makin'."

"That's a convenient story, all right, but I don't know how long it will go over."

"Dry as tinder," said Lew, pumping Exxon into the tank of the Mustang. "I don't allow no smokin' around th' station 'til after we get a good rain."

"Is Harley anywhere to be found?"

"In th' grease rack," said Lew.

"Harley!"

"Rev'ren', how're you comin' along?"

Merely laying eyes on Harley Welch gave him a certain happiness. "Couldn't be better!" he said. "I miss you."

"I miss you back," said Harley.

"Let's get together."

"Yes, sir. When might that be?"

"You and George come over to the house Friday night. I'll make Mississippi barbecue."

There went Harley's toothless grin, meeting behind his head again.

Emma had shown him how to go online, and after painstaking deliberation, he'd chosen an address and a code word.

He thought this address the cleverest, most unique idea he'd come up with in an eon, but someone else already had it. Who else could possibly have chosen such a thing? He went through three additional clever and unique addresses before one was finally accepted. The code word, *Barnabas,* made it through whatever maze these things might contain, which gave him a small comfort.

He sat with her while they e-mailed Walter and Katherine, an act that was guaranteed to blow their minds, then as soon as Emma left, he forgot everything she'd told him and couldn't figure out how to turn it off.

Finding the minuscule glyphs and directions hard to read on the black case, he got out a magnifying glass and finally figured how to turn it off. When he booted it up again to make sure he hadn't broken it, he was confronted with a terrible warning on the screen, a dire prognostication that alarmed him greatly.

He shut it off and clamped down the lid and, in the absence of his wife, who was at a Bible study, went to the Grill for lunch, shaking his head.

"Dry," said Mule. "Th' grass at my place is hist'ry."

Percy set two glasses of water on the table of the rear booth. "My garden's been s' punk, I plowed it up. Got four little t'matoes, a handful of limas, an' three ears of corn I fed to th' squirrels."

"I didn't garden this year," said Father Tim.

"If you were goin' t' skip a year, this was th' year t' skip."

"Profoundly true."

"What're y'all havin'?"

"We're waitin' for J.C.," said Mule. "You can bring me a Diet Coke. No, let's see . . . make that a Pepsi."

"Diet Pepsi," Percy said, writing.

Mule shook his head. "I don't like diet Pepsi."

"So you're orderin' a regular Pepsi? Is that what I'm hearin'?"

"That's it."

"How 'bout you?"

"Water," said Father Tim. "I've got it right here."

"What's th' special?" Mule wanted to know.

"Gizzards," said Percy.

Mule smacked his forehead. "I forgot this is Tuesday. Seem like you ought t' have two specials on Tuesday, to give a man a choice."

"This ain't a four-star restaurant where th' specials outnumber th' reg'lar menu items. It's aggravation enough th' way it is."

"Gentlemen?"

"Reverend Tipton!" Father Tim scooted from the booth and shook hands with Mitford's new Methodist.

"You didn't have to get up for me, Father."

"It's time clergy got a little respect around here."

Mule stood and shook hands with enthusiasm.

"Could you squeeze in one more, or would another day suit better?"

"Always room for one more!"

"Yes ma'am!" said Mule. "Always!"

"We're just waiting for our newspaper editor, J. C. Hogan, he'll be along any minute."

Mule sat down fast and slid to the corner. "Here you go!" he said to Millie Tipton, slapping the seat beside him.

Father Tim was disappointed to note that this forced him to sit on J.C.'s side, usually occupied only by J.C. and, of course, the editor's briefcase, which was loosely the size of a panel truck.

No doubt about it, the new pastor was an attractive woman—tall, dark-haired, eyeglasses on a pearl chain, and looking far better in a black shirt and collar than he ever would.

Millie Tipton, they discovered, was a fount of information. She hailed from Daphne, Alabama, where her parents still resided. She was happy to be in Mitford. She liked Italian cooking, quilting, and reading. And she was living on the road to Farmer in a little stone house with two dogs, a cat, and a bed of dahlias that appeared to be thriving in the drought.

"Looks like we've got a two-collar town goin' here." Mule seemed downright pleased.

"Three-collar," said Father Tim. "Don't forget Father Talbot at Lord's Chapel."

"One stoplight and three collars. That's an unusual ratio." Mule turned and peered at his seat mate. "Never married?"

"Not yet," she said, looking amiable about it.

Percy stepped over to meet Millie Tipton, declaring he'd been raised Methodist, but had fallen away to the Baptists twenty years ago.

"Then you probably know," said Millie, "how many Baptists it takes to change a light bulb."

"No, ma'am, can't say I do."

"At least fifteen. One to change the bulb, and three committees to approve the change and decide who brings the fried chicken."

Percy cracked up.

"I'm a Baptist now, too, but I was raised Lutheran," said Mule, trying to be informative.

"Ah, the Lutherans! Everybody knows how many *Lutherans* it takes to change a light bulb."

She looked around the table, obviously enjoying herself.

"How many?" asked Mule.

"None. Lutherans don't like change."

Guffaws, general hooting. In the front booth, two town councilmen thought the rear booth was helping itself to a mighty loud hullabaloo. . . .

"All right," said Percy. "Y'all got t' git down t' business, I'm short-handed. Let J.C. fend for hisself when he gets here. What're you havin', Rev'ren'?"

"Please call me Millie!"

Percy had no intention of calling a preacher by a first name, especially a good-looking woman preacher.

Millie put her glasses on. "Let's see . . . I'm new at this menu, it'll take a minute. Y'all please go ahead and order."

"I'll have the tuna sandwich on whole wheat," said Father Tim. "Toasted, no mayo, and a side of cole slaw."

"He always knows what he wants," Mule informed Millie.

"Hop to it," said Percy.

"I'm ready for you, buddyroe. Shoot me a hotdog all th' way!"

"Hotdog all th' way."

"Right. No onions, no mustard, an' leave off th' relish."

Percy shook his head; he wasn't going there.

Millie Tipton gave Percy a big smile. "And I'll have the gizzards."

He spent a full afternoon at the Children's Hospital, laughing, crying, telling stories, counseling with a parent, holding small hands, praying. It never failed to be a workout of the emotions; afterward, he was either filled with elation or numb with suffering, and no in between.

It occurred to him to ask Millie Tipton if she'd consider making a weekly visit, as well—she seemed to have enough energy to go around.

In truth, the ratio of three collars to one stoplight was a ratio sorely needed, and then some.

"Father? It's Gene Bolick."

"Gene! God bless you, my friend. How are you?"

"Not too bad, under th' circumstances. Whoa, wait a minute, I forgot I'm tryin' to live *over* th' circumstances, not under 'em."

"Well said!"

"I wanted to tell you somethin'."

"I'm all ears."

"Just wanted to say how much I appreciated your sermon on Sunday."

"Thank you."

"Seem like you were talkin' directly to me."

"I know the feeling."

"How can a man thank God for a brain tumor? That's what I've been askin' myself. But I can thank Him it's brought our daughter closer to us, th' one livin' over in Asheville, and it sure makes me look at every day a whole lot different.

"In other words, it seems to me that God is usin' th' tumor to . . . I guess what I'm sayin' is, a tumor's a bad thing, but I see how it's caused good things to happen." Gene choked up.

"I hear you."

"So, that's about it."

"Thank you, Gene. God loves a grateful heart, He'll bless you for it."

"You doin' all right?"

"I am!"

"Well, you come up and see us anytime. Esther's bakin' apple pies today, she said tell you she'll leave th' sugar out of one if you'll come up an' get it."

"That," he said, "is the best offer I've had all day."

Eager to give another tutorial, Emma stopped by on her way to The Local, showed him again how to retrieve his e-mail, and delivered one of her own.

Dear Mrs. Newland,

We are thrilled and delighted at the prospect of becoming a Sister Village with Mitford. We are writing to enquire your thinking re: how we should exchange delegates to make this happy alliance an official reality.

We expect to send Andrew and Margaret Hart, a charming couple whose unanimous election has been a matter of some rejoicing, as Andrew has relatives living in the eastern part of your state whom he has never met. We feel the months of May or June of next year would be a grand time for the individual ceremonies, if that would be convenient to your own schedule, of course.

The weather in our Mitford is usually very lovely at that season, though last year we had the most dreadful heat wave, and the year prior to that, a perilous flooding that washed our newly-planted rhododendron into the neighbor's ha-ha.

Do let us know.

With greetings to all, we remain . . .

The Mitford (UK) Sister Village Coordinating Committee

"Who do you think should go?" he asked Emma.

"Why, th' mayor, of course, that's th' sort of thing mayors *do*."

"If he can't go, who do you think? Hessie Mayhew?"

"Hessie Mayhew?"

Emma's indignation nearly blew him against the wall. "Why not?"

"*Why not?* She's Presbyterian, that's why not."

"I don't get it."

"I've been workin' with th' Anglicans over there, th' whole thing's bein' done thro' th' *Anglicans*!"

"I see. But don't you think the delegate should be somebody who simply represents the spirit—the heart, if you will—of our Mitford, regardless of denomination?"

"What I really think is, you should be th' one goin'."

"How quickly you forget. I'm not flying across that pond or any other."

"You bought a computer," she reminded him.

"Give you an inch, you want a mile."

"Maybe Esther Cunningham. She was mayor for how many years, eighteen?"

"Esther won't do it, she'd rather be traveling with Ray in the RV. I'd talk to Andrew if I were you, get his thoughts."

"Right," she said.

"You know who I'd send?"

"Who?"

"You," he said.

"Me?"

"It was your idea. It's your hard work that got us to this point. I think you should do it. In fact, I'll mention it to the mayor."

"Fly all that way over *water*?"

"Don't look down," he said. "Get a seat on the aisle."

She frowned. "I'm too fat to go to England. Plus I don't have anything to wear. *Nothin'*. And even though I used to be Episcopalian, now I'm a Baptist."

"Umm," he said.

"An' Snickers . . . I've never left Snickers. I don't know if he could live without me."

"Scared of flying, too fat, nothing to wear, dog will keel over, and a Baptist! You've convinced me. If I were you, I wouldn't go, either."

She peered at him over her half-glasses. He knew that look. She was waiting to be begged, cajoled, wheedled, and coaxed. But no way. Let that job fall to somebody else.

She picked up the e-mail and studied it. "What in th' dickens does this mean . . . 'washed into the neighbor's ha-ha'?"

"A ha-ha is a ditch, a sort of ravine that cows won't cross. Saves on fencing."

"The way they say things over there, you'd think they live in a foreign country."

"They do live in a foreign country."

He went back to paging through the essays she had typed and printed out before the era of his own p.c.

"OK," she said.

"OK what?"

"If th' mayor asks me, I'll go. I'll give up potatoes, gravy, bread, an' ice cream startin' in January. That way, I'll lose ten pounds by May, which means I can get in that blue suit you've seen me wear, th' one with th' gold buttons, and that orange knit dress with a jacket. You remember that orange knit dress with a jacket."

"Can't say that I do."

She took a deep breath. "I should probably give up bacon while I'm at it, an' I'll get a pill from Hoppy, to knock me out over th' Atlantic."

"There you go," he said. "There's more than one way to skin a cat."

"But I'm not gettin' my hopes up," she said. "Andrew will probably go, or he's already got somebody in mind."

"Could be."

"And lookit, they're sendin' a couple. I wonder if that means we should send a couple, to keep things even. I can't imagine who it would be, can you? Not th' Bolicks, he has that tumor. Not th' Harpers, they've just been on vacation. . . ."

He studied the top of the computer screen, pondering the mysteries to be unlocked within File, Edit, View, Insert, Format, Tools . . .

"Besides, who would fix Harold's breakfast?"

"Percy Mosely?" he asked, hoping to be helpful.

"Late February is what th' doctor said. But I hope it's March! If it can wait 'til March th' third, it'll be born on my mama's birthday."

He sat at the kitchen table, counting his pocket change. "Do you know whether it's a boy or a girl?" A dollar forty, a dollar fifty . . .

"No, sir, I don't know an' don't want t' know. What did people do before you could look in somebody's stomach with a camera? They waited 'til it was born, that's what!"

"Will you, ah, be bringing the baby to work?"

"I'm sure not goin' to farm it out! Besides, how do you think it would get to know its granpaw if I didn't bring it to work?"

He thought Puny looked positively radiant.

"A dollar seventy-five, seventy-six, seventy-seven. You've got a point there," he said.

Emma Newland's possible mission to England, and his new grandchild on the way. . . .

Just let somebody try to tell him that miracles didn't happen every day.

Dear Father,

I have seen little Timothy and he's cute as a button. He looks just like Junior, though he has his mother's eyes. We hope you and Cynthia can come and visit soon, and see your namesake for yourself.

I feel like a regular gossip column, but must tell you that Ernie and Mona are going on a cruise and will renew their vows in Honolulu! The wall they built on the yellow line is being used as a community bulletin board, tho' you have to stoop down to read the postings. It's where I found a wonderful old Hoover vac as good as new. I always liked an upright.

Don't forget us!

Best love from Marion and Sam

Timothy! Hail to thee from Tennessee!

Just wait til our package arrives on your doorstep, in thanks for the outstanding gift you made to Backyard. Abner has worked on this marvelous creation for several months and as he is not gifted at drawing or painting, decided to send the forthcoming, instead. Am busting to tell you what it is, but can only say you are a fortunate man! God be with you, let us hear soonest. Send mammon, as ever. In His service, Fr Roland

Teds! Its us, walt&kat@icm.com! We were blown away (to use the vernacular) to receive your e-mail. We can't figure whether your entry into cyberspace is the beginning of an era or the end of one!

The year at Meadowgate sounds like loads of fun, and yes, we'd love to come for a week, will probably drive down and stop along the way. Let's talk soon.

C's trip sounds exhausting but fun, I'm reading her Violet books to my dearlings at the retirement home, as I passionately believe great children's literature is for all ages.

So glad yr health improved. Lots of love and kisses to you and your talented C, and hugs to Dooley

"It's me . . . Betty."

"Betty!"

"I'll do it."

"Great! Wonderful!"

"But no cleaning." He heard the tremor in her voice. It wasn't easy for Betty Craig to lay down the law.

"Absolutely none!"

"And just two meals a day."

"Not a scrap more," he said.

"When do I start?"

"He'll be home tomorrow. Your timing is perfect."

"So I start tomorrow evenin'?"

"Yes, ma'am. Around four-thirty, if you could."

"Will you be there to get me started?"

"I will."

"And Father?"

"Yes?"

"Every time Miss Rose is mean to me, I'm goin' to put a dime in a little bank I made from a Sprite can."

He laughed. "You could quickly become a very rich woman."

"Yes, sir, an' when this job is over, I'll use th' money for a vacation—'cause I'll sure be needin' one."

Father Talbot rang up in the evening. Would the Kavanaghs come to a spur-of-the-moment community-wide covered dish supper on Friday? Bill Sprouse would be there, and Millie Tipton; there would be special music, and they'd do a bit of ecumenical praying-for-rain into the bargain.

Cynthia was up for it.

"Ray Cunningham's cole slaw, Margaret Larkin's fried chicken, and Hessie Mayhew's yeast rolls. Fabulous!" said his wife.

"How do you know they'll even be there?"

"It's worth the gamble," she said. He thought Cynthia Kavanagh had come home as starved as a barn cat.

Father Tim called George and Harley to see if they could reschedule the barbecue for the Saturday before George was to leave. Not a problem. George said he would pass on going to Lord's Chapel, however, and get together with Scott Murphy.

Harley was keen for the church supper.

"What sort of getup?" asked Harley.

"Khakis, I'd say, and a sport shirt."

"You reckon I ought t' bring a pan of brownies?"

"Definitely!"

"Nuts or plain?"

"Nuts," said Father Tim. "And when you take the Saran Wrap off, stand back."

Harley cackled. One of his proudest moments had been when two church ladies begged for his recipe. He'd written it down on the back of a pew bulletin, and now, every time they came by the station, they talked about the brownies that were making them famous all the way to Minnesota, or was it Montana?

Didn't he have to earn his wings sooner or later?

Well, then, why not sooner?

He'd take five minutes while Cynthia dressed for the church supper, and carry forth the dictum laid down by Nike.

Thumping into his desk chair, he opened the laptop and accessed his e-mail. Nothing new. He was pierced by an odd disappointment.

Now. He knew how to retrieve his e-mail, but could he *send* one without Emma standing over him? All he had to do was follow the handwritten directions she'd scrawled on a yellow pad. What could happen, after all, if he did it unsupervised? Could he somehow break the thing that had cost an arm and a leg and thrust him into the twenty-first century?

If so, so be it. . . .

> Dear Emma, just a note to say How much your pesky insistence is appreciated, not to mention your patient Tutorials. I like this sTuff, and yes, You Told Me So. (Lest you gloat overmuch in seeing my bald admission in black and white, tear this up, I pray you, or run it through a shredder.) The Mouse is driving me Ccrazy/
>
> Guess Who

He hit send, holding his breath.

Out of here.

Emma Newland would count this her greatest triumph.

To tell the truth, he felt pretty good about it himself.

At six-thirty, Hope Winchester filled her teakettle with bottled water and placed it on the gas burner. She was wondering whether she'd ever known anyone other than George who was willing to make personal sacrifices for God.

She thought of her mother, who had made desperate sacrifices for her two daughters, but not for God. Her mother didn't appear to believe in God, though Hope remembered the time when her sister, Louise, was running a perilous fever, and her mother had sat at the foot of the bed and wept and rocked herself. "Oh, God, oh, God, oh, God," she had whispered over and over. It had frozen Hope's heart to witness her grief. When she was older, Hope remembered wondering if it had been God who made Louise well.

It was mystifying to her that George would choose to go back to prison, back into despair and hopelessness and even possible danger, when he could have chosen an easy life in Mitford. And yet, she sensed it wasn't in him to choose an easy life.

She walked to the front window of her two rooms above the Chelsea Tea Shop, and looked out to Main Street. The days had grown shorter; already the street lamps were shining against the gathering dusk. Three people passed on the street below, two of them carrying something covered by a tea towel.

A choir member had invited her to the Lord's Chapel supper, and she'd wrestled all day with the invitation. Never in her life had she cooked or baked anything for a covered-dish supper, and the thought of doing it and failing was humiliating.

Worse still, what if she took something and no one ate any of it and she had to carry the dish away, untouched, while everyone else went home with empty platters?

It occurred to her in the afternoon that she might buy a dozen corn muffins before the tea shop closed, and in this notion found a moment of glad reprieve. Bought muffins, however, might be a mark against her in some way she could only sense and not fully understand.

She wished fervently that she'd never been asked, and found that she was wringing her hands again. The bright spirit she'd recently felt had vanished, and she was her old self, the worried, fretful self she'd been before the fall.

She went to her boiling teakettle and looked at the clock on the stove. Six forty-five. As the supper was at seven o'clock, it was too late to worry about it anymore. The whole affair could at last be forgotten.

She instantly felt both an enormous relief and an unexplainable sadness, something like the feeling she had when she realized she wasn't in love with George Gaynor, after all, but counted him a friend.

"And in this mountain the Lord of hosts will make for all people a feast of choice pieces, a feast of wines on the lees, of fat things full of marrow. . . ."

In his blessing of the meal, Father Talbot quoted from the prophet Isaiah, then invited all to break bread together.

"Did you bring your brownies?" Amy Larkin asked Harley, who was ahead of her in the queue to the food table.

"Yes, ma'am," he told the eleven-year-old. "Right over yonder."

"I brought pimiento cheese sandwiches." Her eyes shone. "No crusts."

"Where're they at?"

"Right next to the potato salad in the red bowl," she said. "On the left."

He nodded, respectful. "I'll make sure to have one."

Amy Larkin reminded him of Lace when she was still a little squirt, running to his trailer with a book under her arm. He hated she had grown up and gone off to school, but he knew it was for the best.

He fixed his gaze on Cynthia's lemon squares on the dessert table. He had set his mouth for a lemon square, and hoped he could get to the familiar blue and white platter before it was too late.

"O God, heavenly Father, who by Thy Son Jesus Christ has promised to all those who seek Thy kingdom and its righteousness all things necessary to sustain their life: Send us, we entreat thee, in this time of need, such moderate rain and showers, that we may receive the fruits of the earth, to our comfort and to Thy honor; through Jesus Christ our Lord."

"Amen!"

"Abide with me:
fast falls the eventide;
the darkness deepens;
Lord, with me abide:
when other helpers
fail and comforts flee,
help of the helpless,
O abide with me. . . ."

The words of the eighteenth-century hymnist carried through the open windows of the parish hall and lifted on the mild September air.

A block away, Hope Winchester thought she could hear singing, but wasn't sure. Maybe she heard something that sounded like *abide with me . . .* and something about eventide, but she couldn't be certain.

She stood at her open window for what seemed a long time, listening.

Hélène Pringle heard the faint sound of the basement door closing, and knew that someone had come in.

When she saw Harley this afternoon at the gas station, he said he was having supper at Lord's Chapel. "Are you goin'?" he asked.

"Oh, no," she'd said. "I haven't been invited."

"Ever'body's invited," he'd told her. "Hit's community-wide, you ought t' come!"

But of course she hadn't gone; she'd felt terribly vulnerable last Sunday when the father preached on being thankful and had the odd notion he was preaching directly to her. She tried to recall if she had thanked God for anything, or only asked Him to give her something, as a child might make requests of St. Nicholas.

She had grown fond of those times of talking through the curtain, to the one she supposed to be God. She still had no certainty that He cared or was even listening, but she hoped He was. In truth, it was increasingly important to her that He should listen and care, and that their time together be more than the figment of a spinster's overwrought imagination.

She turned the kitchen light off and was going along the hall when the phone rang. It would be a student, of course, canceling or rescheduling .

"Allo!" she said in the French way.

"Miss Pringle, it's Hope Winchester. How are you this evening?"

"Very well, Hope, and you?"

"Good, thank you. Is . . . George Gaynor there? I hope this is no trouble."

"No trouble in the least! One moment, please, and I'll call down."

She laid the phone on the hall table and walked to the basement door and opened it. "Mr. Gaynor! Are you there?" Though she called Harley by his first name, she had never felt comfortable calling Mr. Gaynor by his.

"Yes, Miss Pringle?" George Gaynor appeared in a pool of light at the foot of the basement stairs.

"You have a telephone call. Will you come up?"

"Yes. Thank you."

"The receiver is on the hall table, just switch on the lamp."

Mr. Gaynor was an arresting figure, she thought, as he appeared at the top of the stairs—quite handsome and dignified, not at all like someone who had spent time behind bars. "Please don't hurry," she said. "I'll be upstairs."

"Thank you again."

It was *étrange,* she mused as she went up, that her next-door neighbor had somehow collected the three of them under one roof—what an odd assortment! She smiled at the thought.

Ça alors! what a day this had been—Barbizon was in the foulest of tempers, and all three of her students had done poorly at their lessons. She would take a hot bath and put on *sa chemise de nuit préférée* and talk to the other side of the curtain.

She paused at the top of the stair, attracted by laughter in the hallway. It was such an unusual sound, a man laughing in her house. . . .

"I said you could call anytime. Yes, it's all right, I assure you."

There was a long silence. Hélène thought she should go to her room, but didn't move from the banister railing.

"Of course. I remember the day when the teachers came in, I was going to tell you about the prayer, but . . ."

Her grandmother's tall case clock ticked on the landing.

"It's a very simple prayer. Sometimes, people think they want something more sophisticated, or even complicated. But if you have a willing heart, it's all you need, nothing more. . . ."

"What will happen? That's a good question."

Hélène heard him chuckle; it seemed a glad sound.

"It would take years to tell you all that happens when you surrender your life to God. Perhaps forgiveness—I think His forgiveness may be the most important thing that happens. . . .

"Yes. Even for the worst stuff. . . ."

Hélène looked at the clock. In less than a minute, it would chime the hour. Her heart beat in her temples.

"Surrendering your soul to Him changes everything. That sounds scary, but I found it downright terrifying when I presumed to be in control . . .

"I understand. I had every reason, also. My uncle was a priest who stole six hundred thousand dollars from the church coffers—with the help of my father. I've found that if we keep our eyes on Christians, we can be disappointed in a major way. The important thing is to keep our eyes on Christ. . . .

"I can't honestly say that I know what *happy* means. Let's say that I'm certain . . .

"About who He is, what life is for, where I'm going, what it means to be given a second chance. . . .

"Yes, you can pray it with me . . . whatever seems right to you."

Hélène heard the movement in the French clock begin to whir.

"Thank you, God, for loving me . . . and for sending Your Son to die for my sins. . . ."

The first hour struck . . .

"I sincerely repent of my sins . . . and receive Jesus Christ as my personal savior."

The second hour . . .

"Now, as your child, I turn my entire life over to you. Amen."

The clock on the landing of the old rectory struck again, seven times.

Hélène stood by the railing, breathless and unmoving, lest she betray to George Gaynor that she was standing there at all.

When at last she went down the stairs to turn off the light, the hall was empty and the basement door was closed.

When Volunteer Fire Chief Hamp Floyd got the call from a neighbor, he ran to his back door and flung it open. Naked as a jaybird and still clutching the cordless, he looked east.

Rooted to the spot, he dialed the fire chief in Wesley.

"It's Hamp," he said, his voice shaking. "Bring both trucks, I'll have a lead car waitin' at the corner of Lilac an' Main."

He dressed in two-point-three minutes and, without kissing his wife, ran from the house to do the impossible.

🐚

Father Tim heard the truck leave the fire station at two in the morning.

He got up quickly and went to the window facing Wisteria, but saw nothing out of the ordinary.

"What is it, Timothy?"

"I don't know. I'm going to throw something on and go down to the porch. Sounds like they're headed north."

"I'll pray," she said.

He pulled on his pants, shoved his feet into his loafers, and buttoned his shirt as he went down the stairs.

"Stay," he said to his dog, who was hard on his heels at the front door.

From the porch, he saw a neighbor running toward Main Street.

"What is it?" he called.

"Fire on the ridge!"

He ran to the sidewalk, hooked a left, and jogged toward Main.

Several neighbors were standing in the street; a group had gathered on Edie Adams's front lawn.

Bill Adkins, dressed in pajamas and a windbreaker, nodded as Father Tim reached the sidewalk at Edie's. "It's a bad one," said Bill.

Father Tim turned and looked northeast, up to the long ridge where fire was turning the dark sky orange, where the clouds appeared lit by an eerie inner glow.

"Clear Day," he whispered.

"Yessir. Looks like the truck went out mighty late."

"I should go." He was suddenly chilled, shaking.

"Nossir, I wouldn't do that if I was you."

"That's a huge fire."

"Yessir, there's no way our truck can handle it, they'll have to get help from Wesley. Lord knows I hope th' woods hadn't caught fire, dry as it's been."

Ninety acres of parched timber bordering eight thousand square feet of heart pine, oak beams, and cedar shakes.

"That yella truck'll have t' do th' work of three or four red 'uns," said an onlooker.

"What if she's up there?" he asked Bill Adkins.

"In Florida would be my guess."

But something told him otherwise.

Stricken, he prayed aloud the prayer that never fails.

"Dear God, Your will be done!"

"Amen," replied a voice in the crowd.

Neighbors in slippers, a few with their hair in curlers, continued to convene along the west side of Main Street, as if gathering for a parade. There were long periods of astonished silence as they looked east to the furnace on the ridge. Then murmurs of disbelief again rippled through the crowd, swelling into agitated talk and laughter.

To Father Tim it seemed an eternity before they heard the twin sirens of Wesley's trucks hauling south toward the Mitford monument. As the trucks came into view and swung left on Lilac Road, cheers went up.

He walked toward home, praying.

"That woman's gettin' back what she's been dishin' out."

"A little taste of what's to come, you know what I mean?"

Laughter.

He walked on.

"Hey, Father."

"Hey, Sam. Will you pray?"

"Yes, sir."

Cynthia would sleep through this; she could

sleep through an air raid. He wouldn't disturb her. But he needed her; he needed her to tell him what to do.

"It's bad, isn't it?"

She was sitting up in bed, waiting, her eyes wide.

"It's Clear Day."

"Dear God . . ."

"I think any effort I could make would be useless. Three trucks, and maybe more coming, I don't know."

"If you went, all you could do is pray; we can do that here. Come, sweetheart."

She held out her hands to him.

He went to her and sat by her side and couldn't stop trembling.

He awoke at first light and lay quiet and uneasy, listening to the snores of his dog in the hallway.

He thought for a while, trying to bring something forth from his befuddled mind, then got up and padded to the wing chair and turned on the floor lamp and picked up his Bible and turned to Isaiah.

Toward the end of the twenty-fifth chapter was the prophet's warning to those who would not trust, the reverse side of the bright verse that Father Talbot had used in his prayer only last night, though it seemed days ago.

"For in this mountain," he read, "shall the hand of the Lord rest . . . and the fortress of the high fort of thy walls shall he bring down, lay low, and bring to the ground, even to the dust."

Without waking Cynthia, he dressed and went downstairs, and made a call from the kitchen.

CHAPTER TWENTY-THREE

A Place of Springs

"They wadn't no fire alarm that went off, is what they say."

Coot Hendrick was occupying the lead stool at Percy's counter, and looking as ragged out as the rest of the early crowd.

Father Tim took a mug of coffee from Percy and sat on the stool beside Coot. "I called Wesley Hospital this morning, on the chance they'd know something. It turns out Ed Coffey drove her over there, and she was picked up by a trauma unit. They flew her to Charlotte."

"Was she burned bad?" asked Percy.

"Wasn't burned at all. A ceiling beam and some of the plaster gave way in her bedroom—it's serious, I think." Clergy shared a few privileges with the press; they were sometimes given information that others couldn't access.

Percy rubbed his eyes. His house afforded one of the best views of the Clear Day property, and sleep had been scarce. "Tim Jenkins was th' first one in this mornin', takin' coffee to th' ridge, said 'er house was about burned t' th' ground when they got there."

"They'll be on th' ridge a while yet," said Coot. "Smoke's comin' off of it, big time."

"Took 'em a good half hour to get to th' house from th' road, Tim said they had t' break down that electric gate she's got, they busted th' bloomin' thing half t' pieces t' get in, then what d'you think?"

"What?" asked Coot.

"Turns out there's a hedge of rhodos on either side of th' road, runnin' from th' gate to 'er house—"

J.C. wheeled in with his briefcase, blackened from head to toe and reeking of smoke. He took a mug of coffee from Percy.

"We were just talkin' about th' rhodo hedge," said Percy.

"Man, what a mess. Th' guys in the trucks didn't know there was a back way to th' house, so they tried gettin' th' trucks in through th' front. Th' rhododendrons have grown together, sides and top, 'til they're tight as a steel culvert.

"But ol' Hamp floored his new truck an' in they went. Only trouble is, they couldn't get very far. There they were, three trucks stalled in that tunnel of rhodos and th' house goin' up like kindling.

"I think Hamp did some damage to his new vehicle before he finally got to th' house." He handed the mug back to Percy. "Shoot me a little cream in there and about a bucket of sugar.

"My take is, all th' heavy equipment she's had on th' place th' last couple of months, they maybe ran over a cable, somehow cut some wires, and took th' security system out—that's why Hamp didn't get a call off th' smoke alarm." J.C. jerked several paper napkins from the aluminum holder and wiped his face. "Man, that was th' worst thing I ever saw, I don't want t' see anything like it again in this lifetime."

"Th' father says Ed Coffey drove 'er to Wesley an' they sent a trauma unit to pick 'er up."

"I got to find Ed," said J.C. "He's th' main man, th' missin' piece. This story's got to run Monday, I got a lot of facts to pull together. What kind of trauma unit?"

"I don't know," said Father Tim. "They said part of the ceiling caved into her bedroom, she was flown out of Wesley about two-thirty this morning."

J. C. swigged his coffee. "I wish we could run color like Gary Barnes's paper over th' mountain. When it comes to a fire, black and white photos don't cut it."

"So how come how Ed didn't get hurt?" asked Percy.

"He lives in th' carriage house out back," said J.C. "Which is prob'bly what saved her neck."

"Looked like the fire was bad enough to take the whole ninety acres," said Father Tim.

"Yeah, well, when th' guys saw th' house was a goner, they went to work to keep th' fire out of th' woods; it was fish or cut bait, accordin' to Hamp."

"So, what're you orderin'?" Percy asked J.C. This CNN news hour could go on 'til the cows came home. A man had to make a living.

"Can you do lunch?"

"Depends on what it is." It was six-thirty in the morning, for Pete's sake.

"Give me a ribeye, well done on a toasted bun, with mayo, steak sauce, onions, an' an order of hash browns—make that a double order. I been goin' like a sonofagun since Hamp hauled by my house at two A.M."

Percy crossed his arms. "I can do it, but it'll be a one-time-only deal."

"An' while you're at it, fry my onions along with th' steak."

Percy had no intention whatever of frying onions at six-thirty in the morning. Let Mister Fat Cat Know-It-All fry his own blooming onions.

On Monday morning, the ashes of Clear Day still smoldered on the ridge; the smell hung over the village like an acrid incense.

Though a number of people couldn't resist being secretly pleased that Clear Day's owner had gotten her comeuppance, most of them kept their mouths shut. As dry as it had been, the fire could easily have spiraled out of control and advanced down the ridge to devour the town, like the Gordonsville fire in 1978. Nossir, you didn't want to go badmouthing somebody at a time like this, especially since your own neck had been spared—they would badmouth Miss High and Mighty after the smoke cleared and the dust settled.

Ridge-Top Home Burns to Ground

Clear Day, the home of longtime Mitford resident, Edith Mallory, burned to the ground at about two-thirty a.m. on Saturday morning of last week.

Fire Chief Hamp Floyd and his squad of hard-working volunteers joined forces with two trucks from our sister station in Wesley. They battled the blazing inferno until seven o'clock Saturday morning, with special emphasis on building a fire screen that prevented the blaze from igniting surrounding woods.

Chief Floyd said a large area of raw ground and a large swimming pool also helped contain the fire. Someone reported that Ms. Mallory was having a helicopter pad constructed on the west lawn of her 90-acre property, once the sight of the log cabin home of Mitford's founder, Hezikiah Hendrick.

"It was a big one," stated Chief Floyd/. "Apparently, the Mallory alarm system had malfunctioned, and we did not get a call from the security company. My call came from Buster Boyd, who had to let his dog out and saw what was happening on the ridge. I would like to personally thank Buster for his contribution."

It was learned that Ms. Mallory suffered severe injuries, though not from fire. Ed Coffey, an employee of Ms. Mallory who returned to the sight for personal belongings from his living quarters, said he could not discuss the specific nature of the injuries. He did say that Ms. Mallory is recuperating in a Charlotte hospital, and will return to her home in Florida in several weeks. He added that new wiring was underway in the attic of the house and may have caused the problem.

We would like to thank all who bravely battled the fire that if not properly contained might have spread to other home sights with tragic results.

The story was accompanied by a large black and white front-page photo showing a crescent moon risen over the enormous conflagration. A piece of garden statuary in the foreground appeared to be of Diana, Goddess of the Hunt. In the confusion of men and equipment, an arm had been broken from the statue and was lying in the grass.

"Lookit!" said Emma.

She pulled something from a shopping bag, unfurled it, and presented a navy blue dress with a white collar.

"England! What d'you think?"

"I like it."

"I decided I'm not going to try an' lose weight, I'll just buy somethin' dark and loose that makes me look thin."

"Brilliant."

"On sale. Half price."

"Brilliant to the max."

He wouldn't exactly call Emma Newland beautiful, no, indeed. But ever since Andrew had insisted she be the one to go, she had looked radiant, a new woman.

"I'm studyin' how to speak English," she announced.

"It's about time."

"*Boot* for *trunk, post* a letter for *mail* a letter, *garden* for *yard,* and *ha-ha* for a *ditch* to put cows in. . . ."

"Spot on," he said.

"Timothy, Stuart. I've got good news and bad news."

"The bad first."

"You know about Edith Mallory?"

"I do. But not many details. It was a terrible fire, a sight I'll never forget."

"You remember I asked if you know how to reach her, thinking we might scare up a gift for the cathedral? She's no longer on the membership list at Lord's Chapel, so we had to trace her. Beth O'Conner—did you know Beth?"

"Yes, she visited Edith several times, came to church."

"We knew she was a friend of Edith's, so we called her. And listen to this . . ."

It had definitely been a while since he'd heard joy in Stuart's voice.

"She's giving us a half million dollars for the choir school!"

"Congratulations! Mazel tov!"

"It's in memory of her son who died of cancer a few months ago. She's been waiting, she said, until God spoke to her heart about where to give it. She loves the idea of the choir school, her son began singing in the choir when he was eleven years old, she may even do something for us again."

"My friend, you sound eleven years old yourself. But I thought you were going to start with the bad news."

"I was, but I forgot and gave you the good stuff instead. Anyway, that's the first specific commitment we've had to the choir school, and I'm frankly beside myself. By the way, thanks a thousandfold for the Kavanagh gift, it means a great deal to have it."

"It meant a great deal to send it."

"The bad news, of course, is that Edith Mallory is in serious condition. Beth says Edith would want it kept quiet, but I thought you should know—both her motor and speech centers have been damaged. There's great difficulty in expressing herself verbally, and she's paralyzed along her right side, something like what happens with a stroke. She'll be in a wheelchair, and the doctors don't know where the brain injury could lead. Right now, Beth says she can only speak gibberish. The doctors call it word salad."

"I'm sorry," he said, meaning it.

"Yes. So am I. She'll be in a rehab center for a couple of months, then down to Florida."

"Do you know where she is in Charlotte?"

"Putney."

"That's good. Thanks for bringing me up to speed. I needed to know."

"It occurs to me that Edith has participated in building the choir school, albeit unwittingly. In any case—moving along to happier themes—I'm encouraged, Timothy. I hope you are."

"I am. Very much."

"God is faithful, Timothy, listen to this—my secretary wrote it on my notepad this morning. 'Those who go through the desolate valley will find it a place of springs, for the early rains have covered it with pools of water.' Psalm Eighty-four."

"Amen and amen."

"Love to Cynthia."

"And love to Martha."

He sat for a time, looking out the window to Baxter Park.

Then he opened the desk drawer and took out his Mont Blanc pen and a sheet of ivory writing paper.

Dear Edith,

He wouldn't speak to her of God. Let God do that Himself.

You are faithfully in our prayers.
  Cynthia and Timothy Kavanagh

"Ugh!" exclaimed his wife, trying to huff the box from the porch bench.

"Here," he said. "Let me get it."

"It's from Tennessee!" she said, as eager as he to see what the delivery contained.

"I must chide Father Roland for shipping UPS when the post office could have done it cheaper."

"Tell him that next time he begs for money."

They sat on the floor of the study, slicing through the laboriously applied tape with an old kitchen knife.

She pulled up the lid and peered inside. "The bundle on top says, 'Unwrap first.'"

"Heave to."

She removed the string and unrolled the paper, and Noah's ark tumbled onto the floor, landing upright.

Tears sprang to her eyes. "Timothy!"

He was smitten at once with the grace and skill of Abner's carving. The long, shoe-box-like vessel had clearly been modeled after the architectural and engineering directions contained in the book of Genesis.

"Amazing!" he said.

"And look!" Two amiable-looking camels rolled from the heavy wrapping paper and into her lap.

"They're wondrous," she said. "Wondrous!"

Unable to resist, he opened a bundle himself. "Geese, by George!"

"No, by Abner!" exclaimed his jubilant wife.

They were children for an hour, unwrapping a buck and a doe, two pigs, two bears, and two mules. They examined each creature, looking at the way the knife had shaped the wood, at the sleepy eyes of the pigs, the erect ears of the horses, the movement of the wood grain.

"If this is any indication," she said, "Back-yard is helping God do something wonderful in Tennessee."

"Absolutely!"

"I have a great idea."

"What's that?"

"It isn't a new idea, of course, Father Roland thought of it ages ago."

"Speak."

"Let's send him some money," she said. "A really generous amount."

"What, and deny him the thrill of hammering us on the head?"

"I'll just go upstairs and get the checkbook."

"And I'll take the envelope straight to the post office," he said.

"I need a joke."

"What for?" asked Mule.

"I'm going to see Uncle Billy, he's back at home and could probably use a laugh."

"I can't remember jokes. They go in one ear an' out th' other."

"Maybe Percy has a joke."

"Come on. Have you ever heard that ol' sourpuss tell a joke?"

"Now that you mention it, no."

"I've heard Coot tell a joke a time or two, but you wouldn't want to repeat it."

"Maybe Harley," said Father Tim. "Once in a while, Harley has a good joke."

J.C. slung his briefcase into the booth and thumped down. "You need a joke?"

"Clean," said Father Tim.

"Here you go. Th' doctor asks the nurse, says, 'How's that little boy doin', the one who swallowed all those quarters?' Th' nurse says, 'No change yet.'"

J.C. looked across the table, raising his eyebrows.

"I don't get it," said Mule.

"Got anything else?" asked Father Tim.

Only a moment ago, in the simple act of walking across her kitchen floor, Hélène Pringle was startled to recognize that God had, in fact, revealed Himself to her.

He had revealed Himself by allowing her to help find Sammy Barlowe, and had arranged for her to stand on the landing while George Gaynor repeated the prayer on the phone.

It was an intimate revelation that gave her a deep gladness, and she thought again of the other evening, the night marked by that terrible fire, when her life had been altered for all time.

She had known it was discourteous to eavesdrop, but apparently God had been willing to overlook this small indiscretion to gain something of far greater importance.

Indeed, her heart had pounded into her throat as she repeated the lines of that simple prayer. She felt as if she'd been electrified.

Afterward, she wanted desperately to go to her room and kneel by her bed and speak to the other side of the curtain. She had instead gone downstairs to turn off the light, for she could not afford the extravagance of a lamp burning unnecessarily.

At the time, she had no idea what might come of the prayer she had uttered silently—perhaps nothing. Yet, she'd known she had to repeat it after George Gaynor; not to have done so would have been unthinkable.

By the time she'd gone up the stairs and into her room, she realized that the curtain so long imagined in her mind had vanished. And though she hadn't actually seen Him sitting on what was once the other side, she hadn't been surprised at all to realize He was there.

Hope Winchester was once again watching George Gaynor leave Mitford.

This time, he wasn't leaving in a car with dark windows, driven by an FBI agent, he was riding with Father Tim and his dog in a red Mustang convertible with the top down.

She stood with Scott Murphy on the sidewalk, in the precise spot she'd occupied more than eight years ago, and waved goodbye as the car moved toward them from Wisteria Lane.

George had been standing at the bookstore this morning, bearing two cups of coffee from the Grill, when she arrived to open up. They had sat in his office, drinking coffee and saying goodbye, and he told her he was honored that she'd imagined herself in love with him, however briefly. They had laughed a little then, and he thanked her once more and said he would write and she said she would, too.

Then Scott had joined them in the office, where he stood with one hand on George's shoulder and the other on hers, and prayed—for the power, consolation, and guidance of the Holy Spirit in George's future, and in the life of Hope Winchester.

The men had embraced then, unashamed and oddly happy, and her own heart had been moved as George left, walking down to the yellow house to meet his ride to the Asheville airport.

As the Mustang drove by now, Father Tim beeped the horn twice and George threw up his hand and looked their way, beaming. Barnabas sat upright on the backseat, gazing straight ahead.

They watched until the red convertible drove around the monument and passed from view.

Scott cleared his throat and turned to her. "I need to pick up a book."

She smiled. "You've come to the right place."

He was paying for the book when he felt a sudden inspiration.

"Hope . . ."

"Yes!" She loved the sound of her name.

"I don't suppose you would . . ."—he paused, looking for just the right word—"consider going to Wesley for dinner and a movie. Sometime."

He knit his brow as if he expected to hear the worst.

"Why, yes, I . . . would enjoy considering it."

She could count on one hand the times she'd been out for dinner and a movie—twice with her mother and sister, and once on a blind date.

"Good!" he said. "Great!"

He'd never before asked anyone out for dinner and a movie. When he was just nine years old, three of his grandparents had been killed in a car accident on their way home from dinner and a movie. Miraculously, his mother's mother had survived, and was still living and active and always eager to hear what was happening in her grandson's life.

He knew that he would call his grandmother tonight.

Although he'd heard the news, he was eager to see it in print, in black and white.

When the September seventh edition of the *Muse* hit their front lawn on Monday morning, Father Tim went out, barefoot, and carried the paper inside to the kitchen, where the coffee was brewing.

He read the headline, set in the largest type he'd ever seen in their hometown journal, and was moved to cross himself.

Portion of Mallory Land to Be Deeded to Town

According to Ed Coffey, employee and official spokesman for longtime Mitford resident, Ms. Edith Mallory, two acres of land at Ms. Mallory's fire-ravaged home site on the ridge above Mitford will be given to the town.

Mr. Coffey states that Ms. Mallory had made legal arrangements to deed this plot of land to the town several days before fire destroyed her 8,000-square foot home in the early morning hours Saturday before last.

"Ms. Mallory has had the plot of land inspected by a team of archaeologists who found positive evidence of five grave sites."

Mr. Coffey presented a written statement to the town, which was shared by Mayor

Gregory with the *Mitford Muse.* It states that the two-acre plot, which lies on the northeast edge of the Mallory property, contains "five visible depressions in the ground." According to the statement, the archaeology team did not disturb the graves proper, as no excavation went deeper than necessary to identify the tops of the grave shafts, "and no remains were disinterred."

Ms. Mallory's gift of the two acres contains several restrictions.

No remains can be disinterred now or in the future. No parking for automobiles will be allowed. Any markers the town wishes to erect may be erected. She especially requests that a marker identifying the founder of the town and pertinent dates be included. A walking trail may be created on the property which is largely wooded "with abundant wildflowers." No admission to the site may ever be charged, and trespassing beyond the site will be strictly enforced.

Mayor Gregory says that town officials are "jubilant" over this act of "unsurpassed generosity." The council will review costs for improving and marking the site and making it ready for public visitation, possibly in the spring of next year.

The Council will also review the cost of purchasing a shuttle bus to ferry visitors to and from the site.

Coot Hendrick, a town official who has worked to gather data on the site and bring its history to public recognition, said the evidence of five graves rather than one, is a credit to the character of his ancestor, Hezikiah Hendrick, founder of Mitford. "for obvious reasons, if you think about it," he said.

Mr. Hendrick stated that he would personally host a small celebration in the town hall for all town employees at noon tomorrow. Cookies and tea will be served. His mother, Mrs. Beulah Mae Hendrick, will sing.

He couldn't believe J.C. had at last improved his spelling. He checked the story again to make certain he was seeing right, then moved along to the next item.

Town Announces Fifty Dollar Fine for Watering Yards

Put your sprinklers away and roll up your hoses.

After Forty days with no rain in Mitford and surrounding areas, CityManager Jim Sherrill has instituted a fifty dollar fine for using town water for lawns, flower beds, or any other outdoor purpose. Residents are also strongly cautioned against using washing machines and dishwashers at peak hours.

"There are no exceptions to the rule," says Town Manager Jim Sherrill. He informed the *Mitford Muse* that our water table is 10 inches below normal.

Mayor Andrew Gregory is in full agreement with the decision to impose a penalty. "In view of the seriousness of our water shortage, the penalty is quite lenient. Everyone's support is needed."

While Cynthia had an animated conversation on the hall phone, he watched the five o'clock news and scrubbed two potatoes for baking.

"Who was it?" he asked his wife as she trotted into the kitchen.

"Guess!" she said, looking ecstatic.

"Please! I hate guessing."

"One guess," she said, just this side of jumping up and down.

He picked up the remote and hit mute. "The mayor decided to send Coot Hendrick to England with Emma, and Emma canceled her trip altogether."

"Sammy wants to come for Thanksgiving and Lon Burtie is bringing him."

"Alleluia!"

"Sammy wants to come here, he doesn't want to see his mother."

"That'll take time. But what good news; we'll call Dooley tonight."

She thumped onto a stool. "I love good news," she said.

He forked holes in the potatoes. "What don't you love, my dear?"

"Labels that scratch the back of my neck, size-eight jeans that don't fit anymore, and baked potatoes without sour cream."

"Not to worry. I just found sour cream on the bottom shelf—it has a couple of hours to go before the shelf date expires."

"Timothy, what's that sound?"

They raised their heads, listening.

"Can it be?" he asked.

"Rain!" She hopped from the stool and ran to open the back door.

The cool, sweet air flowed in through the screen; the drops pounded the steps and the landing.

"Let's go out in it!" she said.

"You go out in it."

"Timothy . . ."

"You mean *out* out?"

"Of course! Walking, singing, whatever. Just this once, before we're old and gray."

"Kavanagh, I *am* old and gray."

"We'll go to Baxter Park . . . look, it's pouring, that's terrific, I always wanted to do this! Nobody will see us in Baxter Park, not a soul, put on your windbreaker. . . ."

"I'll need a raincoat," he said, frowning.

"No, dearest, that's not walking in the rain! Here, take this . . . that's right! Good, darling! Wonderful! You're the best. . . ."

Not since he was a kid in Holly Springs had he been *out* out in the rain.

They hit the back steps running and sprinted east on their side of the hedge, shouting like wild things.

He dumped his sopping clothes on the floor of the bathroom and dried off with a towel while his wife took a shower. For his money, he'd just taken a shower, enough was enough.

She stuck her head around the curtain. "I just remembered . . ."

"What?"

"Today's our anniversary. Did you forget?"

"I did. I'm sorry."

"It's OK. I remembered yesterday and then I forgot again."

"Thank heaven I'm not the only one," he said, meaning it.

"Should we celebrate?"

"We just did." He grinned.

He pulled on a pair of worn sweats and, whistling, went downstairs with his dog to pick up where he'd left off.

He set the dial to 450 and was just popping the potatoes in the oven when the phone rang.

"Hello!"

"Hey, Dad!"

"Hey, son!"

"You won't believe this."

"Try me."

"No, seriously, there's no way you could believe it."

Was it sheer, unbounded joy he heard in his boy's voice? Whatever it was, he had never, ever heard it in Dooley's voice before. It was something like jubilation.

"You've won the lottery!"

Dooley cackled. "Yeah, right." A brief pause. "Lace called me back."

"No way."

"I was walking down the hall and the phone rang and I picked it up, like, 'Hello, Tau Kappa Epsilon,' and she said, 'Dooley?' *Man.*"

"Man!" he echoed.

"She returned my call," Dooley said again, as if trying to fully comprehend the truth.

"Never say never." He was a temple of wisdom, all right.

"It only took her a year and a half."

His grin was stretching clear around his head. "Oh, well, these are busy times."

There was brief silence in which each sought to fully digest the miracle.

"Well, hey, look, Dad, I've got to go. Catch you later."

"Alligator," he whispered, hanging up.

He stood at the kitchen island, looking out to the rain that continued unabated. He'd completely forgotten to tell Dooley about Sammy. Later, he and Cynthia would call and tell him together.

"Timothy . . ."

His wife came into the room, wearing her bathrobe and slippers. "You have tears in your eyes, what is it, sweetheart?"

"Life!" he said. "And love."

He drew her to him, feeling her damp hair against his shoulder. They would talk about the phone call over dinner. It would be a great treat.

Now, he held her close, wordless, rocking her gently in his arms.